... a national writing competition by describing her ideal date: being flown to an exotic island by a gorgeous and powerful man. Little did she realise that she'd just wandered into her dream job! Today she writes for Mills & Boon, and her books feature often stubborn but always to-die-for heroes and the women who bring them to their knees. She believes that the best books are those you never want to end. Just like life...

After spending three years as a die-hard New Yorker, **Kate Hewitt** now lives in a small village in the English Lake District, with her husband, their five children and a golden retriever. In addition to writing intensely emotional stories, she loves reading, baking and playing chess with her son—she has yet to win against him, but she continues to try. Learn more about Kate at kate-hewi...

ONE NIGHT BEFORE THE ROYAL WEDDING

SHARON KENDRICK

PRIDE AND THE ITALIAN'S PROPOSAL

KATE HEWITT

MILLS & BOON

First Published in Great Britain 2021
by Mills & Boon, an imprint of HarperCollins*Publishers*
1 London Bridge Street, London, SE1 9GF

One Night Before the Royal Wedding © 2021 Sharon Kendrick

Pride and the Italian's Proposal © 2021 Kate Hewitt

ISBN: 978-0-263-28233-7

MIX
Paper from
responsible sources
FSC
www.fsc.org FSC™ C007454

This book is produced from independently certified FSC™ paper
to ensure responsible forest management.
For more information visit www.harpercollins.co.uk/green.

Printed and bound in Spain
by CPI, Barcelona

ONE NIGHT BEFORE THE ROYAL WEDDING

SHARON KENDRICK

For the gorgeous Pete Crone,
with thanks for his help and inspiration—
particularly in regard to the Marengo Forest.

CHAPTER ONE

WHO *WAS* SHE?

A puppet, that was who.

Zabrina pulled a face, barely recognising the person she saw reflected back at her. Because the woman in the mirror was an imposter, her usual tomboy self replaced by a stranger wearing unaccustomed silks and finery which swamped her tiny frame. Another wave of panic swept over her. The clock was slowly ticking down towards her wedding and she had no way of stopping it.

'Please don't scowl,' said her mother automatically. 'How many times do I have to tell you? It is not becoming of a princess.'

But at that precise moment Zabrina didn't *feel* like a princess. She felt like an object, not a being. An object who was being treated with all the regard you might show towards a sack of rice being dragged by a donkey and cart towards the marketplace.

Yet wasn't that the story of her life?

Expendable and disposable.

As the oldest child, and a female, she had always been expected to safeguard her family's future, with her hand in marriage offered up to a future king when she was little more than a baby. She alone would be the one able to save the nation from her weak father's mis-management—that was what she had always been told and she had always accepted it. But now the moment was drawing near and her stomach was tying itself up in knots at the thought of what lay ahead. She turned to face her mother, her expression one of appeal, as if even at this late stage she might be granted some sort of reprieve.

'Please, Mama,' she said in a low voice. 'Don't make me marry him.'

Her mother's smile failed to hide her resolve. 'You know that such a request is impossible, Zabrina—just as you have always known that this is your destiny.'

'But this is supposed to be the twenty-first century! I thought women were supposed to be free?'

'Freedom is a word which has no place in a life such as yours,' protested her mother. 'It is the price you pay for your position in life. You are a princess and the rules which govern royals are different from those of ordinary citizens—a fact which you seem determined to ignore. How many times have you been told that you can't just behave as you wish to behave? These early-morning missions of yours are really going to have to stop, Zabrina. Yes, really. Do you think we aren't aware of them?'

Zabrina stared down at her gleaming silver shoes and tried to compose herself. She'd been in trouble again for sneaking out and travelling to a refuge just outside the city, fired by a determination to use her royal privilege to actually *do* something to help improve the plight of some of the women in her country. Poverty-stricken women, some under the control of cruel men. Her paltry personal savings had almost been eaten away because she had ploughed them into a scheme she really believed in. She repressed a bitter smile. And all the while she was doing that, she was being sold off to the king of a neighbouring country—in her own way just as helpless and as vulnerable as the women she was trying to help. Oh, the irony!

She looked up. 'Well, I'm not going to be able to behave as I please when I marry the King, more's the pity!'

'I don't know why you're objecting so much.' Her mother gave her a speculative look. 'For there are many other positive aspects to this union, other than financial.'

'Like what?'

'Like the fact that King Roman of Petrogoria is one of the most influential and powerful men in the world and—'

'He's got a beard!' Zabrina hissed. 'And I *hate* beards!'

'It has never prevented him from having a legion of admirers among the opposite sex, as far as I can understand.' Her mother's eyes flashed. 'And you will soon get used to it—for many, a beard is a sign of virility and fertility. So accept your fate with open arms and it will reward you well.'

Zabrina bit her lip. 'If only I could be allowed to take one of my own servants with me, at least that might make it feel a bit more like home.'

'You know that can't happen,' said her mother firmly. 'Tradition dictates you must go to your new husband without any trappings from your old life. But it is nothing more than a symbolic gesture. Your father and I shall arrive in Petrogoria with your brother and sisters for the wedding.'

'Which is weeks away!'

'Giving you ample opportunity to settle into your palace home and to prepare for your new role as Queen of Petrogoria. After that, if you still wish to send for some of your own staff, I am certain your new husband will not object.'

'But what if he's a tyrant?' Zabrina whispered. 'Who will disagree with me for the sake of disagreement?'

'Then you will work with those disagreements and adapt your behaviour accordingly. You must remember that Roman is King and he will make all the decisions within your marriage. Your place as his queen is to accept that.' Her mother frowned. 'Didn't you read those marriage manuals I gave you?'

'They were a useful cure for my recent insomnia.'

'Zabrina!'

'No, I read them,' admitted Zabrina a little sulkily. 'Or rather, I tried. They must have been written about a hundred years ago.'

'We can learn much from the past,' replied her mother serenely. 'Now smile, and then let's go. The train will already be waiting at the station to take you to your new home.'

Zabrina sighed. It felt like a trap because it *was* a trap—one from which it seemed there was no escape. Never had she felt so at the mercy of her royal destiny. She'd never been particularly keen to marry anyone, but she was far from ready to marry a man *she'd never even met*.

Yet she had been complicit in accepting her fate, mainly because it had always been expected of her. She'd been all too aware of the financial problems in her own country and the fact that she had the ability to put that right. Maybe because she was the oldest child and she loved her younger brother and sisters, she had convinced herself she could do it. After all, she wouldn't be the only princess in the history of the world to endure an arranged marriage!

So she had carefully learnt her lessons in Petrogorian history and become fluent in its lilting language. She studied the geography of the country which was to be her new home, especially the vast swathe of disputed land—the Marengo Forest—which bordered her own and would pass into the ownership of her new husband after their marriage, in exchange for an eye-watering amount of cash. But all those careful studies now felt unconnected with her real life—almost as if she'd been operating in a dream world which had no connection with reality.

And suddenly she had woken up.

Her long gown swished against the polished marble as she followed her mother down the grand palace staircase which descended into an enormous entrance hall, where countless servants began to bow as soon as the two women appeared. Her two sisters came rushing over, a look of disbelief on both their faces.

'Zabrina, is that really you?' breathed Daria.

'Why, it doesn't really look like you at all!' exclaimed little Eva.

Zabrina bit down hard on her lip as she hugged them goodbye, picking up seven-year-old Eva and giving her an extra big hug, for her little sister sometimes felt like a daughter to her. She wanted to cry. To tell them how much she was going to miss them. But that wouldn't be either fair, or wise. She had to be grown-up and mature and concentrate on her new role as Queen, not give in to indulgent emotion.

'I don't know why you don't wear that sort of thing more often,' said Daria as she gazed at the floaty long gown. 'It looks so well on you.'

'Probably because it's not really appropriate clothing for being on the back of a horse,' replied Zabrina wryly. 'Or for running around the palace grounds.'

She hardly ever wore a dress. Even when she was forced into one for some dull state occasion, she wouldn't have dreamed of wearing one like this, with all its heavy embellishments which made it feel as constricting as a suit of armour. The heavy flow of material impeded her naturally athletic movements and she hated the way the embroidered bodice clung to her breasts and emphasised them, when she preferred being strapped securely into a practical sports bra. She liked being wild and free. She liked throwing on a pair of jodhpurs and a loose shirt and jumping onto the back of a horse—and the more temperamental, the better. She liked her long hair tied back out of the way in a simple ponytail, not gathered up into an elaborate style of intricate curls and studded with pearls by her mother's stylist.

Her father was standing there and Zabrina automatically sank to the ground, reluctantly conceding that perhaps it was easier to curtsey in a dress, rather than in a pair of jodhpurs.

'How much better it is to see you look like a young woman for a change,' the King said, his rasping voice the result of too many late-night glasses of whisky. 'Rather than like one of the grooms from the stables. I think being Queen of Petrogoria will suit you very well.'

For one brief moment Zabrina wondered how he would react if she told him she couldn't go through with it. But even if her country *didn't* have an outstanding national debt, there was no way the King would offend his nearest neighbour and ally by announcing that the long-awaited wedding would not take place. Imagine the shattered egos and political fallout which would result if he did!

'I hope so, Papa—I really do,' she answered as she turned towards her brother, Alexandru. She could read the troubled expression in his eyes, as if silently acknowledging her status as sacrificial lamb, but despite his obvious reservations what could the young prince possibly do to help her? Nothing. He was barely seventeen years old. A child, really. And she was doing it for him, she reminded herself. Making Albastase great again—even though she suspected that Alexandru had no real desire to be King.

Zabrina walked through the gilded arch towards the car which was parked in the palace courtyard and, climbing into the back of the vintage Rolls-Royce, she envisaged the journey which lay ahead of her. She would be driven to the railway station where King Roman of Petrogoria's royal train was waiting, with his high-powered security team ready to accompany her. On this beautiful spring afternoon, the train would travel in style through the beautiful countryside and the vast and spectacular Marengo Forest, which divided the two countries. By tomorrow, they would be pulling into Petrogoria's capital city of Rosumunte, where she would meet her future husband for the first time, which was a pretty scary thought. It had been drummed into her that she must be sure to project an expression of gentle gratitude when the powerful monarch greeted her, and to curtsey as deeply as possible. She must keep her eyes downcast and only respond when spoken to. Later that night there would be fireworks and feasting as the first of the pre-wedding celebrations took place.

And two strangers would be expected to spend the rest of their lives together.

Zabrina shot a wistful glance across the courtyard in the direction of the stable block and thought about her beloved horse, which she had ridden at dawn that very morning. How long would it take for Midas to miss her? Would he realise that until she was allowed to send for him one of the palace grooms would take him out for his daily exercise instead of her?

She thought about the bearded King and now her cause for concern was much more worrying. What if she found him physically repulsive? What if her flesh recoiled if—presumably when—he laid a finger on her? Despite her jokey remarks, she had read the book gifted to her by her mother, but she had received most of her sexual education from the Internet and an online version of the Kama Sutra. Even some of the lighter films she'd seen didn't leave a lot to the imagination and Zabrina had watched them diligently, fascinated and repelled in equal measure. She had broken out in a cold sweat at the thought of actually *replicating* some of the things the actors on the screens had been doing. Could she really endure the bearded King's unwanted caresses for the rest of her life?

She swallowed.

Especially as she was a total innocent.

A feeling of resignation washed over her. Of course she was. She'd never even been touched by a man, let alone kissed by one, for her virginity played a pivotal role in this arranged marriage. She thought about another of the books she'd ploughed her way through. The one about managing expectations within relationships and living in the real world, rather than in the fantasy version peddled by books and films. It had been a very sobering read but a rather useful one, and it had taught her a lot. Because once you abandoned all those stupid high-flown ideas of love and romance, you freed yourself from the inevitability of disappointment.

The powerful car pulled away to the sound of clapping and cheering from the assembled line of servants, but Zabrina's heart was heavy as she began her journey towards unwanted destiny.

CHAPTER TWO

'SIR, I URGE you not to go ahead with this madcap scheme.'

Roman's eyes narrowed as he surveyed the worried face of the equerry standing before him, who was practically wringing his hands in concern as they waited in the forecourt of the vast railway station for the Princess to arrive. He wasn't used to opposition and, as King, he rarely encountered any. But then, usually he was the soul of discretion. Of sense. Of reason and of duty.

His mouth hardened.

Just not today.

Today he was listening to the doubts which had been proliferating inside his head for weeks now—doubts which perhaps he should have listened to sooner, if he hadn't been so damned busy with the affairs of state which always demanded so much of his time.

'And what exactly are your objections?' he countered coolly.

Andrei took a deep breath, as if summoning up the courage he needed to confront his ruler. 'Your Majesty, to disguise yourself in this way is a grave security risk.'

Roman raised his brows. 'But surely the royal train

will be packed with armed guards who are prepared to give their lives for me, if necessary.'

'Well, yes.'

'So what exactly is your problem, Andrei? Where is the risk in that?'

Andrei cleared his throat and seemed to choose his next words carefully. 'Will the future Queen not be angry to discover that the man she is marrying is masquerading as a commoner and a bodyguard?'

'Why don't you let me be the judge of that?' remonstrated Roman icily. 'For surely the moods of the future Queen are no business of yours.'

His equerry inclined his head. 'No, no, of course not. Forgive me for my presumption. Your wishes, as always, reign supreme, my liege. But, as your most senior aide, I would not be doing my job properly if I failed to point out the possible pitfalls which—'

'Yes, yes, spare me the lecture,' interrupted Roman impatiently as they made their way towards the red carpet where the Petrogorian train was sitting on the platform in all its gleaming and polished splendour of ebony and gold. 'Just reassure me that my wishes have been understood. Are all the other guards up to speed about what they are to do?'

'Indeed they are, my liege. They have been fully briefed.' Andrei cleared his throat. 'For the duration of the train journey from here to Petrogoria, you have taken on the role of chief bodyguard. A role to which you are well suited, with your expertise in the martial arts as well as your undoubted survival skills.'

'Are you trying to flatter me, Andrei?' enquired Roman drily.

'Not at all, sir. I am simply stating the facts—which

are that you are perfectly qualified to act as a body-guard, for your strength and your sword skills are legendary. And that hitherto you will be known as Constantin Izvor and none of the staff will address you as sire, or Your Majesty. They have also been instructed that under no circumstances are they to bow in your presence or give any clue as to your true, royal identity.'

'Good.'

'And they also know that, along with a female servant, you will have sole access to the Princess.'

'Correct.'

'If I may be so bold, it is also a little strange, sire, to see you clean-shaven.'

Roman's lips curved into a smile, for this was a sentiment he shared with his equerry. He had worn a beard since he was nineteen years old and the thick black growth had always defined him, as had his thick black hair. Even when he had ascended to the throne four years ago, he had not conformed by cutting off the luxuriant mane whose ebony waves had brushed against his collar. The press often commented that it made him look like a buccaneer and sometimes referred to him as the conquering King, and he was not averse to such a nickname. But he had been taken aback by how dramatically a shave and a haircut had changed his appearance and when he'd looked in the mirror, he had been a little startled. He had noticed, too, that many of the palace servants had passed him by without recognising him!

And hadn't that sensation filled him with a sudden sense of yearning and sparked off this brainwave of an idea? He'd realised that this was his first ever taste of anonymity—and that, although it was sweet in the extreme, it was poignant, too. Like being given a glimpse of something very beautiful and knowing you would never see it again. Oh, he had travelled incognito before, especially if he was visiting one of his former mistresses in Europe, but he'd never pretended to be anyone other than a king before, and the sense of occupying the skin of a commoner was curiously liberating.

As he awaited Zabrina's arrival, Roman could sense his aide's surprise showing little sign of evaporating and maybe that was understandable, because he was aware he was behaving in a highly uncharacteristic way. For years he had thought nothing of his long-arranged marriage, for such unions were traditional in royal circles, such as his own. In fact, the only time the convention had been broken had been by his own father, and the disastrous results had reverberated down through the years. It was a mistake he was determined never to replicate, for his parents' short-lived marriage had been enough to sour Roman's appetite for anything defined by the word 'love'.

His mouth twisted. Only fools or dreamers believed in love.

He knew he must wed if he wished to continue the noble line of Petrogoria and it was sensible to select a wife who would fit seamlessly into her role as his queen. Just as he knew that the odds were better if his intended bride was also of royal blood—and this marriage had been brokered many years ago. He would acquire the hugely significant Marengo Forest, and Zabrina's homeland would be bankrolled in exchange. It was a deal designed to satisfy the needs of both their countries and, on paper, it had seemed the perfect pairing. In fact, for many years it hadn't even impacted on his personal life, for he had enjoyed brief relationships with carefully selected women who were chosen for their discretion as much as their shining beauty. His arranged marriage had just been something which was there in the background—like a string quartet playing quietly during a state banquet.

Yet lately, the thought of his impending nuptials to someone who supposedly ticked all the right boxes had started to give him cause for disquiet. A wedding which had always seemed an impossibly long way ahead seemed to have arrived with indecent speed. He had started wondering what kind of woman Princess Zabrina really was and the rumours which had reached his ears about her offered him no reassurance. It was said she was a little too fond of her own opinion, and at times could be feisty. It was also said that she was a rule-breaker and there were claims that she sometimes disappeared and nobody knew where she was. And mightn't that create a problem going forward? Because what if the virgin princess proved to be an unsuitable candidate to sit by his side and help rule his beloved country, and raise his children?

He swallowed and his throat suddenly felt as raw as if it had been lined with barbed wire.

What if she was like his own feckless mother?

A bitter darkness invaded his heart but instantly Roman quashed the feeling. Instead he concentrated on the rather faded gleam of the Princess's Rolls-Royce as it made its stately approach onto the station forecourt, its Albastasian flag fluttering in the light breeze. Soon he would no longer have to rely on conjecture and he would discover what kind of woman Zabrina *really* was.

Beginning with her appearance—which up until now he had only ever seen in pictures in which she often appeared to be glaring suspiciously at the lens, as if she didn't like having her photo taken.

And there she was. The car door was opened and a woman stepped out, the tip of her silver shoe contrasting vividly against the scarlet carpet which streamed in front of her like a rush of blood. She moved rather awkwardly in her silken gown as if she was uncomfortable within its rich folds, and Roman felt a sudden unexpected rush of adrenalin as he surveyed her in the flesh. Because she was…

He felt the inexplicable thunder of his heart.

She certainly wasn't what he'd expected. Small of stature and very slim, she looked much *younger* than he'd imagined, although he knew for a fact that she was twenty-three—a decade less than himself. But right now she looked little more than a girl. A girl with the cares of the world on her shoulders if her sombre expression was anything to go by, for there were lines of worry around her full lips. Her smile seemed almost *forced* as he began to walk towards her, though surely that could not be so, since she must have been aware that there were countless women who would have wished to be in her situation.

Who would *not* want to marry the King of Petrogoria?

As he grew closer he could see that her skin was glowing—unusually so—and his eyes narrowed. This wasn't the protected flesh of a pampered princess who spent most of her time beneath gilded palace ceilings. In fact, she had the high colour of someone who was far more comfortable being outside. He frowned, because didn't that feed into some of the gossip he'd heard about her? Yet he noticed that her eyes were an unusual shade of deepest green—as dark as the tall trees of the Marengo Forest, which would soon be his—and that they widened as he came to a halt in front of her. They were beautiful eyes, he realised suddenly. Rich and compelling, with a flicker of innocence in their depths. Quelling the brief stab of his conscience at what he was about to do—because surely one day they would laugh together about this—he executed a deep bow and stepped forward.

'Good morning, Your Royal Highness,' he said. Only now he wished he weren't masquerading as anyone—because wouldn't his kingly status have given him licence to lift her hand and press those tanned fingers to his lips? To inhale the sweet scent of her skin and acquaint himself with her own distinctive perfume? He cleared his throat, struck by the sudden quickening of his blood. 'My name is Constantin Izvor and I am the chief bodyguard who will be in charge of your safe passage to Petrogoria.'

'Good morning.'

Zabrina's response was steady but inside she felt anything *but* steady. She inclined her head in greeting, mainly to hide her face, aware of a disconcerting cocktail of emotions flooding through her which she didn't want the King's servant to see. Her initial thought was that the chief bodyguard seemed a little *too* confident and full of himself and her second was that he was...

She swallowed.

The second was that he was *utterly gorgeous*.

Her heart missed a beat. He was beautiful, there was no other way to describe him. And he was powerful. Strong. The most incredible-looking man she'd ever laid eyes on. Not that she had a lot of experience in that department, of course, but she'd certainly never seen anyone like him among the dignitaries at official functions, or the palace servants she'd grown up with.

She tried not to stare but it was difficult, because he was better looking than any Hollywood heart-throb and all she wanted to do was to drink him in with her hungry gaze. Zabrina had been taught from birth never to maintain eye contact with anyone—especially not servants—but suddenly that seemed an impossible task. And, since she was surely permitted a closer look at the man who had been charged with her protection, she continued with her rapid assessment.

Night-black hair was cropped close to his head and his skin gleamed, like softly buffed gold. His features were chiselled and exquisitely sculpted—the faint scar on his jaw the only thing which marred their even perfection. A silky cream shirt hinted at the hard torso beneath and close-fitting trousers were tucked into soft leather boots, emphasising every sinew of his muscular thighs and making the most of his sturdy legs. She could see a sword tucked into a leather belt—and, in his other pocket, the unmistakable outline of a handgun. These two weapons made him look invulnerable. They made her think of danger. So why was that filling her with a wild kind of excitement, rather than a natural wariness, which surely would have served her better?

Remembering her instructions, she forced herself to look down again—as if it were imperative to study the nervous fingertips which were brushing fretfully over her silky gown. But his image remained stubbornly burned into her memory. She wished her heart rate would steady and that his proximity weren't sending her senses so haywire. Senses which until now she hadn't known she possessed. She felt raw. Vulnerable. Her body felt as if a deep layer of skin had ripped away from it, leaving her almost...*naked*.

Yet as she lifted her gaze upwards once more, it was the bodyguard's eyes which unsettled her most—because they were not so easy to look at as the rest of him. They were hard and cold. The coldest eyes she'd ever seen. Steely-grey, they cut through her like the sword which hung from his belt and were fringed by liquorice-dark lashes which made his gaze appear piercing and...brooding. Suddenly it was impossible to keep a flush of self-awareness from flooding her cheeks, making her shift from side to side in her silver shoes, wondering what on earth was happening to her.

Because she wasn't the type of person to be blind-sided like this. The only time she could remember having had a crush on someone—and an innocent one at that—had been for her fencing tutor when she'd been just seventeen. Somebody must have noticed her clumsy blushes whenever he was around because the man had been summarily removed from his employment without her even having had the chance to say goodbye to him. Zabrina remembered feeling vaguely sad—a feeling which had been superseded by indignation that her life should be so rigidly controlled by those around her.

But what she was experiencing now was the very opposite of *innocent*. There was a distracting tightening of her breasts and the pulsing of something honeyed and sweet at the base of her stomach. A faint film of perspiration broke out on her forehead and she thought how horrified her mother would be to see her princess daughter sweating like a labourer.

'Is there anything Her Royal Highness desires before we set off?' Constantin Izvor was saying.

And sudden Zabrina was angry at the nature of her jumbled thoughts. Angry at the way her stomach was fluttering with butterflies. With an effort she composed herself, drawing her shoulders back, and determined to inject a suitable note of command into her voice. 'There is nothing I desire, thank you, Izvor. And since I see no reason for further delay, I suggest we get going. We have a long journey ahead of us,' she said crisply, perfectly aware that her observation was actually an order and hoping her brusque words would shatter the debilitating sense of torpor which had suddenly enveloped her.

The bodyguard looked slightly surprised—as if he wasn't used to being spoken to like that—which alerted Zabrina to a couple of possibilities. Was his employer, the King, especially tolerant with his staff? she wondered. Was Izvor one of those tiresome servants who seemed to think that the trappings of royalty were theirs, too—simply by association? Well, he would quickly learn that he needed to keep his distance from *her*!

'Certainly, Your Royal Highness,' he drawled. 'The train is ready to leave. You have only to say the word and I will ensure we are quickly under way, for I am your most obedient servant.'

Something about his words didn't quite ring true and the hint of a smile playing at the edges of his lips made Zabrina feel as if he were actually *mocking* her, but surely he wouldn't dare do that? Anyway, why was she even giving him a moment's thought, when Constantin Izvor was nothing more than one of the many cogs who kept the royal machine smoothly rolling along?

'Good. Consider the word given. Let's go!' With a

quick nod, she began to walk down the red carpet and as the brass band began to play the Albastasian national anthem, Zabrina was surprised by the powerful wave of homesickness which swept over her. From now on she was going to have to listen to the Petrogorian version and, although she had learnt the words by heart, it was not nearly so tuneful.

Constantin Izvor leapt onto the train in front of her, but she refused the helping hand he extended, with a firm shake of her head. Admittedly, it was a very big and old-fashioned train, but she was perfectly capable of negotiating her way up the cumbersome steps into the front carriage without any assistance from the dashing bodyguard. Why, she had spent her life leaping onto the backs of horses which made most people quake!

Yet the thought of him touching her filled her with a disconcerting burst of something which felt like excitement. Why could she suddenly imagine all too vividly how it might feel if those strong fingers tightened around her much smaller hand with a firm grip?

Slightly hampered by the abundant folds of her dress, Zabrina hauled herself up onto the train where a young woman was standing, waiting to greet her. With her blonde hair cut into a neat bob and wearing a simple blue shift dress, she looked more like a member of an airline cabin crew than a royal Petrogorian servant. Constantin Izvor introduced her as Silviana and Zabrina smiled, unable to miss the bodyguard's flicker of surprise when she replied in fluent Petrogorian.

'You speak my language well,' he observed, on a deep and thoughtful note.

'When I am seeking your approval, I will be sure to

ask for it!' Zabrina answered coolly and for some reason Silviana winced, as if she had said something untoward.

'I will be sure to remember that in future, Your Royal Highness,' the bodyguard replied gravely. 'And in the meantime, I will escort you to your salon.'

She followed him along the narrow corridor until he threw open a door which led onto a lavishly appointed salon. Zabrina nodded and walked inside but, annoyingly, the bodyguard showed no sign of leaving. He was still standing on the threshold, his steely eyes gleaming, as if he had some God-given *right* to dominate her space and disturb her equilibrium. Zabrina wondered if she should formally dismiss him—yet the stupid thing was that, despite his presumption and his undoubted arrogance, she was strangely unwilling to see him go. It would be like closing the night-time shutters on a spectacular moon—you wouldn't be sure when you'd see all that beauty again.

'How long do you anticipate we'll be travelling for?' she questioned.

He shrugged, a movement which served only to illuminate the powerful ripple of his shoulders beneath his silky shirt.

'Fourteen hours at most, for the train will halt its journey midway, to allow Her Royal Highness a peaceful night of sleep,' he replied smoothly. 'We should reach the capital of Rosumunte before the sun is too high, where the people are already gathering to greet you.'

'Good,' she said, though the word didn't register her sudden rush of nerves at the thought of crowds of people waiting to see her. Would they like her? Would they consider her worthy to be the wife of their King?

'I trust you'll find everything to your satisfaction,' he said.

Zabrina forced herself to look around, trying to take in her surroundings and act as if she cared about them when all she could think about was him. She tried to acknowledge the splendid decoration. The walls were hung with pale lemon silk and several stunning oil landscapes, which she recognised as being of some of Petrogoria's most famous beauty spots. Woven silk rugs were scattered on gleaming wooden floors, and on a polished bureau she could see plenty of writing materials, along with golden pens in a jewelled container. A bowl of fruit stood on a low table and the two sofas which stood nearby were littered with soft and squashy cushions. Through a carved archway was a door leading to what was probably the bathroom and, beyond that, a wide and sumptuous-looking divan bed, scattered with yet more cushions. The bedroom, she thought, painfully aware of the sudden flush of colour to her cheeks as she prayed the bodyguard hadn't noticed.

'This all looks perfect,' she said, but suddenly all she could think of was how strange and alien it seemed. And how alone she was going to be for the next few weeks before the wedding—so far from home and away from everything which was familiar. She might moan about her family from time to time, but they were still her family, and right now they represented stability.

Constantin bowed. 'In that case, I will take my leave of you, Your Royal Highness. Silviana is here to wait on your every need but if there is anything you discover you don't have—'

'I'm sure there won't be,' she said quickly.

'Anything it is within my power to give you,' he

continued, as if she hadn't spoken, 'then please ring. At any time. I will be stationed directly outside your compartment.'

'You will?' questioned Zabrina nervously. 'Right outside?'

'But of course. Your welfare is my sole preoccupation and only a wall will divide us. Nobody will pass me to gain access to the Princess and I will remain awake for as long as the journey lasts.' He paused, his voice dipping. 'It is usually the custom for the chief bodyguard to eat meals with his or her royal subject.'

'Really?' she questioned.

'But of course. I need to taste your food and make sure it has not been poisoned, or tampered with. Which is why I am proposing to join you for dinner this evening, unless you have any objections to that.' Once again he flickered her a steely grey stare. 'Would such a proposition be acceptable, Your Royal Highness?'

Zabrina's mouth grew even dryer. She was expected to *eat meals* with him? She was expected to sit looking at his beautiful face, while all the time attempting to adopt an air of indifference? It sounded like a forbidden kind of heaven, made worse by the fact that Zabrina knew she shouldn't be thinking this way. She was promised to another man, wasn't she? That was the deal. She should be thinking about Roman and only Roman—beard or no beard. 'Why?' she questioned, playing for time. 'Am I such an unpopular choice to be your queen that I am likely to be poisoned?'

'Of course not.' He gave the faintest wave of dismissal. 'It is simply a necessary precaution. A safeguard, if you like, so that you will be delivered to the King unharmed.'

'I see,' said Zabrina slowly, but his use of the expression 'deliver' only reinforced the doubts she'd been experiencing earlier. Was that how *everybody* saw her—as a commodity? She supposed it was. She might be a crack shot who was fluent in four languages and thoroughly at home on the back of a temperamental horse. She might have devoted a huge portion of her time to working for women's charities and trying to get more equality for them in her homeland. But none of these things counted for anything, not really. And perhaps it was that which made a sudden streak of rebellion influence her decision, even though she had vowed to herself she wasn't going to make waves.

She could have told the autocratic bodyguard she wasn't particularly hungry and was quite happy to miss dinner—both of which were true. She could have hidden herself away in here and not seen anyone until they reached Rosumunte. But she wasn't going to. She glanced around at the sumptuous salon and suddenly it resembled nothing but a gilded cage.

Her gaze was drawn to the spring-like countryside outside—a blur of bright green as the train passed through. She was leaving her old life behind. When she returned here—and who knew when that would be?—it would be as the queen of a foreign country. One which had waged war against her ancestors in the past. And she was one of the spoils of that war. The modern-day virgin princess offered to the grisly king in exchange for a small chunk of his sizeable wealth.

Through the train window she caught a tantalising glimpse of an orchard at its very best. The branches of the trees were covered in thick white blossom, as if a mantle of snow had fallen on them. She found herself thinking of sunshine and birdsong and felt the sudden quickening of her blood.

Was it that which made her bold?

She was about to consign herself to a life of duty with the bearded King and, in essence, this was her last day of freedom. Surely she could have a little harmless fun before that happened? Would it be so wrong to mix socially with someone she wouldn't usually have been allowed anywhere near? Constantin Izvor obviously knew her husband-to-be as only a loyal servant could—and certainly a whole lot better than she did. Perhaps she could subtly learn a few tips on how best to handle the powerful King.

At least, that was what Zabrina told herself.

Just as she told herself it had absolutely nothing to do with the bodyguard's steely eyes and hard body.

'Yes, I suppose that will be okay,' she said carelessly, and then turned away before he saw the telltale flush in her cheeks.

CHAPTER THREE

As HE STOOD outside the ornate door of the Princess's carriage, Roman felt the powerful thunder of his heart. His throat was dust-dry and his body tense as the train hurtled towards the vast forest which divided Albastase from Petrogoria. He felt excited, yes, but the familiar, blood-pumping sensation of desire which raced through his body was one which filled him with foreboding.

Because Princess Zabrina had thrown his thoughts into disarray and caused him to feel more than a little apprehensive. And, try as he might, he couldn't dispel the feeling that he had been short-changed. That he had somehow been misled about what to expect from his future bride.

He had anticipated a little more modesty from the virgin princess. For downcast lids to cover those forest-green eyes—not a challenging stare to be slanted in his direction, which had made the hairs on the back of his neck stand up. He found himself wondering if he had imagined the powerful sizzle of lust which had passed between them. Or had that simply been wishful thinking on his part—because he had looked at her and wanted her and suspected that she wanted him too, because women were never able to resist him? Had he misinterpreted her acerbic response as one of flirtation, when in reality she was genuinely irritated by him—hard as that might be to believe? He curved his lips into an indulgent smile. He would not judge her too harshly. Of *course* she wouldn't have been flirting with him—she would have known perfectly well that any such flirtation should be reserved solely for the monarch to whom she was promised.

But in a way, the fact he was having to ask these questions justified what he was about to do—for what better way to observe his future bride than through the invisible cloak of the humble servant? And when he revealed his true identity to her, he would do it in such a way that could not possibly offend. Even if she was piqued by his elaborate charade, any displeasure would quickly be smoothed away. He would charm her and shower her with the priceless gems he had brought with him and which were currently concealed within his carriage. Because jewels were always a reliable bargaining tool. He had observed the way women behaved with priceless and glittering baubles and doubted his bride-to-be would be any exception.

And he knew this princess was financially astute. Hadn't she already negotiated a fairly hefty personal settlement for herself within the terms of the marriage contract, which his lawyers had expressed some anxiety about? But her greed did not repel him. Instead, it reassured him. This marriage was nothing but a business deal and the Princess recognised that, too.

He rapped on the door and Silviana opened it. Of course she did. Did he really imagine that Zabrina herself would fling it open and ask him inside? He watched as the servant's brow creased above the line of her veil, and wondered if she was resisting the desire to curtsey to him. Probably. She knew his true identity but was too well trained to offer anything but a polite nod of greeting. Roman smiled. His equerry had obviously done his job well in warning the staff not to 'recognise' him. He glanced across to the other side of the room where a table had been set for dinner, right next to the window and the dusky countryside which was hurtling by. Pale, fragrant roses stood at the centre of the linen cloth and pure white candles had already been lit, casting flickering lights which contrasted with the darkening sky outside.

It was, he realised suddenly, a very romantic scene and now he found himself wondering if that was such a good idea.

Was he worried that temptation would assail him?

'The Princess will be with you shortly,' Silviana said. 'She is getting ready for dinner.'

He nodded, lifting the palm of his hand in a gesture of dismissal. 'Excellent. You may leave now, Silviana. We will ring the bell when we wish the meal to be served and after that I wish to be alone with the Princess for the rest of the evening.'

She hesitated for no more than a fraction of a moment but Roman had seen it and raised his eyebrows at her in arrogant query.

'Was there something else, Silviana?'

'No, no, not at all, Constantin Izvor,' she said hastily. 'Please. F-forgive me.'

But Roman barely registered the servant's stumbled apology or her silent departure. He was much too preoccupied by a growing sense of anticipation—an expectation which was allowed to mount during the thirty long minutes it took for Zabrina to arrive.

He was not used to being kept waiting. Nobody would dare make the King cool his heels in contemplation, and Roman quickly discovered he was not overfond of the experience. He had often secretly wondered what it would be like to live as an ordinary man but was fast discovering that perhaps he had been guilty of sentimentalising a life of obscurity. Because this was *boring*—standing to attention while Zabrina took all the time in the world to prepare herself for dinner.

During the hours which had passed since she had closed the door on him earlier, he had allowed himself to fantasise about what she might choose to wear tonight. Was she dressing in one of her fine gowns to dine with him? he wondered, unable to prevent the sudden drying of his mouth. Would the soft rustle of silk precede her, and that tanned skin be complemented by the framing of lavish lace and satin? He felt the heavy beat of desire as he imagined her parading around her bedroom in a variety of different outfits, which banished his boredom just long enough to ensure he was genuinely lost in thought when, eventually, he heard a sound behind him. But there was no rustle of silk or waft of fine perfume as he turned round to survey his future queen.

Roman's lips parted in disbelief as the Princess entered the salon.

Was this some kind of joke?

She had certainly changed from the embellished dress she'd had on earlier but she had not replaced it with something similarly splendid, or regal. No, she was wearing a pair of what he believed were called 'sweatpants', teamed with a loose top which effectively con-cealed her upper body like some kind of monstrous, flapping tent. She had removed the pins from her hair, too, but the intricate styling had not been replaced by a gratifying fall of lustrous unfettered hair. Instead, the thick brown locks were drawn back in a tight ponytail and she looked...

His brow furrowed. She looked like a woman leav-ing the gym!

She walked in and saw him and he observed the wariness in her eyes. 'Oh,' she said, with that same careless tone she'd used last time she'd spoken. 'You're here.'

'Did you think I wouldn't be?'

She shrugged. 'I wasn't sure.'

'I said I would be eating dinner with you, Your Royal Highness.'

'So you did. So you did. Well, you'd better stand at ease, I suppose.' She flopped down onto one of the sofas and Roman noticed her feet were bare and for some rea-son his disquiet was replaced by a mounting indignation that she should be so studiedly *casual* in his company. Because although she was ignorant of his royal iden-tity—surely she shouldn't be so relaxed in the presence of a strange *male* bodyguard. Surely she shouldn't be stretching her arms above her head so that he couldn't help but be transfixed by the sudden pert outlining of her breasts beneath that horrible garment. Instantly, he looked out of the window and gave the darkening sky a searching scrutiny, as if scanning the horizon for potential threats. As if reminding himself that he was supposed to be guarding her and not running his gaze lustfully over her small and perfect body.

'Are we waiting for something?' she questioned.

'Not at all. I shall ring for dinner immediately,' he said, resenting the implicit order as he found himself noticing the curving sweep of her dark lashes which shuttered those amazing green eyes.

'You know, I'm almost tempted to ask if we couldn't have a sandwich or something instead,' she continued, huffing out a small sigh. 'At least that way we could cut the evening short.'

Again, people trying to limit the amount of time they spent with him was something Roman wasn't used to. They usually hung on his every word until he took his leave of them, and he wasn't enjoying the sensation of knowing she was there under *sufferance*. No, he wasn't enjoying it one bit!

'A casual snack would of course be possible, Your Royal Highness,' he answered smoothly. 'Though surely you need to keep your strength up for the long days of celebration and preparation which lie ahead? I am certain that the royal chefs would be deeply disappointed if you didn't allow them to offer you a range of typical Petrogorian delicacies.'

The forest-green eyes were suddenly very direct. 'And is that to be my role for the evening?' she questioned quietly. 'That I am to moderate my behaviour in order to please the catering staff?'

'Of course not, Your Royal Highness,' he said stiffly. 'That was not what I meant.'

Zabrina saw the way the bodyguard's jaw tightened with obvious disapproval and in a way she couldn't blame him, because she probably *was* coming over as spoiled. But her behaviour was motivated more by self-protection, rather than petulance. She had been pacing her room restlessly ever since she had met Constantin Izvor at the beginning of this journey, glad to shut the door on him and mop her hand over her sweating brow. She had peeled herself out of her constricting gown and tried blaming *that* for the acute aching of her breasts and the increased sensitivity around the nipple area, which was making her feel oddly excited but deeply uncomfortable. She had convinced herself that if she dressed down in the comfy clothes she had secreted into her luggage without her mother's knowledge then she would quickly feel as relaxed as she sometimes did when she was gathered together with her sisters and brother, watching American films and eating popcorn in the palace games room.

But she had been wrong.

Despite the slouchy pants and baggy top, all those feelings of earlier were still there, only more so. In fact, she had only to look at the powerful bodyguard for her heart to start racing as if she had been galloping her horse at great speed.

But it was wrong to feel this way about the brooding servant. She was on her way to marry another man!

Conditioned by years of inbred royal etiquette, she sat up straight, put her shoulders back, pressed her knees together, and smiled as she tried to ignore the fake intimacy of the candlelit scene beside the window. 'Forgive me,' she said. 'I am not quite myself. This whole situation is so…'

His steely eyes narrowed. 'So what?' he questioned, as her words tailed off.

She shook her head. 'It doesn't matter.'

'But—'

'I said—' her voice was cool now, and properly regal '—it doesn't matter. And I meant it. Really, it doesn't. So why don't you order supper, Izvor, because the sooner you do, the sooner I will be able to retire for the night and you can go back to your guard post?'

It puzzled her that a look of faint irritation crossed his face and she wondered what on earth his agenda was. Was he so arrogant about his undoubted good looks that he found it hard to believe that a woman would want to cut short her time with him? Maybe she had been right in her initial assessment of wondering if his closeness to the King might have given him ideas above his station. Or maybe he was dating one of the chefs and determined that their culinary skills would be properly appreciated by the new Queen! Was that why he seemed so determined to have her eat an elaborate and possibly heavy meal when that was the last thing she wanted?

And then the strangest thing happened and it took her completely by surprise. A dark streak of something she didn't recognise shot through her body like a sweeping arrow and Zabrina felt her chest tighten as she imagined the bodyguard with another woman in his embrace.

Hugging her.

Kissing her.

She swallowed as he reached for the bell, realising that the emotion was one of jealousy and that she'd never felt it before. It unsettled her even more, because surely to feel such an emotion about a servant was very, very wrong. 'I wonder, could you also organise something to drink for me?' she croaked.

'But of course. Is something the matter, Your Royal

Highness? You look…' His steely eyes narrowed, as if he was suddenly remembering it was not his place to offer his opinion on how she looked. 'I trust you are not ill?'

'No, of course I'm not ill and nothing is the matter. I would just like a drink, if that's not too much to ask!'

She saw his brow darken with what was almost a scowl, before he replaced it with a bland smile.

'Of course, Your Royal Highness. Your wish is my command. Might I offer a little wine, perhaps? I could recommend a superb Petrogorian vintage, ma'am. Some say it is even finer than the finest of French wine— though obviously the French themselves are not among that number!'

Zabrina rarely drank alcohol—not even on high days and holidays—and, much as she longed for something which might help ease the terrible tension which was spiralling up inside her, she knew it would be foolish to accept a drink from Constantin Izvor. Because alcohol loosened the inhibitions—didn't it?—and instinct was warning her that was the *last* thing she needed to do right now.

'International comparisons between alcoholic beverages do not particularly interest me, if it's all the same to you,' she answered coolly. 'But I *would* like a drink of water.'

'Certainly, Your Royal Highness,' he said, a nerve working in his cheek as he rang the bell, as if he were having difficulty dealing with her testy orders. A man-servant answered his summons and took the order, reappearing moments later, carrying drinks on a silver platter, before silently exiting the room.

She watched as Constantin poured sparkling water

into a glass, lowered his head and sniffed it as though he were judging a fine wine and then solemnly sipped.

'Perfect,' he murmured, filling another crystal goblet and handing it to her, and as he did so his fingers brushed against her skin.

And Zabrina could do nothing about the shiver which whipped over her body, even though it angered her. Because wasn't it *insane* that such a brief touch could make her breath catch in her throat? How could something so small and so meaningless make her want to sit there gazing at him in rapt and eager wonder? She was behaving like a love-struck schoolgirl! Lifting up the glass, she took a mouthful, but even as the cool liquid quenched her parched throat all she could think about were the bodyguard's lips, which were gleaming in a way which was making her feel strangely stirred-up inside.

It was worrying.

It was more than worrying.

She was on her way to marry another man and all she could think about was the one standing before her.

More servants appeared, carrying plates and covered dishes, which were placed on the table, and once they'd gone Zabrina shot him a questioning look. 'You have dismissed the rest of the staff?'

He shrugged. 'The train carriage is relatively small, ma'am, and I suspected you would feel more relaxed if you were not being observed by your new subjects. Does my action not meet with Your Royal Highness's approval, for I can immediately rescind it if you would prefer?'

'No, no. That all sounds perfectly…reasonable.' She

risked a glance into those pewter eyes and was immediately beguiled by their smokiness. 'Shall we sit?'

'If you don't mind, I would prefer to stand. And after I have sampled each dish, I will serve you.'

'Yes. Yes, of course,' said Zabrina hastily, terrified that she had broken some unknown rule of food-taster's etiquette. 'Thank you.'

Roman watched as she rose from her position on the sofa and slid onto one of the dining chairs, but as she shook out her napkin and placed it on her lap he thought she looked uncomfortable. As well she might, he thought grimly. She had casually invited him to sit opposite her—as if he were her equal! His mouth hardened. Was this how she *regularly* conducted herself when dealing with servants of the opposite sex—or with men in general? Were they unsuitably relaxed about such matters as correct social distancing, back at her palace in Albastase?

Briefly, he wondered if his judgment of her was unnecessarily harsh. He knew he possessed certain strong views about women and he knew, too, their source. But being aware of his own prejudices didn't mean he was going to blind himself to his future bride's obvious deficiencies!

He took his fork and ate some wild rice studded with pomegranates and pine nuts, and afterwards heaped a small amount on her golden plate, thinking that her tiny frame could surely not accommodate a larger portion than that.

He watched as she put a few grains into her mouth and found himself fascinated by the movement of her mouth as she chewed. It would be no hardship to kiss those soft lips, he thought, with a sudden fierce rush of desire, for he had not been intimate with a woman for well over a year, despite the many invitations which had come his way during his last royal tour. But he had resisted any such overtures, no matter how tempting they had been, aware that it would be unfair to the woman he was soon to marry if he had indulged in any pleasures of the flesh so close to their wedding.

But as a result, his sexual appetite was highly honed and keener than he could ever recall and he seemed to be growing harder by the second.

He cleared his throat. 'A little more, Your Royal Highness?'

'No, no. That was plenty.' She surveyed the selection of platters before her with a rueful smile. 'Especially as there appear to be several other courses to follow.'

He allowed himself a brief smile. 'Indeed there are.'

She lifted her head to look at him and, in the flicker of the candlelight, he was aware of feathery shadows on her honeyed skin, cast by her long lashes. 'Look, why don't you sit down for the rest of the meal, Constantin?' she said. 'It's hurting my neck to have to look up at you.'

Roman hesitated, but not for long, because it was a temptation too powerful to resist. It was a break with protocol, that much was true, but since he was planning to surprise her by revealing his identity before too long—and festooning her with a king's ransom in jewels—surely it wasn't too heinous a crime. Carefully, he removed his sword and put it within reach, before lowering his frame into the seat opposite hers. Then he forced himself to try and concentrate on the food he was tasting, rather than thinking how much he would give to free that magnificent mane of hair from its constricting ponytail and see what it looked like when it was tumbling down over her shoulders. But he comforted himself with the knowledge that it would not be too long before she was in his arms and in his bed. A few short weeks until their wedding and they could enjoy the legal consummation of their royal union. And if in the meantime, fuelled by his fierce hunger for her, that time passed with unendurable slowness, well, that wouldn't be the end of the world, would it? For wiser men than he had written that deprivation was a sure-fire guarantee of pleasure.

He forced himself to return his attention to the meal. Thin slivers of cold fish came next, accompanied by a leafy salad, soft with buttery avocado. She ate this with a little more interest and Roman experienced a small pang of compassion as, gradually, he saw her narrow shoulders relax and some of the tension leave her face and her body.

'You haven't eaten in a while,' he observed.

She looked up from her plate, her eyes narrowed and wary. 'How can you possibly know that? Are you a mind-reader or something?'

'That is one gift I suspect would be a double-edged sword,' he said drily. 'No, it's simply instinct. In the past I have commanded an army and can always recognise the signs when the men are hungry.'

'Oh?'

He shrugged, and as she continued to look at him curiously, he elaborated. 'Food is a necessity. A fuel, not a luxury, Your Royal Highness—although women often regard it as the enemy. And you need to eat. You're slim enough not to have to diet to get into your wedding dress and your brain and body need nourishment, especially when you consider what lies ahead.'

She put her fork down and he could see her lips pressing in on themselves. 'If you don't mind, I'll skip the lecture,' she said. 'Though when I want advice on dieting or nutrition, I'll be sure to come to you.'

'Forgive me for my presumption.'

She bit down on her lip, as if she was itching to say something but trying very hard to hold her words back.

Which made Roman curious. Curious enough to let the silence between them grow into something very real and somehow brittle. He could feel a renewed tension in the air. He could see the distress clouding her forest-green eyes and all of a sudden the words came sliding from her mouth, even though he had not prompted them. Words he had not been expecting to hear, delivered with soft venom, as if she were excising a painful wound and needed all the poison to spill out before she could be healed.

'But what if you have no appetite?' she questioned in a low voice. 'What if you have barely been able to face food for days, because of the fate which awaits you?'

'To which fate do you refer, Your Royal Highness?' he questioned steadily. 'Surely your destiny is one which any princess would envy. Are you not about to become queen of one of the richest lands in the world and to marry its most powerful king?'

'Yes! Yes, I am,' she flared, putting her fork down with a clatter as she jumped to her feet. 'But unfortunately, that's the problem.'

'Problem?' he probed, his brow furrowed with confusion.

And now all semblance of protocol had disappeared

and the face she turned towards him was both mulish with pride and pink with passion. 'Yes,' she breathed. 'A problem to which there is no satisfactory solution, for all my high-born position in life. Because I am being forced to marry a man I have no wish to marry!'

CHAPTER FOUR

ZABRINA WAS SHOCKED to find herself on her feet, staring across the table at Constantin Izvor as the train continued its swaying journey through the countryside. No, that wasn't quite true. She wasn't shocked. She was horrified.

Horrified.

Had she really just announced to the King's chief bodyguard that she had no desire to marry his esteemed boss?

Yes, she had. Guilty as charged.

So now what?

Trying to smooth her scrambled thoughts and work out how to get herself out of this bizarre situation, she walked over to the window to survey the darkening landscape outside. High up in the indigo sky the moon was nothing but a thin, almost unobtrusive slither, which meant that you could see the blaze of thousands of stars which bathed the countryside, illuminating the blossom-covered trees with an unworldly silver light. It was the most beautiful scene she could remember seeing in a long time, yet it felt unbearably poignant. She thought about the same stars shining high over her palace in Albastase and her brother and sisters assembled there, and was surprised by another wave of homesickness which swept through her.

But she couldn't be a coward. She must face the music she had managed to create all by herself. She had just committed what was, in effect, an act of treason. And if Constantin Izvor was determined to denounce her to his boss—which he was perfectly entitled to do—then she would have to accept her punishment and her fate.

Slowly, she turned around and lifted her gaze to his, but to her surprise the bodyguard did not look outraged. In fact, judging by the implacable expression on his devastatingly handsome face, he didn't even seem particularly shocked by what she had just blurted out. Just curious—the way she imagined someone might look if they had just been handed an envelope written in a hand they did not recognise.

'Look, can you forget you heard that?' she began falteringly. 'I was…overwrought. It must have been a lack of blood sugar—like you said.'

'Or not?' he negated.

She looked at him in surprise. 'Not?'

'In my experience, people don't just say things they don't mean. You clearly have some concerns—and concerns should always be addressed. So why don't I ring for these dishes to be taken away, while you go and sit down over there and compose yourself?' His grey eyes narrowed as he lifted the bell and rang it. 'And then perhaps I can put your mind at rest for you.'

He was gesturing towards one of the sofas on the opposite side of the salon and, once again, Zabrina thought he was behaving almost as if *he* were the host, rather than a member of the royal household! But by then a fleet of silent servants had arrived and were taking away all the used dishes, extinguishing candles and lighting soft lamps around the carriage, and by the time they had quietly shut the door behind them, she started thinking quickly. Wondering how she could possibly redeem herself in the light of such an inappropriate outburst, she sank onto the sofa he had indicated, thinking how blissfully comfortable it felt after being seated on that rather hard and ornate chair. Suddenly, the atmosphere seemed attractively inviting and *intimate*. She found herself wishing that the rest of the world would disappear and she could just stay in here, with him, protected and safe from the world. Wasn't that a bizarre thing to be thinking at such a time?

And now Constantin Izvor was moving across the silken rug towards her—this time not apparently requiring any invitation from her—and he sat down on the opposite end of the sofa and turned his head so that she was caught in the penetrating spotlight of that steely gaze.

'So,' he said, his accent sounding pronounced and thoughtful. 'You clearly have reservations about your forthcoming wedding.'

She thought that was probably the understatement of the year. 'Doesn't every bride?' she hedged.

'May I ask why?'

It wasn't really a subject which should be up for discussion but there was something so…so *approachable* about the way he was looking at her that she found herself wanting to tell him, but something held her back. It would be far better to pretend they'd never started this conversation, wouldn't it? She could dismiss him and he would obviously obey and next time she saw him she could act as if nothing had happened. But that wouldn't work for all kinds of reasons. *He* would know what she'd said and he would either pass those words on to his boss, or keep them to himself. If he did the former she would be vilified, and the latter would mean there would be a big secret between the two of them which the King wouldn't be privy to. And both those outcomes would be a disaster.

So couldn't she backtrack a little? Play up her natural worries about marrying a man of the world like Roman, and make out that they were nothing but the natural fears of any innocent bride-to-be?

She lifted up her shoulders and felt her ponytail whispering against her back. 'I realise it came out all wrong—'

The brief shake of his head indicated his lack of agreement. 'It came out the way it did because it was something you were feeling at the time. But please be aware that I am not planning to judge you, Your Royal Highness, for it is not my place to do so. Or to tell tales,' he added coolly. 'I am simply interested in your reaction and thinking that perhaps you need to get something off your chest. Certainly before you arrive at the royal palace,' he concluded softly. 'For I know it can be an intimidating place at the best of times.'

'But I grew up in a palace!' she defended quickly. 'And I'm used to that kind of life.'

'Perhaps you are, but no palace in the world can equal the size or splendour of the Petrogorian citadel,' he said, eyeing her with a shuttered look. 'Look, why don't you consider me like a priest in the confessional, knowing that anything you say to me is bound by the rules of confidentiality and will go no further than these four walls?'

Anyone less like a priest, Zabrina couldn't imagine—because surely holy men weren't supposed to inspire thoughts of…of… She swallowed. Thoughts she didn't understand properly, but which were bubbling away inside her and making her want to squirm uncomfortably beneath his seeking gaze.

Yet hadn't one of her initial thoughts on meeting him been that he would know the King better than anyone? What better person to allay her fears about her future husband and put her mind at rest, than Constantin Izvor?

'I have heard that the King is very…ruthless,' she said at last.

His thin smile was followed by a shrug. 'Some might say that an element of ruthlessness is necessary for any monarch and particularly for a man as successful as Roman the Conqueror. He has increased our country's wealth by some considerable margin since coming to the throne, and brokered peace in a region which has a history of being notoriously unstable. As you know, Petrogoria has often come under siege from its neighbours in the past.' He flicked her a candid look. 'Including from your very own country, Your Royal Highness.'

Zabrina nodded. She wasn't going to defend the actions of her ancestors and their dreams of conquest—how could she, when they had planted the Albastasian flag on disputed territory, which they had claimed as their own and which was now being returned to its rightful owner?

'I know all that,' she burst out. 'I just wish I wasn't being offered up as the human sacrifice in all this! If you really want the truth, I wish I wasn't getting married to anyone—but certainly not to a total stranger.'

The look he shot her was pensive. 'But you will gain a massive financial package as a result of the marriage,' he observed. 'Plus, you understand all the privileges of royal life as well as its constraints. And do not most princesses want to marry a king?'

'It was a decision made for me by someone else.'

'Alas, that is one of the drawbacks and also one of the strengths of an inherited monarchy. That the needs of the country are put ahead of personal need.'

'And the King is perfectly happy with this arrangement?' she questioned tentatively, thinking that *satisfactory* somehow sounded insulting.

'The King is governed by facts, not emotion. He knows perfectly well that a marriage of blue blood is preferable,' said Constantin, a sudden harshness entering his voice.

'The King's father married a commoner, didn't he?' probed Zabrina as she found herself remembering things she'd heard about him, and when he didn't answer, she persisted a little more. 'Was that one of the reasons why they had that terrible divorce? When he was so young? Didn't she leave, or something?'

The bodyguard's mouth twisted, as if he had just tasted something unspeakably sour. 'Something like that,' he agreed bitterly, before his face cleared and he looked at her with that oddly detached expression, as if it had been wiped clean of all emotion. 'Such an experience inevitably scarred him, but some say that boyhood pain makes for a powerful man.'

It was an aspect of the King's reputed character which Zabrina had never considered before, but there was another one which she had. One which naturally made her wary. 'Is he cruel?' she questioned suddenly.

He didn't answer straight away. His dark brow knitted together and his eyes narrowed, as if he had seen something outside on the horizon he wasn't sure he recognised. 'No.'

'You sound very sure.'

'That's because I am sure and, believe me, I know him better than anyone. It is true that some women have gone to the press and given interviews which imply cruelty,' he said eventually. 'But maybe that's because he has been unable to provide them with what they most desire.'

'And what do women most desire?' she questioned, into the silence which followed, feeling suddenly out of her depth.

'Can't you guess?'

'S-sex?' she questioned, with more boldness than she had ever displayed in her entire life.

'No, not sex,' he said softly, with a short laugh. 'Sex is easy.'

Zabrina blushed. 'What, then?'

'Love,' he said, and when she made no comment, he carried on. 'That nebulous concept which drives so much of the human race in hopeless pursuit and brings so much misery in its wake. I find that women are particularly susceptible to its allure. How about you?' He arched his black eyebrows questioningly. 'Do you rate love very highly, Your Royal Highness?'

'How would I know how to rate it when I have no experience of it?' she said quietly.

'Then you should consider yourself fortunate, for some say it is nothing but a madness and others do not believe in its existence at all,' he asserted, before giving his head a little shake. 'But forgive me, for I digress. I don't know how we got onto this subject. Were we not supposed to be talking about the King?'

'Yes,' she said, a little breathlessly. 'I suppose we were.'

'You will find Roman exacting and demanding at times, as most highly successful men are,' he continued. 'But he asks of people no more than he is prepared to give himself. He certainly drives himself too hard—his people often say that he defined the term *workaholic* before the word became widely used. But, at heart, he is a good man.'

Zabrina was aware that her lips had grown dry and that her heart had begun to skitter and suddenly her lack of desire to meet the King was growing. 'That's hardly the most glowing recommendation I've ever heard.'

'I am trying to be honest with you, Princess. Did you wish for me to spin you a fairy tale—to make him into the kind of man you would wish him to be? You are not being promised rainbows and roses, no, but something far more solid. You will be embarking on the tried and tested situation of the arranged marriage, which offers the highest chance of success.'

'And so, in order to guarantee this "highest chance", I am to be immersed in your culture, without outside influence. I am being taken to Petrogoria, without family or servants to comfort or reassure me. I am being prepared for your ruler, as a chicken would be prepared for the pot.'

She had spoken without thinking but, surprisingly, the comment made him laugh and Zabrina was shocked by how much that sexy sound affected her. It whispered over her skin like rich velvet. It made her want to curl up her toes and sigh.

'Ah, but an uncooked chicken is cold and lifeless,' he said softly as he removed his gun from its holster and laid it on the low coffee table in front of the sofa. 'While you are warm and very, very vibrant.'

The unexpected compliment shocked her and made her react in a way she hadn't been expecting. It made her breasts tighten beneath her sloppy sweatshirt and her heart begin to pound. She knew that what was happening was inappropriate, but somehow Zabrina had absolutely no power over what her body was doing. She looked into the steely gleam of his pewter eyes and felt a clench of something low in her gut. She'd experienced something like this a bit earlier, but this felt different. It was more powerful. It seemed to be eating her up from the inside and suddenly she was overcome with an aching regret that she would never know what it was like to be held within the powerful circle of Constantin Izvor's arms, or to be kissed by him.

She thought of all the photos she'd seen of her future husband. On horseback, wielding a sword. At an official function in New York with presidents and other dignitaries, or wearing a black tie and tuxedo at some glittering charity event. She'd seen images of him dressed in ceremonial robes and army uniform, and others of him working hard at his desk.

And not one of those images had provoked the faintest glimmer of desire in her.

'He's a grisly bear of a man,' she found herself whispering, dimly aware that Constantin's eyes were suddenly very bright and that he was actually sitting much closer to her than she'd thought. 'With a beard. And...'

There was a pause. A heartbeat of a pause.

'And?' he prompted smokily.

Zabrina looked at him and knew it still wasn't too late, even though she had already said far too much. She could send the bodyguard away and retire to her room and take whatever consequences came her way. But she couldn't seem to move. Not only couldn't, but didn't want to, despite the undeniable thrum of danger in the air and the sense that something momentous was about to happen. She just wanted to sit there, drowning in the smoky grey light from his eyes and letting his velvety voice wash over her. 'And I hate beards,' she added, her voice suddenly fierce.

Roman nodded in response to her bitter words. He should have been angry. It was surely his *right* to be angry but that was the last thing he was feeling. Maybe because the defiant face which was turned to his was so irresistible. Maybe because he wasn't used to such candour, not from anyone. He could see the urgent flicker of a pulse beating at the base of her neck and could sense all the latent resentment which had stiffened her slender frame. But there was something else he could see in her eyes and that something was desire—a sexual hunger which surely matched the one which was pulsing around his veins. It had been present from the moment they'd met and now it was plainer than ever.

She didn't want the man she was promised to, he realised—and yet she wanted *him*.

He shook his head slightly, knowing what he should do. He should immediately absent himself from her company and address the disturbing aspects of her character this had raised in the cold, clear light of morning. But he knew he wasn't going to. He was going to kiss her. He *had* to kiss her because she was drawing him to her like a magnet. He was dazzled by the light which shone from her eyes. As he looked into her face his overriding sensation was one of intoxication. Or maybe he had just been celibate for too long and was woefully unprepared for any kind of temptation.

All he could see was the gleam of her lips. The rise and fall of her breasts and the whisper of her unsteady breath as she looked at him, those forest-green eyes soft and molten with hunger. The subtle scent of desire hung like a musky perfume in the air and he felt it wrapping him with silken bonds. He knew he should tell her the truth. Tell her who he really was. But how could he possibly explain his dilemma when right then he wasn't sure *who* he was? No longer an ice-cold monarch or masquerading bodyguard, but a man whose senses had been invaded with a potency which had taken him by surprise, leaving his nerve-endings clamouring and urgent with need.

It felt visceral.

It felt all-consuming.

As if everything he'd ever known before that moment had been forgotten and was focussed in the hard, sweet throbbing at his groin.

He must have moved, for his shadow threw her slender body into shaded relief and his face hovered above her startled, yet hungry expression. And suddenly he was responding to the glint of invitation in her eyes. He was bending to brush his lips over hers, fired up by the groan of pleasure which passed from her mouth to his as he kissed her. He told himself that any moment now she would come to her senses and push him away, but that wasn't happening. Her fingers were on his shoulders. They were digging into his flesh and she was pulling him closer, as if she wanted him to go deeper. And he did. God, he'd never kissed a woman as deeply as this before. The pressure of their seeking mouths was like lighting the touchpaper of a firework. He could feel her breasts pressing against his chest. His tongue laced with hers and she was moaning softly—moaning like someone in the middle of an erotic dream who was just about to come.

Was she?

Or was *he*?

Maybe.

Roman slipped his hand beneath her baggy top and a groan of pleasure escaped him as he cupped her breast in his palm, luxuriating in the lace-covered feel of it. He kneaded the soft flesh, thinking how much more luscious it was than it had appeared beneath her embellished dress of earlier. He grazed a negligent thumb over one pert nipple and heard her little moan of joy.

His lips on her neck, he ran the tip of his tongue over her skin and felt her shiver in response and, as he tasted her flesh, he felt utterly bewitched by her. His hand moved down towards the waistband of her sweatpants and she was circling her hips towards him, like a dancer on a podium inviting men to throw money at her. And all the questions he should have asked—not just of himself, but of her—suddenly seemed to evaporate.

Hadn't he told her that everything which was said would remain between these four walls for ever—and didn't that count for everything they *did*, as well?

'Princess,' he intoned huskily. But it was more than an undeniable purr of appreciation. It was also an unspoken question which they both understood as he stared deep into her eyes.

Zabrina stilled as she heard the use of her official title, but even that brief brush with reality wasn't enough to dampen her desire for him, which was off the scale. He was tacitly asking if she wanted to continue and she knew only too well what she ought to say. Despite her inexperience, she could sense that things were getting rapidly out of control, yet she was doing nothing to stop him—and it was pretty obvious why. All during dinner she'd been fascinated by him. She had been deeply attracted to him on a physical level, yes, but there had been a huge element of trust, too.

He had told her she could confide in him and for some reason she had believed him—because the light shining from his grey eyes had looked genuine and honest. So she had. She'd told him more than she'd ever told anyone. But all those confidences now seemed like a double-edged sword. It had been good to get things off her chest and vocalise her doubts to someone outside her immediate family, yet the freedom of doing such an *unroyal* thing had made her feel strangely restless and…incomplete.

It had made her long for the freedom to do more of the same. It had made her wish she weren't a princess who was being sold off to a man she didn't know, but a woman who had the ability to make her own choices about things. Like, about who she would give her body to, when she chose to have sex for the first time. Constantin had tried to put her mind at rest by explaining that Roman was an *exacting* rather than a cruel king—but that didn't cancel out the fact that she didn't fancy him, did it?

But she fancied Constantin.

Her heart pounded almost painfully. She fancied him more than she could say. Especially as he was now peeling back her sweatshirt and bending his mouth to the mound of her breast. She tipped her head back and a helpless shudder ran through her as he sucked at the nipple through the flimsy barrier of her new bra. And now he was beginning to stroke her belly and she wanted more. Much more. She could feel the molten heat building between her thighs, along with a hungry pulse of need which had started flickering there. Her mouth dried to dust because he was igniting a yearning deep inside her and it felt so incredible that every cell of her body was screaming to let him carry on.

So she did.

She told herself it would only be for a minute. Certainly no longer than that.

His hand slipped further down and he pushed aside the centre panel of her panties, which were almost shockingly wet, and Zabrina gave a little cry as he made contact with her aching flesh. She swallowed. Was it so wrong for his finger to be skating urgently over that most intimate part of her? And for that same finger to alight on the exquisitely sensitised nub before beginning to move in delicate rhythm? How could it be wrong when it felt like nothing she'd ever experienced before? When it felt so *good*…

She closed her eyes as the light movement made her catch her breath, then blindly she lifted her face to his, and his responding kiss made her feel as if she were drowning in honey.

'Princess?' he groaned again against her lips.

Again she sensed that some new barrier was about to

be crossed and he was seeking her permission. Maybe if he'd said her name then common sense might have prevailed, but his repetition of her title made her feel slightly disconnected and uncaring of the consequences. As if this were not happening to her but to someone else—someone she didn't know very well. A wild stranger who was briefly inhabiting her body and demanding that this fierce sexual hunger be fed.

'Yes,' she said, in her own language, her next words muffled by the sweatshirt he was pulling over her head. 'Yes, please.'

CHAPTER FIVE

HE WAS UNDRESSING. Or at least, he was freeing himself from his clothes. There was very little ceremony involved. Zabrina watched as Constantin Izvor impatiently removed his long leather boots and kicked them aside, before peeling off his dark trousers and sending them in the same direction, after first extracting a mysterious packet of foil.

His shirt followed, exposing the honed magnificence of his bare chest—but there wasn't really time to appreciate it because the bodyguard was turning his attention to her once more. He splayed his palms over her hips, her slouchy pants were swiftly disposed of and it wasn't until she felt the rush of cool air against her legs that it suddenly occurred to Zabrina that Constantin was completely naked, while she was still wearing her underwear.

His eyes narrowed as if he had suddenly tuned into her thoughts. 'We don't seem to be very equally matched,' he murmured.

It was almost enough to destroy the mood, because Zabrina knew they would *never* be equally matched, because, no matter how vaulted his position, he was still a servant and she a royal. But by then she didn't care, because he was deftly unclipping her bra and her reservations were dissolved by the delicious sensation of her breasts sliding free. She liked the way that made her feel, just as she liked the way his eyes had darkened in response.

His gaze roved to the only remaining barrier to her nakedness—a tiny triangle of pink lace panties, which matched the bra—and she saw his mouth harden with something she didn't recognise. Something which looked faintly disapproving. Surely not—for hadn't part of her pre-wedding sexual education reinforced the fact that men liked provocative lingerie and it was a wife's duty to heed such desires?

Zabrina chewed on her lip. Perhaps he was perplexed by her extravagant underclothes, particularly when worn underneath such a deliberately unglamorous outer layer. She wondered what he'd say if he knew that the flimsy garment was completely unlike the sleek black briefs she normally favoured, which made horse-riding so much easier.

But now was not the time to start thinking about the trousseau which had been acquired by one of her mother's stylists. Not when he was hooking the sides of her panties with his fingers while making a low, growling noise at the back of his throat. For one crazy moment she thought he was about to rip them off and wasn't there an unknown and rather shocking side to her character which actually hoped he *would*? But she had been mistaken, because he was removing them conventionally enough, sliding them down over her knees—though with hands which were slightly unsteady.

His watchful eyes burned into her as he ran a questing finger over her thighs, lightly stroking the goose-pimpled flesh in inciting circles which made them tremble even more. And suddenly Zabrina found herself parting her legs for him, as if his pewter gaze was compelling her to do so—and he was…he was…

She gave a startled gasp as Constantin Izvor bent his head down between her thighs. His tongue began to dart over the exquisitely aroused flesh and he gently hushed her with a single, 'Shh!'

It was an impossible order. How could she possibly stay silent when he was working such magic? When he was making her feel like this—as though she were rapidly soaring towards an unknown destination? Some place of unbelievable sweetness which was beckoning to her with honeyed fingers. It felt shockingly intimate. Decadent and delicious. It felt *perfect*.

Helplessly, Zabrina writhed beneath the featherlight accuracy of his tongue, scarcely able to believe that it could get any better. But it did. It was getting better all the time. It was so good that she felt as if she were going to faint with pleasure. She bit back a cry of disbelief mingled with joy, and just as her body started convulsing he pressed his lips against her pulsating core. Bunching up her fist, she dug her teeth hard into her fingers and bit on them as the flick of his tongue intensified the blistering sensations. One delicious spasm was followed by another and never had she felt quite so vulnerable—or so powerful—as she did in that moment. Time stretched and suspended and she found herself strangely reluctant to float back down to earth.

Her eyelids parting, she saw Constantin opening the foil packet he'd retrieved earlier and Zabrina suddenly understood what it contained. She'd never even seen a contraceptive before—why would she?—and she'd always imagined she might feel a mixture of terror and embarrassment when eventually she did. But the only thing she was experiencing right now was a warm anticipation as he moved to lie on top of her. His flesh was silky and hard. She could feel the muscled weight of his body and his satin tip nudging against the core he had just kissed so intimately. She could detect a faint perfume in the air, and as he lowered his head to kiss her she could taste the scent on his tongue and realised that the taste was *her*.

'Constantin,' she said, almost brokenly.

'What?'

For a moment she felt him grow still against her, as if he was having second thoughts.

Was he?

Should *she* be having them?

Of course she should.

A lingering remnant of common sense reminded her of the insanity of what she was about to do—yet her body was so greedy for more of this incredible pleasure that it refused to contemplate any other alternative than what was about to happen.

'What is it?' he demanded again, his voice raw and ragged with need.

'N-nothing.' If she wasn't careful she would start putting doubts in his mind, and the King's servant would realise what a compromising position they were in. And if he decided to call a halt to it could she really bear it? No, she could not. Was that what made her instinctively thrust her pelvis forward, so that his tip entered by a fraction and he gave a soft roar as he thrust into her more deeply?

Zabrina sucked in a disbelieving breath as he filled

her and she was amazed at how quickly her body adjusted to his possession—as if she had been waiting all her life for this man to be inside her. She let out a slow shudder as he began to move and, very quickly, could feel an escalation of that now-familiar bliss with each powerful thrust he made. But as his mouth fixed itself on hers and she felt the lace of his tongue again, she suddenly became aware that this was about more than the purely physical. It felt as if the two of them really had become one—in every sense. Did she feel that connection because he'd convinced her to confide in him? Or because he'd made her feel almost normal—less like a princess and more like a woman?

And that had never happened before.

'Oh,' she whimpered.

He raised his dark head, his eyes seeming unfocussed. 'Oh, what?'

'It feels…amazing.'

'I know it does.'

What was that sudden edge to his voice as he drove even deeper? Zabrina wasn't sure but right then she didn't particularly care, because it seemed that instinct was guiding her movements again. Why else did her thighs lock with familiar ease around his back, and why else did she move her pelvis to meet each hard thrust? The low moans of pleasure he gave thrilled her immeasurably. Did that mean he liked the way she was responding to him? She hoped so because she liked everything he was doing to her.

Everything.

She liked the way his teeth teased her nipples into diamond points. The way he smoothed his fingers over her arching flesh, as if discovering every centimetre of her body through touch alone. Each thrust he made took her deeper, and then deeper still, into a new and intoxicating world which was becoming familiar to her. In her befuddled mind she saw the twitch of a colourless curtain, behind which was a glimpse of that rainbow place again. And suddenly it became real, and all those incredible sensations were swamping her in tantalising waves.

It couldn't be happening, Zabrina thought dimly. Not…not again.

But it could, and it was.

Oh, it *was*.

As her body began to clench around him, he drove his mouth down on hers—as if recognising that kissing was the only way of stemming the euphoric cry which was bubbling up inside her. Zabrina yelped softly into his mouth as his movements became more urgent—until at last he jerked inside her, his head tipping back as he shuddered out his own moment of fulfilment.

It felt like an intensely private moment but she was so dazed and spellbound that she risked a glance at his face.

He looked enraptured. There was no other word for it. As if he'd just discovered the most delicious thing imaginable. And for a few silent seconds, Zabrina allowed herself the pointless luxury of fantasy.

What if he'd realised—like her—that this type of connection was rare? So rare that she would be prepared to give up her destiny for it. For him. She could tell him that she'd meant what she'd said about his boss—that she had no desire to marry him, nor even any desire for him. She could renounce her royal title and they could run away together. There would be a terrible scandal, yes, but people would get over it and the world would move on. He was strong and resourceful. He could build them a cottage in the woods and she would bear his children. She would cook meals and grow vegetables and he would come home every night and take her into his arms, and... She frowned. It was true that she'd never cooked anything in her life, but she would soon learn!

'Constantin,' she said softly, and as she said his name an astonishing transformation seemed to come over him.

The first thing he did was to withdraw from her, as if he couldn't wait to put some distance between them. But not before she'd detected the way he had begun to harden inside her once more...and she sensed he was having to fight the urge not to thrust inside her again. She wished he would. She wanted to ask him if something was wrong but her inexperience warned her to wait a little. Because he might be awash with feelings of guilt and regret at what they'd just done—feelings she knew she should share, but somehow she just couldn't. How on earth could she possibly feel guilty or regretful about something which felt as if it had been written in the stars?

His back to her now, he peeled off the condom and dropped it on top of his discarded trousers, as if this was something he had done a million times before. He probably had, Zabrina reasoned, though she needed to understand that his life before he'd met her was none of her business and she must not question him about it. Not when they had more than enough questions of their own they needed to address. In fact, he was probably wondering where the hell they went from here, so surely it was up to her to put his mind at rest and reassure him that she wasn't intending to pull rank.

'Constantin?' she repeated softly.

He turned to face her then and Zabrina almost wished he hadn't, because...

Surely there had to have been some kind of mistake? Surely someone couldn't have travelled from bliss to contempt so quickly. But eyes which had been soft and smoky with lust now resembled chips of grey ice and his face looked as if he had pulled on a dark mask of anger. Was he anticipating the repercussions of what they had done?

She frowned. 'Is...is something wrong?'

'What do you think?' he snapped, his voice as cold as his eyes.

She swallowed. 'I know we shouldn't have—'

Roman shook his head, unable to contain his anger for a second longer. Anger at the naked princess who was still tempting him unbearably, yes, but far more potent was the anger he was directing at himself. How could he have lost control like that? How *could* he? 'Damned right, we shouldn't,' he snarled.

She was sitting up in bed and smoothing down her hair, shiny strands of which were tumbling from its constricting ponytail and falling tantalisingly over her bare breasts.

'Look, I don't have any experience but I do know that these things happen,' she whispered.

Her wide-eyed expression was completely at odds with the foxy euphoria he'd witnessed when she'd been orgasming underneath him and now Roman felt another spear of anger directed at the erection which was stirring at his groin. 'Oh, please. Don't insult my intelligence by playing the wounded innocent, when nothing could be further from the truth!'

She blinked at him in confusion and it almost looked real. She was a good actress, he'd say that for her.

'What are you talking about, Constantin?'

The way she spoke his name made another wave of anger wash over him. 'What do you think I'm talking about?' Furiously, he rose from the bed and grabbed at his clothes, rapidly pulling on his trousers before heading towards the bedroom at the far end of the compartment. From there, he tugged a silken coverlet from the bed and walked back into the salon before tossing it to her. 'Cover yourself up,' he said, striding over to the door and turning the key in the lock.

Thankfully, she did as he asked, concealing her delicious body from his hungry eyes with the aid of the bedspread. That was one less distraction at least, Roman thought grimly as a pert pink nipple was covered by a ripple of silk, though he couldn't deny his faint sense of deprivation. His mind was buzzing but all he could see was the fearful gaze she was directing at the door before looking back at him, as if she had only just realised where they were and what they had been doing.

'Oh, my goodness. We could have been discovered,' she was breathing in horror. 'Anyone could have walked in at any time.'

Roman shook his head. He had been wondering how he could tell her what she needed to know—he just hadn't been sure how to go about it. But now he was. There was a perfectly simple way of alerting her to the simple fact which was going to change her fate for ever. His, too. Yet wasn't there a part of him which felt a kind of *relief* at the prospect that he would no longer need to marry her? No need to marry *anyone*.

'Nobody would have walked in,' he declared, with icy certainty.

She gave a nervous laugh. 'You can't possibly know that.'

'Yes, I can.'

'How?'

The stab of conscience he had all but eliminated made another brief attempt to unsettle him, but Roman quickly quashed it. Because surely her deception was far greater than his? He looked into her forest-green eyes and sucked in a deep breath.

'Because my name is not Constantin Izvor and I am not the chief bodyguard to the royal household. I am—'

'You are the King,' she interrupted suddenly, her face growing as white as a summer cloud. 'You are King Roman of Petrogoria.'

CHAPTER SIX

'How the hell do you know who I am?' he demanded.

Zabrina felt a flicker of pleasure that she'd taken him by surprise because surely her sudden realisation of the King's true identity gave her back a modicum of control over this awful situation.

But only a modicum.

Keep cool, she told herself fiercely, as the train continued to rattle through towards the border which divided their two countries. Don't let him guess at your thoughts or your feelings. Because if he does—*if he does*—that will give him even more power than he already possesses. If he realised, for example, that her primary feeling was one of hurt and betrayal, then wouldn't that run the risk of making her appear even more foolish? She shuddered as she forced herself to recall her stupid imaginings. Had she seriously been considering renouncing her title and her life to live in a country cottage with him? She must have been out of her mind.

'How long have you known my true identity?' he questioned coldly.

She forced herself to glare at him instead of drinking in his steely beauty, which she had been doing until just a couple of minutes ago. Why, if she was capable of winding the clock back even by a minute, she would still be in that dazed place of sensual fulfilment, her body all glowing and tingly. And wasn't it crazy that, even now, she was finding it difficult to remain immune to his physical allure? It was very difficult to concentrate on anything when she noticed he'd left the top button of his trousers undone. 'You mean, how long is it since I found out that you've been deceiving me, since even before I boarded this royal train?'

'You dare to talk to me of deception?' he flared back. 'When you were planning to arrive in my country to great fanfare and acclaim and then to marry me, having had sex with someone you believed was my bodyguard?'

Zabrina felt completely wrong-footed by his icy accusation, which was presumably his intention—because everything he'd said was true. She *had* done all those things. But it was all becoming much clearer now. When she had met the man who had introduced himself as Constantin Izvor, she had quickly noticed his autocratic bearing and had thought he was a little full of himself. *Of course he was.* He had been trying to behave like a commoner, when all his life he had occupied one of the most powerful positions in the region. No wonder he had struggled with humility. No wonder he had such strong traces of arrogance. She had thought that at times he seemed almost regal—because he was! Oh, why hadn't she trusted her instincts and found out more about him, instead of taking everything he said at face value? Why the *hell* had she trusted him? Hadn't she learnt ever since she was barely out of the cradle that men were selfish creatures who were not to be trusted?

'You started it!' she declared. 'You started the whole seduction process!'

'How?'

'By telling me...' Oh, how trite it sounded now and how gullible she had been. 'By telling me that my skin was soft and silky—'

'And do you respond to all men who compliment you like that?' he snapped. 'If, say, one of the servants had admired the colour of your eyes, would he have been allowed to put his head between your thighs and be in the position I now find myself in?'

'How dare you?'

'It's a simple question, Zabrina. All it needs is a yes or a no!'

'I shouldn't even dignify that question by responding, because you know very well what the answer is. The answer is no, of course it is. Because I was an innocent,' she elaborated, when he continued to look at her coldly.

'What the hell,' he iced out, 'are you talking about?'

Zabrina had thought it couldn't possibly get any worse than it already was, but she had been wrong. She looked at the contemptuous curve of his lips and a terrible truth began to dawn on her—one so awful that initially she wouldn't allow herself to believe it. Surely he didn't think...? 'I was a virgin,' she repeated—and wasn't it another stupid side-effect of the situation she now found herself in that she should feel embarrassed about having a clinical discussion about something so personal, when in his arms she had behaved completely without inhibition?

'Oh, please.' His laugh was bitter. 'We may have both committed the sin of deception, but that time has gone, and from now on perhaps we should agree to speak only the truth.'

'That's exactly what I am doing.'

'I'm giving you time to think about what you've just said and to modify it accordingly. You were no virgin, Princess. So please don't insult me by pretending that you were!'

Instinctively, Zabrina's fingers dug into the silken coverlet as his gaze raked over her and she wondered if she had imagined that sudden brief darkening of his eyes. Was that because she was naked underneath it? she wondered. And did he still want her as much as she wanted him? How inconvenient desire could be, she thought bitterly, aware of her hardening nipples in response, and the molten heat which clenched so tantalisingly at the base of her belly. 'Are you saying I *lied* to you about my inexperience?'

'If it makes you feel better, I'll be generous and put it down to you being creative with the facts. I can understand your reasoning because obviously you want to protect your reputation. But it won't make me think any worse of you if you admit to the truth,' he added. 'It certainly won't change the outcome of what I am about to do next.'

Maybe she should have addressed the slightly sinister portent of 'what I am about to do next', but Zabrina was so horrified by his accusation that she briefly forgot his words. 'Why are you saying that?' she whispered, and then, as a sudden horrified thought sprang into her mind, she glanced over at the sofa to quickly put her mind at rest, relieved to see that it was as pristine as before. 'Because there was no evidence? Were you hoping to fly the bloodied sheet from the palace balcony in Rosumunte on our wedding night? Aren't we royals supposed to have moved on from those days?'

'Please do not try to distract me with inappropriate sarcasm!' He glowered at her. 'Because I *know* how a woman behaves when it is her first time with a man. She is shy. She is tentative. She is often overwhelmed by what is happening to her.'

'How encyclopaedic you sound, *Roman*. Which leads me to conclude that you must have had sex with many virgins before?''

'Some.' He shrugged. 'Not many.'

'And is that supposed to make me feel better?'

'I don't imagine anything would be able to do that at the moment,' he commented wryly and gave a sudden, heavy sigh. 'But if it's any consolation, I feel pretty much the same.'

'It isn't!' she snapped. 'I'm not interested in consolation, even if you were capable of providing any, which I suspect you aren't. And as for knowing how a woman behaves when it is her first time—don't you suppose that any shyness on her part might have something to do with the fact that you're a powerful king? Except when you're pretending not to be, of course.' She gave a short laugh. 'Surely your crime was worse than mine, since you knew exactly who I was. Was that your intention all along, *Roman*? To seduce me? Was this some sort of primitive test of my character to see how much temptation I could take before submitting to you?'

'Which I have to say you failed quite comprehensively, Princess.'

'Well, maybe you shouldn't be so skilled at seduction!'

There was silence for a moment before eventually he expelled a long sigh. 'Look, I can see with hindsight that it's unreasonable of me to apportion blame,' he said, lifting the palms of his hands in what looked like a gesture of conciliation.

'Why don't you say that as if you mean it?' she demanded, thinking that here was a man who was a stranger to the word *apology*. But weren't all powerful men like that—especially kings? They only said sorry if they were forced to—the way her father had done in the past, when he'd been found out in his latest dalliance. They might go through the motions, but they never really *meant* it.

'I have had sexual partners before,' he continued. 'So I guess it's not unreasonable that you should have done the same.'

'But?' She raised her eyebrows. 'I sense there's a "but" coming.'

Again, a shrug—but this time there was no accompanying hint of apology. 'We both know that the unwritten clause in our marriage contract is that you should have known no lover other than me, Zabrina. It's how these things work. Sexual equality may be alive and well in most of the world, but it has yet to reach either of our two countries. And I'm certain your grasp of royal history is thorough enough for you to realise that there can be no possible question over the legitimacy of any future progeny, which can only be the case if my bride is pure.'

'*Pure?*' Zabrina stared at him, tugging the band from her hair and giving her ruffled mane an angry shake. 'Look, believe or don't believe that I wasn't the cowering little innocent you were hoping for—I don't particularly care either way. But please don't illustrate your prejudices with such ridiculous euphemisms. You make me sound like a bar of soap!'

For a moment Roman almost smiled at her outburst, until he remembered the gravity of the situation in which he now found himself. A situation which must be resolved as quickly as possible. He shook his head. If only he could just walk out of the salon now and pretend that this had all been like a bad dream.

Or an irresistibly sweet one…

But he couldn't. That was the trouble. Nobody could rewrite the past, no matter how much power they possessed at their fingertips. And unfortunately, the past wasn't his only dilemma—not when the present was haunting him in a way he hadn't anticipated. He found himself wishing she were someone else. Someone anonymous, with whom he had no projected future, so that he would have no qualms about going back over to the sofa on which she reclined and ravishing her over and over again as he hungered to do. What wouldn't he give to feel her soft thighs wrapped around his back one more time, and hear her soft moans of joy as he thrust into her with wild abandon? He swallowed, looking into her defiant face and realising she didn't look in the least bit *chastened*—which he might have expected in the circumstances.

Until he forced himself to remember that this was not a virginal princess who was grateful to marry the mighty King who had been selected for her. No, this was a princess who had betrayed, not only him, but both their lands. And now she would pay the ultimate price for her folly.

Yet he remembered what it had felt like to touch her

and he felt a bitter regret that he would never experience it again. Sex had never felt like that before. As if he would die if he didn't possess her. As if his very life had depended on being deep inside her. He remembered the battle which had raged within him as he'd fought to conquer the terrible desire she had unleashed in him. To stop what was happening before it reached the point of no return. But he had been unable to turn away from her sweet temptation and prevent himself from stripping them both bare, before losing himself in her delicious honey. As he had entered her, he had looked deep into her eyes and seen a powerful yearning which had matched his own and a random thought had briefly speared his mind. A thought which contradicted everything he had been brought up to believe.

That this woman was his equal.

But he forced himself to focus on the truth instead of fantasy.

Yes, she was a woman who would have made a superb mistress.

But a thoroughly unsuitable wife.

He wondered if she would save face by exiting their embryo relationship with the minimum of fuss or whether she needed him to spell it out for her. He thought perhaps she did since she was studying him with an impassive expression, almost as if nothing had changed. When everything had changed.

But he knew that this was a delicate situation which required careful and diplomatic handling, if the fallout was to be kept to a minimum.

'You have many attributes, Princess,' he said slowly. 'You are a beautiful and intelligent woman and I am certain you will find another man who is willing to marry you. Perhaps not one as highly connected as I am, it is true.' He glimmered her a smile, trying to reassure her, yes, but also trying to convince himself that nothing would be gained from making love to her again. He tried to take his mind off his throbbing groin. 'And you must rest assured that what I said earlier was true. Nothing which has passed between us will go any further than these four walls.' He gave her a swift, businesslike smile. 'Your secret will be safe with me.'

Some of the impassivity left her face. 'My…secret?'

'Nobody will ever know what happened between us, Princess. It will be like closing the chapter of a book.'

Zabrina flinched and not just because his words were filling her with fury, but because they were managing to turn her on at the same time. How did he *do* that? For a few brief seconds she felt almost powerless over the effect his cool stare was having on her. Why else would she find herself recalling how amazing it had felt to have him peeling off her panties? Or remembering the expert flick of his tongue against her throbbing bud until he had brought her to orgasm? She swallowed as she remembered the second orgasm when he'd been deep inside her. Just the thought of what he'd done was making her stomach dissolve and her skin grow heated. Surely, if she wasn't careful, he would guess at the effect he was having on her.

And that was something she simply couldn't afford to let happen.

Setting her mouth into a firm line, she stared at him. 'You mean, you are no longer planning to marry me?' she verified.

His sigh sounded genuinely regretful—it was just a pity the steely glint of relief in his eyes didn't match the sentiment. 'I cannot marry you, Princess—for the reasons I have already expanded upon and which I am sure you understand. Because if you are being honest with yourself, can you really be hypocritical enough to exchange public vows with a man you theoretically betrayed, even before you'd met him?'

'I—'

'The wedding must be called off as quickly as possible. We just need to work out the best way to go about it and how best to return you to your country.' A new and gritty note entered his deep voice. 'A damage-limitation exercise, if you like.'

If she *liked*?

Zabrina could hardly comprehend the audacity of the man. How did he have the nerve to start talking about *damage limitation* and coolly state that he was about to send her back to Albastase like some reprimanded schoolgirl? She bristled with indignation. And wasn't it funny how contrary human nature could be? Earlier that day she would have sold off the few humble jewels she possessed if someone could have guaranteed her a get-out clause for her marriage to the grisly King.

Except that he wasn't grisly.

He was anything but. He was gorgeous enough for her to have eagerly surrendered her virginity to him—a virginity he didn't believe she'd possessed. So not only had he deceived her, he had also accused her of lying! His list of crimes against her was long, but could she afford to dwell on them, or take offence? No, she could not. She needed to keep her eye on the bigger picture and not on whether or not her feelings were hurt, because at the end of the day that didn't matter. Feelings passed. They waxed and waned like the moon whose cold, silver crescent now looked like a scythe hanging outside the train window.

She thought about the different choices which lay ahead of her. She and Roman could agree a joint statement which could be put out by both their countries, stating that the wedding would not take place. They could fudge a reason—although it was difficult to see what that reason might be. Incompatibility was hardly going to work as a believable concept, because the underlying understanding within an arranged marriage was that compatibility had to be *worked* at.

She swallowed. Then there was all the expense involved—all the lavish celebrations which would need to be cancelled—not to mention the disappointment of their subjects, who were looking forward to a three-day holiday of feasting and dancing, once the wedding had taken place. But those things paled into insignificance when she remembered the real purpose behind this union…

Her country badly needed an injection of funds to bring it back from the brink of economic ruin.

And wasn't she the only person who could do it?

If the wedding was called off, she would be seen as a failure. No matter how they spun it she would always be known as the Jilted Princess, unwanted by the highly desirable and powerful ruler. She would be the one who would be judged negatively, because in this region men were seen as more important than women. Her father would be furious that she had failed to provide the goose that laid the golden egg, but ultimately wouldn't it be her brother and her sisters who suffered as a result of a cancelled marriage?

Zabrina sucked in a determined breath. No. No mat-

ter what the provocation, the luxury of escaping her
fate with the arrogant King was simply not an option.

'But I don't want to call off the wedding,' she informed him quietly.

His eyes narrowed, but not before she'd seen the
flicker of astonishment glinting in their pewter
depths—as though someone disagreeing with him was
something he wasn't used to. Zabrina could almost see
the cogs of his brain whirling, as if he was trying to decide the best approach to take to kill off her rebellion,
before it had a chance to grow.

'I'm sorry to disappoint you, Princess, but that's
what's going to happen.'

'No. I think you misunderstand me, Roman. I am not
disappointed. This is a decision I have made using my
head, not my heart. This has nothing to do with emotion, because emotion has no place in this marriage of
ours. It never did. I never particularly wanted it, if the
truth were known, but I was willing to accept my fate.'

'Do you realise how much you insult me?' he
breathed.

'It was not said with the purpose of insulting you. I
said it because it was true. But the past is irrelevant.'
She drew in a deep breath. 'The union must still take
place. It has long been agreed. My country will benefit.
Yours, too. Aren't you forgetting how much you desire
that piece of land?'

'And aren't you forgetting something?' he snapped.
'Something less pragmatic than matters of finance and
territory? It was always intended that my future queen
should be—'

'*Pure?*' she interjected sarcastically. 'So you keep
saying. Maybe it was and maybe I should be a lot more

offended than I actually am that you don't believe I was. But I find I'm not offended at all—which I can only put down to the fact that I set the bar very low when it comes to my expectations concerning men!'

'Your negative opinions about men do not interest me. And I don't think you're hearing me properly, Zabrina. You are not what I consider to be a suitable partner and I do not want you as my wife.'

'And you're not hearing *me*,' she countered fiercely. 'You said yourself that my virginity was the unwritten clause in our wedding contract, and anyone who knows even a little bit of law realises that an unwritten clause means nothing!'

His eyes hardened. 'So you wish to force me to marry you? Is that what you really want? A man you have hounded to the altar? And all because your ego can't take perceived rejection.'

'It has nothing to do with my ego and everything to do with securing a prosperous future for my country!'

'And then what?' he demanded. 'Being with someone who doesn't want you is hardly a recipe for life-long contentment, is it?'

For a moment Zabrina was perplexed by his words—because surely he wasn't foolish enough to believe in fairy tales like *life-long contentment*. A relationship of polite civility and tolerance was the best that could be hoped for, because that was how these things worked. A royal marriage was about what the couple *represented* rather than the relationship which existed between them. She had even known she would be expected to turn a blind eye to his behaviour—to the liaisons with other women he would undoubtedly have—and she had been prepared to do that, because that had always been the case for the wives of kings.

She looked at him and thought about his words. 'But in some ways you *do* want me,' she said slowly.

'I'm not talking about sex!' he snapped.

'But isn't that also important? I mean, is what happened between us just then usual?'

'No, it isn't *usual*,' he said. 'You must know that.'

Zabrina nodded. She'd thought that to be the case. Perhaps in a different situation she might have been pleased by his acknowledgement of the powerful chemistry which existed between them, were his words not tinged with such obvious bitterness. And, of course, accusation. That subtle jibe about her supposed sexual experience hadn't escaped her. But she had lived a life where unfairness was something you just learned to live with and there was no reason why this should be any different.

'So why not just go through with it? It's not ideal, I know. But understand this, Roman. I've spent years preparing for my fate and if I hadn't, I might have lived my life very differently. I don't want to go back to Albastase as the Jilted Princess, and when you think about it you'll have to go to all the trouble of finding another bride who can provide you with an heir—that all-important means to securing and continuing your line of inheritance. Someone else who might just happen not to pass your exacting vetting process.'

There was silence for a moment. 'You mean you wish to bear my children?' he questioned slowly.

It had always been a given that she would do so and deep down Zabrina had always longed for children of her own. She thought of the fierce love she felt for her sisters and brother and how much she was going to miss them. Producing a family was an essential part of an arranged royal marriage, when you stopped to think about it, and yet it wasn't the kind of thing you spoke about in polite society. Yet as Roman asked the question, Zabrina felt a surge of something which felt like hope. Something which warmed and stirred her heart in a way she hadn't expected, but she kept her expression deadpan, because she suspected that somehow it would be more appropriate. That passion or eagerness might scare him.

'That has always been part of the deal, hasn't it?' she questioned quietly. 'We could make this marriage work, if we wanted it to. We don't seem to have a problem with communication and maybe that could work in our favour. We don't shy away from discussing things other people might find difficult. And neither of us believe in love, only duty. We have no foolish illusions, do we, Roman? No secret dreams ripe to be shattered. So, if you were to agree, we could continue on this train to the palace at Petrogoria and I could prepare for my life as your queen, as planned.'

There was a long pause before he spoke. 'Just like that?'

'Why not?'

His eyes narrowed, the silver gaze slicing through her like a blade. 'You've got it all worked out, haven't you, Princess?'

She wished he wouldn't use her title in that mocking way, because she liked it. She liked it more than she should. 'Let's just say I'm making the best of a bad situation.'

'And if I refuse? What then?'

His voice was silky but the note underpinning it was anything but. Zabrina imagined that tone might have intimidated many people, but it wasn't going to intimidate her. She shrugged, hearing the rhymical sound of the train as it thundered through the darkness towards Petrogoria. If she had been somebody else she might have threatened to go to the newspapers, because imagine all the money the press would pay for a juicy scoop like this—a respectable king pretending to be someone else and seducing the virgin princess! But she wouldn't do that—and not just because such a disclosure would drag both their names and their reputations through the mud. No. There were some things she would push for and some things she realised were pointless, because on an instinctive level she recognised that a man like Roman the Conqueror would never give in to something like blackmail.

'I don't think you will refuse,' she said, her gaze very steady. 'Because I think you need this marriage as much as I do.'

CHAPTER SEVEN

THERE WERE FLOWERS EVERYWHERE. Bright flowers which filled the air with their heady scent. Roses and gerbera. Delphinium and lilac. Pink and blue and red and orange and every conceivable shade in between. Swathes of them festooned the railway station at Rosumunte and yet more were waved by the packed crowds lining the roads to the palace. Petals were thrown towards their open-topped car and most fluttered to the ground but some were captured by the inert wipers and lay against the car's windscreen, where already they were beginning to wilt in the warm sunshine.

And there were so many *people*. In the pale blue silk dress which had been specially chosen for this occasion, Zabrina sat bolt upright beside the King, who was raising his hand to his adoring subjects, and she forced herself to follow suit. 'Gosh,' she breathed, her heart missing yet another beat. 'This is…'

He turned to her, his face shadowed and enigmatic despite the bright sunshine. 'What?'

She swallowed but somehow turned the movement into a small smile, the sort of smile her new subjects would expect to see, because she wasn't supposed to be inside her own head, thinking about the man whose thigh was so tantalisingly close to hers. She was supposed to be thinking about other things. Like that sweet little girl by the roadside, who was waving like crazy in her direction. Zabrina lifted her fingers in response and the child's smile widened.

But it wasn't easy to rid her thoughts of the devastatingly handsome King, because it took some getting used to—seeing him in uniform when before she'd only ever seen him in billowing shirt, trousers and long boots. And naked, of course. She mustn't forget that. But the Petrogorian army uniform was dark and formal and did incredible things for his already impressive physique. It emphasised the hard, honed body, while the peaked cap drew attention to the shadowed jut of his jaw and the proud posture which made his shoulders look so broad. Zabrina cleared her throat. 'It's massive,' she breathed. 'I wasn't expecting all these people to turn out to greet me.'

'You are their future Queen. Of course they wish to welcome you.'

'I know, and I appreciate that. It's just that you can be aware of something intellectually, but, when it happens, it doesn't feel how you thought it would feel.'

'And how does it make you feel? Nervous?'

She folded her hands together in her lap, terrified he would notice the tell-tale dampness of her palms, because hadn't she fought for this? To be Roman's future queen and to bear his children? In which case it would be inappropriate to showcase a quivering mass of uncertainties which seemed to have come at her out of nowhere. 'I was told many years ago that nerves have no place in the life of a princess.'

'And did you believe everything you were told, Zabrina?'

'I suppose I did,' she said carefully, resolutely ignoring the trace of mockery in his voice. 'Doesn't every child put their faith in the adults who form their view of the world?'

His laugh was unexpectedly bitter and the lines around his mouth became deep and tense. 'Not necessarily. Not if they've discovered such an exercise to be futile.'

'Is that what happened to you?'

'I don't dwell on the past, Zabrina. It's pointless.'

She wanted to argue that the past informed the present and to tell him that she needed to get to know him better, but something told her now was not the time and her immediate concerns were of a far more practical nature. Soon they would arrive at the palace and, if her own father's exalted position was anything to go by, the King would quickly be surrounded and swept away by a cohort of aides and equerries. And she would be on her own. Alone in a place where she knew absolutely no one.

Except him.

She moistened her lips with the tip of her tongue. 'So what happens when we reach the palace? What's the set-up there?'

He shrugged. 'The set-up will be exactly as was always planned. You will have your own staff. A private secretary with their own office, plus various ladies-in-waiting who will provide you with anything you need. You will obviously wish to explore as much of Petrogoria as is possible in the run-up to the marriage and to acquaint yourself with your new country and its people.

Some of these visits we will do together, some you will perform solo and, once we are married, we will tour nearby Greece.'

She touched one of the waxy blooms of the lily-of-the-valley bouquet she had been presented with on embarkation and fixed her gaze on his. 'I was told that it would be possible for my horse to be brought here. And before you start telling me that you have the finest stable of horses in the world—it's not the same as having a mount you've owned ever since he was a young foal.'

'Of course you can have your horse here. I will set the process in motion,' he said, his eyes narrowing, as if he had picked up some of her apprehension. 'The aim is to make you feel at home, Zabrina, not alienate you, and all efforts have been made to do this. Your suite of rooms is in the southern end of the palace, where the outlook is particularly fine. I am sure you've heard about the fabled gardens here, which have inspired some of the nation's finest poets and—'

'Of course I have,' she interjected quickly, because he was the last person she could imagine enjoying poetry and just the thought of that was more than a little distracting. 'But what about you?'

'Perhaps you could be a little more specific, Princess.' His grey eyes gleamed with yet more mockery. 'What *about* me?'

'Is your...?' A lump seemed to have inconveniently lodged itself in her throat, making her next words come out as a thready whisper. 'Is your own section of the palace nearby?'

'Why, is that what you were hoping for?'

'Of course not,' she said crossly, but her burning cheeks ran the risk of making her words seem like a sham.

'I have decided that there will be no resumption of intimacy until we take our vows, as tradition demands. So I'm afraid you will just have to survive on the memory of how good it can be, Princess.'

'Does anyone know?' she questioned, in a low voice.

'You mean, are my staff aware that we've already had sex?'

'Keep your voice down!' she hissed. 'How…how are you going to explain the fact that you were even *on* my train when it arrived this morning, when I was supposed to meet you for the first time at the station? I could tell the crowds were surprised when they saw you jumping off in front of me and then lifting me down.' She raised her hand to wave to the crowds, her serene smile belying the rapid thunder of her heart. 'A completely over-the-top response, in my opinion.'

Roman expelled a reluctant sigh as the sunlight splashed pale gold streaks over her dark hair, because the reworking of the original plan had given him cause for concern. He had considered having the train make an unscheduled stop just outside the capital, and for one of his grooms to have a horse saddled and ready for him to ride to 'meet' the Princess for the first time. But the thought of any more subterfuge had been wearisome and he couldn't guarantee how Zabrina would react to such a suggestion—negatively, he suspected. And besides, he was the King. If he occasionally broke the rules, so what?

'I've already spoken to my aides and given them a story.'

'A *story*?'

'Don't look so shocked, Princess. Isn't that what everyone does?' He saw an old woman lay her hand across her heart as he passed by and he gave a courteous nod of acknowledgement. 'Reality is just an interpretation of facts,' he continued smoothly. 'And no two people ever see things the same way. I told them I was determined to protect my future bride and the most effective way of ensuring that was to guard her myself.'

'Right. Because the real facts—the true facts—that you were secretly doing a character assassination of me, wouldn't play out very sympathetically for you, would they, Roman?'

'Possibly not,' he mused. A flurry of rose petals drifted into the car and as one of them lodged itself beneath a pearl clip which gleamed in her hair, Roman had the strongest desire to smooth it away with his finger. But he didn't. He didn't trust himself to touch her again. At least, not yet. And certainly not in public, where his every action would be forensically scrutinised. What if some clever camera lens managed to capture his gnawing frustration at the way control seemed to be slipping away from him whenever he was around her?

Because none of this was turning out as he'd expected. He had thought, after deciding to go ahead with the marriage, that they might spend the remainder of the night on the train, blissfully exploring each other's bodies. There had certainly been plenty of sexual tension fizzing between them, after she'd given him all the reasons why they *shouldn't* call off the union. In a way, he had almost admired her dogged determination to get her own way. It had certainly turned him on. And while he was aware that sexual propriety would have to be observed once they reached the palace and they wouldn't be intimate again until their wedding night—

surely that was even more reason to have capitalised on the strange circumstances which had led to that first delicious encounter. Silviana the servant could have been dismissed for the night and he could have locked the carriage door and let bliss take over.

But it had seemed that Zabrina had other ideas.

In fact, he had conducted the remainder of the journey standing to attention in the rattling corridor of the train, right outside her salon.

'If you're so determined to pretend to be a bodyguard, then maybe you'd better start acting like one!' she had hissed, before slamming the door in his face—something which had never happened to him, not in all his thirty-three years.

Outside his stint in the Petrogorian army or those heart-knotting times after his mother had deserted him, it had been the longest night of his life—not helped by the thought of Zabrina lying in bed only a few metres away. At the beginning of his long shift, thinking about her and what they had done together had been a welcome distraction—until it had become a self-induced form of torture. He had found himself wondering whether she slept naked. He had begun picturing her tiny frame and the slender curves which had wrapped themselves around him so accommodatingly, and his body had stiffened with such a hard jerk of desire that a passing guard had looked at him with concern and asked if he was okay.

Of course he hadn't been okay! He had been frustrated in more ways than one—furious at having been wrong-footed by the foxy Princess. A part of him still was...

'And do you still think it was a good idea?' she questioned suddenly, her soft voice breaking into the muddle of his thoughts. 'To pretend to be someone you weren't, just to find out what I was really like?'

He looked at her. It would have been easy to say no, that he regretted all the subterfuge and deceit, and surely that would dissolve some of the strain which had tightened her features. But a defining—and possibly redeeming—feature of their relationship had emerged during the short time they had known one another. She had said so herself. They had no illusions of love. No foolish dreams to shatter. Couldn't total honesty elevate this arranged marriage into something which didn't need hollow and placatory words to survive?

'Perhaps the manner of execution wasn't ideal,' he mused. 'But if you're asking whether I regret having got to know you in that way, then the answer would have to be no. If we had been introduced in the traditional way, then all kinds of barriers would have been erected. We would have made polite small talk and been forced to endure a stilted courtship. And yes, it is going to be something of a farce and frustration to deny ourselves physical satisfaction in the run-up to the wedding, but it will certainly hone our mutual desire.' He turned and slanted her a complicit smile. 'Which is presumably why you kicked me out of the carriage last night.'

'I did that because I didn't trust myself not to kick you literally!'

He could feel the flicker of a smile tugging at the edges of his lips. 'If you want me to be perfectly frank, it was something of a relief to discover you were sexually experienced.'

'It was?' she verified, her voice growing a little faint.

'Undoubtedly.' He turned and waved to someone in the crowd who was calling out his name. 'To be honest, virgins are hard work.'

'Hard work?' she echoed dully. 'In what way?'

He shook his head. 'It doesn't matter.'

'Oh, I think it does.'

'You don't want to know.'

'Oh, but that's where you're wrong, Roman. I do. I thought we were going to be frank with one another. I don't want you to spare my feelings.'

He shrugged. 'If you want the truth, virgins need constant reassurance. They don't seem to realise that if you're constantly asking a man whether or not he likes it and whether or not you're doing it properly, it's a bit of a turn-off.'

'I see.' She pressed her lips together in what he was now coming to recognise was one of her determined smiles. 'Well, I'm glad we've got that out of the way! Thanks very much for the enlightenment.'

Roman's eyes narrowed. In many ways she surprised him as well as amused him, but there was something about her which was… He shook his head, unable to define what it was he was feeling and that did not sit comfortably with him. And surely it was simpler to push such feelings aside… He cleared his throat. 'If you look straight ahead,' he said unevenly, 'you'll get your first view of the palace, with the Liliachiun mountains behind.'

The iconic towers of the Petrogorian palace soared into view, but Zabrina could barely focus on the pale-hued magnificence of the ancient building ahead, so great was her anger towards the man by her side. He was…

unbearable. He was the most unspeakably arrogant man it had ever been her misfortune to meet and if she was now committed to spending the rest of her life with him, she had only herself to blame.

So how come she still fancied him like crazy, even though some of the things he came out with made her want to scream with rage?

His damning assessment of virgins and their *constant need for reassurance* had been unbelievable! Was that how he regarded everyone who came into his orbit? In terms of how they impacted on him? Why, he'd made it sound as if he found some women boring even while he was actually having sex with them! Her heart missed a beat as an annoying flash of jealousy shot through her like a dark flame at the thought of him being intimate with another woman, but, once it had passed, her overriding emotion was one of relief. Thank heavens she hadn't asked him if she was pleasing him! Or if she was 'doing it right'.

But it hadn't been like that, she remembered. There had been no sense of inequality when they had both lain naked on that sofa. It hadn't felt as if he was the super-experienced one—which he clearly was—while she didn't have a clue, because she had never done it before. Because everything which had happened seemed to have happened so naturally. As if, on a physical level at least, they *knew* one another.

She shook her head a little because thoughts like that were dangerous. Fanciful. If she wasn't careful, she would start believing her own stupid fairy-tale version of what had happened. And Roman had tacitly warned her not to do that. He'd said that reality was just a personal interpretation of facts. So she'd better be careful not to misinterpret them.

Surreptitiously, she wiped her palms over the skirt of her silk dress and looked ahead. She could see even more crowds gathered outside the gilded gates of the palace and a huge cheer went up as the open-topped car began to make its stately progress up the wide, tree-lined boulevard.

'Do you like it?' Roman was saying. 'Your new home?'

Zabrina's eyes narrowed as they grew closer. She had seen pictures of the palace, of course she had, for it was widely acknowledged to be one of the finest examples of imperial architecture to be found anywhere in the world. The walls were the colour of rich cream, the conical towers rose-gold. Arched windows were edged with pale stone and a pair of intricately carved columns stood on either side of the vast main doors. In the distance she could see a glimpse of the famous gardens and parkland and, beyond that, the soaring splendour of the Liliachiun mountains.

'It's…beautiful,' she said truthfully, but then almost regretted the sincerity of her words because they had caused Roman to smile with genuine pleasure, and she was ill prepared for the impact of that smile. Did he realise it was like the sun coming out from behind a thunder-dark cloud? He must do. Someone in the past must have told him that when he smiled like that it was like discovering something you'd never realised existed. As if you'd just looked up into the sky and noticed that a second sun had suddenly made an unexpected appearance.

And then he went and spoiled it.

'So you think you will be able to tolerate your position here?' he questioned coolly. 'As the wealthiest consort on the planet, with untold riches at your disposal.'

'How greedy you make me sound,' she reflected, but the stupid thing was that it hurt. She didn't want it to be all about money. She wanted it to be about feelings.

But his steely gaze was completely lacking in emotion. 'Not greedy, Zabrina,' he said calmly. 'Just practical. We're both going into this marriage because of what we stand to gain. And I think it's wise to acknowledge that, don't you? I read the prenuptial contract thoroughly before signing. I saw the clause your lawyer insisted on inserting—that you would be guaranteed a private income of your own.'

His black brows were raised in arrogant query as if demanding an explanation, but Zabrina was damned if she was going to give him one. She had her reasons for wanting that money, but she wasn't ready to share them with him and maybe she never would be. He probably wouldn't believe her anyway. And wasn't there something a bit sad about someone who insisted on pointing out what a do-gooder they were? She didn't trust him, he didn't trust her, so maybe they should just leave it at that.

She shrugged. 'And I noticed your lawyer inserted a rider to that clause, saying that I would only get the money for as long as the marriage lasted.'

'Of course he did. Otherwise there would be no incentive for you to make the marriage work, would there? You could just take the money and run.'

He said something harsh beneath his breath, and Zabrina frowned.

'Did you just say…"*just like my mother*"?' she asked slowly.

She spoke without thinking and must have hit a raw nerve because a flash of something dark ravaged the carved beauty of his face. It was as if he'd put on a savage mask which made him almost unrecognisable, but it was gone in an instant, his features shuttered and emotionless again—as if he was all too aware that the prying lenses of the cameras were trained on them.

'I had forgotten that you spoke fluent Petrogorian,' he bit out. 'Perhaps I would do well to guard my tongue in future. But even so, do you consider this is an appropriate time to ambush me with such questions?'

Zabrina was aware that she had either hurt or angered him but she hadn't meant to do either. It hadn't been intended as a point-scoring exercise, or a desire to catch him off-guard—she'd just wanted to find out more about the man she was to marry.

'Roman—'

'Let's just concentrate on what we're supposed to be doing, shall we?' he interrupted, his lips barely moving as he edged out the words—presumably to foil any would-be lip-readers. 'And smile. No, a *big* smile, Princess. Act like you really mean it. We're here.'

The powerful car drew to a halt in front of the applauding palace staff and Zabrina glanced up to see figures clustered at upstairs windows high above, capturing the image on their cell-phones. Roman leapt from the car and opened her car door himself and as he held out his hand to help her down, Zabrina was aware of two things. Firstly, that the brief touch of his fingers was enough to send soft shivers of desire rippling down her spine, making her wish he would lift them to his lips and kiss them. But he didn't.

Because the second thing she noticed—and this was the one which stayed with her for the rest of the day— was that the grey eyes which were turned in her direction were as empty and as cold as ice.

CHAPTER EIGHT

SOFT SUNLIGHT FLICKERED over the profuse spill of roses, bathing the famous gardens in a rich golden glow as Zabrina stared out of the vast windows.

But no matter how hard she tried to concentrate on the beauty outside, or on the small dish of fruit on the table in front of her, it was difficult to focus on anything other than the devastatingly handsome man who was seated opposite. The morning light was glinting on his cropped dark hair, making her realise how much it had grown, and his snowy white shirt emphasised the muscular width of his shoulders.

Suddenly he pushed his empty coffee cup away and leaned back in his chair to study her. Was he aware she'd been watching him with a hungry desire which wouldn't seem to go away? And did that fill him with a sense of triumph—and power?

'Today's the big day, isn't it?' he said.

Zabrina gazed at him blankly. The only 'big day' which seemed to be on everyone's lips wasn't for another three weeks—unless somebody had brought the wedding forward and not bothered to tell the bride. She hoped not, because there were still what looked like five million seed pearls to sew onto her traditional Petrogorian wedding dress and sequins which needed to be scattered all over her tulle veil. She picked up her silver spoon, still trying to get used to the enormous emerald and diamond engagement ring which felt too heavy for her finger. 'Big day?' she repeated.

'Your horse,' he said. 'What time does it arrive?'

'He. The horse is a he, not an it,' Zabrina corrected, watching as a servant silently moved forward to refill the King's cup with inky-black coffee. 'And his name is Midas.'

'Ah!' He picked up a sugar cube. 'Named after the king who wished for an excess of gold and almost ruined his life in the process?'

'That's the one.'

He lifted his dark brows in arrogant query. 'Perhaps there is an allegory in that story for us, Zabrina.'

'Let's hope not,' she said darkly.

A brief smile curved the edges of his lips as he dropped the sugar into the cup and began to stir and Zabrina found herself mesmerised by the circular movement of his fingers, wondering how he could make such a simple action look so insanely sexy. But then, he made just about everything he did look sexy. Was that deliberate? Was he taunting her? Reminding her of that heart-punching intimacy they'd shared on the Petrogoria-bound train, which was now being put on hold until they were married?

Stop it, she thought. *Just stop it. You are supposed to be having a polite breakfast conversation about the day ahead.*

The kind of measured diary conversation they'd been having every morning since she'd arrived in Petrogoria last week. This was the public face of their formal engagement, as opposed to the private anxieties which plagued her every night when she was alone in bed.

Over coffee, fruit and eggs over easy—for him—they would go through the various royal duties which had been mapped out for them by their private offices—some together and some apart. Solo duties she welcomed. In many ways, it was less distracting when Roman wasn't by her side distracting her with his powerful presence.

Hadn't she thought—hoped—that he would go back on his determination for their nights to be spent separately? But she had been wrong. He hadn't and now she had started to wonder if his reluctance to touch her meant he was having second thoughts about the wedding. But rejection was something she wouldn't countenance—not now—and so she threw herself into her new charities with fervour, hoping that her engagements would make her fit in and feel easier about her place here.

Because Roman had been right. Or rather, Roman when he had been masquerading as Constantin and answering her questions with an alluring frankness, leaving her wondering which of them was the real man. The understanding and passionate bodyguard, or the cold, disciplined king?

It didn't matter.

The fact remained that the royal palace of Petrogoria *was* intimidating, just as he'd warned her.

For a start it was big. Way bigger than she'd imagined and everything was on a much larger scale than what she was used to. It made her childhood home seem like a matchbox lined up next to a shoebox. And it wasn't just the size—it was all the contents. There was more of *everything*. More Old Master paintings, more

ancient books and precious artefacts. The scaled-up
fountains sprayed bigger and more impressive plumes
of water and the corridors seemed endless. And these
weren't the familiar corridors of home—the ones which
she'd run along and explored and hidden in, from when
she'd first learned to walk. These were impossibly wide
marble passageways, lined by inscrutable servants who
bowed or curtseyed whenever she passed them. Here
there were no friendly cooks or grooms who'd known
her since babyhood and who had treated her with a
slightly modified version of informality, which she'd
always found comforting.

Roman had described it as home.

It just didn't feel like *her* home.

Life here was like being part of a beautifully choreo-
graphed dance—with the King positioned at its glittering centre. Everything revolved around him. Sometimes
Zabrina felt like a satellite to his blazing sun—as if she
were an insignificant and very distant star. Each day
they took their meals together in different dining rooms,
all of them exquisite. They ate breakfast overlooking the
fabled rose gardens and lunch was taken in a huge win-
dowed chamber, decorated in a dizzying spectrum of
blues. Dinner was served either in the supposedly more
low-key Rose Room—which wasn't low-key at all—or,
if they had company, in the highly ornate Golden Dining Room. Because if people were coming to eat in a
palace as famous as this one, they liked to really feel
they'd had the whole palace 'experience'.

After dinner she and Roman might have a nightcap—
rare—before retiring to their separate suites, though
she gathered from remarks which Silviana had made
that the King often worked in his study until the early

hours of the morning. Whatever he did, it didn't involve her. In fact, none of his life did. Not physically, at least. Amid the careful carving out of her role as his future queen and the increasingly frenetic arrangements for the wedding, there had been no rerun of that heady sensual episode on the train.

The King of Petrogoria had not laid a finger on her since she'd walked over the threshold of his glittering golden palace.

Had she thought it might be different?

Yes, of course she had.

Had she offended him hugely by kicking him out of her carriage that night, when it had been obvious that—after all the dust had settled—he had wanted to stay and carry on with more of what they'd been doing? Probably. She had felt so strong and so sure of herself at the time. She'd been infused with a powerful sense of self brought about by that magical sexual encounter and had felt no qualms about castigating him for his deception, and for refusing to believe that he was her first lover.

Yet the annoying thing was that her show of defiance seemed to have backfired on her—because he had taken her at her word, quite literally! And by keeping his physical distance, he had managed to fill her with a lingering sense of uncertainty. The brief and heady authority she had felt when he had been in her arms had shifted, and now *he* was the one who seemed to possess all the power. She wondered if she had wounded his pride and ego in such a way that he now found the thought of touching her unpalatable. Should she ask him?

Roman, don't you find me sexually attractive any more?

Roman, don't you want to take me to bed?

No. Because deep down she knew the answer to that, no matter how insecure she sometimes felt. It was made plain by the smoky hunger which flared in his eyes whenever she inadvertently caught him watching her, before quickly composing his handsome face into its more habitual impassive mask. He still wanted her, all right. That mutual desire showed no sign of abating. Predictably and potently, it fizzed between them whenever they were in the same room together. Like a flame, she thought, with equal longing and despair—bright and vital—yet tantalisingly ephemeral.

His grey gaze was fixed on her questioningly. 'So is he gold?'

'Who?' She looked at him in confusion, trying to gather together the scramble of her thoughts. 'Oh, you mean Midas?'

He made no attempt to hide his sardonic smile. 'Isn't that what we've just been talking about?'

She flushed, wondering if he had any idea what had been preoccupying her. She hoped not. Though what did she know? Probably any woman who found herself alone with him spent the majority of their time fantasising about what he was like in bed. It was almost a pity that she had actually experienced it—because didn't that make it harder to shift the tantalising images from her head?

She cleared her throat and forced herself to concentrate on her beloved horse. 'No, he's not really golden. More of a bay. An Akhal Teke, actually. But when I first got him it was my birthday and I was taken down to the stables early in the morning and there he was, with the sunshine glinting off his coat like metal—and he looked...well, he looked magical really. Like a living golden statue.' She paused, the iced mango in her bowl forgotten as an unexpected wave of nostalgia washed over her and she looked at him rather sheepishly, surprised by the narrowed interest in his grey eyes. 'I don't know what made me tell you that.'

But she did know. It was just a long time since she'd allowed herself to think about it.

It had been one of those unusual periods of her upbringing when an air of something like calm had settled over the palace, mostly because her father had returned into the bosom of his family after his latest affair. After one of these interludes, her mother's overriding reaction would always be one of profound relief that everything could be 'normal' again. Often, this would provide the ideal opportunity for the palace to release a photo depicting happy family life. It was also one of the reasons why her father would overcompensate—materially, at least—and overspend even more than usual. Thus, Zabrina had been gifted a beautiful and very expensive horse with a scarlet ribbon tied around his neck and the cake they had all eaten later for her birthday tea had been ridiculously big.

The memory of that monstrous gateau made her feel a little nauseous and she pushed her half-eaten dish of mango away, forcing herself to change the subject. But maybe she should capitalise on the fact that Roman seemed to have let his guard down and this was the most relaxed he'd been. There were a million questions she wanted to ask him but instinct told her that she needed to tread carefully. Maybe he was like a prized thoroughbred, who needed careful handling. 'Can I ask you something, Roman?'

Instantly, his eyes narrowed with caution. 'You can ask. I won't guarantee that I'll answer.'

She wondered if he had been a lawyer in a previous life. 'Are you planning to do anything with the Marengo Forest after our wedding?'

Roman sat back in his chair as he stared into the long-lashed beauty of her green eyes. She could be quite…unexpected, he conceded. He had imagined her mind to be flapping with those tiresome thoughts women so often entertained and had been anticipating her demanding to know how he 'felt' about her. And that was the last thing he wanted to answer. Because the bizarre truth of that was he didn't really know and there was no way he wanted Zabrina to realise that.

She seemed such a contradiction. Sometimes seasoned, sometimes innocent, sometimes spoiled and at others sweetly thoughtful. Her complexity intrigued him and he had no wish to be intrigued, because that wasn't what this union was supposed to be about. She unsettled him and he didn't like being unsettled by a woman. Hadn't he vowed that was never going to happen to him again? That no woman should have any kind of power over his thoughts and his feelings?

That was one of the reasons why he hadn't touched her since he'd brought her to his palace. Why he hadn't given into the silken tug of desire even though every time he saw her he grew exquisitely hard. He swallowed. Before her arrival, she had been allotted a separate suite at the opposite end of the vast palace complex. At the time he had accepted there would be no sex before marriage because the Princess was a virgin and tradition demanded it. And even though her subsequent behaviour had meant there was no reason for such a restriction, he saw no reason to change the existing plan, because he could see a definite advantage to denial—no matter how frustrating he might find it.

Because hadn't Zabrina of Albastase smashed down all his carefully erected defences that night? Hadn't he found himself unable to resist her in a way which had been mind-blowingly unique? His mouth hardened. She had made him lose control in a way which was alien to him, transforming him into a man he didn't recognise, or particularly respect. In her arms he had felt as if he had died and gone to heaven and it had been terrifying and delicious. But he realised it had put her firmly in the driving seat and he wanted to shift the balance of power back in his favour. And *that* was why he continued to distance himself from his future bride, no matter how great the cost to his equilibrium.

She wanted him. Of course she did. Every woman had always wanted him, ever since he'd reached puberty. But what he felt for her was right off the scale. It was as though provocative and carnal invitation thrummed from every pore of her delicious body. At times it became almost too much to bear and he was tempted to throw caution to the winds and take her in his arms. His fantasy involved either the slowest removal of lingerie in the history of the world, or ripping off her panties and plunging deep into her syrupy heat as her little cries of encouragement urged him on.

But he wasn't going to do that. He was going to make her wait, even if he half tortured himself with frustration in the process. He would demonstrate icy control and defer delight until the appropriate time and that would be an invaluable lesson in self-denial. Zabrina would come to him on their wedding night, humbled by his restraint and eager to taste pleasure once again. Because delay heightened hunger.

His mouth twisted.

Or so he'd heard.

He looked at the gleam of wavy dark hair which fell so abundantly over her shoulders. At the green silk dress which matched her eyes and clung so enticingly to the small and perfect breasts. He'd thought about those breasts a lot recently, especially at night when he'd been lying in his lonely bed, sleeplessly staring as the shifting moon painted the walls silver. Just as he'd thought about her strong, slim thighs and the way his head had fitted so perfectly between them.

'Of course I'm planning to *do* something with the Marengo Forest,' he said, reluctantly dragging his thoughts back to the present, knowing he had no one but himself to blame for the hard throb of his erection. He cleared his throat. 'Its return has been in my sights for a long time and I have big plans for it.'

She looked up from where she had begun to pleat her napkin with those tanned fingers which had worked such magic on his shuddering flesh. 'You do?'

He frowned. 'Why else do you think I should go to so much trouble to acquire it? Why I'm prepared to pay such a monumental amount of money for it, in the form of your dowry?'

'I hope you think I'm worth it.'

He saw her cheeks colour and momentarily felt a little bad as she made the sardonic comment, but only for a moment. Hadn't they both agreed to be pragmatic about the situation? 'It's a deal, Zabrina,' he said simply. 'Remember? And this is not just about territory— about me having some hypothetical need to return the

Petrogorian flag to its rightful place. I want to build an airport nearby—it's a pristine, natural wilderness which is ripe for sympathetic eco-tourism.'

'Oh.' Her fingers stilled on the napkin, the white linen folds making her skin look like softest gold. 'Oh, I see.'

'So what makes you appear so crestfallen?' he enquired idly. 'The price I'm paying for that piece of land is more than you could have ever hoped of achieving, if you'd sold it on the open market. Even you must realise that.'

'Yes, of course I do. It's not that.'

'What, then?'

'It doesn't matter.' She shook her head. 'It won't be of any possible interest to you.'

'Why don't you let me be the judge of that?' He took a sip of coffee. 'I'm interested to know what's making you bite your lip as if you have all the cares of the world on your shoulders.'

Imprisoned in the grey spotlight of his narrowed eyes, Zabrina hesitated. Should she tell him what she'd been thinking? This was to be nothing but a marriage of 'convenience', which presumably meant they could keep things on a very superficial level. But what was the point of keeping everything buttoned up inside her? Wasn't one of the benefits of a live-in relationship supposed to be that you were at liberty to confide in your partner? And surely it would be good to talk to someone who might actually *listen*, rather than her mother—on whose deaf ears Zabrina's concerns had always fallen, so that she'd given up expressing her fears a long time ago.

'If you must know, I admire your ambitious plans about a region which has lain neglected for so long...'

'But? I suspect there's a "but" coming?'

'I guess I'm also slightly frustrated that my country didn't think of doing it first.'

'Either nobody considered it, or they didn't have the wherewithal to carry it out. Presumably the latter.' He looked at her with a steady gaze. 'It usually boils down to hard finance, Zabrina.'

'I know it does.' She puffed out an unsteady breath. 'I suppose I'm also concerned about the amount of money you're paying for the land. And for me,' she finished drily.

He raised his eyebrows. 'You don't think it's enough?'

She gave a short laugh. 'Nobody in the world could think that. It's an extremely generous amount of money. I'm more worried about what's going to happen to it when it lands in my father's bank account.'

'He could spend it wisely. Make sure it's ploughed back into the country.' He gave a shrug. 'You know. Invest in some new infrastructure.'

Zabrina could feel her cheeks colour as she wondered whether it might be wise to close the subject down. Anyone who had been to Albastase knew it was getting very frayed around the edges, but few people knew just how inept the King was at managing finances. Sometimes she wished this money had been transferred directly to the government, bypassing the royal coffers, giving him little opportunity to fritter it away—but she could hardly denounce her own father.

'I hope so.'

'You don't sound very convinced.'

She had obviously failed to inject a tone of enthusiasm into her voice but Roman's perception surprised her. She hadn't thought of him as a student of nuance.

Just as she hadn't expected him to continue to regard her with what looked like genuine interest.

And somehow she started telling him about it. Stuff which she never talked about with her family, because there had been no point. Her mother could not or would not act, her sisters were too young and uninterested and her brother... Zabrina swallowed. Her brother was already having difficulty coming to terms with the fact that one day he would be King and she didn't want to be the one to add to those concerns. They had been like the family of someone with an unacknowledged drinking problem...as if by ignoring it, the problem would somehow go away.

'My father can sometimes be...extravagant.'

'That is surely one of the perks of being a king.'

Her jaw worked and somehow all her fears about leaving everyone back home to fend for themselves came tumbling out. 'No. This is more than having a garage full of fancy cars, or a fleet of racehorses which he keeps overseas.'

'I'm glad about that,' he said wryly. 'Or I might find myself the subject of your obvious disapproval.'

She shook her head slightly impatiently. 'It's more than extravagance. He's surrounded by a coterie of stupid advisors and the trouble is that he listens to them. They keep getting him to invest in their friends' supposedly amazing business schemes, only they never quite work out the way they're supposed to and he gets his fingers burned. Every time.'

'Then one has to ask the question as to why he keeps doing it,' said Roman coolly. 'Don't they say that the definition of madness is to keep repeating the same mistake, over and over again?'

'Because he doesn't believe in his own fallibility and when it happens, he needs something to reassure him that he's as clever as he thinks he is,' said Zabrina quietly. 'Which is why, after every failure, he grabs at that guaranteed age-old ego boost so beloved of men.' And wasn't it crazy that she *still* felt a sense of guilt as she admitted the truth to the man she was soon to marry, as if she were wrong to criticise her own father. Yet in the midst of all these misgivings, it felt a huge relief to be able to confide in him like this.

'And you're worried because your country is gradually being run down?' Roman questioned.

'Of course I am. But I'm more worried that by the time my brother Alexandru inherits, there won't be anything left. He's a delicate young man,' she whispered. 'And super-sensitive. I'd hate for him to take on the burden of kingship if he was also saddled by an enormous debt!' she finished, her lips wobbling a little with the impact of expressing all that usually bottled-up emotion. She looked into the King's face but, as usual, its cool impassiveness gave nothing away.

Instead he raised his fingers and the servant brought him another cup of coffee, before Roman indicated he should leave—signalling that this breakfast might go on longer than anticipated. And that surprised Zabrina, because usually these meal times were strictly regulated and chaperoned—as if the man she was to marry couldn't bear to be alone in her company a second more than he needed to.

'I can understand that,' he said slowly. 'But now you've triggered my interest.'

'Oh?'

He lifted his gaze to hers. 'What *exactly* is the age-old ego boost your father always resorts to?'

She guessed they'd always needed to have this discussion, so why not now, even though it wasn't really the kind of thing she'd ever imagined discussing calmly over the muesli? Because Roman was a king and what she was about to talk about was what all kings did. It came with the territory and she was surprised he even needed to ask.

'Affairs,' she said simply. 'He has affairs.'

CHAPTER NINE

ROMAN STUDIED ZABRINA'S expression with a curiosity he didn't bother to hide, because something about the calm acceptance he read there surprised him. 'Explain,' he clipped out. 'About your father's affairs.'

She shrugged with studied carelessness, but he didn't miss the fleeting look of apprehension which crossed her eyes.

'They usually come about as a reaction to one of his disastrous business investments,' she began slowly. 'You see, he loses huge amounts of money and promises himself it will never happen again.' She stared at the pink roses in the vase at the centre of the table, before lifting her gaze to his again. 'But in the meantime he needs something to make him feel better—to take his mind off what he's done. And women can do that. They can fill that emotional hole—just like a drink or an unnecessary plate of food. And, of course, he's a king. So he can do what the hell he likes.'

'Isn't that a rather sweeping generalisation?'

She laughed. A sound he had heard only infrequently and usually he was forced to steel himself against its soft lure, but now it was edged with the hard ring of cynicism.

'I'm only basing my comments on experience, Roman.'

'Of observing your father, you mean?'

She shook her head. 'No, not just that. Don't forget my mother is a princess herself and she and her sisters all married monarchs and, according to her, they have all "strayed". I always thought that was a funny expression to use,' she added reflectively. 'It reminds me of a horse or a cow somehow managing to get out of its enclosure.'

He guessed that was supposed to be a joke but the brittle note in her voice suggested she wasn't as comfortable with the subject as she wanted him to think.

'So your mother just accepted this state of affairs, if you'll excuse the pun?'

She didn't laugh, just shrugged. 'In a way. She said it was easier to accept than to constantly rail against something she couldn't change. She told me that husbands always returned—eventually. Especially if there was a calm and non-accusatory welcome for them to come back to. And especially if there were children involved.'

He felt the chill of something dark. The indelible shadow of his childhood making itself known without warning. His heart clenched with pain but he was practised enough to be able to eject the thought and corresponding emotion as far from his mind as possible, and to continue to subject Zabrina to a steady stare instead. 'And what about wives?' he questioned softly. 'Do they also stray?'

Either she was genuinely shocked by his question or she was a superb actress, for her lips fell open and she frowned.

'Well, no. She never did.'

'Why not?'

'Because men are different.'

'In other ways than anatomically, you mean?' he challenged, disproportionately pleased to see the blush which made her cheeks colour so thoroughly.

She glared. 'That's not funny. It's a biological thing, or so my mother always said. I'm not saying that infidelity is necessarily a good idea—more that it's understandable. Nature's way of ensuring the human race continues, because men—'

'I get the idea, Zabrina. There's no need to spell it out,' he interrupted drily, taking a final sip of coffee before pushing his cup away. 'So will your extremely liberal views on fidelity impact on our own marriage?'

She paused. For effect, Roman suspected, more than anything else. Because surely she must have given this subject *some* consideration in the light of her own experience.

'This is a duty marriage,' she said at last. 'And I don't have any unrealistic expectations about that side of it. I know that men often get bored when they have been intimate with one woman for any length of time, and that they crave new excitement.'

'Who the hell told you *that*?'

'My mother. She's a very practical person.'

Roman thought these views cynical rather than practical, but he didn't say so. 'I see.'

'What's important to me is providing a secure base for the family we both hope to have.'

'Well, that's something, at least,' he said and maybe some of his own cynicism had become apparent because she shot him a quick and rather worried look.

'You do *want* a family?' she verified. 'I mean, I know we touched on it on the train—'

'We did a lot of touching on the train, Zabrina.'

'That's not funny.'

'No?'

'No.' Her voice was bitter. 'I wish I could forget that trip.'

'So do I,' he said, with more force than he had intended.

'All I ask…'

He could see her throat constricting and she appeared to be conducting a struggle to find the right words. 'Don't upset yourself,' he said, with a sudden wave of empathy which surprised him. 'We don't have to talk about this right now.'

'But we do. We need to get all these things out of the way. All I ask,' she continued stolidly, 'is that you're discreet—both before, during and after any affair you may choose to have. That you don't rub my face in it.'

'This is extraordinary,' he breathed, raking his fingers back through his shorn hair which, thankfully, was beginning to grow a little. 'You're basically giving me carte blanche to be unfaithful?'

She didn't appear to be listening, for her gaze was locked to the movement of his hand and he found himself remembering the way she had pressed her fingers into his scalp when she'd been coming, crying out something softly in her own language. He wondered if she had been remembering it too. Hell. Why think about that *now*? He shifted uncomfortably in his chair, thankful that the sudden jerk of his erection was concealed by the snowy fall of the tablecloth. But his thoughts quickly shifted from desire to evaluation. He tried to imagine how other men in his position would react if confronted with the astounding fact that their wife-to-be was prepared to look the other way, if he were ever unfaithful. But her words gave him no heady rush of freedom or anticipation—in fact, his overriding feeling was one of indignation and a slowly simmering anger.

'Why, Zabrina?' he demanded. 'Are you planning to do the same? To take other men as your lovers and expect me to be understanding in turn?'

'Of course not! If you want the truth, I can't imagine ever wanting any other man but you.'

He sat back in his chair, surprised by her candour. This wasn't the first time this particular sentiment had been expressed to him by a woman—yet instead of his usual irritation he found himself ridiculously pleased by her sweet honesty. 'I see,' he said, again.

'Obviously I would prefer our marriage to be monogamous, because I've seen the havoc these affairs can wreak. I've seen the damage they can inflict on a couple's relationship.' She tore off a fragment of croissant and lifted it to her mouth before seeming to change her mind and putting it back down on the plate again. Her eyes were very dark and very direct. 'And since we're on the subject. You haven't told me anything about your own parents.'

Instantly he was on the defensive. 'There's nothing much to tell. It's all on the record, as I'm sure you know. I imagine you've seen it for yourself.' Roman could feel his throat thicken and cursed the pain one woman's desertion could still cause him. No wonder he never talked about it. No wonder he had closed his mind to it a long time ago. 'My mother left when I was three years old and I never saw her again,' he said baldly. 'My father never remarried.'

'But—'

'But what?' he interrupted, forcing all the bitter emotion from his words and replacing it with a tone of cool finality. He reminded himself that this was a conversation they needed to have only once and he could make it as short as he wanted. 'Those are the facts, Zabrina. I've never gone in for analysis and I don't intend to start now.' He stared down at the inky brew in his coffee cup before lifting his gaze to hers. 'And since we're being so remarkably frank, there's something else we should address. I think we both need to know where we stand on the subject of divorce, don't you?'

Zabrina grew still as his words filtered across the table towards her, stabbing at her like little arrows. She should have been prepared for this question but, stupidly, she wasn't and as a result she found herself filled with another rush of uncertainty. Had she thought that if she was so reasonable on the subject of fidelity, Roman might declare she would be his wife for life? And wasn't there some inexplicable part of her which *wanted* that—because while she might feel unsettled around him, weirdly she felt really *safe*? As if Roman could protect her from some of the terrors of the world. That as long as he was by her side, nothing really bad could happen.

Why think something as irrational as that?

She stared at the sunny gleam of her half-eaten mango, trying to work out what had changed inside her, but it was difficult to put her finger on, mainly because she didn't understand the softening of her feelings towards the man she was soon to marry. It wasn't just the amazing sex they'd shared on the train—although that had obviously been the most incredible thing which had ever happened to her. It was more to do with his subsequent behaviour and the conversations they shared whenever they took their meals together. He spoke to her as if she were his equal. She realised that sometimes Roman could seem as sympathetic as 'Constantin' had been. He made her feel as if her views counted. As if she was an intelligent person worthy of consideration. And nobody had ever done that before.

But that didn't mean she should allow herself to be lulled into a false sense of security, because, although his attitude towards her might sometimes be sympathetic, his feelings hadn't changed. He didn't *have* feelings towards her, remember? Of *course* he would wish to address the subject of divorce, because it was relevant. This wasn't an emotional discussion, she reminded herself, but a practical one. They were a modern monarchy and there wasn't a royal family in the world which hadn't been affected by marital breakdown. Divorce no longer held any real stigma—other than the devastating heartbreak her auntie had told her about after she'd gone through it herself. Perhaps that was what had made her mother so determined to hang onto her own marriage, no matter what. And surely she couldn't be condemned for that.

'I don't know about you,' she said, meeting the question in his eyes, 'but I would prefer to avoid divorce, especially if there are children involved. Though obviously,' she amended hurriedly, 'if circumstances were to change—'

'In what sense?' he questioned coolly.

The words were threatening to stick in the back of

her throat, so that each one felt as if it had been coated with tar. 'If, say, you were to meet another woman,' she began. 'And to fall in love with her. Then obviously I wouldn't stand in your way, if you wanted to end the marriage.'

His face was shuttered. 'How very understanding of you, Zabrina. I had no idea I was marrying such a libertarian.'

'Why, what would you prefer me to do?' she demanded. 'Display an undignified rage and rake your cheeks with my fingernails?'

'Honestly?' He gave a short laugh. 'Right now what I would prefer you to do involves being locked in my arms.'

But it was less of a question and more of a statement and the short silence which followed was broken by the smooth glide of his chair against the marble floor. Zabrina's heart began to thunder and she felt the curl of excitement low in her belly as he rose to his feet.

'Roman,' she said—and this too was a statement, because he was walking around the table towards her, moving with a natural grace and stealth which was incredible to watch, and the look of intent on his sensual features cried out to something deep inside her. Something which scared and excited her. She tried to bat the feelings away but somehow it wasn't working. Beneath her silk dress, she could feel her nipples tightening into hard buds and surely he must be able to see that too? There was a syrupy tug in her belly and suddenly she longed for him to touch her there. She swallowed and felt her cheeks colour. Yes, *there*—where the aching was at its most intense. Did he see her blush? Was that why his lips curved into that seeking smile?

He was beside her now. Reaching down and lifting her clean off the chair—or was she reaching up to him? She didn't know, and afterwards she would find it impossible to remember. All she knew was that there were no servants present—for he had dismissed them all— and that this was the first time they had been alone since she had stepped off that train in Rosumunte.

And that they seemed to be in the middle of some crazy sexual power game.

'Roman,' she whispered.

'We're done talking,' he husked. 'Just kiss me.'

It was an uneven request which went straight to her heart but Zabrina needed no such instruction because her lips were already seeking his, and, oh, that first touch of his skin against hers made her gasp. How could a simple kiss feel like this? How come that already she wanted to explode with pleasure? One of his hands was tangled in the fall of her hair while the other was on her peaking breast, his thumb circling the pebbled nipple with dextrous provocation which was making her want to squirm. Sanity implored her to call a halt but she couldn't. She didn't want to.

Her hands explored the width of his powerful shoulders then reacquainted themselves with his chest, her nails scraping hungrily against the fine linen of his shirt. She could feel the faint whorl of hair against his muscular torso and, as he cupped his palms possessively over her buttocks, he deepened the kiss. He was pulling her even closer, so that his body was imprinted on hers. She felt the rocky outline of his erection and remembered what it had been like when he had been naked and proud, and she shuddered in his arms.

'Sweet heaven,' he husked, and never had she thought

that a man so powerful could sound so helpless. 'How the hell do you do that?'

'Do what?'

'I don't know,' he grated, almost angrily, as he circled his hips against her, his voice dipping to a silken murmur. 'Do you like that?'

'You know I do,' she whispered back.

The words seemed to stir him into action, for he began to move. He was backing her across the room, his mouth not leaving hers, until she could feel the coolness of the wall pressing against her back. His mouth was on her neck. Her jaw. As she looped her arms around his neck and arched herself into the hardness of his body he gave a low laugh, and the sound of his exultation thrilled her even more. And now his fingers were rucking up her dress and lightly tracking over the goose-pimples which were rippling over her thighs. Any minute now and he would reach her panties, whose moist panel felt like an unbearable barrier, denying him the access she was so desperate to grant him. She squirmed in expectation and he gave an unsteady laugh.

'Do you have any idea of how much I want you, Princess?' he bit out in a tone she'd never heard him use before, and in that moment Zabrina felt a wave of the same heady power which had flooded her the first time he'd made love to her. *She* could make him feel like this.

But that random thought was her undoing—or maybe her salvation.

Because he hadn't 'made love' to her, had he?

He'd had sex with her while pretending to be someone else! He'd thought—and presumably still did—that she had a comprehensive backlist of lovers! He'd tried to wriggle out of marrying her!

Reality shattered the tension like a rock hurled through a window, but she tried to block it because she didn't want to think about those things right now. She didn't want to destroy the pleasure she was feeling. But, infuriatingly, she couldn't keep them at bay any longer—and one thought dominated everything. Wasn't this just another example of Constantin/Roman amusing himself with her as if she were his own, personal plaything? And was she prepared to go along with that?

No, she was not.

Somehow Zabrina untangled herself from his arms and took a step sideways, needing to put some space between them, terrified that any closer and she'd be tempted to carry on. But hot on her frustration came a sudden wave of irritation when she saw just how *composed* Roman looked. Why, he might have been doing nothing more strenuous than reading the financial pages of the newspaper!

'That's enough,' she said, in a low voice.

'So I see. But you're not going to deny how much you were enjoying that, are you?' he challenged softly.

Oh, if only that were the case—but Zabrina was no hypocrite. She wished she knew what she wanted. Or what she didn't want. Deep down she wanted to make a success of this arranged marriage, but everything seemed to be in such a muddle. *She* was in a muddle and she didn't know what do.

She wanted to burst into tears and laugh out loud, all at the same time. She wanted to rush from the breakfast room—yet she wanted him to lock the door and finish what they had started. But she mustn't. She really mustn't. The King of Petrogoria had spent the last week treating her with polite and considered detachment. He

hadn't shown a single jot of desire for her. He had behaved as if she were some convalescing relative who'd
come to stay at the palace, not the flesh and blood woman
he was soon to marry. Only now he seemed to have become bored with that particular course of action—and
presumably that was why he had kissed her. Was this
all some sort of game to him? Did he think she was like
one of those old-fashioned dolls her grandmother used
to have—the ones you wound up so they would obedi-
ently walk and talk for you?

'You know I was enjoying it. But we both know
the rules. Or rather, I thought we did. No...' Her voice
trembled a little but she forced herself to say it. Why
be shy of saying something they'd actually *done*? 'No
sex until we're officially man and wife.'

'That didn't seem to bother you on the train, Zabrina.'

'I wasn't... I wasn't thinking straight on the train,'
she said, smoothing the crumpled skirt of her dress with
palms which were clammy. 'And we were lucky not to
have been caught. We might not be so lucky this time.
So if you'll excuse me, I'm going. I want to get down
to the stables before my dress fitting and check everything is ready for Midas's arrival.'

'As you wish.' He was looking at her thoughtfully—
as if he knew perfectly well that her composure was
nothing but a façade. But the hard gleam of his eyes
was underpinned with something else and she couldn't
quite work out what it was. 'Oh, and I'm going away
for a few days.'

And Zabrina was surprised by the sudden sinking
of her heart. He was going away without her, leaving
her alone in the palace? 'Where?'

'I'm taking a short trip to the Marengo Forest. I want

to meet with a few people there so we can get the ball rolling on the airport development as soon as the wedding takes place.'

She nodded her head. Of *course* his mind was fixed on his shiny new acquisition—wasn't that the main reason he would soon be sliding a golden band on her finger? And, while he might have been momentarily distracted by that passionate encounter, he wasn't obsessing about it, like her. He wasn't reading all kinds of things into it which simply didn't exist. So show him how independent you can be. Don't be such a *limpet*. She nodded. 'In that case, I'll see you when you get back. Have a good trip.'

He had started walking ahead and when Zabrina realised he was pulling rank on her, she had to resist a childish urge to race him to the door! But just as he reached the door, he briefly turned his dark head.

'Oh, by the way, you'll find some jewellery waiting when you get back to your suite.'

'What kind of jewellery?'

'Just a necklace. I thought you could wear it to the palace ball on Saturday.'

CHAPTER TEN

'JUST' A NECKLACE, Roman had said. But this wasn't just any old necklace, Zabrina had quickly realised. This was a glitzy waterfall of sparkling emeralds and diamonds which was too big and too heavy and completely swamped her. But she supposed it was exactly the sort of accessory people would expect a future queen to wear and she had to admit that the jewels matched perfectly her green ball gown. And how strange it was that as she had slithered into the silk creation earlier, she had felt a slow building of anticipation rather than dread. From someone who had hated dresses she had found herself wondering if Roman would approve of her outfit. It came as something of a shock to realise she was dressing for *him*.

The candlelit ballroom was decked with fragrant white roses and now, as the remains of the seven-course banquet were cleared away and the Petrogorian Chamber Orchestra started to play, Roman led her from the table to begin the dancing. The other guests had formed a circle around the dance floor like spectators at a bullfight, to watch the newly engaged couple on their first formal outing. But Zabrina was aware that every eye in the golden ballroom was fixed on *her*. People's gazes were running over her assessingly. Possibly critically. She worried that the high-flown members of Petrogorian society wouldn't approve of the Princess who was shortly to become their Queen. She found herself wishing she'd worn higher shoes because she barely reached Roman's shoulder and surely the discrepancy in their height must make them look faintly bizarre as a couple.

Her sudden attack of anxiety wasn't helped by the recognition that some of the most beautiful women she'd ever seen were gathered in this sumptuous ballroom, along with their powerful husbands. But her smile hadn't faltered as line after line of Roman's loyal subjects had filed in front of her before dinner, and the Prime Minister had seemed favourably impressed when she'd quoted from one of his country's ancient poets.

Zabrina could feel the loud skitter of her pulse as Roman put his arms around her and she tried not to let her inner excitement show too much. The King had been away in the Marengo Forest for three whole days and she was taken aback by how pleased she'd been to see him again. To touch him again. Wasn't it crazy how being on a dance floor allowed you to be intimate with a man in a way which would be forbidden anywhere else? And she had missed him. Missed him more than she should have done, considering she'd barely known him a fortnight. More than anything, she wanted to talk to him because they'd been seated at opposite sides of the table during the sumptuous banquet and had barely exchanged a word all evening.

'So, when did you get back?' she asked a little breathlessly as they began to move in time to the music, because she was acutely aware of the indentation of his fingers at her waist.

'This morning.'

'Oh.' A stupid sense of disappointment washed over her. He'd been here all day and hadn't bothered to let her know? She wanted to say, *Why didn't you come and find me?* Or, *Why didn't you join me for lunch?* But maybe that would have been presumptuous. As if she were laying down terms, or revealing expectations he might stubbornly refuse to meet if he were aware of them. Instead she strove to find just the right, light touch. To sound like the kind of undemanding partner he might wish to spend more time with and not one who was immediately haranguing him with demands. 'I've been with Midas for most of the day.'

'I know you have.' There was a pause. 'I came down to the stables to see you.'

She turned her face upwards, aware of the faintly shadowed jut of his jaw and the sensual curve of his lips. 'But you didn't come over and say hello?'

'You looked as if you were preoccupied. I didn't want to disturb you. I watched you riding for a while and that kept me…entertained. You are quite something on the back of a horse, Zabrina.'

Something in his tone spooked her—but not nearly as much as the thought of Roman quietly observing her, his pewter eyes glinting from within the concealment of the stable yard's many shadows. She wondered how long he had been there for. She wondered if she would have behaved any differently if she'd known he was watching.

'How was the Marengo?' she said, changing the subject.

'The Marengo was fine,' he replied evenly. And then,

'You didn't tell me that your groom was planning on coming to Petrogoria, too.'

She stiffened a little. 'That's because I didn't know.'

'You didn't *know*?'

'Well, that's not strictly true. Not specifically. I knew one of the grooms would travel with him and Stefan has known Midas since he was a foal, so I guess it made sense that he should have been the one to make the journey. But when he got here…well.' She shrugged, feeling the heavy weight of the jewels scratching against her skin and she wished she could just rip them from her neck and drop them to the ground. 'It seemed silly for him to go back immediately, so I gave him permission to stay. Just to get the horse properly settled in, of course.'

'Of course,' echoed Roman, his words non-committal as he spun her round, thinking that she was as light as a cloud. He glanced down at the loose dark hair which spilled over her shoulders. At the dark green silk which clung to her slender frame, making her appear pristine and perfectly princess-like, especially when adorned by the priceless glitter of his gift. He contrasted that with the carefree image he had seen on horseback earlier, trotting out of the yard with a banner of a ponytail floating behind her. She had tipped back her head and laughed at something her groom had said and something dark and nebulous had invaded his soul. Something which had been eating him up ever since.

Was it jealousy?

No. He felt the slippery silk of her dress beneath his fingertips and his jaw tightened. It couldn't be.

But just because you'd never felt something before, didn't mean you wouldn't be able to recognise it when you did. And if that *were* the case didn't he only have himself to blame? Despite not being the sort of princess he had ever imagined himself marrying, she had persuaded him into going ahead with the union and he had allowed himself to be persuaded, because the pros had outweighed the cons. Or so he had convinced himself. Theirs was to be an unemotional business arrangement. He knew that and she knew that. She had implied that she was prepared to be 'reasonable' if he sought solace in the arms of another woman, as kings had done from the beginning of time, and by implication that meant he couldn't rule out her doing the same, despite her protestations to the contrary. So why did he feel the primitive throb of dark possession when he even considered that option? Why did he want to roar out his anguish at the thought of her ever being in another man's arms?

But his face betrayed nothing, for an implacable countenance had been drummed into him for as long as he could remember. A king must never show his feelings and, in order to guarantee that, it was preferable not to have those feelings in the first place. It had been one of the first things his father had taught him when he had woken on that bleak, black morning to find his mother gone.

It had been a useful lesson in survival.

'Do you want me to ask him to leave?' Zabrina was saying. 'Is that what you want?'

He looked down, steeling himself against the forest-dark beauty of her eyes and resenting the fact that he found her so enchanting, even while inside he was quietly simmering with rage. 'This isn't supposed to be about what *I* want, Zabrina,' he said coolly. 'This is supposed to be your home, not a prison, and if you want your groom to stay on then that, of course, is your prerogative.'

The music came to an end and the Petrogorian Prime Minister stepped in to ask Zabrina to dance and willingly she resumed her progress around the floor with the portly leader, even though she wanted to stay with Roman and ask him…

She swallowed.

Ask him what? He was being perfectly reasonable, wasn't he? Telling her she was free to do as she wished. Telling her Stefan could stay as long as she wanted. She didn't imagine it would go down very well if she started quizzing him about why he was adopting that tone of voice.

What tone of voice was that?

Dark?

Disapproving?

Yes, both those things.

But if he felt that way, then surely that was his problem. If she tried to accommodate him—to gauge his mood and to modify her behaviour accordingly—wouldn't that be setting an awful precedent, turning her into the kind of woman she didn't really like? Or respect. And it wasn't going to be that kind of marriage, she told herself firmly. A meeting of minds and bodies, hopefully, yes, but ultimately it was a transaction. She needed to keep her independence and sense of self-worth, or else she suspected she could easily fall into a deep hole of useless yearning for someone who saw her simply as a means to an end.

She did her best to put on a credible show as a future queen that night—her mother would have been proud of her. She danced with everyone who asked but made sure she conversed with plenty of the women too, admiring their gowns and jewels and talking about various charitable endeavours. But with Roman there was no more dancing. She told herself it wasn't deliberate and that she was imagining his cool and sudden distancing himself from her. But as the clock chimed out midnight, and she and the King left the ballroom to the tumultuous applause of their guests, Zabrina realised that she hadn't really had a chance to talk to him again.

Servants converged on them, walking both ahead and behind as they made their stately progress towards her suite. But when they arrived outside her door, Zabrina turned to the King, licking her lips and slanting him a nervous smile. 'I wonder, shall we have a…nightcap?'

If she had suggested that he suddenly broke into an impromptu rendition of the Petrogorian national anthem, he couldn't have looked more—not *shocked*, exactly, but certainly slightly appalled. As if she had just come out with a highly irregular proposition and had somehow let herself down.

'Unfortunately that will not be possible. I have work which I need to attend to,' he said coolly, briefly lifting her fingers to his lips and bowing his dark head as he kissed them. 'I will see you at breakfast tomorrow.'

The imprint of his mouth on her hand was all too brief and suddenly Silviana was ushering her inside and helping remove her necklace, before undoing all the little buttons at the back of her ball gown.

'Shall I run you a bath before you retire, mistress?' she ventured.

Zabrina shook her head. 'No, thank you. To be honest, I'd just like to be left on my own now.'

'Is something…forgive me for my presumption, Your Royal Highness, but is something *wrong*?'

Zabrina was biting the inside of her lip but she forced herself to smile. Because what if she answered that question honestly? What if she dared to admit even to herself that she was scared of the way Roman could make her feel? She didn't want his disapproval and yet she didn't want to go seeking his approval like some tame puppet. So where did that leave her?

'No, nothing is wrong.' She widened her smile, hoping it looked more reassuring than it felt. 'It's just been a long day and that was my first official introduction as Roman's future bride.'

'All the servants were saying how fine you looked, mistress,' cooed Silviana. 'And that you will make a wonderful queen.'

'That's very sweet of them. Go now and make sure you get a good rest. You've waited up very late.'

But once the servant had left, Zabrina found herself unable to relax and, even though she undressed and climbed into bed, the adrenalin which was rushing around her body made it impossible for her to sleep. She stared at the ceiling. She stared at the necklace which lay discarded on her dressing table, the pile of stones glittering in the moonlight like a handful of shattered glass.

She thought about Roman, working in his office, no doubt. And then she thought about Midas—because that was easier on her heart than thinking about Roman—and was suddenly overcome with an urgent need to see her beloved horse. She could put her arms around his neck and give him the kind of unconditional love she'd never felt comfortable channelling anywhere else apart from to her siblings.

Sliding on a pair of jodhpurs and a fine wool sweater, she slipped silently from her room, listening for a moment as the door opened soundlessly, her gaze darting down the wide marble corridor. But there was nobody around and maybe that wasn't so odd. Servants had to sleep.

She made her way towards the stables, moving as noiselessly as she could and sticking mainly to the shadows but thankfully encountering nobody along the way. Outside in the fresh air the moon was still waxing— every night getting bigger and brighter—and the stable yard was bathed in ghostly silver. Ignoring the heavy sounds of breathing and occasional snorts coming from the King's thoroughbred horses, Zabrina made her way to Midas's loose box and peered inside.

To her surprise, the horse was lying down, fast asleep—which meant that he must be much more contented in his new home than she'd imagined. But he must have had one ear pricked up and heard her, for he instantly picked himself up and came over to nuzzle her. She petted him for long minutes, murmuring to him in Albastasian sweet talk, and felt much better as a result. It was only when she decided that she really did need to get some sleep and reluctantly began to walk back towards the palace that she saw a silhouette standing motionless on the other side of the yard. She did not jump but carried on walking towards the shadowed figure because she assumed...and that was her first mistake.

'Stefan?' she whispered. 'Is that you?'

'Why, is that who you were hoping for?'

Instantly, Zabrina knew who was speaking and it wasn't Stefan. Because although the groom was young and articulate, he did not speak with a velvety Petrogorian accent, nor have such an aristocratic delivery. Nor would his words ever have been tinged with unmistakable accusation.

'Roman,' she breathed.

He stepped out of the shadows and she was appalled by her body's instant response to all that powerful masculinity, because surely her overwhelming emotion in such a scenario shouldn't be one of desire... He was still wearing the formal suit he'd had on at the ball, though she noticed he had removed his tie and loosened the collar. Just as she noticed the brooding quality of his darkened features and the censure which hardened his sensual lips.

'Surprised?' he taunted softly.

'A little. Have you been spying on me, Roman?'

'You dare to accuse *me*?'

'Too right I do! I want to know what you're doing here. Why you suddenly sprang out of nowhere at this hour.'

'But you weren't scared, were you? You didn't scream and raise the alarm as many women in your situation would have done.'

'So I am to be rebuked for reacting maturely and not like some hysteric?'

'Don't try and change the subject!'

'Then perhaps you could try getting to the point. How did you know where I'd be?'

'Did you really think you could wander the palace at the depths of night without being detected by anyone,

Zabrina? That my corridors would go unguarded and my servants not have your welfare at heart?' He gave a bitter laugh as his gaze flicked over her. 'When one of Andrei's aides came rushing to my office and told me that the Princess was out exploring at the dead of night, I knew immediately where you'd be.'

Her heart was thumping painfully but she tried to put a flippant face on it. 'Really? Since you're not a practising clairvoyant as far as I'm aware, perhaps you'd like to let me into the secret of how you "knew" where to find me.'

'Where is he, Zabrina?'

She wanted to say *Who?* but she knew exactly who he meant and to pretend she didn't would surely imply guilt. 'I suppose you're talking about Stefan,' she said slowly. 'What did you imagine, Roman—that I would creep down here to have sex with my groom at the first available opportunity?'

He flinched. 'Did you?' he grated and Zabrina wondered if she had imagined the shudder of pain in his voice.

She stared at him, not bothering to hide her incredulity. Did he really think she'd be interested in a man like Stefan—indeed, in any man—when the only one she had ever wanted was standing right across the yard from her? What kind of women had he dealt with in the past if his level of distrust was so deep and so instant?

'I am hugely insulted,' she said, her voice shaking, 'that you have made so many negative assumptions about me and should believe me capable of such terrible behaviour. What makes you think so badly of me, Roman?'

There was a long pause before he answered, his voice seeming to draw each word out reluctantly. 'I told you. Rumours about you had started reaching me a few months ago—rumours which ignited my curiosity.'

'You mean that I was occasionally guilty of voicing my own opinion?'

'Yes, that.' He narrowed his eyes. 'But I find that trait is not as unappealing as I imagined it would be.'

'Wow,' she said sarcastically. 'This is progress indeed. But much as I would like to applaud your sudden emergence from the Dark Ages, I'm more interested to know what else it was you heard about me.'

He shrugged. 'That you had a habit of disappearing. That the Princess Zabrina would sometimes ride out at first dawn with her groom and not return until the noon sun was high in the sky.'

'And so you came to the conclusion that Stefan and I were galloping off together to enjoy some sort of illicit encounter?'

'Something like that.'

'How dare you? How dare you accuse me of such a thing, Roman?' All pretence at light-heartedness now abandoned, her voice had begun shaking with rage. 'Do you really think I could be so duplicitous that I would agree to marry one man, while being intimate with another?'

'Of course I can!' he flared. 'Because you had sex with Constantin, didn't you, Zabrina? You weren't thinking about Roman then, were you? So how can you explain that?'

She spoke without thinking. She spoke from the heart. 'I can't,' she said simply.

There was a pause. 'Neither can I.'

They stared at each other in silence and all Zabrina could see was the gleam of the moon in his shadowed eyes.

'I tried to resist you,' she said quietly. 'Or rather, I tried to resist Constantin, because I had never met anyone like him before. Surely you must have noticed how deliberately rude and abrupt I was towards you at the beginning?'

'I thought that was a game you were playing.' He gave a short laugh. 'Don't you realise that a head-strong and stubborn woman is exceedingly attractive to a man?'

She shook her head. 'I don't know what happened to me that night and I don't really want to think about it now. But I hold my hands up—I *did* used to ride out with Stefan. If you really want to know what I was doing, then I'll tell you—but we certainly weren't having sex.'

'Really?' He spoke carelessly, but Roman could do nothing about the sudden punch of hope to his heart, even though he despised his visceral reaction to her words.

She nodded and in the moonlight he saw her face assume an expression of fierceness. 'In my country I had a list of charities of which I was patron and which my sister Daria is going to take over, now that I'm no longer there. I was obviously invested in all those charities but there was one in particular which was very close to my heart. It was…' She hesitated. 'It was a refuge on the outskirts of the city. A refuge for women who have suffered domestic violence.'

His eyes narrowed. 'So why all the cloak-and-dagger stuff?'

She nodded, as if this was a topic with which she was familiar. As if she was used to accusation.

'My parents didn't approve of my involvement with these women. It was something else they turned a blind eye to. To admit that women suffered at the hands of men and were made impoverished if ever they chose to escape from abusive relationships—well, they were both of the opinion that the women didn't try hard enough to save their marriages!'

'Good heavens,' said Roman faintly.

The look she threw him was challenging. 'What, is that a bit hardcore old-fashioned, even for you?'

He didn't like being held up as someone completely out of touch with the modern world, just as he didn't like the way she was looking at him. It made him feel... *uncomfortable*. Kings were rarely forced to say they were sorry but Roman knew he needed to say it now. 'I shouldn't have leapt to those conclusions,' he said gruffly. 'Will you forgive me?'

Her absolution wasn't instant. She waited just long enough for him to entertain a little doubt in his mind— and didn't part of him admire her for her strength of character?

Eventually, she nodded. 'Yes, I forgive you,' she said. 'But, going forward, I'd prefer it if you didn't just leap to conclusions. And that it's probably better if you don't just brood about something, but ask me outright.'

She smiled then and the deepening dimple in her cheek drew his gaze, so that suddenly it looked like the most beautiful thing he had ever seen.

Roman swallowed. Her lips were gleaming irresistibly and looking unbearably kissable. He knew what he should do. Escort her back to her suite and bid her goodnight. Just as he knew what he wanted to do, which was to pull her into his arms and then lay her down in one of the dark corners of the stables and make love to her over and over again. And then he thought of all the reasons why he shouldn't—but the one which dominated them all was duty.

Duty.

It was a word which had been drummed into him from the moment he'd been born. A concept which had driven him all his life. It had been duty which had made him focus himself on his lessons and fencing skills, rather than give in to the bitter tears of a deserted child. Duty which had made him fulfil his end of this marriage bargain with the young Albastasian Princess.

Couldn't he—for once—take a break from the crushing weight of royal expectations? Suddenly, he felt a jolt of his own power as he looked at her. 'I want so badly to make love to you.'

He saw her bite her lip and gaze at the ground, as if seeking an answer amid the strands of silvered straw which lay there, and when she raised her head again, her face was serene and very solemn, as if she had come to some swift conclusion of her own. 'I want that, too.'

He sucked in an unsteady breath, his body warming as he acknowledged her instant capitulation. 'And I suspect that if I drew you into the shadows now and laid my hands and my lips upon your body,' he continued, 'you would again be mine.'

'R-Roman,' she said shakily, but she didn't contradict him.

'But we aren't going to do that.'

'We…aren't?'

Was he wrong to enjoy her obvious disappointment?

No, he was not. For didn't her response indicate that the balance of power between them was more equal than he'd thought, and perhaps that was something he needed to address.

'No, we aren't.' He paused just long enough to give *her* a taste of doubt, because wasn't uncertainty one of the most powerful aphrodisiacs of all? 'Instead, I will come to your suite tomorrow. At midnight.'

Her eyes widened. 'But you can't! You know you can't. Tradition states—'

'I don't give a damn what tradition states because *I* am King now and I make the rules.' He lowered his voice, even though there was nobody within earshot. 'I have no intention of broadcasting my movements to palace staff but neither do I intend to have sex with you on a sofa, or rammed up against a wall, or lying on the dusty ground of the stables, even though the prospect of not doing that right now is almost unendurable. I want to share your bed—properly. As Roman, not Constantin. As the man I am and not the man I was pretending to be. But I need you to be certain that this is what you want too, Zabrina.' He paused. 'This is to be no hot-blooded and hasty liaison, fuelled by rampant hormones and frustration, which is why I'm giving you adequate time to think about it. Because if, for any reason, you decide that you would prefer to wait for our wedding night to be intimate with me again then you must send me a signal.'

'How?'

His eyes gleamed like the blade of a sword. 'If you wish me to share your bed, then you should light a lamp in your window tomorrow night, and leave it unshuttered. If the light flares, then I will come to you. But if shutters are closed then I will not, and we will never refer to the matter again. It will be as though we never had this conversation. Do you understand what I'm saying to you, Zabrina?'

'Yes,' she said, in a voice so quiet he could barely hear her response. 'I understand.'

CHAPTER ELEVEN

ZABRINA SHIVERED AS she positioned the light in the centre of her bedroom window, thinking how strange life was. One minute you could be watching a film about a mermaid and wondering how she could possibly keep her hair looking that shiny when it was constantly immersed in salt-water, and the next...

She licked her dry lips.

Next you could be sending out a secret and silent message as you waited for your lover.

And she didn't have a clue what she was getting herself into.

Should she be in bed, waiting for Roman to arrive? Surely it wouldn't be a very attractive sight if she were caught anxiously pacing the floor—even if she *was* clad in a delicate nightgown which she had plucked from her trousseau with trembling fingers. Maybe she ought to be in bed, carefully positioned against the pillows, with her newly washed hair falling artfully over her shoulders. No. No, she couldn't do that. She would feel like a fraud—an imposter—and it would make the situation even more unreal than it already was.

There was a light rap on the door and then, without any prompting from her, it silently opened and closed again and there was Roman in her suite, dominating the space around him, dominating everything with his aura of alpha masculinity. For a moment Zabrina said nothing—but her breathing was so erratic she doubted she'd be able to speak any kind of sense in any case. Because, as always, his brooding beauty stopped her in her tracks. For once his muscular body was clothed in muted colours—presumably so he would melt into the background as he made his way from his part of the palace to hers. But no matter what he wore, his aristocratic bearing always shone through, like a diamond in a pile of rubble.

Yet her own royal status suddenly seemed to count for nothing. She felt like a fraud despite standing before him in her provocative lingerie, which was presumably perfect for an assignation such as this. But how she looked on the outside wasn't how she felt on the inside. Her fluttery excitement kept morphing into worry that she wouldn't be able to handle the way he made her feel, because wasn't the underlying message she was getting from him that this was supposed to be about sex, not emotion?

The King probably thought she knew how these midnight encounters worked, when the truth was she didn't have a clue. So did she have to go through another humiliating disclosure about her lack of experience and hope he'd believe her this time—or did she pretend, and try to pick things up as they went along?

Yet wasn't the whole point of their relationship supposed to be honesty?

'Roman—'

'Shh. Just let me take you to bed, Princess. Because I don't think I can wait for a moment longer.'

His soft words shushed her. They bathed her in silk.
The slight cracking of his voice was hugely flattering
and suddenly Zabrina was in his arms and his fingers
were pushing back through the spill of her hair and
he was kissing her as she'd never been kissed before.
Stars splintered at the backs of her eyes as she kissed
him back, as if they couldn't get enough of each other.
He groaned against her mouth and then suddenly he
scooped her up into his arms and carried her into the
bedroom, the mattress dipping beneath her as he laid
her down on the huge divan.

Without taking his eyes from her face he began to
unbutton his shirt, but still she said nothing. For hadn't
his soft words been a tacit order not to break the spell
of what was about to happen—and wasn't the truth that
it really *did* feel like magic?

Zabrina watched as he peeled off his clothes until
his golden flesh was naked and rippling in the lamp-
light. Her mouth dried as he joined her on the bed and
he pulled her against his powerful frame. He let out
a long sigh as his fingers began to reacquaint themselves with her aching body but there seemed a different kind of urgency about him tonight as he kissed her.
Her nerves were quickly dissolved by the sweetness of
his mouth roving over her neck, her hair and her breasts
and Zabrina was writhing with impatience when at last
his hand moved beneath the delicate nightgown and
began to ruck up the slippery fabric.

'Was this for your honeymoon night?' he murmured.

'Y-yes,' she whispered back, her skin prickling into
goose-bumps.

Did she imagine the brief darkening of his face before he peeled it off with such infinite care, so that in

that moment she felt almost...*treasured*? *Cherished.* Zabrina's heart clenched with something which felt unbearably poignant—as if she'd been given a glimpse of something which could never be hers. Something elusive and fragile and wonderful. Was this what *love* felt like? she found herself wondering wistfully. Until she reminded herself fiercely that love was irrelevant. Emotion was superficial and sensation was key to what was happening. So she turned her attention to the satin of his skin, and his deepening kisses indicated just how much she was pleasing him. The pace began to change and quicken. The air crackled with rising tension and musky desire. She felt him reach for protection, heard the rough tearing of foil before he stroked her thighs apart with beguiling fingers. And then he moved over her and she was lost.

Roman groaned as he entered her. She felt so *tight*. Tighter even than she had done on the train—or was that because he was so unbelievably turned on tonight? He thrust deep inside her honeyed flesh, taking her to the brink again and again, until she cried out his name in a ragged plea and he gave her what she wanted. What she needed. What he needed, too. And didn't a distinctly primeval satisfaction wash over him as he heard her shudder out his name, so that he was forced to silence her frantic cries with another kiss? She was still spasming around him when he started coming himself and never had so much seed spilled from his loins before.

Afterwards, drained and empty, he felt the powerful beat of his heart as she lay slumped against his sweat-sheened shoulder, her own hair damp with exertion. He heard the sudden catch in her breathing and wondered if she was crying. And even though it was definitely not his style to probe a woman's mood, he found himself doing it.

'Zabrina?'

She shook her head as if she didn't want to engage. 'Shh,' she said, the sound mimicking the very one he'd made earlier.

It was a get-out clause. An escape route. But surprisingly, Roman paid it no heed. He rolled on top of her again, smoothing the tousled tendrils of hair away from her flushed cheeks. Her eyes were closed as if she didn't want to have this conversation, which would normally have suited him fine, but he found himself unable to ignore the sudden stab of his conscience.

'Zabrina?'

Her lashes fluttered open and he found himself staring into forest-dark eyes.

'I know,' he said softly and nodded his head resolutely. 'I know I was the first man for you. The only man. And I'm sorry I accused you of all those things.'

She drew back, her eyes wide. 'I don't understand.'

'It's hard for me to understand myself.'

'Well, try.'

He traced his forefinger along the tremble of her lips and resisted the urge to kiss them. 'When I saw you waiting for me tonight, you looked so sweet and so nervous.' He shrugged. 'And so obviously out of your depth. You certainly weren't behaving like an experienced woman of the world. Deep down, I realised that on the train, when you told me—only it was easier to think you weren't. To paint you as someone who was wanton, and free.'

'And why was that, Roman?' she questioned softly.

He shook his head, afraid of what he might say, what he might reveal in an unguarded and totally irrelevant post-orgasmic moment. But he had been the one who had started all this, hadn't he?

'Because it would be easier to keep me at a distance?' she guessed, when still he said nothing.

He furrowed his brow into a frown. He didn't want her to be right, just as he didn't want her to be this perceptive. But he wasn't going to tell a lie. 'Maybe,' he admitted. 'And maybe because it gave me permission to make love to you under the guise of another man. I should never have done that, Zabrina.'

'Maybe you shouldn't,' she said slowly. 'But I wanted you to. I wanted it more than I can ever remember wanting anything.'

It was an unexpected display of candour, but to his surprise it didn't repel him or make him want to run. The look in her eyes seemed to be beguiling him even more than before and Roman tensed. The atmosphere was getting claustrophobic and in danger of suffocating him if he wasn't careful.

He swallowed. So what was he going to do about it?

He reached down to play with one of her nipples and felt himself grow hard as it puckered beneath his touch. He kissed her and guided her hand between his legs, biting back a moan of pleasure as she began to whisper featherlight fingertips up and down his aching shaft.

'I want you to teach me,' she said softly. 'About the things you would like me to do.'

Already, he felt as if he could explode. 'You don't seem to need any advice from me. You're doing just fine,' he growled.

He had been about to show her how to pleasure him

but it seemed that his princess was an instinctive expert where his body was concerned and a feeling of anticipation rippled over his body as he reached down and began to finger her in turn.

He closed his eyes.

Because this type of feeling he could cope with, but only this.

Maybe that was the only lesson he needed to teach her.

When Zabrina awoke, he had gone. She turned to look at the imprint of his head on the pillow and felt her heart give a wrench. Of course he had gone. That was the deal. He had crept from her bed under the velvety cloak of darkness, to slip back unnoticed through the palace corridors.

Lying amid the warm and rumpled sheets, watching dawn as it filtered through the unshuttered window, she allowed herself a moment of erotic recall.

It had been...

She swallowed.

It had been divine on every level, bar one. She had been nervous about having sex with the King, wondering if it would be the same as having sex with his alter-ego bodyguard. But it had been incredible. Perhaps because so many different layers of their characters had been peeled away, it had felt deeper than what had happened before. It had been intense. Powerful. Almost *transforming*. Every single time. Once, when he had been deep inside her pulsing out his seed, she had wanted to weep from pure joy. She had wanted to trace her fingertips over the shadowed graze of his jaw and thank him for making her feel this way. But instinct had warned her against such an over-the-top reaction and instinct had proved her right. Because just before Roman had returned to his own quarters, rising gloriously and boldly naked from the sheets, she had thought he seemed more…

She frowned as she tried to think of a word to describe it. Remote, yes—that was it. Almost as if the intensity of their physical interaction had made him want to instinctively push her away. Maybe she was reading too much into it. After all, what did *she* know about how men behaved once they had shared a woman's bed? And hadn't his last words been a husky promise that he would come to her later that night? She smiled as she plumped up the pillows and afterwards fell asleep and when next she awoke, the sun was up and Silviana was busying herself in the suite, laying out all her clothes for the day.

Leaving her hair loose, she put on a floaty dress the colour of apple blossoms, but she definitely felt nervous as she walked into the breakfast room, to find Roman already seated and looking at his phone. She wanted him to say something or do something. To send out some secret acknowledgement of what they had shared during the night by slanting her a complicit look. But when he glanced up from his phone and smiled, his face looked nothing except composed.

'Good morning,' he said. 'Did you sleep well?'

Maybe it was irrational but Zabrina was disappointed at the lack of unspoken communication passing between them. She wondered how he'd react if she blurted out the truth. *No, not really. How could I possibly sleep when you were deep inside my body for most of the night?* But, of course, she didn't. She simply sat down while a servant shook out a napkin and placed it on her lap, and attempted to match her fiancé's cool air of self-possession.

'Very well, thank you,' she answered. 'You?'

'Mmm,' he said, non-committal as he put his phone face-down on the table, as if he were making a great sacrifice. 'So, what are you doing today?'

'I have a dress fitting, and I need to finalise the design for the top layer of the wedding cake.' She lifted up her spoon to scoop up a cinnamon-dusted strawberry and shot him a look. 'Would you like to give your input? Any favourite recipes from your childhood?'

His expression suddenly grew stony and shuttered. 'I've never been much of a cake-eater, Zabrina. So why don't I leave that side of it to you?'

She wanted to ask what had made his face darken like that, but she didn't do that either. The mood in the room was too fragile for those sorts of questions. *She* was too fragile—like a piece of honeycomb which had been placed in the path of an approaching pair of feet. The brief insecurity which had washed over her in bed earlier that morning now grew heightened. In a flash it came to her that she wanted more than erotic intimacy. She wanted other intimacies, too. She wanted them to grow close and to be a real couple—not spend her life tiptoeing around his feelings. She looked at the proud jut of his aristocratic jaw.

So make it happen.

Don't crowd him.

In public at least, give him space.

Zabrina dug her spoon into another strawberry and nibbled at the fruit delicately, even though she would have preferred to have picked it up with her fingers. But she knew how palace life worked. Beneath the careful scrutiny of the servants she would play the royal game which was expected of her. She would make small talk and discuss generalities about the day ahead and that would have to do for the time being. But there was nothing to stop her from breaking down Roman's barriers whenever she got the opportunity. Surely that was essential if she wanted to discover more about this complex man she was soon to marry.

And where better than when they were alone in bed?

CHAPTER TWELVE

'YOU NEVER REALLY talk about your past, do you, Roman?'

Roman kept his eyes tightly shut, hoping his forbidding body language would stem the Princess's infuriating line of questioning. Because this wasn't the first time she'd tried to quiz him after one of his delicious midnight visits to her bedroom. Chipping away as she tried to get to know him better, as lovers inevitably did—no matter how many times he discouraged them. He guessed that with Zabrina he had been unusually indulgent—and at least their powerful sexual chemistry meant it had been easy to distract her. He'd been able to deflect her annoying queries with a foray into mutual bliss, but this time he heard the note of stubborn determination in her voice which made him suspect the subject wasn't going away.

It didn't.

'Roman?' Soft fingertips began to stroke distracting little circles on his forearm. 'I know you're not asleep.'

Reluctantly, Roman opened his eyes, his vision instantly captured by the sight of the naked woman lying in bed next to him. He felt the instant thunder of his heart as he drank in her slender curves. If this were anyone else he would simply leave but with Zabrina he couldn't—and not just because he was due to marry her in ten days' time. Because wasn't the truth that he simply couldn't bear the thought of leaving her bed? Not when there were still several hours available to them before daybreak, which he intended to put to the best possible use. Starting with the judicious use of his tongue, which he would trickle down over her belly until her nails were scrabbling against his scalp and she was moaning helplessly and bucking beneath him.

But despite the hungry clamour in his groin, his desire was tinged with the flicker of resentment, because he knew that in many ways he had become unexpectedly addicted to her. Didn't he sometimes despair of the way she effortlessly seemed to weave her spell around him? He gave an impatient sigh. Maybe his attempts at evading her questions were simply delaying the inevitable. Maybe his future wife had the right to ask him things which had been forbidden to other lovers.

'Which particular part of my past particularly interests you, Princess?' he questioned coolly.

Her answer came straight back, as if she'd been rehearsing it.

'Your parents.'

'My parents,' he repeated slowly.

'Everyone has them at some point in their life, Roman. You know all about mine but I know nothing about yours. I mean, I know that your father died four years ago and that your parents got divorced, but I don't know any more than that because you've never said.'

'And don't you think there's a reason for that?'

She wriggled up the bed a little, so that her dark hair shimmered down, rather disappointingly concealing the rosy nipple which had been on display.

'So why don't you tell me what that reason is?' she said.

The look in her eyes was compelling, the expression on her face serene as she calmly returned his gaze. And all at once it felt as if there was no hiding place. No place left to run—and the weirdest thing was that Roman didn't *want* to run. He wanted to confide in her. To tell her things he'd never discussed with another soul. A pulse began to beat at his temple. Why *was* that? Why did he suddenly feel as if he had been carrying around an intolerable burden and this was his chance to put it down for a while?

But it wasn't easy to articulate words he'd spent a lifetime repressing, or to expand on them, and for a while he just listened to the sound of silence, broken only by the distant ticking of a clock.

'My mother left when I was three,' he said at last. 'After that, it was just me and my father.'

'What was she like?'

It was a simple question but something he'd never been asked outright and, stupidly, he wasn't expecting it. Forbidden images of a tall blonde woman with a worried face swam into his mind and Roman realised just how long it had been since he'd thought about her. Since he had *allowed* himself to think about her. 'I don't remember very much about her,' he said. 'Only that she used to read me bedtime stories in a low and drawling voice. She was American. She came from Missouri and she used to wear a necklace with a bluebird on it.'

'What else?'

She looked at him and he wondered if her inquisitiveness was inspired by curiosity or horrified fascination. Because a mother who deserted her child always excited people's interest—particularly women's. A mother who left her child was seen as a monster and the child as unloved and unwanted. His preference would have been to have shut the subject down but suddenly he realised that some day he and Zabrina were going to have to explain the lack of a paternal grandmother to their own children, so maybe she *needed* to know. 'What kind of thing do you want to know?'

'Like, how did they meet?'

He raked back through the things he knew, which were surprisingly sketchy. 'They met when my father was on a world tour. She was working as a waitress and I think he just became obsessed by her and swept her off her feet. He proposed, she accepted and he brought her back here with almost indecent haste.' His voice hardened into flint. 'It's why I became an advocate of arranged marriages, Zabrina. He should never have made her his wife.'

She pushed a strand of hair out of her eyes and blinked at him. 'Because she was a commoner?' she said slowly.

'Almost certainly. She couldn't deal with royal life or all the restrictions which accompany it. Or so my father told me afterwards. She never settled into life here—not even when she had me. I remember that sometimes she seemed too scared to hold me and seemed to leave most of my care to my nurse, Olga.' He flinched as the memories came faster now. A black spill of memories he couldn't seem to hold back. 'Even when she read to me at night, she would slip into my room under cover of darkness. I noticed she started being around less and less and sometimes I would spot her heading towards me in one of the corridors, only she would turn away and pretend she hadn't seen me. Don't look at me that way, Zabrina, because it's true. And then one day, she left. She *left*,' he repeated, angry at the hot twist of pain in his heart. Angry with himself because surely it shouldn't still hurt like this. 'She just walked away and never looked back.'

She didn't respond to that and he heaved a breath of thanks, thinking she'd taken the hint and would ask him no more. He was just about to pull her into his arms and lose himself in the sweetness of her body when she propped herself up on one elbow and screwed up her nose. 'So what happened after that? I mean, how did you find out she'd gone?'

'Is this really necessary?' he demanded.

'I think it's important,' she clarified quietly. 'And I'd like to hear the rest of the story.'

'I'll tell you how I found out.' His voice grew quiet now. So quiet that he saw her lean forward fractionally to hear him. 'I woke up one morning and couldn't find her and when I asked Olga where she was, she told me I must go and speak to my father. So I went downstairs and discovered my father calmly eating breakfast. He looked up and told me my mother had gone and wouldn't be coming back, but I didn't believe him. I remember I ran from the room and he let me go. I remember searching every inch of the palace until I was forced to accept that the King had spoken the truth and she really *had* gone.'

He tried to focus himself back in the present but the memories were too strong and they overwhelmed him like the heavy atmosphere you got just before a storm. He remembered the dry sobs which had heaved from his lungs as he'd hidden himself away in a shadowed corner. He hadn't dared show his heartbreak or his fear, for hadn't his father drummed into him time after time that princes should never show weakness or emotion? Olga had eventually found him, but he had turned his face to the wall as she'd tried to tempt him out with his favourite sweets, still warm from the palace kitchens. But the usually tempting smell of the coconut had been cloying and it had been many hours before he had relented enough to take his nurse's hand and accompany her back to the nursery.

The silence which followed felt like a reprieve, but not for long because Zabrina's soft voice washed over him with yet another question.

'And did you ever hear from your mother again? I mean, surely she must have written to you. Sent a forwarding address so you could contact her.'

'Yes, I had an address for her,' he confirmed bitterly. 'And I used to write her letters. At first they were simple, plaintive notes, asking when she was coming back.' It made him curl up with disgust to think how he had humiliated himself by begging her to return, seeking solace from a woman who had rejected him outright. 'After a while, I just used to send her drawings I'd made, or tell her about my horse, or my fencing lessons.'

'But you never heard back?'

Was that disapproval he could hear in her voice, or incredulity? Or just the loathsome pity he had always refused to tolerate? 'No, I never heard back,' he clipped back and then shrugged. 'So in the end, I just gave up. My father never remarried, and brought me up to the best of his ability. It wasn't great. He wasn't a particularly easy man and it certainly wasn't what you'd call a normal, nuclear family but we adapted, as people do.'

'And, of course, you had Olga.'

He didn't answer straight away, just stared out of the window, noticing that the silver moon was almost full. 'No. Actually, I didn't.'

It was the first time she had looked truly taken aback. 'But—'

'My father sacked her.'

'He *sacked* her?'

The lump in his throat made it hard for him to speak, yet somehow the words just kept coming. 'He thought we were too close. As he explained, Olga was a servant and she didn't seem to know her place where I was concerned. He said you couldn't have a nursemaid who was acting like a quasi-mother and, anyway, he was done with commoners.'

'Oh, Roman, I'm so sorry,' she breathed, and he steeled himself not to react to the crack of compassion in her voice. 'That's terrible.'

'No, it was not terrible. It was manageable,' he said fiercely, daring her to contradict him, because he didn't want to dwell on the pain of that double rejection or how cold and how empty his life had seemed afterwards. 'After that I had a series of nurses and nannies who looked after me—sometimes men and sometimes women—all of them experts in one field or another.' But despite the variety of staff who had been engaged to help with his upbringing, they all had one thing in common. They never hugged him. Rarely touched him. Sometimes he'd suspected they'd been instructed to behave that way, but he didn't investigate further because the thought of that made him feel slightly sick. And anyway he didn't care, for in the end it had done him a favour and allowed him to view his brave new world with different eyes. Because at least you knew where you were with those people. *They* would never let you down.

He shot Zabrina a speculative look. 'Satisfied now?' he questioned, not bothering to conceal the note of warning in his voice. 'I don't think there's anything else you need to know.'

Zabrina bit her lip. She was aware he wanted her to leave it—why, his body language couldn't have been more forbidding if he'd tried. But how could she stop asking when there was still so much she didn't know? There were so many gaps in his story and she needed to fill them, because otherwise he would remain a stranger to her and she suspected she might never get another chance like this.

'Is she still alive? Your mother, I mean.'

His body tensed. She thought it looked like rippled marble in the moonlight.

'I have no idea,' he answered coldly. 'I stopped writing when I was thirteen and never heard of her again.'

'And you never tried to have her found, not even when you acceded to the throne? I mean, a king has access to the kind of information which would make that sort of thing easy.'

'Why on earth would I do that, Zabrina?' His lips curved disdainfully. 'Unless you're one of those people who believes that continued exposure to rejection is somehow character forming?'

'And Olga?' she questioned, deciding to ignore his bitter sarcasm. 'What happened to your nurse?'

'That I *did* discover,' he conceded, giving a brief, hard smile. 'She went back to live with her family not far from here, in the mountain town of Posera.'

'And do you—?'

'No! No, that is it!' he interrupted furiously. 'You have tested my patience too long and too far, Zabrina, and I will not be subjected to this any longer!'

Without warning, he rose from the bed and began reaching for the scattered clothes which had been discarded when he had arrived soon after midnight.

'What are you doing?' She was acutely conscious of the note of alarm in her voice but she couldn't seem to keep it at bay.

'What does it look like I'm doing? I'm getting dressed. I'm going back to my own room.'

'But it's still early.'

'I'm perfectly aware what the time is.'

'Roman, there's no need—'

'Oh, but that's where you're wrong, Zabrina. There is every need,' he interjected coldly. 'Because I'm not doing this again. Not ever again.'

'You mean...' She could feel the sudden plummet of her heart. 'You mean you won't be coming to my bed again?'

'I don't know.' There was a pause. 'That's up to you.'

'I don't...' Her fingers dug into the rumpled sheet. 'I don't understand.'

'Don't you?' He waited until he had finished pulling on his soft leather boots before flicking her an emotionless look which had replaced the ravaged expression of before. 'Then let me make it crystal clear for you, just so there won't be any misunderstandings in the future. A future you need to make a decision about, because you need to know which direction you want to take.'

'What are you talking about?' she whispered.

'I'll tell you exactly what I'm talking about. I think

we have the makings of a good team,' he said slowly. 'In public we just need to turn up and wave and fulfil the worthwhile causes close to our hearts. And in private I certainly have no complaints about what takes place between us, because I would be the first to admit that you completely blow my mind. But as for the rest.' His face grew dark and brooding again. 'All this other *stuff* you seem intent on dredging up with your endless probing and questioning. That has to stop and it has to stop right now. I'm not interested in analysing the past or its effect on me—because the past has gone. And neither will I contemplate the kind of future where you do nothing but needle away at me. I can't and I won't tolerate such behaviour. Either you accept the man I am today, or the wedding is off. No more questions. No more analysis. Do you understand what I'm saying to you, Zabrina?'

There was a long silence. She could hear the muffled pounding of her pulse as she looked at him. 'That sounds like an ultimatum.'

'Call it what you want. I'm not going to deny it.'

It felt as if someone had taken a heavy, blunt instrument and smashed it into her heart. It was illogical to think he might have reacted any differently, but logic was having no effect on the way his words were making her feel. Zabrina's head was spinning. He had wanted to call off the marriage once before but she had insisted on going through with it because her homeland badly needed this union, and she'd convinced herself they could make the marriage work and produce a family.

But now she could see it wasn't as simple as she'd first thought.

She'd used her parents' marriage as a template for

her own behaviour—but she didn't *like* her parents' marriage! Her father's affairs indicated a total lack of respect and regard for his wife and her mother's tacit acceptance of his behaviour was tantamount to a nod of approval. Yet she had calmly told Roman she would be prepared to react in a similar way, because she accepted that was what kings 'did'. Had she been out of her mind? Zabrina's stomach churned. Had she really imagined she'd be content to sit back and watch while Roman behaved that way, when the thought of him having sex with another woman made her want to scream out her horror and her distress?

She realised something else, too. She wanted a real marriage. She wanted to be a wife to Roman in every sense of the word, and for him to be a proper husband. She didn't know if that was possible, but surely she had to give it a try. Because when he had been telling her his sad story about his mother, it had sparked off flickers of recognition inside her. It had made her think of other stories which she had heard so many times before. She might be wrong, but there might be a reason why Roman's mother had disappeared in such a dramatic fashion and maybe she should try to discover if what she suspected was true.

The King was now standing fully dressed in his traditional night-time clothes of jeans and a dark sweater and she could sense the air of impatience radiating from his powerful frame as he waited for her answer. But there was more to Roman than his sometimes intimidating exterior suggested. If she looked beyond his arrogant sense of entitlement, she could detect the deep wound which had been inflicted on him as a boy and which had never been given the chance to heal.

Could she help him do that? Would he accept her help, even if such a thing were possible?

Deliberately she lay back against the pillows. 'I'm not going to address ultimatums—and certainly not when they are delivered in the middle of the night,' she said, with a carelessness she was far from feeling. 'Speak to me about it in the morning.'

She wouldn't have been human if she hadn't enjoyed the very real flash of shock and frustration which gleamed from his eyes—presumably because he was never obstructed quite so openly—before leaving the room without another word. And she suspected he might have slammed the door very loudly, if there hadn't been a continuing need for silence.

CHAPTER THIRTEEN

'SILVIANA?' ZABRINA MADE a final adjustment to the collar of her silk blouse as, with a raised hand, she waylaid her lady-in-waiting just as she was leaving the dressing room. 'Did you ever hear of a palace nurse called Olga?'

The servant lifted her head, her thick, blonde bob swinging around her chin as she did so. Did Zabrina imagine the caution she saw written on her lovely face or was she just getting paranoid?

'Of course I have heard of her, Your Royal Highness. My own mother knew her very well.'

Zabrina nodded. 'I understand she lives in a place called Posera. Is that very far from here?'

Silviana shook her head. 'No, Your Royal Highness. It is a little village nestled in the foothills of the Liliachiun mountains.'

'I was wondering…' Zabrina swallowed, nervous about saying this, but she *needed* to say it. For Roman's sake. For all their sakes. She forced a smile. 'I would like to visit her. This morning. Right now, in fact.'

'Now?' Silviana looked alarmed. 'But you are already late for breakfast with His Imperial Majesty.'

Zabrina shook her head. 'I won't be taking breakfast this morning. Perhaps you could have someone send word to that effect to the King.' And it wasn't just the thought of food which was making her throat close up. She couldn't face walking into the breakfast room under Roman's indifferent gaze and pretend that last night had never happened. Because it had. He had basically told her that if she wasn't prepared to accept the most superficial of marriages, then the wedding was off. *And that was a decision she wasn't prepared to make just yet. Not until she was fully equipped with all the facts.* 'I would like to set off immediately. I'm sure that can be arranged?'

'No doubt the King would be happy to—'

'No,' Zabrina interrupted firmly. 'I don't… I don't want the King to know about this. I need you to arrange a car to take me there, Silviana, and for the driver to be sworn to secrecy. You can tell him that I am arranging a surprise for His Majesty.' Which was true, she thought grimly. The only trouble was that she had no idea if her hunch was correct—or how it would be received if it was.

Her heart was pounding hard in her chest as she accompanied Silviana through the palace and she didn't begin to breathe normally again until she and her lady-in-waiting were driving through the streets of Rosumunte, towards the famous mountain range which dominated the capital city.

Zabrina tried to concentrate on what she was seeing but found herself not *wanting* to love the elegant trees and lush foliage as the car skimmed through the green countryside. Because what if she was exiled after all this? What if the wedding was called off because Roman was angered by her taking such a bold initiative? Could she cope with the emotional and financial fall-out of not securing a marriage deal?

She was going to have to.

Before too long, they drew up in front of an old-fashioned cottage with a thatched roof, just like the ones she'd seen in a book she'd once had, all about England. To the front there was a beautiful garden and in the distance was a goat grazing in a meadow. A young woman came running out of the house when she heard the car, her look of curiosity changing to one of shock as Zabrina stepped from the car, and hastily she sank into a deep curtsey.

'Your Royal Highness!' she gasped. 'This is indeed an unexpected honour.'

'Forgive me for this unannounced intrusion,' replied Zabrina. 'But I was wondering if I might have a word with your…grandmother? Alone, if I may.'

'Of…of course, Your Royal Highness. If you would just give me a moment to inform my *bunica* and quickly prepare the cottage.'

Zabrina could hear the murmur of voices and the clattering of china before being ushered inside the surprisingly large and very comfortable cottage, and minutes later she was sitting opposite a sprightly looking old lady in a chair which rocked before a blazing fire, despite the sunshine of the day outside.

'When you get old, you get cold,' the old lady said.

Zabrina nodded. 'I hope to have the good fortune to discover that for myself one day.' But her voice was a little choked as she spoke, her chest tight with emotion as she realised that this woman had rocked the infant Roman, had held his little hand and watched as he'd learned to walk. And then she had been summarily dismissed from his life. 'Thank you for seeing me.'

Olga's still-beautiful eyes were a little faded, but they narrowed perceptively as her gaze took in the enormous emerald and diamond engagement ring which glittered on Zabrina's finger.

'You are Roman's woman?' she asked, very softly.

This was a tricky one to answer, but how could Zabrina possibly demand the truth, if she was not prepared to speak it herself?

'I want to be.' The words came out in a rush. 'I so want to be.'

Olga folded her hands together on her lap. 'I wondered when you might come.'

Roman stared out of the window, but the sweeping beauty of the palace gardens remained nothing but a green and kaleidoscopic blur. He turned back to find Andrei regarding him with an expression of concern he hadn't seen on his aide's face in a long time. Probably not since he had masqueraded as Constantin Izvor on that fateful journey from Albastase to Petrogoria, he thought grimly.

'*Where*,' he repeated furiously, 'has she gone?'

'We don't know, Your Majesty.'

'What do you mean, you don't know? How can you not know?'

'Is the Princess not free to travel at will?' Andrei asked mildly.

Roman glared. 'Of course she is. It's just...'

Just what? Had he expected her to be pale-faced and remorseful over breakfast this morning, telling him she'd been too intrusive with her questions last night and promising him it wouldn't happen again? Yes, he had. Of course he had. For he wasn't blind to the effect he had on her—women were notoriously bad at hiding their feelings when they had begun to care deeply for a man, and he knew that cancelling their wedding was the last thing Zabrina wanted.

At first he had even been prepared to overlook her lateness, aware that she was going to have to lose face by backing down and was probably dreading making her entrance and her apology. But as his coffee had grown cold and the servants had hovered around the table anxiously, he had realised that she wasn't going to show up at all. Not only had she failed to appear, but she had neglected to do him the courtesy of informing him until much later. Wasn't such an act towards the monarch completely unacceptable?

He had gone to his offices and tried to lose himself in his work, but for once his grand schemes had failed to excite him. Even the prized Marengo Forest seemed to represent nothing but a cluster of trees which had forced him into making the most stupid decision of his life by agreeing to marry the stubborn and foxy Princess who refused to conform to his expectations of her!

Now it was getting on for midday and still she hadn't returned and his slowly ignited temper was in danger of erupting. He could hear Andrei talking quietly on his cell-phone and then the aide gently cleared his throat as he finished the call.

'Your Majesty?'

'Yes, what is it?'

'The Princess's car arrived back at the palace a short time ago and she—'

'Have her sent here as soon as she—'

'You don't have to have me *sent* anywhere,' came a voice from behind him. 'I came all of my own accord!'

He whirled around to see Zabrina standing there, a look of challenge sparking from her green eyes which matched the faint sarcasm underpinning her words. Her cheeks were flushed with roses, as if she had been outside in the fresh air, but there was no contrition on her face, he noted. No sense that she had offended him on so many levels he didn't even know where to begin.

'Where have you been?' he questioned coldly.

She opened her mouth as if to respond and then looked at Andrei.

'If you will excuse me, Your Majesty, Your Royal Highness?' said the aide smoothly, backing out of the double golden doors with indecent haste.

Roman wanted to demand that his aide stay, or that Zabrina return later, when he might deign to schedule in a slot to see her. Or even to suggest she wait until they were having lunch—because any of those propositions would demonstrate very firmly who was in charge. But the glint of determination flashing from her eyes made him realise that any such request would be futile. And besides, why not get it over with?

'So,' he said coolly, once the doors had closed behind Andrei. 'Are you going to answer my question and tell me where you've been?'

She made a big show of wiggling her shoulders so that her dark hair shimmered against the yellow blouse—the fine fabric hinting at the slender but muscular body beneath. Had she done that deliberately to emphasise her allure? he wondered achingly. To remind him how much in thrall he was to her agile physicality?

'No ideas, Roman?' she asked, with equal aplomb.

'You aren't going to accuse me of trying to seduce my new, Petrogorian groom?'

'Hardly,' he snapped. 'Since you were seen leaving by car, with Silviana!'

For a moment she looked as if she was about to smile, but then seemed to change her mind for her face took on a completely different look. Softer. Thoughtful—almost gentle. And that put the fear of God in him like nothing else, because gentleness was alien to him and he didn't trust it. Very pointedly, he lifted his arm to glance at his watch. 'Whatever it is, will you please hurry up and tell me because I haven't got all day?'

'Roman, I went to visit Olga. I found out where she lives.'

A barrage of feelings hit him. Cold fear, dark dread and anger. But anger was the overriding emotion which made him shoot out his response to her. Because wasn't it easier to focus on that, rather than confront the sudden blackness which was hovering at the edges of his mind? 'What the hell did you do that for?'

'Because I was confused by some of the things you told me.' She licked her lips. 'I guess I found it hard to believe that your mother never even wrote back to you.'

'You think all women are fundamentally good—and mothers in particular?' He gave a bitter laugh. 'In that case, I pity you your naivety, Zabrina. I lost faith in your sex a long time ago.'

But she shook her head as if he hadn't spoken. 'Some of the things you said didn't add up,' she continued. 'Why she used to hide away. Why she used to only come to you under cover of darkness. It seemed to me that Olga must have known something and she did. That was another reason why she was sacked.'

Roman's heart clenched as if some malevolent iron fist were squeezing it tighter and tighter. He wanted to turn and run, or to put his hands to his ears like a child and block out whatever was coming. But that would be the behaviour of a coward, and he was no coward. And hadn't he weathered the worst of the storm all those years ago? What could possibly be left to hurt him now? 'What did Olga know?'

She sucked in a deep breath and now he saw the flicker of fear and darkness in her own eyes. 'Your father used to abuse your mother,' she said. 'Mentally and physically.'

'No!' The word thundered from his lungs. 'That is not possible.'

'Why not?'

'Because I would have known.' He could hear the break in his voice as he shook his head in denial. 'I would have protected her.'

'No, Roman. You would not have known, because your mother wouldn't have wanted you to know. She wanted to hide her pain and distress from you. She wanted to protect *you*, which is a mother's instinct. And how could a small boy possibly save a woman from the wrath of his powerful and autocratic father? That would only have put you in danger and that was the last thing she would have wanted.'

He curled his fingers into his palms so hard that he could feel the deep imprint of his nails, but the sharpness of that didn't come close to the fierce stabbing of his heart. 'How could you possibly know what she wanted?' he raged. 'Are you the one who is now capable of reading minds?'

'No. But I have helped many women like your mother at my refuge in Albastase—'

'Poor women?' he demanded in disbelief.

'Yes, poor women—and some rich ones, too. As well as all the others in between. Because abuse knows no age or class boundaries, Roman, and there are victims everywhere. Olga told me that your mother often used to have black eyes. That was why she would read your bed-time story in darkness and why she sometimes ducked out of sight if she saw you walking down the corridor. It was why she had to leave, because she knew she was incapable of being a good and loving mother towards you, if she was constantly being beaten down.'

'Then why…why didn't she take me with her?'

Zabrina heard the raw note of anguish in his voice as he whispered out that stark and heartbreaking question and she wanted so much to comfort him. To take him in her arms and hold him. But not now. Not yet. Because didn't he need to *feel* this? To *really* feel it—to have the ugly wound laid wide open after all these years, so he would be able to recover from it at last? Afterwards—maybe once he'd heard the whole story—that would be the time to offer him solace. If he still wanted her. 'She tried to take you,' she said simply. 'But, of course, your father discovered her plans and made sure she was spir-ited away in his private jet in the dead of night, while you were fast asleep. I don't know if you can imagine how different those times were, but a waitress from Missouri would have had no clout against one of the most powerful men in the world.'

'She never got my letters?' he questioned suddenly.

Zabrina bit her lip, because, oh, how she wished she could sugar-coat this one. But she couldn't do that either. 'I don't think so. I suspect the letters might have been destroyed as soon as you dispatched them,' she said. 'But she wrote to *you*.'

He narrowed his eyes and the flare of hope he was so desperately trying to repress made her heart turn over with love and sorrow.

'She wrote to you through Olga, but the letters only got through after your father died. I have them.'

There was a long silence while Roman digested this and he could feel the powerful thunder of his heart as he looked at the Princess who stood before him, her green eyes wide with compassion. 'Why did I never receive them?' he demanded, but deep in his heart he knew the reason.

'Olga tried to contact you after your father's death,' she said gently. 'But she was blocked every time. By you.'

He nodded, painfully aware of his own contribution to what had happened. 'Because the thought of seeing and speaking to her again after all those years was more than I could endure,' he said slowly, almost as if he had forgotten she was in the room with him. Was that why he did nothing to conceal the bitter break in his voice? Or because he know that his Princess would understand? 'I couldn't bear the thought of reliving...' He swallowed. 'Of reliving all that pain.'

'I realise that,' Zabrina whispered. 'And so does she. She knows you were responsible for the anonymous donations paid into her bank account for so many years and she thanks you for your generosity.'

'I want to hate my father for what he did,' he said, his voice changing into a rasp. 'In fact, I *do* hate him.'

'Well, don't,' she whispered. 'Just let it go, Roman. For hate brings nothing of value to anyone's life and you don't know the truth about his own upbringing, I assume?'

He shook his head. 'No. No, I don't. He never wanted to discuss it. He never wanted to discuss anything.' His father had never *talked* to him, not properly. It had been like living with an automaton who had demanded increasingly high levels of perfection from his only child. Had he ever felt guilty about the way he'd treated the woman he had married? Could that have been the cause of the unexpected tears he had shed, just before shuddering out his final breath, his hand tightly clutching that of his son? Roman gave a heavy sigh because Zabrina was right. He needed to forgive, or there would be no peace in his own heart. His thoughts cleared and he looked into her clear, bright gaze, his mouth feeling as if it had been crammed full of stones as he asked the question he had been dreading.

'And my mother?' he asked, bracing himself for the inevitable reply.

'She's alive,' Zabrina said, very quietly.

He froze. 'Are you serious?'

She nodded. 'Totally serious. Your mother is alive and well, Roman. She sent you this.'

She bent and reached into her handbag and pulled out a small pouch and inside was a delicate necklace—a cheap silver chain with a blue enamel bird dangling from the end. 'It's a bluebird,' she whispered, as she let it spill into his open palm. 'The symbol of Missouri state, where she comes from. She sent it to Olga, with one of her first letters. She wants to see you. We could invite her to the wedding, if you like. Or you could go and see her on your own, if…if you don't want the wedding to go ahead.'

His fingers closed around the little locket. 'You're saying you want to call it off?' he husked.

Zabrina closed her eyes in despair as she watched him replace the necklace in the pouch and put it in his pocket. How could he be so *dense*? How could he fail to see the evidence which was before his eyes, that she wanted him so much she would walk to the ends of the earth for him? But deep down she knew the answer to that. Because he hadn't been shown enough love in his life—that was why he couldn't recognise it. His trust in love had been destroyed and this was her chance to help him rebuild it, and she had to take it, no matter what the outcome. Even if he felt she now knew too much about him, to be comfortable with them sharing a life.

'Calling it off is the last thing I want to do,' she said. 'I want to be your wife more than anything in the world, because I love you, Roman. I think I've loved you from the first time I saw you, when you were Constantin Izvor. I loved you as the man, not as the King, but I love the King too—if that makes sense. You make me laugh and you bring me joy, and, yes, you can be infuriating at times but I'm sure I can, too.'

'Zabrina—'

'No. Let me finish, because this bit is important,' she said in a low voice which, infuriatingly, had started shaking. 'When I told you all those things about what I expected from our marriage, I was wrong. When I said I would turn a blind eye if you wanted to have affairs with other women, I don't know what I was thinking. Well, I do actually, but I wasn't being honest with myself. Because the truth is that I would be beside myself with jealousy and rage if you ever touched another woman. I want you exclusively, Roman, maybe even a bit possessively. So if that isn't your idea of what you want out of a royal marriage, then—'

'Zabrina, Zabrina, Zabrina.' He pulled her into his arms and smoothed his thumb down the side of her face as if he were seeing it for the first time. 'I never wanted that kind of marriage and the thought of you being with anyone other than me repels me. In fact, the idea of you being jealous is rather reassuring—because we both know that I'm capable of feeling it, too.' He paused and his voice was a little unsteady. 'Except that I will never give you cause to be jealous, because I love you, Princess.'

'You don't have to say that,' she whispered.

'I know I don't. I'm not in the habit of saying anything I don't mean and I don't intend to start now. But learning how to express myself is a whole new skill set, so you will have to make allowances for me.'

She smiled. 'Oh, I think I could manage to do that, my darling.'

She touched her fingers to his jaw and Roman could see the wonder shining from her face and her sweet expression smote at a heart which was already full and somehow all the pain was just draining away from him, leaving him feeling as if he'd shed a heavy burden he hadn't even realised he'd been carrying. It would have been so easy to kiss her and allow their bodies to help heal the pain and take away the sense of time wasted, and a mother's love denied. But this was too important to take the easy way out. He needed to find the right words to say to her and make sure she believed them. 'Just like you,' he said slowly, 'I fell in love the first time we met and wished you weren't a princess so I could just go ahead and seduce you.'

'But you seduced me anyway!'

'So I did.' He sighed. 'I don't know if you can appreciate just how out of character that was for me, Zabrina—to shrug off my sense of duty and make as if it didn't matter. And I resented you for that. I resented your power over me.'

'You never wanted a woman to have that perceived power over you again,' she guessed slowly. 'Because you didn't want to risk being hurt again. I understand that. But I will never hurt you, Roman—certainly not intentionally—and if I do, then you must tell me and we'll talk about it.'

He felt his heart lurch. 'I want to marry you,' he breathed. 'If I could marry you here and now, then I would. And because these words do not feature in the official Petrogorian ceremony I will say them to you now. You are the most beautiful woman I've ever met—both inside and out. You are brave and strong and caring and I am blessed to have you in my life. I love you with every fibre of my being, Zabrina. Believe me when I tell you that.'

'Oh, I do,' she whispered, the break of emotion in her voice fracturing her response. 'I so do.'

EPILOGUE

'OH, ZABRINA, YOU look so beautiful.' Eva clapped her hands over her mouth as she stared up at her big sister. 'Like a real queen!'

'That's because,' said Daria, glancing at the diamond-encrusted watch which had been a bridesmaid gift from her future brother-in-law, 'in approximately an hour's time she will *be* a queen! Are you nervous, Zabrina?'

Zabrina shook her head so that her tulle veil shimmered. 'Not nervous,' she said softly. 'Just happy.' She sighed. So very happy. Because Roman made her happy every second of every day. Soon she would legally be his wife and she couldn't wait. She wanted to start on this new phase of life with him. The two of them, together, as man and wife. She heard the sound of distant trumpets playing a triumphant Petrogorian fanfare and, turning to both her sisters, she gave a smile so wide it felt as if it might split her face in two. 'Shall we go?'

As they nodded, she reached out and took the fragrant white bouquet from Silviana, the gilded doors were flung open and she began to make her way down the aisle towards her beloved King. Embroidered with over one thousand tiny pearls, the train of her dress was heavy, which meant she had to walk slowly. But she *wanted* to walk slowly. She wanted to make the most of every second of her wedding day to her one true love. To the powerful soulmate who had emerged from all the turmoil and heartbreak as a different man, once all the barriers with which he'd surrounded himself had come tumbling down. She could see him standing waiting for her beneath an arch of flowers, his pewter eyes dark, a gleam of anticipation in their depths as he watched her approach.

Faces turned as she walked—some she recognised but many she didn't. Her parents were there, of course. Her mother sitting bolt upright in her recently cleaned 'best' crown and her father paying rather too much attention to the busty redhead seated at the end of the row. Zabrina found herself wondering how they would adapt to being grandparents. Maybe a brand-new generation would bring a little light and freshness into their cynical relationship. You could but hope.

Along the aisle she moved, watching heads incline and women curtsey. There were members of the Albastasian aristocracy alongside their Petrogorian counterparts— as well as royals from Maraban, from Greece and from Britain. There were A-list actors and academics—and a devastatingly handsome but rather dangerous-looking Sheikh called Zulfaqar, whom Daria had been flirting with all during the rehearsal last night. Zabrina intended have a stern word with her sister after the ceremony and warn her off, because apparently the desert King had a terrible reputation with women. But for now, she just wanted to reach her beloved Roman and say her vows.

Her heart was beating very fast as she handed her

bouquet to Daria, and as she saw Olga sitting in the front row, with three of her grandchildren, Zabrina felt a great tremble of emotion. Maybe she *was* more nervous than she'd thought. But the moment Roman grasped her fingers within the warmth of his, she felt nothing but a powerful sense of excitement and contentment filling her heart.

'You look beautiful,' he murmured.

She could feel her cheeks grow warm. 'Beautiful for you.'

His eyes narrowed as he looked down at her and she realised that he wasn't seeing the spectacular white gown, or the white tulle veil held in place by a glittering diamond crown. Instead, his gaze was fixed on the chain which hung from her neck. A cheap little silver chain from which dangled a tiny bluebird. Her 'something blue', worn by every traditional bride.

Roman's mother hadn't come to the wedding. During a very exciting video call, she had explained that it was *their* day and she didn't want to take any attention away from that. But they were planning to visit Missouri during their honeymoon and Zabrina's brother was very jealous because Kansas City was the setting of one of his favourite films. And Roman was still getting his head around the fact that he had three half-brothers!

He had also invited her three siblings to stay during the long vacation and said he intended to do this every year if they were keen—and to instruct Alex in the art of kingship at the same time. He was also quietly intending to put a diamond mine in trust, so that her brother should have no financial woes, should he ever inherit a large national debt.

And when Roman had revealed that the priceless emerald and diamond necklace she'd worn on the night of the ball—and which she *hated*—had been a placatory gift intended to make amends for his deception on the train, Zabrina had wasted no time in chiding him. But not for very long. She had asked if she might sell it and use the funds raised to open a women's refuge in Rosumunte and Roman had agreed. As she had observed, the world was going through a bit of a crisis at the moment and people like her needed to lead by example. Because she didn't need *things*. The only thing she needed was him.

He lifted her fingers to his lips and as the trumpets gave their final flourish, he spoke against her skin, but so softly that only she could hear.

'You bring me utter joy, Zabrina. Do you know that?'

'Sssh,' she said. 'The congregation will be reading your lips.'

'I don't care—let them read to their heart's content. I need to say this and I need to say it now. I think you know how much I love you, my Princess. Just as I think you know I always will.'

Blinking back tears, she nodded, trying to compose herself in preparation for the sacred vows she would shortly make. Later, she would bring him even more joy when she told him about the baby growing beneath her breast. A baby they hadn't planned quite so soon, but something told her Roman was going to be a wonderful father.

She wanted to laugh and she wanted to cry. She was caught in the crossfire of so many powerful and conflicting emotions that suddenly she didn't care about lip-readers either.

'I love you too, my darling Roman,' she whispered. 'I love you so very much.'

And a single tear of happiness rolled all the way down her cheek and dripped onto the tiny enamel bluebird.

* * * * *

PRIDE AND THE ITALIAN'S PROPOSAL

KATE HEWITT

Dedicated to all the P&P fans out there—
may you find your Mr Darcy!

CHAPTER ONE

'YOU'LL NEVER GUESS who just walked in!'

Liza Benton looked at her younger sister's flushed face and laughed. 'I'm sure I won't,' she returned with a smile. 'Considering I don't know a single person in this place.' She glanced around the busy bar in Soho, its interior all sleek wood and chrome stools, pounding music and bespoke cocktails. Right now it was full of glamorous people who had a lot more money and fashion sense than she did, and they seemed to be taking delight in showing both off.

Liza had only moved to London from rural Herefordshire six weeks ago and she was still feeling a bit like a Country Mouse to a whole load of sleek Town Mice. But her younger sister Lindsay, visiting for the weekend with their mother Yvonne, was determined to be the belle of whatever ball—or bar—they frequented.

It had been Lindsay who had assured Liza and their older sister Jenna that Rico's was the place to be. 'Everyone who's anyone goes here,' she'd said with a worldly insouciance that belied her seventeen years. Considering she'd hardly ever left their small village in Herefordshire save for a few school trips, Liza wasn't sure how her sister would know such things, but she seemed confident that she did. Of course, Lindsay was confident—perhaps a bit too confident—about everything, including her own youthful charms.

Looking around Rico's now, Liza didn't think it looked all that special, although she acknowledged she didn't know much about these things. She hadn't been to many bars, and hadn't particularly wanted to. Her twenty-three years had been spent helping out with her large family and then getting her degree; socialising or romance hadn't played much part at all, save for one unfortunate episode she had no desire to dwell on.

'So who walked in?' her older sister Jenna asked with a little laugh as Lindsay collapsed breathlessly onto the banquette next to her, determined to maximise the melodrama. Their mother took a sip of her violently coloured cocktail, eyes wide as she waited for her youngest daughter to dish. She loved a bit of gossip as much as Lindsay did.

'Chaz Bingham,' Lindsay announced triumphantly. Liza and Jenna both stared at her blankly but Yvonne nodded and tutted knowingly.

'I saw him in a gossip magazine just last week. He's recently inherited some sort of business, hasn't he? Investments, I think?' Her mother spoke with the same worldly air as her daughter, although she left Herefordshire even less than Lindsay did. All her knowledge was gained from TV chat shows and tabloid magazines, and treated as gospel.

Lindsay shrugged, clearly not caring about such details. 'Something like that. I know he's loaded. Isn't he *gorgeous*?'

Liza met Jenna's laughing gaze as they both silently acknowledged how their younger sister's excited voice carried. The sophisticated occupants of the table next to theirs exchanged looks, and Liza rolled her eyes at Jenna. She'd never had time for snobs, and she'd encountered a few over the years, people who thought her family was a little too different, a little too loud—her lovably eccentric father, her exuberantly over-the-top mother, and the four Benton girls—pretty Jenna, smart Marie, fun Lindsay…and Liza. Liza had no idea what her sobriquet would be. Quiet, perhaps? Normal? *Dull?* She knew she possessed neither Jenna's looks nor Marie's brains, and definitely not Lindsay's vivacity. That had been made apparent to her on more than one occasion, often by well-meaning people, but once…

She really had no desire to dwell on that now, when they were having so much fun and apparently someone exciting had walked into the bar, even if she'd never heard of him.

'Where is he?' their mother asked, her eyes on stalks as she rubbernecked for a glimpse of the mysterious but apparently impressive Chaz Bingham.

'There.' Lindsay pointed towards the entrance of the bar, and Liza muffled a chuckle.

'Shall we make an announcement on the Tannoy system?' she asked wryly, and her sister gave her a blank look.

'Liza, a bar like this isn't going to have a *Tannoy*.'

'Silly me,' she murmured, and Jenna smiled before she suddenly let out a soft, wondering gasp that had Liza curious enough to see who all the fuss was about. She glanced towards the entrance of the bar and her breath caught as her gaze snagged on the man who had just come in. Now that she'd seen him, it was impossible *not* to notice him. Not to feel as if he took up all the space and air in the place.

He was half a head taller than anyone else in the room, with ink-black hair pushed away from a high aristocratic forehead. Steel-grey eyes under hooded brows scanned the room dismissively, a cynical twist to his sculpted mouth that Liza could see all the way from across the room. Cheekbones like blades and a hard chiselled jaw worthy of any of the steamy novels that Lindsay loved to read.

His powerful physique was encased in a snowy-white dress shirt, unbuttoned at the neck to reveal a bronzed, alluring column of throat—how a *neck* could be sexy, Liza had no idea, and yet it was—and narrow black trousers, an outfit that would suit a waiter, and yet such a thought was laughable when it came to this man.

Everything about him exuded power, wealth, influence and, most of all, arrogance. He looked as if he not only owned this bar, but the entire world. Normally Liza hated conceit of any kind—and she had good reason for it—but this combination of blatant sex appeal and innate arrogance was both compelling and disturbing and, unable to make sense of her thoughts, she forced herself to look away.

'Did you see him?' Lindsay demanded, and Liza jerked her head in a nod. How could she *not* have seen him? Even now, looking away, she could still visualise him perfectly— from that twist of his lips to the powerful shrug of his shoulders. He was emblazoned on her mind's eye, which was another disturbing thought. Why had she reacted so viscerally to a stranger?

'Jenna, I think he's noticed you,' Yvonne whispered excitedly, although her whisper was as loud as Lindsay's, especially after two of her fancy cocktails. Jenna smiled and flushed.

Liza glanced up; the dark-haired Adonis wasn't looking anywhere near her sister, but a friendly-looking man with rumpled blond hair and ruddy cheeks was, with obvious interest. *This* was Chaz Bingham? Then who was the other man?

Unthinkingly, she looked for him, only to find herself suddenly speared on his sardonic gaze for a terrible second, his steely eyes blazing into hers and branding her with their knowledge before, indifferently, he looked away.

'He's coming closer!' Lindsay squealed and, turning away from the man who had so casually dismissed her, Liza wished her sister wasn't *quite* so loud.

Amazingly, Chaz really was coming closer to their table. Liza braced herself, wondering if he was going to ask them to lower their voices, or maybe if he could have the chair they'd piled all their coats on, but he did nothing of the kind. He gave Jenna an immensely appealing smile before turning to them all, including them easily in his friendliness.

'I say, may I buy you a drink?'

'Oh…' Jenna was blushing prettily, and Liza smiled at the man's gentlemanly charm, as well as his obvious interest in her beautiful sister. With her long, tumbling blonde hair and vivid blue eyes, not to mention her curvy figure, Jenna had never been without admirers. Amazingly, her beauty hadn't made her vain in the least; she'd barely had a boyfriend, and she always seemed surprised by the attention she received. Liza, however, was not, and she had never resented her sister's popularity…even when it had caused her pain.

'Yes, *please*,' Lindsay said, elbowing Jenna meaningfully, and the man—Chaz—smiled and took their orders.

'Of all the women in the whole room,' their mother whispered triumphantly when he'd gone to the bar, 'he chose you!'

'Mum, he's just buying me a drink,' Jenna protested, but Liza saw how her gaze tracked Chaz as he headed towards the bar. Her own gaze moved instinctively to the *other* man in the room, a man who created a tingling awareness all through her body even when he wasn't looking at her. He was clearly with Chaz, for he'd joined him at the bar, propping one elbow upon it as he talked to him, his bored, sardonic gaze moving slowly and disinterestedly around the room.

Really, the look on his face was rather ridiculously arrogant, almost a parody of what Liza imagined some lord of the manor would look like as he gazed down upon his peasants. She felt a thorny spike of annoyance pierce her; why did such a good-looking man have to be so *proud*? Looks weren't everything and yet, Liza acknowledged with an inward sigh, in this world they certainly counted for a lot. She'd discovered that to her detriment—plain Liza compared to pretty Jenna for most of her childhood—and when it had mattered.

'When he comes back,' their mother instructed Jenna,

interrupting Liza's thoughts, 'for heaven's sake, invite him
to sit down.'

'*Mum*—'

'Of course she's going to invite him to sit down,' Lindsay interjected with a scoffing laugh. 'And if she won't, I
will. I tell you, he's *loaded*.'

'I don't think he'll appreciate the invitation quite as
much, coming from you,' Liza interjected with a smile,
and her sister gave her a fulminating look. Liza reached
for her white wine, which only had one sip left in the glass;
she'd declined Chaz Bingham's offer of a top-up. Would
Chaz sit down with them if he was asked? she wondered.
And if he did, would his dark, proud friend join him? Her
heart tumbled over at the thought, and she decided she
needed to fortify herself with more wine.

'Liza, where are you going?' her mother demanded, pulling on her sleeve. 'Chaz will be coming back any second—'

Already it was Chaz, she thought wryly. He hadn't even
introduced himself yet. 'I've decided I want a glass of wine
after all,' Liza said, and with her heart fluttering a little
she headed towards the bar—and the intriguing man leaning against it.

'Why on earth did you choose this place?' Fausto Danti
glanced around the crowded bar with a grimace of distaste.
Having arrived in London from Milan only that afternoon,
he'd been hoping for a quiet dinner in a discreet and select
club with his old university friend, not a booze-up in a bar
that looked like it was full of tourists and college students.

Chaz glanced at him, full of good humour as always.
'What, you don't like it?' he queried innocently. Fausto did
not dignify his question with a reply. 'You've always been
something of a snob, Danti.'

'I prefer to consider myself discerning.'

'You need to loosen up. I've been telling you that since

our uni days. And come on.' He nodded meaningfully towards the table with its bevy of squawking women. 'Isn't she the loveliest creature you've ever seen?'

'She's nice enough,' Fausto allowed, because he had to admit the woman Chaz had set eyes on the second they'd walked through the door was really rather beautiful. 'She's the only pretty one among them.'

'I thought her sisters were nice enough.'

'Sisters?' Fausto arched an imperious eyebrow. 'How do you know they're not all just friends?'

Chaz shrugged. 'They all have a similar look about them, and the older one is clearly their mother. Anyway, I intend to get to know them all. And you can do the same.'

Fausto snorted at such an unlikely suggestion. 'I have no desire to do any such thing.'

'What about the one with curly hair?'

'She looked as plain and boring as the other, if not more so,' Fausto replied. He'd barely glanced at any of the women; he had no intention of picking someone up in a place like this, or even picking up someone at all. His stomach tightened with distaste at the thought.

He'd left such pursuits behind him long ago…and for good reason. He was here in England to deal with the fallout of the London office only, and then he was returning to Italy, where his mother was hoping he would soon announce his choice of bride. His stomach tightened again at *that* thought, although he knew there was no question of not fulfilling his duty.

'Oh, come on, Danti,' Chaz insisted. 'Relax, if you can remember how. I know you've been working hard these last few years, but let's have some fun.'

'This is generally not how I amuse myself,' Fausto replied as he took the tumbler of whisky from the bartender with a terse nod of thanks. 'And certainly not with a couple of obnoxious, gold-digging women who look poised to fawn over your every word.' He'd heard the younger one jabber about how much money Chaz had, not even caring who might be listening.

'Fawning over my every word? That's more your style, mate.' Chaz patted him on the arm and Fausto gave him a tight-lipped smile, even as he felt an uncanny frisson of— something—ripple through him, an awareness he didn't understand, but certainly felt.

He turned swiftly, expecting someone to be standing right next to him, but no one was. He scanned the crowded room but saw only the dull mix of middle class Londoners out for an evening of cocktails and fun.

'Come on,' Chaz said as he hoisted the drinks he'd bought for the motley crew of women, including a revolting-looking cocktail that was garnished with a pink umbrella and no less than three maraschino cherries.

With the utmost reluctance, Fausto followed his friend towards the table of eagerly waiting women. The blonde Chaz had set his sights on was indeed attractive, if in a rather simple way. There was no guile in her clear gaze, no depths to discover in her open face. Yet, Fausto concluded fairly, he would not necessarily consider her looks insipid.

The second sister, who looked to be still in her teens, was all flash and flare, her make-up overdone, her light brown hair pulled into a high, tight ponytail, a tight cropped top emphasising her curvy figure. The look in her eyes was what Fausto could only call avaricious, and his stomach tightened once more in sour anticipation of a most unpleasant evening.

The mother, he saw, was cut from the same cloth as the sister, and dressed in almost as revealing an outfit— but hadn't there been another at the table? Briefly Fausto recalled curly chestnut hair, a pair of glinting hazel eyes. They were no more than vague impressions, but he held the distinct certainty there had been a fourth woman at the table. Where was she?

Chaz set the drinks down with a gentlemanly flourish and, predictably, the pretty blonde stammered an invitation for him to join them, which Chaz did, sliding into the booth next to her. Fausto was left with no choice of seating other than next to the teenager with a lusty look in her eye, and so he coolly informed them he would prefer to stand.

'I'm sure you would,' a voice quipped near his ear, as the woman he realised he'd been looking for walked briskly by and slid into the booth next to her sister. 'To tell the truth, you seem as if you couldn't get out of here fast enough.'

Fausto locked gazes with the hazel eyes he'd recalled, and they were just as glinting as he remembered. Even more so, for right now they were flashing fire at him, and he wondered why on earth this Little Miss Nobody was looking at him with such self-righteous anger.

'I admit this was not my first choice of establishment,' he returned with a long, level look at this slip of a woman who dared to challenge him. Her hair was the colour of chestnuts and tumbled over her shoulders in a riot of corkscrew curls.

Large hazel eyes were framed with lush chocolate-coloured lashes, and her mouth was a ripe cupid's bow. She wore a plain green jumper and jeans and, all in all, Fausto decided after a moment's deliberate perusal, she was nothing remarkable.

The woman raised her eyebrows as he held her gaze, her angry expression turning to something more mocking, and with a disinterest that was not as legitimate as Fausto would have wished, he flicked his gaze away.

Chaz was making introductions and Fausto turned to listen, although he doubted he would ever have the need to address any of these women by name.

'Jenna… Lindsay… Yvonne… Liza.' Chaz looked as delighted as if he'd just done an impressive sum in his head, and Fausto shoved his hands in the pockets of his trousers. So now he knew her name was Liza, not that it mattered.

'And your name?' the mother, Yvonne, trilled. It was obvious she already knew who he was—Chaz graced enough of the gossip rags and society pages, with his pedigree, wealth and cheerful attendance at many social occasions.

'Chaz Bingham, and this is my good friend from university, Fausto Danti. He's here from Milan to head up his family's London office for a few months.'

Fausto gave him a coldly quelling look; he did not need these people knowing his business. Chaz smiled back, completely unrepentant as always.

'What do you think of our country, Mr Danti?' the mother asked in a cringingly girlish voice. Fausto gave her a repressive look.

'I find it as well as I did when I was here for university fifteen years ago,' he answered coolly, and she gave an uncertain laugh and then blushed, before gulping down her ridiculous cocktail.

Instinctively, unwillingly, Fausto glanced at the woman—Liza—and saw she was glaring at him with unbridled fury. This time she was the one to look away, a deliberate snub which he found both irritating and unsettling. It wasn't as if he *cared*.

Chaz was chatting animatedly to Jenna, which left the four of them—Fausto and these three tedious women—to sit through an insufferable silence. At the start Lindsay attempted a few flirtatious forays of conversation which Fausto shot down unreservedly. He was tired, out of sorts, and he had absolutely no interest in getting to know these people, not to mention a seven a.m. start tomorrow. After fifteen excruciating minutes, he looked pointedly at his watch. Chaz caught his eye and then blithely ignored him. Fausto ground his teeth.

He didn't want to be here, but neither did he wish to be unapologetically rude and leave his friend flat—although perhaps that was what Chaz wanted, all things considered. Fausto glanced at his watch again, even more pointedly this time.

'I'm so sorry we're keeping you,' Liza remarked acidly, and Fausto glanced at her, unperturbed.

'Actually, Chaz is keeping me,' he returned, and she let out a huff of indignation.

'He seems like he's having a good time,' she said with a nod towards Chaz and Jenna, their heads bent together. 'I'm sure he wouldn't mind if you chose to leave.' Her eyebrows lifted and Fausto saw a definite spark of challenge in her eyes that caused a ripple of reluctant admiration to pass through him. Here was a woman with a bit more fire than her beautiful sister, a few more depths to discover. Not that it mattered even remotely to him.

'I'm inclined to agree with you,' he replied with a short nod. 'And so, in that case, I will make my goodbyes.' He gave another nod, this one of farewell, his impassive glance taking in all three women before he nodded at Chaz, who gave him a shamefaced grin and kept talking to Jenna.

Fausto couldn't keep from giving Liza one last glance before he left, and as their eyes met something shuddered through him—and then, as dismissive as he had been at the start, she looked away.

CHAPTER TWO

LIZA STARED AT her bedroom ceiling as the autumn sunlight filtered through the curtains and lit her tiny room with gold. She didn't take any notice of it, however, because in her mind she was picturing Fausto Danti, with his steel-grey eyes and his sculpted mouth, his midnight hair and his disdainful look.

Jerk. Rude, arrogant, irritating *boor*.

Her fists clenched on the duvet as she remembered his aristocratic drawl. '*She looked as plain and boring as the other, if not more so.*' She'd heard his damning statement, so indifferently given, when she'd gone to the bar, and the words had scorched through her, branding her with their carelessly cruel indictment. Reminding her that she wasn't anything special—something she'd always felt, had been told to her by someone she'd thought she'd cared about, but to have it confirmed so ruthlessly, and by a *stranger*…

It felt as if Fausto Danti had ripped off the barely healed scab covering the wound she'd done her best to hide from everyone, even herself. She'd always known she wasn't beautiful like Jenna, or intelligent like Marie, or spirited like Lindsay. But to have it confirmed *again*…

After Fausto's callous comment, Liza had raced back to her table, furious and hurt, before he could see her. It wasn't as if she cared or even knew the man, she told herself, and he obviously didn't care at all. The way he'd looked down his nose at them all…as if they were so uninteresting that he simply couldn't be bothered even to make the most basic of pleasantries for a few minutes.

And the way he'd looked at *her*… Liza's fists clenched harder and her stomach did too. There had been something simmering in his iron-coloured eyes that had made everything in her seem to both shiver and heat. As much as she wanted to hate him, and she did, of *course* she did, that look had created a sweet, surprising longing in her she couldn't deny even as she strived to, because she knew it couldn't lead to anything good.

Yet, based on what he'd said, she'd obviously misread that look completely, which added another humiliation to the whole sorry story. Of course he hadn't looked at her like *that*. She wouldn't even know what *that* kind of look was like. She had certainly misread one before.

As for her own humiliating reaction, all heat and awareness…so the man was attractive. Any woman with a pulse would respond to his looks, that much was certain, although after Chaz had left, having exchanged mobile numbers with Jenna, the excited chatter between her mother and sisters had all been about him rather than Fausto Danti.

Would he call? Would he ask Jenna out? When? Where? The deliberations had gone on for half the night, until Liza had finally retreated to bed, unable to contribute to the excitement but not wanting to lower the mood.

She had no doubt that all the conversation today would continue to be about Chaz. No one had even mentioned Fausto Danti last night, which seemed rather incredible considering both his undeniably good looks as well as his undeniably bad manners. But no, her mother and sisters had only wanted to talk about Chaz. Handsome, polite, perfectly nice Chaz Bingham, who was clearly halfway to being head over heels in love with Jenna. And meanwhile Liza couldn't stop thinking about Fausto Danti.

With a sigh she rose from her bed. She had a feeling it was going to be a long day.

* * *

By Sunday night, when she said goodbye to her mother and sister who were heading back to Herefordshire, Liza felt it had been a very long two days. They'd shopped on Oxford Street, had tea at The Ritz and seen a West End musical. They'd gone out for curry, strolled through Hyde Park and had makeovers at Selfridge's, and all the while they'd talked of Chaz, Chaz, Chaz.

How rich was he? How many houses did he have? Where had he gone to school? Lindsay had done countless searches on her phone, trumpeting every gleaned fact with triumph while Jenna had murmured something appropriately modest and blushed.

By the end of it all, Liza was heartily tired of even thinking about Chaz Bingham—as well as Fausto Danti. She'd thought about him far too much while her family wittered on about his friend. Why had he been so rude? Who did he think he was? Had she been imagining some sort of… spark…in the look he'd given her? She must have, based on what he'd said to Chaz about her. Of course she had. She was ridiculous to think—*hope*—she hadn't, even for a second. Ridiculous and pathetic.

In any case, they were all futile questions because Liza knew she'd never see him again. In fact, she thought he'd most likely make sure of it, and if he didn't, she would. She *would*.

Still, thoughts of the irritable and inscrutable man dogged her as she headed to work on Monday. Although her position as an assistant to the editor of a tiny, obscure publisher of poetry paid peanuts, Liza loved it.

She loved everything about her job—the elegant, high-ceilinged office in Holborn, with its many bookcases and tall sashed windows overlooking Russell Square. She loved her boss, an elderly man named Henry Burgh, whose grandfather had founded the business a hundred years ago. He was holding onto it now by the skin of his teeth—as well as his generous but dwindling inheritance.

Liza had no idea who bought the slender volumes of poetry with their silky pages and ink-drawn illustrations, but she thought they were the most beautiful books she'd ever seen, and she loved the combination of older canonical poetry with works by refreshingly modern poets.

It annoyed her that as she worked at her desk in that beautiful room, she was *still* thinking about Fausto Danti. Wondering why he was so arrogant—and if there was any chance whatsoever that she might see him again. She really needed to stop.

'You seem a bit distracted,' Henry commented as he came out of his office to give her some manuscripts to copy edit. As usual he was wearing a three-piece suit in Harris tweed, a gold pocket watch on a chain in his waistcoat pocket. For a man nearing eighty, Henry Burgh certainly had style.

'Sorry.' Liza ducked her head in apology. 'Busy weekend. My family visited.'

'Ah, and how did they find the city?' He raised shaggy grey eyebrows as he gave her a kindly smile.

'They loved it, but I knew they would.' Liza thought Lindsay had been waiting all her life to get to London, to the business of living among fashionable people, socialites and YouTubers and the wealthy elite. A school trip to Paris at age twelve was the furthest adventure Lindsay had had so far, and she was most certainly ready for more when she started university next September.

'I'm pleased,' Henry told her. 'The next time they come, you must bring them here to meet me.'

Liza murmured her agreement, although privately she doubted her mother or sisters would want to visit her workplace. None of them, not even Marie, were interested in reading poetry. Her father would, she thought, but he was reluctant to leave the former vicarage in Little Mayton that he'd bought for a song thirty years ago and done up slowly. He loved his home comforts—his study, his workshop, his garden. Unlike his daughters, he had no hankering for adventures outside the home.

What would Fausto Danti think of the place where she worked? Liza wondered after Henry had gone back into his office. Was he a man who liked books? Poetry? Of course she had no idea, and yet somehow she suspected he might. There had been a quiet, contained intensity about him that suggested a man with at least some kind of an inner life, although perhaps that was stupidly wishful thinking on her part. Why should she think the man had depths, just because he had a sexy scowl? No, of course he didn't. He was just a jerk.

Smiling to herself at the thought, Liza reached for the stack of manuscripts.

'Liza!'

Jenna threw open the door of their tiny flat as soon as Liza had reached the top of the stairs, causing her to put her hand to her heart in alarm.

'What's wrong—?'

'Nothing's wrong,' Jenna declared with a chortle. 'Everything is wonderfully right. Or at least—I think it might be! *Look*.' She thrust her phone so close to Liza's face that the screen blurred and she had to take a step back. 'It's from him,' Jenna explained, although Liza had already figured that out.

'If you're free this weekend,' she read, 'I'd love for you to come to a little house party I'm having in Surrey.' She glanced up at Jenna. 'A house party? Really?'

Jenna bit her lip, doubt flickering in her blue eyes. 'Why not?'

'You've met him once, Jen. And now he wants you to go

to his house? Doesn't it seem…' Liza struggled for a way to explain her concerns that didn't sound too harsh '…a bit much, a bit too soon?' she finished helplessly.

'There will be loads of other people there. And it's only for the weekend.'

'I know, but…'

'This is what people like him do, Liza. Just because we've never been to house parties doesn't mean it isn't the usual thing.'

'I suppose.' Liza handed back the phone as she headed into their flat. She was tired and her feet ached from her walk from the Tube. She was looking forward to an evening of ice cream and maybe some Netflix, but it was clear her sister wanted to talk about Chaz. Again. Not that she'd begrudge Jenna anything, because her sister was her best friend and just about the most genuinely sweet person in the world. She was the one with the attitude problem.

'Do you think I shouldn't go?' Jenna asked as Liza opened the fridge to peruse its meagre contents. 'I won't if you don't think I should.'

'It's not for me to say…'

'But I need your input,' Jenna protested. 'I trust you, Liza. Do you think it's a crazy idea? I barely know him. It's just he seems so *nice*.'

'He does,' Liza admitted, because that much was certainly true.

'And I do like him.' Jenna bit her lip. 'More than I probably should, considering how little I know him.'

'There's no reason not to go, really,' Liza said as she closed the fridge and started examining the contents of their cupboards. 'We came to London for adventure, after all. Now you're having one.'

'Yes…' Jenna still looked uncertain. The truth, Liza knew, was that her older sister had never been particularly adventurous. It had been more Liza's idea than Jenna's to come to London, desperate for a new start, after she'd been offered the job of editorial assistant. Jenna had found a position as a receptionist at an accountancy firm, and Liza had bowled them both along. It wasn't like her older sister to step out on her own. It never had been. 'I know,' Jenna said suddenly. 'What if you go with me?'

'What?' Liza turned from her disappointing perusal of the cupboards. 'Jenna, I can't just show up without an invitation.'

'I'm sure I could bring a plus one.'

'I'm sure Chaz Bingham is counting on you *not* bringing a plus one,' Liza returned dryly. 'There's no way I can just turn up like a spare part and act as if I was invited.'

'Please, Liza.' Jenna's eyes widened appealingly as she gave Liza a pleading look. 'You know how nervous I get on my own. I'm no good at these kinds of things…'

'We've never *been* to this kind of thing—'

'Parties. Social events. You *know*. I never know what to say, and I go all shy and silent. I need your support.'

Liza shook her head resolutely. 'Jenna, if you're too nervous to go on your own, you shouldn't go at all. You could always go and then leave if you really don't like it. But I cannot, and will not, turn up uninvited.' She suppressed a shudder at the thought. If Chaz Bingham was having a house party, there was a chance Fausto Danti would be there and she could only too well imagine the incredulous and disdainful look on his face if she appeared unexpectedly, an obvious hanger-on. He might think she was trying to attract his attention, *and* she'd be seeming to confirm the unkind remark he'd made about them being gold-diggers. No, thank you!

'I don't know…' Jenna murmured, fiddling with her phone, and Liza reached for a packet of pasta, realising this conversation might take the entire evening and she was going to need sustenance for it.

*   *   *

It took three days of deliberation, but on Thursday morning Jenna finally decided to accept the invitation. Liza helped her word a polite but reserved text back to Chaz.

By Friday afternoon Jenna was packed, and Liza saw her off on the train to Chaz's family estate in Surrey, trying to squelch that treacherous flicker of envy that Jenna was going somewhere exciting and she wasn't. Of course Chaz wouldn't have invited *her*, and Fausto Danti wouldn't have extended an invitation either. The idea was utterly ludicrous; it wouldn't have even crossed his mind, and it was shaming that it had crossed hers, even for an instant.

Besides, Liza reminded herself as she headed back to her flat for a quiet weekend alone, she wouldn't have wanted to go anyway. If either man had invited her, she would have refused. Politely, but most definitely firmly. The last thing she needed was a man in her life making her feel inferior, unwanted. Undesirable.

Although, to be fair, Fausto Danti hadn't been quite that bad. No, she was projecting onto him the feelings she still had about being so thoroughly rejected by Andrew Felton. Liza closed her eyes, determined not to think of the man she'd convinced herself she'd been love with, only to have him laugh at her, and worse.

It had been a long time ago now—well, eighteen months—and she hadn't been that hurt. She hadn't even loved him, not really, even if at the time she thought she had.

It was stupid to think of Andrew just because Fausto Danti had been similarly snide. Fausto Danti, Liza acknowledged, was a million times more attractive—and therefore a million times less likely to be interested in her. The sooner she got that through her head, the better.

As one of four sisters, Liza was used to being around people, but she had never minded her own company and she would normally be perfectly content to spend a weekend alone, even if the weather was dire—as cold and rainy an October as there had ever been.

This weekend, however, the hours seemed to drag and drag. There were no texts from Jenna even though she'd promised to tell her how she was getting on and, with the weather so miserable, Liza decided to stay inside. On Saturday afternoon, with little else to do, she began to blitz clean the flat; two hours into her efforts, when she was sweaty and dirty and covered in dust, her phone finally buzzed with a text from Jenna.

Liza, HELP! I've come down with the worst cold and everyone here is such a snob. I'm soooo miserable. Please, please come and rescue me.

'Check.'

Chaz let out a groan as he looked down at the chessboard. 'How did I not even see that?'

'You never see it,' Fausto remarked dryly. 'In all the times I've played you in chess.'

'Too true. I think we should try another game.'

'Go Fish?' Fausto suggested and Chaz laughed.

'That's about my speed.' He glanced out of the window at the rain streaking relentlessly down the long diamond panes, the view of Netherhall's park shrouded in gloom. 'This weather is horrendous.' He rose from the unfinished game and began to prowl about the elegant confines of the study.

'If you're going to have a house party in October,' Fausto remarked, 'you should expect rain.'

'It's not that.'

Fausto leaned back in his chair as he surveyed his old friend. 'Let me guess,' he said. 'It's the fact that your so-called guest of honour is currently laid up in bed.'

Chaz turned to him with his usual ready smile, eyebrows raised. 'So-called?'

Fausto lifted one shoulder in a negligent shrug. 'Did you *meet* her mother?'

Chaz did not bother to defend the woman in question, which did not surprise Fausto. The woman had been too appalling, with her breathy voice and her avaricious manner, not to mention her revolting cocktails. The same with the younger sister. Gold-diggers, the pair of them, and he certainly knew how to recognise one. Admittedly, he couldn't fault either Liza or Jenna, although he still had his suspicions. A woman could seem sweet on the outside and be thinking only about money and prestige.

Look at Amy…

But he refused to think of Amy.

'So?' Chaz answered with a shrug, drawing Fausto out of his grim recollections. 'I didn't invite her mother.'

'Still, it's telling.'

'Of what?'

Fausto toyed with the queen he'd taken off Chaz a few moments earlier, his long fingers caressing the smooth white marble, memories of Amy still haunting his mind like ghosts. 'They're not exactly people of…class.'

Chaz let out a huff of disbelieving laughter. 'You sound about a hundred years old. This isn't the eighteen-hundreds, Danti.'

It was an accusation Fausto had heard before from his friend. People weren't supposed to talk about class any more, or the fact that someone with a position in society had a duty to uphold it.

But it had been drilled into him since he was a child, by both his parents—ideas about respect, and dignity, and honour. Family was everything, and always came first—above happiness, pleasure, or personal desire. He'd rebelled against it all once, and it had cost both him and his family greatly. He had no desire to do it again.

For a second he saw his father Bernardo's proud and autocratic face, turned haggard and wasted by disease. Fausto could almost feel his father's claw-like fingers scrabbling for his own. *'Family, Fausto. Family always comes first. The Dantis have been the first family of Lombardy for three hundred years. Never forget that. Never dishonour it. You carry our name. You represent it everywhere...'*

It was a responsibility he'd shirked once and now took with the utmost seriousness, a burden he was glad to bear, for the sake of his father's memory. It defined who he was, how he acted, what he believed. He would never forget he had a duty to his father, to his family, to himself. A duty to act honourably, to protect the family's interests, to live—and to marry—well, to carry on the Danti name, to run the vast estates that bore his name.

Chaz, he knew, did not feel the same sense of responsibility that he did. His friend wore his wealth and privilege lightly, carelessly, and he did not let himself be weighed down by expectation or tradition—not, Fausto acknowledged, that his parents, currently living in the south of France, cared too much for either. They were new money, a family of socialites, eager to enjoy their wealth. Yet, for all that, Chaz was as friendly and unpretentious a person as any Fausto had ever met.

'In any case, you're not serious about this woman, are you?' he asked.

'I don't know,' Chaz returned thoughtfully. 'I might be.'

Fausto chose not to reply. He couldn't see his friend marrying such a nobody, beautiful though she might be, but if he wanted to amuse himself with an affair, that was his own business.

'Hopefully she'll take some paracetamol then,' he remarked. 'So you can at least see her before she has to go home.' Jenna Benton had shown up at the house late on Friday afternoon, soaking wet and sneezing. She'd barely said a word at dinner, shooting Chaz beseeching looks, and had been holed up in her room ever since.

The other guests Chaz had invited—the usual tedious selection of socialites and trust fund babies—had been as insipid as Fausto had expected. He should have stayed in London and worked through the weekend, but he'd allowed Chaz to convince him to come. Clearly a mistake.

'Perhaps I'll check on her now,' Chaz said, brightening at the thought. 'Make sure she has tea and toast and whatever else she needs.'

'By all means, go and play nursemaid.' Fausto replaced the queen piece on the chessboard before gesturing to the door.

Chaz smiled wryly. 'Are you going to closet yourself in here all weekend? You could have gone into Guildford with everyone else, you know.'

'In the pouring rain?' Fausto shook his head. That afternoon the other three guests had gamely gone into town, but Fausto had refused.

'I know my sister in particular is hoping you'll venture out,' Chaz remarked slyly. 'She was the one to insist you come along.'

'I'm sorry to disappoint her.'

Chaz let out a laugh. 'I don't think you're sorry at all.'

Fausto decided in this case discretion was the better part of valour. As much as he liked Chaz, he had very little patience with his twittering and vapid sister, Kerry. Chaz laughed again, and shook his head.

'All right, suit yourself. I'm going to check on Jenna.'

'Good luck.'

As Chaz headed upstairs, Fausto rose from his chair by the fire and walked about the room, as restless as Chaz had been a moment ago. Perhaps he would make his excuses and return to London tonight.

Danti Investments' London office had been in lamentable shape when he'd arrived last week, a fact which still made him burn with futile fury for its cause. It would take all his time and effort to get it to the productive place it needed to be before he returned to Milan. He didn't have time to waste enduring the company of people he actively disliked.

For a second an image flitted in his mind of someone he didn't actively dislike…someone he didn't actually *know*. Corkscrew curls, hazel eyes, a mocking smile, a willowy figure. Jenna's sister Liza had been occupying too many of his thoughts since he'd first laid eyes on her last weekend.

It was absurd, because she was of absolutely no importance to him, and yet he kept thinking about her. Remembering the pointed sweetness of her tone as she'd sparred with him, the lively intelligence in her face, the sweetly enticing curves of her slender figure. It was aggravating in the extreme that he kept thinking about her, especially when he had no desire to.

When he married, it would have to be to a woman of appropriate status and connections back in Italy, from one of the ancient families he'd known for many years, who held the same values of honour and respect that he did, who knew how to be his partner in running the vast Danti empire. That had been the promise he'd made to his dying father, and he intended to keep it.

As for other, less honourable, possibilities…he had no desire to get caught up in some run-of-the-mill affair that would undoubtedly run its short and predictable course, and in doing so become messy and time-consuming. Sexual gratification could be delayed. Work—and family—were far more important than such base needs.

The sonorous chimes of the house's doorbell echoed

through the hall and Fausto stilled, wondering what unexpected guest might be making such a late appearance. He waited, but no one came to answer the door; Chaz had to be busy with Jenna, and the staff were no doubt occupied elsewhere. The doorbell rang again.

With a hurried exhalation of annoyance, Fausto strode out of the study. It was most likely only a delivery man or some such, but he hated rudeness or impunctuality, and not answering the door was both.

The large entrance hall was empty as he walked through it, towards the front door. Rain streamed down the windows; it really was a deluge out there. Barely reining in his impatience, Fausto threw open the door with a scowl—and then blinked at the bedraggled figure standing there, looking woebegone and forlorn and very, very wet.

He gaped for a second before his mouth snapped shut and he stared at her, eyebrows creasing together, his mouth drawn down into a disapproving frown.

'Liza Benton,' he stated coolly. 'What on earth are you doing here?'

CHAPTER THREE

OF ALL THE people to answer the door. Liza blinked through the rain streaming down her face at the sight of Fausto Danti glaring at her so predictably. He didn't seem like the kind of man who lowered himself to answer doors, so Liza had no idea why he was standing here before her, looking down his nose at her just as he had before.

What she did know was that she was freezing cold and dripping wet, her clothes sticking to her skin, her hair in rat's tails about her face as she shivered visibly. When she'd answered Jenna's summons and arrived in the village of Hartington by train, she'd been told Netherhall was only five minutes' walk from the station. It was more like fifteen, and thirty seconds after she'd started it had begun to bucket down with rain. So here she was, soaking wet and staring at Fausto Danti. Perfect.

'I'm here to see Jenna,' she said with as much dignity as she could muster, which she feared wasn't all that much. 'She texted me and asked me to come because she wasn't feeling well.' It sounded lame to her own ears. *Why* had she hared off so impetuously after receiving Jenna's text?

She'd grabbed her purse and coat and been at the train station in less than twenty minutes, without a thought or care in the world. It was only now, as Fausto Danti regarded her with such chilly hauteur, that she realised how ridiculous—and possibly scheming—she must seem. It wasn't as if Jenna was at death's door. She had a *cold*. Did Danti think she'd come here for him? Liza squirmed inwardly at the humiliating possibility.

'By all means, come inside,' Fausto said and he stepped aside so Liza could enter, dripping muddy water all over the entrance hall's gleaming parquet floor. She felt entirely at a disadvantage—wet, cold, dirty and, worst of all, uninvited. And all the while Fausto Danti lounged there, his hands in his pockets, his expression one of unveiled incredulous condescension.

'I'm sorry to come unannounced like this,' Liza said stiffly. 'But Jenna sounded completely miserable, and I didn't want her to be alone.'

'She is hardly alone.'

Any other man, Liza reflected, any normal, polite, kind, well-brought-up man at least, would have graciously dismissed her apology and insist that she needn't have made it. He would have ushered her in, offered her a cup of something warm and told her she could stay as long as she liked. She was quite sure that was what Chaz Bingham would have done. Why couldn't *he* have answered the door? Or his blasted butler? Surely he had one.

Anyone but Danti. *Anyone.*

'You are very wet,' Fausto observed.

'It's raining.'

'You didn't take a cab?'

'It wasn't raining when I left the station,' Liza returned with some asperity. 'And I was told it was a five-minute walk. And,' she flung at him for good measure, sensing it would annoy him somehow, 'I'm not in the habit of wasting money on cabs.'

'It would have been five pounds, at most,' her adversary returned mildly, 'but I take your point. Why don't you come into the study? There's a fire in there and you can dry off.'

This unexpected kindness appeased Liza somewhat, but she was still miffed by his high-handed manner and, moreover, stepping into a study with him felt a bit like entering the lion's den without either weapon or armour. Besides, she wanted to see her sister.

'I'm here to see Jenna,' she said, aware that an irritating note of petulance had entered her voice. Fausto raised his eyebrows, his mobile mouth quirking in the smallest of mocking smiles.

'You can hardly see her sopping wet. Besides, Chaz is with her now, and I'm quite sure you don't want to interrupt whatever *tête-à-tête* they might be having.'

Liza frowned at him, trying to gauge his tone. No, she didn't want to interrupt them, but the sharpness in Fausto's voice made her feel uneasy and defensive. What was he implying? Another stupid antiquated reference to golddigging?

'Very well,' she said, not wanting to pursue the point, and she followed him into a pleasant wood-panelled room where a fire was burning cheerily. Fausto gestured her towards the blaze and as she started towards it, anticipating its wonderful warmth, his hands came to rest on her shoulders.

She stiffened in shock as an electric awareness pulsed through her, starting from the warmth of his hands on her shoulders and racing to every extremity with disturbing force and speed.

'Your coat,' he murmured after an endless unsettling moment, and Liza closed her eyes in mortification. He just wanted her *coat*. What had she been thinking—that he was making a move on her? As if…! Surely she knew better than to think such a thing. She prayed he hadn't noticed her humiliating reaction.

'Thank you,' she muttered, and she shrugged out of the wet garment. She turned, and the sight of Fausto Danti with her battered, sopping jacket in his hands, his expression rather bemused, made her suddenly laugh out loud, that moment of unsettling awareness thankfully dissipated.

He raised his eyebrows in query. 'What's so funny?'

'The sight of you with my poor coat in your hands. It just looks rather…incongruous.'

He glanced down at her coat, five years old and bought off the bargain rack, and then with a shrug draped it over a chair. His hooded gaze swept over her, his face as inscrutable as ever, but all the same Liza was conscious of her very wet clothes; without the protection of her coat, she realised they were clinging rather revealingly to her body, and she plucked uselessly at her sodden jumper.

'You should change,' Fausto said abruptly. 'Did you bring any spare clothes?'

'No,' Liza admitted. 'I—we—won't be staying.'

His eyebrows lifted once more. 'It's already six o'clock in the evening. You can hardly be returning to London tonight.'

Liza shrugged, defensive again. 'Why not? It's not as if we're in the sticks out here. There are trains running to London all the time.'

'Not from Hartington. They stop at four in the afternoon. And in any case I'm sure Chaz won't hear of it. He hasn't spent any time with Jenna yet.'

'If she has a cold…'

'I have no doubt some paracetamol and a bit of TLC will perk her right up,' Fausto replied, his tone so dry that Liza prickled again. Why did he have to sound so cynical? What was he accusing Jenna of—just wanting Chaz for his money? It was an ugly idea, as well as a ludicrous one if he'd spent two minutes with her sister. 'I'll fetch you some clothes,' he stated, and turned towards the door.

'I can borrow Jenna's—' she protested, but Fausto silenced her with a look.

'Nonsense. You can't remotely be the same size.'

Liza blushed at that, for the truth was Jenna was far curvier than she was, as well as a good four inches taller. Still, it annoyed her that Fausto presumed to know their sizes.

Before she could make any further protest, however, he was already gone, the door clicking decisively shut behind him and leaving Liza alone in the room.

Restless and edgy, she paced the study, glancing at the leather-bound books lining the walls—all very distinguished tomes—and then at the chessboard set in front of the fire, clearly an unfinished game, with black at a distinct advantage.

She was still studying the board when Fausto returned with a bundle of clothes under his arm.

'Do you play?' he asked, sounding so sceptical that some sudden contrary instinct made Liza widen her eyes innocently.

'Sometimes. Do you?'

He gave a terse nod, and that impish instinct inside her gave voice once more. 'Perhaps you would give me a game?'

Fausto looked startled, and then he thrust the clothes at her. 'Perhaps you should get dressed first.'

'Very well.' Of course he wasn't going to play a game of chess with her. She'd only asked to tease him, which had been stupid of her. Fausto Danti did not seem like a teasing sort of person. Flushing from the humiliating ridiculousness of it all, Liza turned away.

Everything about this situation was so very *odd*, she reflected rather grimly as she took the clothes and Fausto gave her directions to a powder room down the hall. It didn't seem to be much of a house party since the house, enormous as it was, appeared empty.

She found the powder room, which was as big as her flat's living room, without trouble and groaned at the sight of her reflection in the gilt-edged mirror—hair in a frizzy mess, cheeks and nose reddened with cold and the jumper and jeans which had been perfectly respectable when she'd put them on this morning now clinging to her like a second skin. No wonder Fausto Danti had been looking at her so disdainfully.

With a dispirited sigh Liza peeled off the wet clothes and hung them on the towel rail to dry. Dubiously she inspected the outfit she'd been given—a modest yet clinging dress in cranberry-coloured cashmere.

It slid over her chilled skin as soft as a whisper, making her wonder whose it was. She scrunched her hair and blotted her face, knowing there was little else she could do to repair the damage wrought by the rain. She still looked very much like a drowned rat, if a little less so than before. She supposed it didn't really matter. She could hardly hope to impress him, and she certainly wasn't going to humiliate herself by trying. She knew how that would go.

As Liza headed back to the study, she wondered yet again where everyone was. She felt like Goldilocks stumbling upon a castle rather than a cottage, and instead of three bears there was merely one incredibly intimidating—and attractive—man.

Having no idea what to expect of this encounter, Liza pushed open the door of the study and peeked in. To her surprise, Fausto was sitting at the chessboard in front of the blazing fire. He'd set the board up for a new game, and he gestured to it as she entered the room.

'Well?' His heavy-lidded gaze swept over her figure, clad in the clinging red dress, her feet bare, but he made no further remark. Liza pushed her damp hair away from her face.

'You want to play?' she asked incredulously.

'I believe you asked for a game.'

'So I did.' Her stomach fizzed with sudden expectation and excitement. She hadn't thought Fausto would humour her in such a way, and she had no idea why he was, but as she took her seat across from him she realised in a scorching instant why she'd come all the way to Netherhall in the pouring rain. It hadn't been to rescue her sister, as much as she loved her. It had been to see *him*—the incredibly attractive, arrogant, frustrating and fascinating Fausto Danti.

Fausto studied his opponent from under his lashes as she considered the board. They'd played the first moves in silence, and he'd noted her predictable use of the Spanish Opening, attacking his knight on the third move. Basic but acceptable, and about what he'd expect from someone who played chess but was still a beginner. At least she didn't call the knight a horse.

He was reflecting on whether to put her out of her misery right away or prolong the game simply for the pleasure of seeing her sitting across from him—the dress he'd taken from Chaz's sister's wardrobe fitted her just as he'd hoped it would, skimming her slender curves with an enticing delicacy, making her look warm and so very touchable.

Her legs were bare, slim and golden, one foot tucked up under her, her hair, as it dried from the warmth of the fire, curling up into provocative ringlets about her heart-shaped face. Everything about her was utterly delectable.

Fausto didn't wish to consider what contrary impulse had led him to agree to her suggestion of a match, but he suspected it was a rather base one. The sight of the firelight glinting on her still-damp curls, the pretty flush on her face as well as the gentle rise and fall of her breasts…it was all a distraction he did not need, and yet even so he found he was enjoying it immensely and he could not be sorry.

'I've never been to a house party,' Liza remarked as she unexpectedly—and, Fausto thought, amateurishly—moved her bishop, 'but I always assumed there would be guests involved.' She looked up at him with laughing eyes. 'Where is everybody?'

'They've all gone to Guildford,' he replied as he moved his knight. 'Since they were so bored here, with the rain.'

'Except for Jenna and Chaz?'

'Jenna stayed because of her purported cold, and Chaz stayed because of Jenna.' Fausto spoke tonelessly, refusing to let his own suspicions colour his words, but Liza frowned anyway, her eyes crinkling up as she cocked her head.

'Purported?' she repeated a bit sharply.

'I have not seen her, so I cannot judge for myself.'

'And yet you judge no matter what,' she returned tartly as she flicked her hair over her shoulders and moved her queen. 'Regardless of the situation.'

'I judge on what I see,' Fausto allowed as he captured her queen easily. She looked unfazed by the move, as if she'd expected it, although to Fausto's eye it had seemed a most inexpert choice. 'Doesn't everyone do the same?'

'Some people are more accepting than others.'

'Is that a criticism?'

'You seem cynical,' Liza allowed. 'Of Jenna in particular.'

'I consider myself a realist,' Fausto returned, and she laughed, a crystal-clear sound that seemed to reverberate through him like the ringing of a bell.

'Isn't that what every cynic says?'

'And what are you? An optimist?' He imbued the word with the necessary scepticism.

'No, that's Jenna. I'm the realist. I've learned to be.' For a second she looked bleak, and Fausto realised he was curious.

'And where did you learn that lesson?'

She gave him a pert look, although he still saw a shadow of that unsettling bleakness in her eyes. 'From people such as yourself.' She moved her knight—really, what was she thinking there? 'Your move.'

Fausto's gaze quickly swept the board and he moved a pawn. 'I don't think you know me well enough to have learned such a lesson,' he remarked.

'I've learned it before, and in any case I'm a quick study.' She looked up at him with glinting eyes, a coy smile flirting about her mouth. A mouth Fausto had a sudden, serious urge to kiss. The notion took him so forcefully and unexpectedly that he leaned forward a little over the game, and Liza's eyes widened in response, her breath hitching audibly as surprise flashed across her features.

For a second, no more, the very air between them felt tautened, vibrating with sexual tension and expectation. It would be so very easy to close the space between their mouths. So very easy to taste her sweetness, drink deep from that lovely, luscious well.

Of course he was going to do no such thing. He could never consider a serious relationship with Liza Benton; she was not at all the sort of person he was expected to marry and, in any case, he'd been burned once before, when he'd been led by something so consuming and changeable as desire.

As for a cheap affair…the idea had its tempting merits, but he knew he had neither the time nor inclination to act on it. An affair would be complicated and distracting, a reminder he needed far too much in this moment.

Fausto leaned back, thankfully breaking the tension, and Liza's smile turned cat-like, surprising him. She looked so knowing, as if she'd been party to every thought in his head, which thankfully she hadn't been, and was smugly informing him of that fact.

'Checkmate,' she said softly and, jolted, Fausto stared at her blankly before glancing down at the board.

'That's impossible,' he declared as his gaze moved over the pieces and, with another jolt, he realised it wasn't. She'd put him in checkmate and he hadn't even realised his king had been under threat. He'd indifferently moved a pawn while she'd neatly spun her web. Disbelief warred with a scorching shame as well as a reluctant admiration. All the while he'd assumed she'd been playing an amateurish, inexperienced game, she'd been neatly and slyly laying a trap.

'You *snookered* me.'

Her eyes widened with laughing innocence. 'I did no such thing. You just assumed I wasn't a worthy opponent.' She cocked her head, her gaze turning flirtatious—unless he was imagining that? Feeling it? 'But, of course, you judge on what you see.'

The tension twanged back again, even more electric than before. Slowly, deliberately, Fausto knocked over his king to declare his defeat. The sound of the marble clattering against the board was loud in the stillness of the room, the only other sound their suddenly laboured breathing.

He *had* to kiss her. He would. Fausto leaned forward, his gaze turning sleepy and hooded as he fastened it on her lush mouth. Liza's eyes flared again and she drew an unsteady breath, as loud as a shout in the still, silent room. Then, slowly, deliberately, she leaned forward too, her dress pulling against her body so he could see quite perfectly the outline of her breasts.

There were only a few scant inches between their mouths, hardly any space at all. Fausto could already imagine the feel of her lips against his, the honeyed slide of them, her sweet, breathy surrender as she gave herself up to their kiss. Her eyes fluttered closed. He leaned forward another inch, and then another. Only centimetres between them now...

'Here you are!'

The door to the study flung open hard enough to bang against the wall, and Fausto and Liza sprang apart. Chaz gave them a beaming smile, his arm around a rather woebegone-looking Jenna. Fausto forced a courteous smile back, as both disappointment and a very necessary relief coursed through him.

That had been close. Far, far too close.

CHAPTER FOUR

LIZA'S SENSES WERE still swimming as she blinked her sister and Chaz Bingham into focus. Had that really happened? Had Fausto Danti almost *kissed* her?

She touched her tongue to her lips, as if she could feel the press of his lips against hers still, even though he hadn't actually touched her at all.

She had been able to imagine it so thoroughly, even as she recognised she could not truly envision it at all. In her twenty-three years, Liza had had a handful of casual dates, and one total disaster. None of it had, thankfully, gone too far, although she was still reeling from the emotional fall-out of her almost-fling with Andrew Felton, even if she pretended otherwise.

Still, none of her experience, those few kisses, had been as memorable, as mind-blowing, as she was sure Fausto Danti's would be. As even the *possibility* of his had been.

But he hadn't kissed her and, looking at him now standing in front of the fire, his expression as austere as ever, she thought he never would.

She had a sudden, awful certainty that she'd imagined the whole thing; it had been a fabrication of her fevered mind, of the utterly inconvenient longing she'd felt for this man since she'd first stepped into Netherhall. Even now she felt overwhelmed by the height and breadth and power of him, the sight and sound, even the *smell* of him, a sharp, woodsy aftershave that made her senses tingle, along with everything else.

But of course he wasn't interested in her. He couldn't be.

Realisation scorched through her. He must have been teasing her, toying with her, and she'd fallen for it completely.

'Liza!' Jenna exclaimed, and started towards her.

Feeling clumsy and stiff, Liza hugged her sister. 'Are you okay?' she asked.

Next to her, Fausto drawled, 'It *was* just a cold, wasn't it?'

Liza threw him a glare that was meant to be mocking. Jenna let out a wobbly laugh.

'I think I've made a fuss over nothing. Chaz gave me some paracetamol and a cup of tea and I feel *so* much better.'

Jenna smiled adoringly at Chaz, who puffed his chest out as if he'd scaled Mount Everest rather than doled out a couple of tablets. Liza could not keep from glancing again at Fausto, whose inscrutable expression still managed to relay his arrogant assurance that he had been entirely correct about the nature of Jenna's *purported* cold, and she fumed inwardly. How could she dislike a man and yet want him to kiss her so much? *So much she'd imagined the chemistry that she'd felt pulsing between them?*

'I'm sorry I made you come all this way,' Jenna said with a guiltily apologetic look for Liza. 'I was just feeling so low.'

'I'm sure you were,' Liza murmured. She could not deny the awkwardness she felt now at having gate-crashed, and she felt it most from Fausto, even though he didn't say a word. When she dared look at him again he looked so severe and unimpressed that she felt quite overwhelmingly that she could not continue to stay there. She would not fulfil Fausto Danti's obviously low expectations of her and her family; she would not let him tease her for another instant with his mocking looks and his almost-kisses.

'Then it looks like I don't need to be here at all,' she said in a voice of patently false brightness. 'I'll call a cab to take me to Guildford—the trains will still be running from there.'

'Oh, no,' Chaz exclaimed, just as she'd feared he would. 'We can't send you away now. Stay the weekend, along with Jenna. I'm sure we could all use the company.'

'I can't...' Liza began. She knew insisting on leaving now would be rude, but she was frustratingly, furiously aware of Fausto's fulminating silence, and she wondered if he thought she and Jenna had orchestrated the whole thing, for some nefarious, mercenary purpose, no doubt. *Gold-diggers*, the pair of them. How she disliked the man, even if she *still* wished he'd kissed her.

'You can certainly stay,' Chaz insisted, and then, to Liza's humiliation, he turned to Fausto. 'Can't she, Danti?'

'Liza must do as she pleases,' Fausto replied with a shrug. Inwardly, everything in Liza writhed with humiliation at his dismissive tone.

'Then it's settled. You'll stay.'

'I don't have any clothes or toiletries,' Liza protested, determined to make one last attempt at departure.

'That's no trouble.' Chaz airily waved away her concern. 'We've got loads of extra shampoos and things like that, and you look about the same size as my sister Kerry. In fact, I think she has a dress just like that one.' He smiled easily, as carefree as a little boy, while Liza flushed. So that was where Fausto had found the dress.

'Thank you, this is really kind of you,' she said dutifully, because she knew she could give no other response.

'I'll show you to our room,' Jenna suggested, and Chaz nodded.

'Yes, we're eating at eight—not too long now. I'll see you then?' He smiled hopefully at them both, and Liza nodded.

'Thank you,' she said again, and she turned away, making sure not to catch Fausto Danti's eye.

As soon as they were upstairs, Jenna launched into a

glowing description of all Chaz had done for her. 'He's so nice, Liza, I mean really nice. You don't often meet people who are good all the way through.'

'You are,' Liza said with a smile. Her sister was so big-hearted, so generous with her time and talents, that Liza felt small for ever having resented her for a millisecond. Andrew Felton was *not* Jenna's fault.

Jenna had ushered her into a room that was twice as big as their flat, with huge windows overlooking a terraced garden, the kind you'd normally have to pay to look at.

'I mean it, though,' Jenna insisted, as if Liza had contradicted her. 'He really is a good person.'

'I believe you.' Liza reached for her sister's toiletries bag and started to tend to her frizzing hair. 'That being the case, though,' she asked mildly, 'why did you send me that text?'

Jenna had the grace to grimace guiltily. 'I'm sorry. I don't think I should have, really. It's just I was feeling so low. My head was aching and everyone besides Chaz seems so…well, I don't like to criticise, but they're…'

'Snobs?' Liza filled in succinctly and Jenna shrugged.

'I suppose, although they're all very nice on the surface, Chaz's sister Kerry in particular. She was cosying up to me right from the beginning, acting *so* sweet, but I had the feeling she'd talk behind my back the second I was out of the room.'

'She probably would,' Liza agreed.

'You've never even met her,' Jenna couldn't help but protest, and Liza sighed.

'I don't need to, but you're right, I should reserve judgement until I do.' Not that Fausto Danti ever did. Checkmating him had been one of the greatest pleasures of her life, although in truth she would rather he'd kissed her.

The thought appalled Liza as soon as it had formed in her head. No, of course she wouldn't have wanted *that*. She couldn't. She actually loathed the man, even if she was helplessly attracted to him.

And if he'd kissed her it would have been either to toy with her or mock her, not out of genuine desire. Of that she was sure. He liked her even less than she did him, and worse, he made her feel so *small*, and she hated that most of all. She had vowed never to feel like that again, and yet here she was.

'You'll meet them all at dinner, anyway,' Jenna said. 'And then you can see for yourself.'

'Do you have anything I can wear? This dress belongs to Chaz's sister, and I really don't feel like turning up in it.'

'I only brought one dress,' Jenna said apologetically. 'And I think it's going to pale in comparison to what everyone else is wearing. They're all millionaires, Liza. They all went to the same private schools, and know the same small group of people. Some of them have such toffee-nosed accents I can barely understand them.'

'Oh, *deah*,' Liza mocked, putting on a drawling aristocratic accent as she planted one hand on her hip. '*Howevah* will we manage?'

Jenna smiled and then let out a giggle, and Liza rolled her eyes. 'Honestly, I think these people are ridiculous, looking down their noses at us just for being *normal*. They're the odd ones, really.' She gestured to the enormous bedroom with its sumptuous silk hangings and ornate furniture. 'Who really lives like this any more?' She wasn't going to be cowed by all the money. She didn't care about it. And she certainly wasn't going to let Fausto Danti think she or her sister were gold-diggers…not that she could do anything about that, unfortunately.

'They do, obviously.' Jenna narrowed her eyes as she regarded her shrewdly. 'These people,' she repeated, 'or just one man in particular?'

Liza stilled, willing herself not to blush, but she did anyway. 'I don't like Fausto Danti,' she said frankly as she turned away to focus on her hair, and hide her flushed face from her sister. 'He's an arrogant snob.'

'A *gorgeous* arrogant snob. When we came into the study, it almost looked as if he was about to kiss you.'

'He wasn't!' Liza exclaimed, her face ever hotter. She scrunched her curls with firm, hard hands. 'We were just looking at the chessboard. I'd checkmated him.'

'That's no surprise,' Jenna answered. 'I can't remember the last time you lost a game.'

'He's annoying,' Liza declared. 'I suspect he thinks we're here as gold-diggers or something like that.'

'Gold-diggers!' Jenna sounded horrified at the prospect. 'He didn't actually say that, did he?'

Liza decided not to mention the comment she'd heard last week at the cocktail bar. She knew it would only distress her sister. 'He didn't have to.'

'Oh, Liza.' Jenna shook her head. 'Sometimes I think you're as snobby as him, only in reverse.'

'I'm not,' Liza insisted. 'I just want to take people as they truly are.' Not, she thought darkly, as someone like Fausto Danti saw them. She didn't judge the way he did, and she wasn't nearly as proud. She wasn't proud at all. In fact, quite the reverse. She knew she struggled with her self-esteem, not that she'd ever apprise Fausto of that fact.

'Well, take them as they are in an hour,' Jenna said with a sigh. 'We'll have to face everyone at dinner and even though I feel better now I'm glad you're with me. It's like going into the lion's den sometimes.'

Just as she'd felt with Fausto. Liza continued to fluff her hair as she met her sister's gaze in the mirror and smiled with determination. 'I'm glad I'm here too,' she said, and she hoped she meant it.

* * *

Fausto sipped the pre-dinner sherry one of Netherhall's staff had served as he observed the other guests circulating in the drawing room before dinner was called. Chaz was talking to Oliver, one of his rather bumbling friends from prep school, a keen cricketer who had far more money than sense. Chaz's sister Kerry was whispering with her friend Chelsea, a hotel heiress in a slippery gold sheath dress. Both of them kept shooting him coquettish looks which Fausto chose to ignore. Where were Jenna and Liza? It was three minutes past eight. They were late.

Not, Fausto told himself as he tasted the sweet sherry with a slight grimace, that he was eagerly awaiting their arrival. Of course he wasn't. The afternoon with Liza had been surprisingly pleasant, and he'd spent the intervening hours thinking far too much about her—from that electric almost-kiss that had been, in its own way, a more satisfying and passionate experience than the last time he'd actually been with a woman—to the fact that she'd trounced him in chess in just a few short minutes. She was, he admitted reluctantly, a superior sort of woman. Sadly, that still didn't make her suitable for a man in his position, with his responsibilities, his expectations. *His past.*

'Jenna!' Chaz sprang away from his friend as the sisters came into the drawing room. Jenna was wearing a rather worn-looking black dress, the kind a hostess at a restaurant might wear, and Liza was still in the cranberry knit dress Fausto had given her, although at least she'd found a pair of flats and styled her hair into a loose knot. Compared to the other women in their designer cocktail dresses and stiletto heels, the Benton sisters looked woefully underdressed, and yet he still found he preferred Liza's unadorned simplicity to the other women's obvious attempts.

Chaz had put his arm around Jenna as he ushered her into the room, and Liza came in behind them, head held high, gaze averted from Fausto's in what he suspected was a deliberate snub, a fact which both amused and annoyed him.

'Goodness,' Kerry remarked in a clipped, carrying voice. 'You aren't wearing my dress, are you?' She let out a tinkling little laugh, like the breaking of glass.

Liza flushed and lifted her chin another inch; any further and she'd be staring at the ceiling. 'I think I probably am,' she admitted with stiff dignity. 'I'm afraid I arrived without a change of clothes, and I was caught in the rain.'

'I gave it to her, Kerry,' Fausto interjected in a deliberately bored drawl. 'I didn't think you'd mind.'

Kerry could hardly say she did mind, and so she contented herself with merely raising her eyebrows and giving Chelsea a disbelieving look. Chelsea tittered, and Liza flushed harder but to her credit said nothing. Fausto realised afresh how much he disliked Chaz's sister.

'Perhaps you should consider giving it to her,' he remarked. 'I think it suits her colouring far more than yours.'

'I'm sure it doesn't,' Liza intervened quickly. 'But thank you, Kerry, it's very kind of you to lend your clothes to a stranger.'

'We're not strangers now,' Chaz insisted in a jolly voice. 'Since we're spending the rest of the weekend together. Now that we're all here, let's eat!'

The dinner was, as Fausto had expected, quite interminable, save for the pleasure of looking upon Liza when he could. She'd purposely seated herself as far from him as possible, which again gave him that push-pull sensation of both annoyance and amusement. Was she putting herself out of the way of temptation, or did she really dislike him that much? What he knew she didn't feel was indifference, and that knowledge satisfied in a deep and primal way.

The chatter and gossip during the meal bored him completely, however, and he stayed silent through it all, despite Kerry's obvious attempts to engage him in flirtatious conversation. He hoped his silence was discouragement enough, but he suspected with a woman like Kerry it would not be. Still, that was a problem for another day.

As for Liza…she ate her meal quietly, gaze lowered and yet alert, and he sensed she was listening to every word and finding it all as tedious as he was, a thought that gave him unexpected pleasure.

After dinner they all retired to the house's high-tech media room, where Chaz put on music and Kerry mixed cocktails. Chelsea draped herself over a leather sofa as artfully as possible, and Oliver sprawled on another as he scrolled through his phone. Jenna was chatting to Chaz, and Liza sat alone, looking serenely composed. Fausto walked over to her.

'How are you finding the company?' he asked, and she looked up at him, hazel eyes wide and clear, her mouth curving into a slight smile.

'I find them as I see them.'

'A scathing indictment, then.'

'Actually, I've found the whole evening quite entertaining. You all live in your cosy little world, don't you?'

Fausto drew back at that matter-of-fact remark. 'What is that supposed to mean, exactly?'

Liza shrugged slim shoulders. 'Only that this is quite a rarefied way of living. You don't seem to have any of the paltry concerns most people do.'

'Is that a criticism?'

'Merely an observation.'

'I suppose you're right, in a way,' Fausto said after a moment. He didn't know whether he felt glad or irritated that she'd chosen to highlight their differences. It was a needed reminder, in any case. As much as he enjoyed Liza's company, he could never consider her seriously. His family obligations as well as his own history made sure of that.

'You certainly don't seem to be enjoying the evening,' Liza told him with a laugh. 'I've been watching you scowl. Do you find everyone disagreeable, Mr Danti?'

'You should call me Fausto.'

'I've been calling you Fausto in my head,' she admitted blithely, 'but you seem like the sort of person who would want everyone to address you appropriately.'

'I don't need people to bow and scrape, if that's what you mean,' Fausto said sharply. He might have ideas about his position, and of respect and honour, but he had absolutely no need for people to be servile. The thought was repugnant to him. 'But if you really do want to get it right, it's Conte, not Mr.'

She looked startled, but then her expression cleared and she smiled and nodded. 'Of course it is,' she said, and Fausto felt frustratingly inferior for having mentioned his title. He hadn't intended to; he rarely used it. 'In future I shall address you as such. Is that Conte Danti, or the Conte of Something-or-Other?'

'Conte di Palmerno,' he bit out. 'But, as I said, there is no need. I am not accustomed to being addressed that way and, in any case, it's a courtesy title only. Officially, nobility was abolished in Italy in 1946.'

'In that case, it's Fausto all the way,' Liza quipped, and Fausto gave a tight-lipped smile. He could not help but feel she'd somehow got the better of him in the conversation.

'What I really want to know,' he said as he stepped closer to her, 'is how did you get so good at chess?'

Her eyebrows raised as her smile widened. 'You weren't expecting it.'

'You led me to believe you were a beginner.'

'I did not,' she returned. 'You assumed it.'

He paused, and then realised she was right. He h*ad* assumed it, but it had seemed like a very justifiable assumption to make. 'You're very good,' he remarked.

'Better than you,' Liza agreed, her eyes sparkling, and Fausto let out an unwilling laugh.

'Perhaps we should have a rematch.' He hadn't meant those words to be so laden with innuendo…had he? Because now he wasn't thinking about the pieces on the board, but the kiss that had so very nearly happened over it. The kiss he wanted—*needed*—to happen again.

This rematch, he realised, was merely a pretext to get her alone, and as Liza looked up at him, eyes wide, lips slightly parted, he thought she must know it.

'Are you sure you're up for a rematch?' she asked softly, and there was no mistaking the subtext in the tremble of her voice, the way her gaze lowered and her chocolate-coloured lashes skimmed her cheeks. He ached to touch her.

'Quite sure,' he said, his low voice husky. 'Quite, quite sure.'

'What on earth are you two talking about?' Kerry called from the cocktail bar. 'You look *awfully* serious.'

'We were talking about chess,' Liza called back lightly, although her voice wavered a little. 'Fausto is insisting on a rematch after I trounced him.'

'You did not *trounce*,' Fausto felt compelled to point out.

She turned back to him with glinting eyes. 'Oh, no? You thought I'd lost my queen for no good reason.'

That much was true, and he could not deny it. He inclined his head in acknowledgement instead, and Liza laughed out loud.

'Come have a cocktail, Fausto,' Kerry said petulantly. 'I've made you a gin sling.'

'I only drink whisky and wine,' Fausto replied. 'But thank you anyway.'

'I'll drink it, if you like,' Liza offered, and with a challenging spark in her eyes she walked over to the bar, her gaze meeting Fausto's as she tossed back the cocktail. He watched her, caught between admiration, amusement and an overwhelming, heady desire. He didn't care whether she was suitable or not. He just wanted to be with her alone.

'Delicious,' Liza pronounced to Kerry, but she was still looking at Fausto. He nearly groaned aloud at the invitation in her eyes. Did she even know it was there? How did everyone in the room not see and feel what was practically pulsing between them?

'That rematch,' he said, the words bitten out. 'Now.'

'For heaven's sake, it's only chess,' Chaz interjected with a laugh.

Kerry was regarding them both with narrowed eyes. 'Why don't you bring the board in here?' she suggested all too sweetly. 'We can all play, have a tournament.'

'You don't play, Kerry,' Chaz pointed out, and Kerry shrugged impatiently.

'I know the rules, at least.'

Fausto didn't think Kerry had any interest whatsoever in playing chess, but he wasn't about to belabour the point. 'As you wish,' he said instead, and then he turned to Liza. 'Will you help me fetch the board and pieces?'

A flush rose on her cheeks as she nodded. At last they would have a few minutes alone.

With eyes only for Liza, Fausto left the room, his breath coming out in a relieved rush when she followed.

CHAPTER FIVE

THEY WALKED IN silence from the media room, down a long, plushly carpeted hall towards the study. The house yawned darkly in every direction, silent and empty. Liza wondered if Fausto could hear the thudding of her heart.

She couldn't believe how flirtatious she'd seemed, how confident. Something about Fausto's manner, his undivided attention, had made her sparkle, and she relished the feeling even as she tried to caution herself. Not to read emotions into a conversation where there weren't any, because heaven knew she'd done that before.

'Why on earth would you think I was interested in you, even for a second?'

She banished the mocking voice of memory as she focused on the present. She didn't think she'd been imagining the undercurrent of sexual innuendo in her and Fausto's conversation. At least, she hoped she wasn't. Every time Fausto looked at her, her whole body tingled. She felt as if she were electrically charged, as if sparks might fly from her fingers. If Fausto touched her, she'd burn up.

And yet he *had* to touch her. She couldn't bear it if he didn't. She might dislike the man, but she needed him in a way she had never needed anyone before—elementally, at the core of her being. And he seemed to need her in the same way, at least in this moment. And being needed, even if just for now, just for *this*, was a powerful aphrodisiac. She wouldn't let herself think about anything else.

Finally they were at the study, and Fausto pushed the door open so Liza could step first into the darkened room, her shoulder brushing his chest as she passed him. She heard him inhale sharply, and she thrilled to the sound. She felt dizzy with desire, and yet he hadn't even touched her yet.

But he would…wouldn't he? He *had* to.

She walked towards the table in front of the fire where the chessboard lay, Fausto's king still toppled from their match. Unthinkingly, she picked it up, the marble cool and smooth in her fingers. She felt Fausto standing behind her, a powerful, looming presence, and then she turned.

She could barely see him in the shadowy room, but oh, she could feel him. The chess piece fell from her fingers with a clatter as Fausto laid one hand against her cheek. His palm was warm and rough and frankly wonderful.

For a suspended moment they were both silent and still, his hand on her cheek, his gaze burning into hers. Silently asking her permission. And she gave it, leaning her face into his palm for a millisecond before his lips came down hard on hers. Finally, *finally*, he was kissing her.

And what a kiss it was. Hard and soft, demanding and pleading, taking and giving. Liza had never, ever been kissed like this. She backed up against the table, and then Fausto hoisted her right onto the chessboard, scattering the pieces as he deepened the kiss, plundering her mouth and claiming her as his own.

Her hands fisted in the snowy white folds of his dress shirt as he pressed his hard, powerful body against hers and the kiss went on and on. She tilted her head back as he began to kiss her throat, his hands sliding down her body to fasten on her hips.

Her breath came out in a shudder as his lips moved lower, to the V-neck of her dress. Everywhere his lips touched her, she burned. Her whole body felt as if it were on fire, as if she had only just finally come wonderfully, twangingly alive.

And then a voice, as petulant as always, floated down the hall. 'Fausto? Where *are* you?'

They both froze for a millisecond and then Fausto stepped quickly away, pushing his hair back from his forehead as he strove to control his breathing. Liza leapt off the chessboard, humiliatingly conscious of her dishevelled clothes, her flushed face and swollen lips, not to mention the fact that she'd been sprawled across a chessboard of all things, ripe for the taking.

'Forgive me,' Fausto said in a low voice as he stooped to gather the chess pieces, and Liza realised that wasn't at all what she'd wanted him to say in such a moment.

She began to gather some of the fallen pieces as well, and just a few seconds later the light flicked on and Kerry was standing in the doorway, her hands fisted on her hips.

'Well.' She let out a high, false laugh. 'If I didn't know any better, I'd think something had been going on here.'

'Don't be ridiculous,' Fausto said shortly, and Liza did her utmost to school her expression into something bland. *Don't be ridiculous*?

Of course it was ridiculous, for something to have been *going on* between them. Ridiculous to him. She didn't have the space or time to be hurt by Fausto's instantaneous denial, and so she focused on gathering up the pieces while he grabbed the chessboard. No one spoke, but the air felt thick with tension.

Liza's body still tingled everywhere. Her lips both trembled and stung. She'd never been kissed like that in her life. She felt as if she'd been changed for ever, branded somehow, and the intensity of her reaction scared her.

I don't even like him, she reminded herself rather frantically, but the words seemed hollow even in the privacy of her own mind.

'So, a tournament,' Fausto said without any enthusiasm,

and Kerry gave him a narrow look while Liza looked away. She wanted this evening to be over.

Unfortunately, it wasn't; the three of them trooped back to the media room where everyone was swilling cocktails. Chaz had put on a film that no one seemed to be watching, and the prospect of a chess tournament was dismissed without a word. Fausto stood in the back of the room, his hands in his pockets, while Liza went over to Jenna.

'I think I'll go upstairs,' she whispered. 'It's been a long day.'

'Oh, but...' Jenna glanced at Chaz, and Liza patted her arm.

'You stay. I don't mind an early night.' It wasn't even that early by her standards, already nearly eleven, and she felt more than ready for bed.

She said her goodnights to everyone, ignoring Fausto, who was scowling by the door; she had no choice but to walk by him on her way out. She tensed as she passed him and for a second she thought he'd speak, but he didn't, and neither did she.

Liza walked out of the room and upstairs on unsteady legs. Her whole body felt like a bowlful of jelly, wobbly and weak. As she closed her door and then collapsed onto the king-sized bed, she had an urge both to laugh wildly and burst into tears. *What had just happened?*

Well, she knew what had happened, of course. Fausto Danti had kissed her senseless. And while it would be a wonderful memory to hold onto, she was sensible enough to realise—at least she hoped she was—that it hadn't *meant* anything. Fausto disdained her as much as he ever did, and she disliked him. Mostly. Flirting a little over chess of all things certainly didn't change that.

And yet...and yet...the feel of his lips on hers, his *hands* on her...the wild passion and yet the surprising tenderness...

'Oh, come *on*,' Liza muttered to herself as she punched her pillow. 'Don't be like this again. Get a grip.'

She wasn't going to fall for the first pair of pretty eyes that made her feel special. Not like she had with Andrew, when she'd believed his flattery and made a fool of herself. She had promised herself she wouldn't fall for that again, and so she hadn't.

She knew very well that Fausto wasn't interested in her, not really, and in any case there hadn't been any simpering compliments involved, not like there had been with Andrew.

Just overwhelming mutual physical attraction…

With a groan, determined to put it all out of her head, Liza got ready for bed. She folded up Kerry's dress and took a T-shirt of Jenna's to sleep in, the excitement of the kiss draining out of her like flat champagne as she realised all the awkwardness that would likely ensue as a result. Fausto's 'Forgive me' most certainly meant he'd regretted his actions almost immediately; tomorrow he would apologise again, if he didn't just ignore her completely. Both prospects made Liza feel miserable, and she wished, quite desperately, to go home.

Eventually she fell asleep, barely stirring when Jenna came in several hours later, and then waking up a little after dawn, a feeling like lead in her stomach. She did not want to see Fausto Danti again. She had an awful feeling when she did he would be colder than ever, as disdainful and dismissive as he'd been that first night at Rico's, only this time, instead of annoying her a little, it would actually hurt.

She knew she wasn't particularly desirable or interesting; she'd already felt a bit lost in the shuffle even before Andrew had dealt her self-confidence its seeming death blow. To think, even for a moment, that she could hold the interest of a man like Fausto Danti…

Of course she couldn't. And she wouldn't let herself want to.

In any case, none of it turned out as Liza had expected. Jenna was brimming with shy excitement about her evening with Chaz, and his promise to take her out to dinner when they were back in London, and no mention was made of Fausto at all.

By the time Liza headed downstairs, dressed in an outfit of Jenna's that swam on her smaller frame, her stomach was seething with nerves and she only picked at the generous buffet that had been laid out for breakfast. She jumped every time someone spoke or came to the door; Kerry strolled in, yawning and bored, and Chelsea and Oliver were both clearly hung over, although Chaz was in as good spirits as ever.

Liza wasn't brave enough to ask where Fausto was, and it was only as they were planning their activities for the day that she learned the truth.

'It's too bad that Danti had to leave this morning,' Chaz said with unaccustomed gloominess. 'He promised me he'd stay until tonight.'

'Why did he leave in such a rush?' Kerry asked with a pout, and Liza stared down at her plate. Chaz mentioned something about him needing to work but she was afraid she knew the truth. Fausto Danti had left because he couldn't bear to see her again.

Fausto shrugged off his coat as he strode through the office of Danti Investments, located in a beautiful Georgian building overlooking Mayfair. It was empty on a Sunday morning, which suited him perfectly because he wanted to work. He wanted to work and forget a beguiling sprite named Liza Benton even existed.

It had been, Fausto had ample time to reflect on the journey back to London, utterly foolish to have kissed her, and kissed her so thoroughly at that. In the moment he'd been inflamed by his desire and he'd completely lost any power of rational thought. It was only afterwards, when Kerry had come in looking so suspicious, and Liza had looked so dazed and overwhelmed, that he'd realised what a mistake he'd made.

The last thing he needed was gossip—or any kind of attachment, physical or otherwise. He didn't want to act dishonourably, and neither did he wish to hurt Liza, and he feared he had by sending out an entirely wrong signal. He wasn't interested in her, didn't care about her, and had no desire to make it seem as if he did.

And yet... Fausto sat back in his desk chair, his unseeing gaze on the gracious view of Mayfair out of the window; his mind's eye was occupied entirely by one woman.

Perhaps he was attributing too much tender feeling on Liza's part. Heaven knew he'd made that mistake before, with Amy.

Amy... For a second he pictured her laughing eyes, her long golden hair, the way she'd smiled and teased and made him feel so light-hearted, as if anything was possible, as if for once the weight of his world and all the responsibility he bore didn't rest so heavily on his shoulders.

Then he thought of her look of regret when she'd said goodbye to him, with his father's cheque in her hand. Yes, he knew about gold-diggers, and how guileless they could seem. Look at Jenna, with that overblown cold she'd dreamed up to take Chaz's attention. It had, to his mind, been glaringly obvious. Was Liza's response to him some of the same? Were both sisters hoping to snag rich husbands, or perhaps just rich benefactors?

Maybe all these tender feelings he feared she had for him were nothing more than a blatant ruse to keep him dangling on the hook so she could reel him in. Maybe he didn't need to worry about Liza Benton's feelings at all.

The prospect brought both a necessary relief and an unsettling irritation. He didn't like the thought that Liza was mercenary, and deep down he didn't truly believe she was. Yet the alternative was to think she might care about him, and that was just as unwelcome a thought. He never should have kissed her, even as he was thinking about doing it again.

What he should do, Fausto acknowledged irritably, was forget the whole episode completely, and yet somehow that seemed impossible. With a grimace of disgusted impatience, he pulled his laptop towards him and started to work.

Fausto managed to convince himself that he hadn't thought of Liza for an entire fortnight—almost. The energy and thought he expended in *not* bringing her to mind might have told another story, if he cared to listen to it. He did not.

He worked long hours that precluded thought about anything other than the business at hand, and he returned home to the townhouse that had been in the Danti family for over a hundred years with nothing in mind except food and sleep. And so two weeks passed well enough.

In fact, Fausto kept Liza Benton so well out of mind that when he stopped by his godfather's business one Friday afternoon in mid-November to fulfil a promise of saying hello, he stared in complete and utter incomprehension as Liza herself looked up from her desk and stared back at him in the same way.

'What...?' Her voice was a faint thread of sound. 'What on earth are you doing here?'

She looked so achingly beautiful, and he thought he saw a spark of hope in her eyes, but the feeling of being completely wrong-footed in the moment had him retreating into chilly reserve.

'I'm here to see my godfather, Henry Burgh. I had no idea you worked here.'

Something flashed across Liza's face—Fausto thought it was hurt—and then she drew herself up. 'And I had no idea you were his godson,' she answered. 'How did that come to be?'

'Henry was my father's tutor in university,' Fausto said, his voice decidedly cool. 'They were very close. I've known him all my life.'

'I see.' She rose from behind her desk, slim and elegant in a navy pencil skirt and ivory blouse, her usually wild hair pulled up into a neat chignon, although a few wayward curls escaped to frame her lovely face. 'I'll let him know you've arrived.'

Fausto watched in frustrated silence as she crossed the room, the only sound the click of her heels on the parquet floor, and knocked on the door of Henry's office. As she opened the door he turned away, determined to act uninterested. He *was* uninterested. He hadn't thought of her once these last few weeks, after all, and it was far better that they resorted to being nothing more than acquaintances, which was in fact all they were.

He was studying the volumes on the floor-to-ceiling shelves when Liza returned. 'He's on a telephone call, but he'll see you shortly. He said to make yourself comfortable.' She gestured to one of the two leather settees facing each other, her face blank and composed.

Fausto resumed his deliberation of the shelves for a few more moments before he took a seat. 'How long have you been working here?' he asked as he sat down.

Liza had retreated behind her desk and made a great show of getting on with her work, pulling a pile of papers towards her and studying them intently. 'About two months.'

'That's not very long.'

'It's when I moved to London.'

'From Herefordshire, as I recall?'

'Yes, a small village in the middle of nowhere.' She lifted her head to look at him, her chin raised a little, a spark in her eyes that was definitely not hope. Was she angry with him? He supposed leaving so abruptly from the house party might have been construed as rude. He hadn't meant it as some sort of snub, not exactly. He'd just needed to get away. Not, of course, that he had any intention of explaining his reasons to her, or how much of a temptation she had been.

'Have you been very busy with work?' Liza asked after a moment, all frosty politeness, and Fausto gave a terse nod. 'Yes.'

'Chaz and Jenna have seen quite a bit of each other in the last few weeks. I suppose you know?'

He shrugged indifferently. 'I don't keep tabs on all my friends, and in any case I've been too busy to go out these last few weeks, but he did mention that he'd seen her.' And rhapsodised about how much he liked her, while Fausto had made no response.

'I think it might be serious,' Liza flung at him like a challenge.

He glanced at her, noting the steely glint in her eyes. 'I'm sure Chaz is well on his way to falling in love with her,' he agreed coolly. 'It's his habit, after all.'

Liza pursed her lips. 'Does he fall in love very often?'

'More than I do.'

'Ah.' She sat back, her arms folded, eyes still flashing. 'Is that a warning?'

Startled, he spared her a wary glance. He didn't trust her in this mood. 'It wasn't meant to be,' he said, although he realised as he answered that it wasn't exactly true. It had been, at least in part.

'Don't worry,' Liza assured him. 'I'm not in any danger of falling in love with you.'

Fausto stiffened in both surprise and affront. 'I was under no illusion that you were.'

'Well, that's a relief,' Liza drawled. 'Here I was, worried you'd raced away from Netherhall because you were heartbroken.'

He didn't know whether to feel amused or outraged by her absurd statement. 'Trust me, that was not the case.'

'No,' Liza said softly, and for a moment the mask dropped, her face fell, and she looked unbearably sad, which was even worse than her anger. 'I didn't think it was.'

The door to Henry's office opened and the older man emerged, his wrinkled face wreathed in smiles. 'Fausto! What a delight to see you after so long.'

Fausto rose and they shook hands while Liza watched, narrow-eyed, although she managed a smile when Henry turned towards her.

'Liza, I insist you take the rest of the afternoon off. I've made a reservation for afternoon tea for the three of us at The Dorchester.'

'What...?' There was no disguising Liza's shocked alarm. 'Oh, Henry, I don't think...'

'Nonsense,' her employer answered with a smile. 'You're on the clock for another hour anyway. I really do insist.' Henry's smile was both genial and steely and, managing a lukewarm smile, Liza murmured her assent.

Fausto knew better than to object to any of it, and in any case he could certainly suffer through an hour's conversation with Liza. Perhaps it would go some way to smoothing things over between them. If the opportunity arose, he decided, he would apologise for the kiss. That was the honourable thing to do, and then they could both put it firmly behind them—not that it was entirely necessary, since he didn't think they would ever see each other again. Still, it was the right decision, and one he felt satisfied with.

Yet as Henry locked up the office and they headed outside into the chilly dusk of a late autumn afternoon, Fausto was honest enough to acknowledge he was deceiving himself if he thought that was the only reason he'd agreed to this afternoon. The truth was, he was simply enjoying being with Liza again…far too much.

CHAPTER SIX

LIZA WALKED WITH Henry and Fausto towards The Dorchester in a daze. This was the last thing she'd expected. The
very last thing! For Fausto to walk into her office…and
now to be taking tea with him… She didn't know whether
it was the stuff of dreams or nightmares.

Certainly he'd featured in her thoughts, both waking
and sleeping, far too much these last few weeks. She'd
tried not to think about him at all, but it was hopeless. A
girl couldn't be kissed like that and then just forget about
it. At least, Liza couldn't.

Still, she'd managed to give herself a very brisk and
practical talking-to about the nature of that kiss, and how it
had, of course, been only physical attraction, nothing more.
Base and animalistic and easily dismissed on both sides. Or
so she'd kept telling herself and she was almost convinced,
until Fausto had walked through the door.

Now, sliding sideways glances at him walking down the
street, she remembered how powerful his shoulders had felt
under her questing hands, how hard and strong his chest
was, how soft and warm his lips…

Everything about him made her buzz and come alive.
Still. Just thinking about that kiss had her tautening like a
bow as yearning arrowed through her. Two weeks of disciplined thought flew right out of the window, and she
feared she was setting herself up for disappointment and
hurt—again.

Henry was chatting with Fausto, which made it easy for
Liza to lag behind and say nothing. She'd stay for an hour,

no more, and then make her excuses. After that she'd never have to see Fausto Danti again.

Why did that thought make her feel so depressed? She couldn't deny that seeing him again had lit her up inside like a firework, even though she hadn't wanted it to. She glanced at his profile—the hard, smoothly shaven jaw, the straight nose, those sculpted lips. He was like a Roman bust come to life, all aristocratic angles and sharp lines. *And just as cold.*

They arrived at the hotel and a tuxedoed waiter ushered them to a private parlour off the main dining room, already set with silver, crystal and linen for a high tea.

Liza took her seat, trying to quell the nerves fluttering in her stomach. She had a feeling the next hour was going to be unbearable.

'Fausto runs Danti Investments, out of Milan,' Henry explained to her as they all placed their napkins in their laps and the waiter brought a fresh pot of tea.

Liza glanced at Fausto, unsure how to handle the conversation. Was he going to pretend he'd never met her before? Why did that thought hurt her so much?

'Liza and I met a few weeks ago,' Fausto said smoothly, answering her silent question. 'At a house party. She trounced me in chess.'

'I thought I *didn't* trounce you,' she said before she could think better of it, and Fausto smiled faintly.

'I must give credit where it is due. But we haven't had our rematch.'

Liza stared at him in confusion, unsure if he was flirting or not. His voice was so light, his expression so bland, it was impossible to tell, although she told herself as sensibly as she could that of course he wasn't flirting. He couldn't be. She was just misreading signals—again—because she wanted to. The realisation shamed her although she did her best to rally.

'If you hadn't had to leave early, perhaps we could have,' she said after a pause, and he inclined his head in acknowledgement.

'Unfortunately, I really had no choice.'

What was *that* supposed to mean? Liza's head was spinning from the subtext, even as she wondered if she was reading too much into everything Fausto said. Discomfited, she reached for her teacup while Henry watched them both in smiling bemusement.

'It's always delightful,' he pronounced, 'when people I enjoy spending time with have already become acquainted with one another. Sandwich, Liza?'

Liza nibbled a cucumber sandwich while Henry and Fausto caught up on all their mutual friends, thankful not to have to contribute to the conversation. She'd barely had that thought when Henry turned to her with a smile.

'Have you ever been to Italy, Liza?'

'No, I'm afraid not.' She hadn't been anywhere. With four children and a large house, her childhood had been happy and full, but money had always been tight, trips abroad out of the question. 'I haven't really travelled,' she admitted with a rather defiant look at Fausto. She had a sudden contrary urge to remind him of how different they were, before he did. 'Or done much of anything. There hasn't been the money or opportunity, I'm afraid, but I've never minded. I've lived a very quiet life, really.'

'Perhaps that will change,' Henry suggested, and Liza gave him a small smile.

'Perhaps,' she allowed with another glance at Fausto's inscrutable face. 'Although I don't think so.'

The conversation moved on, thankfully, and Liza did her best to contribute as little as possible without seeming rude. Finally, after an hour, she rose from the table and made her apologies.

'This has been so lovely, Henry, but Jenna and I have

plans tonight and I really should get back. Thank you.' She spared Fausto the briefest glance possible. 'It was nice to see you again.'

She barely listened to his murmured reply before she hurried out of the room, a breathy sigh of relief escaping her as soon as the door shut behind her.

When she got back to the flat, Jenna was already dressed to go out.

'Get your dancing shoes on,' she told Liza gaily. 'We're meeting Chaz at a new bar in Soho, and it has live music.'

'We are?' Liza couldn't help but sound unenthused. When Jenna had asked her to go out tonight she'd been hoping for a sisterly chat over a glass of wine at their local.

'Yes, and I really do want you to come. You've been moping for the last two weeks, Liza. It's time to have some fun.'

'I haven't been *moping*.' At least, she thought she'd been doing a better job of hiding the fact.

'It'll be fun,' Jenna insisted, and reluctantly Liza went to change. At least she didn't think Fausto would be there. He hadn't mentioned anything that afternoon and he'd made a point of saying how little he'd seen of Chaz, and how busy he was with work. She was safe on *that* score, even if the realisation brought its own treacherous flicker of disappointment.

The bar was pulsing with music and people as Fausto pushed through the door, blinking in the neon-lit gloom of a place that was too trendy for its own good. He hadn't wanted to come, telling Chaz he needed to work, but once again his friend had insisted and after keeping his nose to the grindstone for the last few weeks Fausto had decided it might be enjoyable to relax for one evening, even if it was in a place like this.

The fact that Liza had mentioned she had plans and

could very well be here tonight naturally had nothing whatsoever to do with his decision.

He forced himself not to look around for her as he made his way to the bar and ordered a double whisky. The afternoon with Henry and Liza had been, to his own annoyance, both unbearable and invigorating.

He'd done his best not to look at her, and yet even so his gaze had been drawn to her again and again, as helpless as a hapless moth to the habitual dangerous flame. With her hair pulled up, he hadn't been able to help noticing how slender and delicate her neck was. He hadn't been able to help imagining kissing the nape of it either.

He'd barely been able to conduct a conversation with his godfather with Liza seated across from him; every time he drew a breath he'd inhaled her perfume, a light floral scent that teased his senses with its subtly sweet notes.

Somehow, through it all, the conversation had got away from him. He'd intended to make some sort of apology to Liza for their kiss, but the words wouldn't come, especially with Henry present. While he'd done his best to be friendly, she'd done her best to ignore him. The hour had been endless and yet when she'd left in such a hurry he'd felt a deep sense of disappointment as well as frustration. He wanted to make things right between them, but he was uncertain as to how—or if Liza would even let him.

Perhaps tonight, if he saw her, he'd have a chance.

'Danti!' Chaz clapped him hard on the shoulder. 'Good to see you.'

'You're looking cheerful,' Fausto remarked as he leaned against the bar and took a sip of his drink. Chaz grinned.

'I am! You remember Jenna?' He ushered forth Liza's sister, who gave him a perfunctory smile.

'I do.'

'Jenna has given me the brilliant idea of having a Christmas ball at Netherhall,' Chaz declared. 'Wouldn't that be a laugh? Fancy dress, dancing, the works. We'll all pretend we're straight out of Charles Dickens or something.'

'More like Jane Austen.' Fausto glanced coolly at Jenna, who fidgeted and avoided his gaze. So she'd suggested Chaz host a ball? Already practising at playing Lady of the Manor, it seemed. The suspicions he hadn't wanted to give voice to began to harden into certainty. He knew how women like this worked—was Liza one of them too? He didn't like to think of it, and yet he'd been duped before.

'You'll come, won't you?' Chaz asked. 'I'm inviting everyone. All of Jenna's family too.'

'All of them?' Fausto glanced again at Jenna, who flushed. She really was shamelessly inserting herself into Chaz's circle if she was asking him to invite her ridiculous mother and sister along with the rest of her relatives.

'I'll invite yours too,' Chaz declared grandly. 'What about that lovely little sister of yours, Francesca?'

'She's in Italy,' Fausto stated coolly. 'Thank you for the invitation, though.'

'She could hop over on a flight…'

'I don't think so.' The last thing he needed was seventeen-year-old Francesca having her head turned by some useless lout she met at a ball. Again.

'Well, you'll come, at least,' Chaz insisted, and Fausto gave a tight-lipped nod. He wouldn't be so rude as to refuse, although he was tempted to, especially if he had to deal with the other members of the Benton family shamelessly promoting themselves as they had when he'd first met them. Chaz clapped him on the back again before moving on with Jenna, leaving Fausto to drink his whisky in peace.

His gaze moved slowly, inexorably, over the crowded room, looking for those bright laughing eyes and that wild tumult of curly hair. He wasn't going to bother with the paltry pretence of trying to convince himself he wasn't looking for her; he was. He wanted to see her. He would apologise for the kiss, find a way to start afresh, as friends. She deserved that much. He did too. Liza Benton had caused him far too much aggravation and uncertainty. It was high time to put the whole thing to rest and prove to himself that he was master of his own mind, or at least his libido.

He did another sweep of the room, fighting an alarmingly fierce sense of disappointment, only to have his heart skip and his stomach tighten when he suddenly caught a glimpse of her in the corner of the bar, perched on a stool. Her head was tilted to one side, her hair wild and loose, and even from across the crowded space Fausto could see the sparkle in her eyes, the teasing curve of her lips. She looked as if she was *flirting*.

Instinctively, needing to know, he craned his neck to catch sight of whomever she was talking to, and then everything in him turned to incredulous ice when he saw the man in question—his smoothed-back blond hair, his easy manner, the open-necked polo shirt and expansive gestures so irritatingly familiar. *Jack Wickley*. What the hell was that bastard doing here? And why was he talking to Liza?

Fausto's fingers tightened on his tumbler and he tossed down the last of his whisky, appreciating its burn all the way to his gut. He could hardly approach Liza now. He couldn't come within ten feet of Wickley without wanting to punch the man. He turned back to the bar and ordered another double.

An endless hour passed with Liza talking to Wickley for most of it, before she left the corner she'd been perched in and came to the bar with her empty wine glass. Fausto, who had been tracking her every move, saw when she caught sight of him—her eyes widened as her gaze locked with his and her step faltered before she determinedly started forward again, her gaze skimming over him as if he wasn't there.

As she approached the bar she angled herself away from him, and incredulous indignation fired through him. Was she actually going to *ignore* him?

He leaned forward and he caught the scent of her perfume, which made him dizzy. 'I thought you'd be here tonight.' She gave a brief nod without looking at him, and resentment flared hotly. How dare she ignore him? 'Have you been enjoying yourself?' he asked, hearing the aggressive tone in his voice and wondering at it, but he *felt* too much to care.

'Yes, as a matter of fact I am.' Liza turned, and Fausto started at the obvious derision he saw in her eyes. Why was she looking at him as if she loathed him? She'd been sharp with him that afternoon, yes, but she hadn't looked at him like *that*.

She reached for the fresh glass of wine the bartender had poured for her. 'I hope you are as well,' she said in a final-sounding tone, clearly ending the conversation.

'I wanted to talk to you.' Liza raised her eyebrows, and Fausto struggled to find the right words, hardly able to believe that he—*he*—was being put at such a disadvantage. 'I wanted to apologise,' he said stiffly.

'For what, exactly?' she asked, looking distinctly unimpressed.

'For kissing you. It shouldn't have happened.'

'Noted.'

'I trust we can move beyond it.'

Her smile widened as she informed him with acid sweetness, 'I already have.'

And then, while Fausto could do nothing but gape and fume, she took her wine back to Jack Wickley, who was waiting for her with an all too smug smile.

Fausto swore under his breath. From the moment he'd

laid eyes on Liza Benton he had not been himself—acting
on impulse, saying and doing things he continued to regret.
Acting the way he had with Amy, or even worse, which was
utterly appalling. No more. For the sake of his family, for
the sake of his own pride, not to mention his sanity, it was
time to finally forget Liza Benton ever existed.

CHAPTER SEVEN

'LIZA, HURRY OR we'll be late.'

Liza glanced at her reflection one last time in the hotel room mirror as nerves zoomed around in her belly. Her family had taken temporary residence in a small hotel outside Hartington, for tonight was Chaz's Christmas ball.

Tonight she'd see Fausto Danti again and even though she'd come to despise the man she couldn't deny some contrary part of her was looking forward to seeing him once more—and she definitely wanted to look her best when she did.

Her unease around Fausto had deepened considerably over a month ago, when she'd met Jack Wickley at the evening out with Chaz and his friends. She'd been sitting in the corner of the bar sipping wine when he'd come in with Chaz's group and, seeing she was alone, he'd approached her.

Liza had been wary of him at first; he'd looked too slick and assured for her taste, and there was something a bit too brash about his manner. She'd learned not to trust men like that. Men like Andrew.

Yet after a few minutes of chatting she'd thawed a bit; he had known Chaz from some party or other, and he was funny and charming and it was rather nice to talk to someone who wasn't giving her coldly disapproving looks half the time.

Then, after about twenty minutes of aimless chitchat, he'd stiffened, and Liza had followed his gaze to the sight of Fausto Danti glowering by the bar. Her heart had lurched towards her throat at the sight of him, even as an undeniable pleasure unfurled inside her like a flower.

'Do you know him?' she'd asked, and Jack had let out a humourless laugh.

'Fausto Danti? I should say so.' She'd waited for more, and he'd given it immediately. 'I grew up with him. My father was his father's office manager in Milan.' He'd paused, his lips twisting. 'We went to the same boarding school, in fact.'

'Oh.' She'd eyed him uncertainly for there could be no disguising the bitterness twisting his features. 'I only met him recently.'

He'd turned to her with an ugly sort of smile. 'And what did you think of him?'

Liza had hesitated. 'He can be a bit cold, I suppose,' she'd said, and then felt oddly disloyal for the remark.

'Cold?' Jack had sounded as if he wanted to say much more. 'Yes, I suppose you could say that.'

'Why do you sound as if you don't like him?'

Jack had thrown back the rest of his drink, and then shrugged. 'I don't. I don't want to bias you against the man, but you sound as if you already dislike him.'

'I do,' Liza had said, and then felt even worse.

'Not as much as I do,' Jack had stated grimly. 'Fausto Danti cheated me out of my inheritance. Our fathers were great friends—mine died, and then his did, and it had always been an understanding between them that I would inherit part of the estate, and be given a senior position with Danti Investments. I staked my future on it—and Fausto refused to honour either agreement, even though he knew, as I did, that his father wanted nothing more than to see me take over at least part of the family firm.' He put his glass down with a final-sounding clink. 'He's also bad-mouthed me to everyone he knows, so I haven't been able to be hired by anyone decent, even in an introductory role.'

Liza had stared at him, horrified. 'But why?' She might have disliked the man, but she'd thought he possessed a fundamental core of honour, even if it was of his own particular brand.

Jack had shrugged. 'Because he was always jealous of the way his father preferred me. They never had a close relationship. And because he's petty and mean-spirited, but I'm sure you can find that out for yourself.' He'd smiled at her, shrugging aside all the bitter words. 'But never mind about all that. He's the last person I want to talk or even think about. Another drink?'

Liza had insisted she'd get it herself, mainly because she wanted to see Fausto up close, even if she didn't speak to him, and judge for herself what sort of man he was, after all that Jack had told her. She'd faltered when they'd locked gazes and he'd glowered at her, but then she'd continued on.

To her surprise, he'd apologised for their kiss, which had both irritated and gratified her. She supposed he thought he was being kind, but was a kiss something to apologise for, especially when they'd both so clearly enjoyed it? Or was he apologising because he regretted it so much, since she was so clearly not the sort of woman he'd ever kiss, never mind actually date or marry? He'd certainly made that obvious.

In any case, she'd chosen to end the conversation; Jack's words were still echoing in her ears and she'd realised that everything he had said had confirmed her own instinct about Fausto Danti—he was a thoroughly arrogant and unpleasant man.

'Liza? Come *on*!'

Taking a deep breath, Liza turned away from the mirror. She was worried her dress was a bit over-the-top, but her mother had taken everyone to Hereford for a shopping trip, and all her sisters had insisted she try this one on. Crimson in colour, it had a bodice of ruched satin before it fanned out in a full-length skirt that made her feel like Cinderella at the ball. But if every other woman was wearing a cock-tail dress she'd feel a bit ridiculous.

As Liza joined them in the hallway she tried not to let her alarm show at her mother's dress—a perfectly nice eve-ning gown in royal blue, except Yvonne had insisted she was still a size fourteen when she hadn't been for at least twenty years. She looked like a tube of toothpaste that had been well and truly squeezed.

Lindsay's dress was even more alarming—a long slinky skirt of silver lamé with a double slit nearly up to her crotch and a matching bikini top. She'd insisted it was the latest fashion, and that her favourite YouTuber had worn some-thing similar, but to Liza it just looked inappropriate.

As she gazed at them both she realised she was think-ing like Fausto Danti, all coldly disapproving—and of her family! Who cared if her mother's dress was too tight, or Lindsay's too sexy? They thought they looked beauti-ful, and so did Liza. She hated how Fausto had somehow wormed his way into her thoughts, changed the way she looked at her family, even for a moment.

'And now to the ball!' Yvonne declared grandly. She'd been so thrilled to have the invitation from Chaz that she'd talked about nothing but the ball since. When Liza had come home for Christmas she'd listened to her mother's plans for dresses, hotel rooms, and her hopes that every single one of her daughters might find true love in Neth-erhall's ballroom.

Jenna, at least, was almost a certainty; she and Chaz had been practically inseparable for the last month and Liza didn't think she'd ever seen her sister look so happy, elegant in her ice-blue off-the-shoulder dress. Lindsay would no doubt be on the lookout, but Liza wouldn't be surprised if Marie spent the whole evening in the corner with a book.

As for herself…? True love, she was quite sure, would be nowhere to be found.

As she followed her family outside the hotel, Liza did a double take at the sight of the white stretch Hummer her mother had ordered for the occasion, complete with champagne and Christmas carols blasting.

She knew she should get into the fun festive spirit of the thing, but once again she imagined Fausto's look of disdain and she could only cringe. Why was she letting him affect her this way, even when he wasn't here? She had to stop it.

'Oh, isn't everything beautiful!' Jenna exclaimed as they entered Netherhall a short while later. A twenty-foot Christmas tree decorated tastefully with silver and blue glass baubles stood between the double staircases in the house's main hall. Ropes of evergreen and branches of holly decorated every available surface, while a string quartet played Christmas carols in the ballroom and members of staff handed out crystal goblets of mulled wine. It was all incredibly elegant, and her family, Liza couldn't help but feel, stuck out like a lamentably sore thumb.

Well, who cared about that? She straightened her shoulders as she gazed around the crowded ballroom with determined defiance. She didn't care what these people thought. They were ridiculous themselves, caught up in their own privileged little world, just as she'd told Fausto back in October. They liked to look down at people who hadn't been born into the kind of society and money that they had, and the whole thing was utterly absurd. Who even cared?

She was, she decided, going to have a lovely evening dancing and chatting and having fun, and she wouldn't care what anyone else thought...especially Fausto Danti.

He knew the moment Liza entered the ballroom, even though he didn't see her. He felt her, like a frisson in the air, and he broke off his conversation with an acquaintance of Chaz's to look around the ballroom with an almost hungry air.

Fausto hadn't seen Liza since the night in the bar over a month ago, and while he'd been determined to banish every thought of her from his mind, he'd failed. He'd thought about her all too often in the nearly six weeks since he'd seen her, and he was certainly thinking about her now. *Where was she?*

His gaze snagged on the sight of a young woman in the most absurd outfit he'd ever seen—a skin-tight silver two-piece ensemble that looked as if it belonged in a strip club rather than a ballroom. With a jolt, he realised it belonged to Liza's sister Lindsay. Amazingly, he'd managed to forget just how obvious and showy she really was. His gaze moved further to Liza's mother, who was looking both uncomfortable and excited in a dress that was far too tight for her. Fausto's mouth thinned. But where was Liza?

Then he saw her, standing slightly apart, holding a glass of mulled wine and looking a little wistful. Looking utterly *beautiful*. Her dress was nothing like those of her sister or mother—a princess-like confection of crimson satin, it flowed over her in a simple river of fabric. Her hair had been pulled up into an elegant chignon, but a few curls fell artfully about her shoulders; another brushed her cheek. Fausto started walking towards her without even realising he was doing so.

Liza remained where she was, looking around the ballroom, until she turned slightly and her eyes flared as she caught sight of him walking straight towards her. Fausto didn't know if he saw it or simply felt it, but a tremble went through her. Her fingers tightened on the stem of her glass. He kept walking.

The whole room seemed to fall away—the crowds, the music—as she remained steadily in his sights. Her eyes were fixed on him, seeming huge in her pale face, and yet she was so very lovely. Always so lovely.

Weeks of not seeing her had only sharpened his hunger,

given focus and piquancy to the desire he'd done his best to banish. He stopped and stood before her, his gaze sweeping over her in silent admiration. She looked up at him, waiting.

'Dance?' he queried softly, and her eyes widened further, lush lashes sweeping her cheeks as she looked down for a moment to compose herself.

The animosity he'd felt from her the last time they'd met—the kiss, the apology, the unsuitability and the desire, the sparring and the wanting—all of it seemed to matter both more and less in this moment. Right now it felt amazingly simple and yet infinitely complicated—he wanted to dance with her. He wanted to take her in his arms and feel her body against his. Everything else could wait.

Finally, wordlessly, she nodded. Fausto took her halfdrunk glass of mulled wine and handed it to a passing staff member. As if on cue, the string quartet struck up a sonorous tune. And as he'd been wanting to do all evening, all *month*, he took her into his arms.

Her dress seemed to enfold him as she swayed lightly against him, one slender hand resting on his shoulder, another clasped in his. They moved to the music, but only just. Fausto was conscious of nothing but her.

They moved together, unspeaking, needing no words. At least Fausto didn't need them. It was enough to hold her in his arms, press his cheek against her hair and feel her lean into him.

The song ended and another began, and still they danced. If people noticed or cared, Fausto wasn't aware. They hadn't said a word to one another, but he felt speaking might break the web they'd woven around themselves, a fragile cocoon of silent intimacy.

Desire flowed through him, but also something deeper. Something more elemental and yet more profound. He realised in this moment that he *cared* about Liza Benton—

cared about her more than he had ever cared about any other woman.

The thought was utterly alarming. He couldn't care about her, not like that. Not like he had for Amy, when his honour, along with his heart, had been smashed. He couldn't give in to emotion or desire, not with so much at stake. Besides, his mother was expecting him to marry someone suitable from home, someone his family had known for decades if not centuries, someone capable and assured who could manage his estates and appear at his side without a qualm.

And yet, despite all that, or perhaps because of it, he knew he wanted simply to treasure this moment—the feel of her against him, the sight and sound of her, even the smell of her. His senses reeled.

Then the music stopped and they were forced to come to a standstill. Fausto kept his arms around her for a moment longer before he felt compelled to drop them. She stared at him uncertainly, and he realised he was scowling. He hadn't wanted the dance to end.

'May I get you a drink?'

'Since you took my last one off me,' she answered with a small smile, 'yes, you may. Thank you.'

The mulled wine had been replaced by champagne, and Fausto fetched two flutes. 'You seem in a better temper with me tonight,' he remarked as he handed Liza one, then wished he hadn't said anything.

'It's a ball, and it's almost Christmas,' she answered after a moment. 'I'm in a good temper with everyone.'

'That's a relief to hear.'

'You have been busy working this last month, I suppose?' He nodded and she continued. 'I don't actually know what you do. You're a Count, I know that much, but you have a business as well?'

'Yes, Danti Investments. It is one of the oldest banks in Italy.'

'Ah, yes, Henry said. Very noble.' She nodded, and he couldn't decide if her tone was genuine or not.

'How is Henry?' he asked. 'I haven't seen him since that afternoon at The Dorchester.'

'He's very well.'

'Good.'

They both lapsed into silence as the music struck up again; the spell that had been cast over them during the dance seemed to entirely be at an end. Fausto wished he could dispense with these meaningless pleasantries. There was so much he wanted to say, and yet all of it remained unformed, vague thoughts and feelings he could not give words to, no matter how much he wished it.

He was more than half inclined to take her by the arm and steer her out of the ballroom, back to the study, which would be quiet and dark. There he'd forget about the mere ruse of the chessboard and any possibility of a rematch— he'd take her in his arms and kiss her even more thoroughly than he had before. Kiss her, and then lead her upstairs...

'You're very quiet,' Liza remarked, and Fausto blinked at her, the fantasy he'd been constructing in his head falling to pieces.

'I have never been inclined to idle chatter.'

'Sometimes idle chatter can be pleasant,' she returned. 'Where will you spend Christmas?'

'In London.'

'By yourself?'

He shrugged. 'My family is in Italy.'

'You don't want to see them?'

'I need to sort out matters here. The London office has needed some attention since my father's passing.'

She raised her eyebrows. 'Don't you have an office manager?'

'I did, but he left a year ago. Where are you spending Christmas?' He did not want to talk about business matters with her, or even inadvertently allude to the disaster that had unfolded in the London office, thanks to his father's blind faith and old age—and one man's egotistical evil.

'I'll be in Herefordshire, with my family.'

'Ah, your family.' He couldn't keep his tone from sharpening slightly, even though he hadn't meant it to. His gaze roved around the ballroom and came to rest on Lindsay, who was holding a glass of champagne aloft as she twerked to the sounds of the string quartet.

Liza followed his gaze and blushed at the sight of her sister dancing with a suggestiveness that looked unbearably obscene from afar. Even from across the ballroom, it was clear that people standing nearby were either laughing at her or making shocked faces of disapproval.

'She's young,' she murmured, her face almost as scarlet as her dress, and pity stirred inside him.

'So were you once, but I doubt you ever behaved like that.'

'You sound so judgemental,' she flashed, and then strove to lighten her tone. 'Are you implying I'm not young any more?'

'How old are you?'

'Twenty-three.'

'And I'm thirty-six. So if anyone is to accuse anyone of being old…' He smiled, hoping to lessen any tension and also simply because he wanted her to smile back. She did, after a moment, and he was about to ask her to dance again, already imagining holding her and having the whole world fall away once more, when a carrying voice had them both stiffening.

'Liza, there you are! And oh, it's that Italian. Donato, isn't it—'

'Danti,' Fausto said as he turned to Yvonne Benton with a cool smile. 'It's Fausto Danti. So lovely to see you again.'

CHAPTER EIGHT

LIZA WATCHED HER mother eye Fausto with blatant curiosity—
there were practically pound signs in her eyes—and she
tried not to squirm. Fausto's lips quirked, and she couldn't
tell if he was amused or annoyed by her mother's blatant
scrutiny. He arched an eyebrow in silent enquiry, inclin-
ing his head, but her mother didn't notice.

Several glasses of mulled wine and a generous helping
of hors d'oeuvres had not helped her dress situation, Liza
noticed. Her mother looked as if it wouldn't take more
than one deep breath to have her popping out, something
she seriously hoped wouldn't happen. As she glanced at
Fausto she saw his brows draw together in a frown and she
suspected he was thinking the same thing—and hoping it
wouldn't happen even more than she was.

'I've seen so many interesting people here,' Yvonne declared as she fanned her flushed face. 'So many *names*. I've
recognised several people from *You Too!*.' She turned to
Fausto. 'Do you ever read that magazine?'

He kept his face straight as he answered, 'I do not.'

'Well, you should. You'd recognise so many people if
you did! Lindsay told me there was some YouTuber here,
but I'm not sure if I believe her. There are some people
with titles—proper titles! You know, Lord or Lady This or
That.' Yvonne sounded breathlessly impressed. 'Liza, did
you see the Farringdons? He used to be a footballer and
they have a gorgeous house up in Yorkshire. *You Too!* did a
whole spread on it a few months ago—the most enormous

kitchen with a beautiful family room, everything in white leather. Just amazing.'

'I must have missed that one,' Liza murmured. She wished she could find some way to steer her mother away from Fausto, or at least away from talking about all the guests as if they were celebrities to be gawked at. Had her mother's voice always been so *loud*? It seemed ridiculously so right now, and yet she felt ashamed that she cared. Still, anyone in a twenty-foot vicinity could hear them. Easily.

And, judging from the either amused or disapproving glances that were being slid their way, people were listening. And judging, just as Fausto was. Just as *she* was.

'And I must say,' Yvonne continued without a care for who was around, 'I think things are looking very promising for Jenna and Chaz. *Very* promising.'

'Mum…' The last thing Liza wanted was for her mother to start talking about wedding bells for Jenna and Chaz. She dreaded to imagine what Fausto would think about *that*. She tried to give her mother a pointed look but Yvonne just smiled.

'They've been in each other's pockets for two months now, haven't they? And don't tell a soul—' a rather ridiculous request considering how loudly she was speaking '— but I caught Jenna looking at bridal magazines the other day.'

'Mum!' Liza shook her head. She was quite sure Jenna had been doing no such thing but, even if she had, she would not want the news trumpeted about the ballroom.

'Just a peek, but still. Won't she have a lovely time doing this place up? It *is* looking a bit shabby, I have to admit. Some of the furniture is so old.'

'I believe it's called antique,' Fausto interjected politely.

'Oh, yes, antiques. They're all well and good, but everyone likes a bit of modern, don't they? So bright and clean.'

'There's nothing modern in our house, Mum,' Liza said

a bit desperately. Their home was a hodgepodge of car boot sale and charity shop chic, with a few battered family heirlooms thrown in.

'Oh, yes, but if I had the choice I'd do it all up properly. Get everything modern. Of course I don't have the money Chaz has.'

'Where's Dad?' Liza blurted. Surely her father would put a stop to her mother's runaway tongue. She knew her mum meant well, and she might have had a little bit too much to drink, but the conversation, with Fausto listening to every word in that disdainful way of his, was beyond humiliating.

'He's dancing with Marie,' Yvonne said. 'He managed to get her on the dance floor, although she's got a face like a sour lemon. Why can't she have fun the way Lindsay does?'

Which made them all turn to Lindsay, who had her hands in the air as if she was at a rave, her champagne glass tilted at an angle that caused drops to spray anyone who was standing nearby.

'Your daughter does seem to be enjoying herself,' Fausto remarked.

'Lindsay's always known how to have a good time.'

'Indeed.'

Liza could take no more. She hated that her family was embarrassing themselves, but even more she hated that she cared so much. She hated that Fausto was looking down on them, and she hated herself for minding something she'd never even considered before.

'I'm going to get some air,' she said, turning away from them both, although what her mother might say to Fausto when she got him alone Liza did not dare to think.

She slipped through the crowd of guests, barely aware of her surroundings—the gorgeous Christmas decorations, the sharp scent of evergreen, the candlelight and the elegant antiques her mother had called shabby. *Shabby*. Liza let out a huff of despairing laughter.

The entrance hall was as crowded as the ballroom and, mindful that she should hardly be snooping about the house, Liza went into the one room she was most certainly familiar with—the study.

It was dim inside, the chessboard still on the table by the now-empty grate, the room blessedly quiet. Here she could collect herself, but she couldn't, because when she looked at that blasted chessboard all she thought about was Fausto.

Fausto kissing her with thrillingly urgent passion…

Liza turned away from the board and went to the window. As she laid one hand upon the glass she realised it was actually a French window that led out onto a terrace that wrapped around the entire back of the house, and with one wrench of the handle she opened the window and stepped outside into the cold, clear evening.

Her breath came out in frosty puffs as she stood on the terrace under a sky full of stars and tilted her head to take in the slender crescent of moon.

In the distance she could hear the strains of the string quartet, the sound of chatting and laughter, but it felt thankfully far away. She wanted to be alone. Tears of shame stung her eyes, although she wasn't even sure what they were for. Lindsay's dancing? Her mother's blabbing? Or the fact that Fausto had been standing there, looking down his nose at them all, silently judging them as somehow unworthy. Judging her.

Or maybe she was crying for herself, for feeling so ashamed and disloyal. She loved her family. Yes, they could be a bit OTT, she'd always known that, but they had *fun*. She thought back to camping trips when they were little, and how her mother had washed all their underclothes and draped them over the trees and bushes, heedless of the nearby campers inspecting their rather raggedy pants.

The annual tradition of the Christmas quiz at the pub in Little Mayton—they were the loudest, most raucous team, and no one minded *there*. Yvonne always brought a big bottle of pink champagne as a thank you to Darren, the pub's landlord.

Countless family dinners or chaotic barbecues in the garden, impromptu singalongs and games of rounders—she'd had a happy childhood in a busy home, and right now she felt ashamed of it all and she absolutely hated the feeling.

It was all Fausto's fault.

'Liza.'

His voice, a low thrum in the darkness, made her start and she wondered if she'd imagined it because she'd been thinking about him. Cursing him.

But no, she hadn't been imagining it, for as she turned around he stepped towards her from the study door, a dark figure in his tuxedo, the moonlight casting his features into silver.

'What are you doing here?'

His mouth quirked slightly. 'Talking to you.'

'How did you find me?'

'I followed you.'

She huffed impatiently, turning around so her back was to him as she stared out at the darkened garden. 'I came out here to be alone.'

'You're shivering.'

She was, because it was freezing and her arms were bare, but she simply shrugged off his words. She felt too muddled up in her head, too tangled in her heart, to offer any sort of coherent reply, never mind have an entire conversation.

Then she heard his footsteps behind her and his jacket dropped over her shoulders, enveloping her in his woodsy scent. He rested his hands on her shoulders, just as he had before, and just as before a pulse of longing raced through her, nearly made her shudder.

'You didn't need to do that,' she said quietly and he dropped his hands and stepped back.

'You were clearly freezing.'

Liza shook her head, closing her eyes against the night. Against him. 'Why are you really here, Fausto?'

It was a question he couldn't answer. *Why* had he followed her out onto the terrace? It wasn't like him at all, but since meeting Liza Benton he hadn't acted anything like his usual self—calm, reserved, *controlled*. He lost it all when it came to this woman.

'I wanted to speak to you,' he said finally.

'What about? My ridiculous mother? Or my worse sister? Or the fact that you think Jenna is some absurd gold-digger? I know you still do—I saw it in your eyes. Maybe you think I am one too.' She let out a little cry as she shrugged impatiently. 'Oh, it doesn't matter. I don't want to talk to you.'

'I have not said a word against your family.'

'You didn't need to! I saw you looking down your long aristocratic nose at them all. You think we're so beneath you.'

Fausto clenched his fists as he fought a rising frustration. He might not have known why he'd come out here, but it certainly wasn't to talk about the less salubrious members of the Benton family.

'I admit I find the behaviour of some of your family members to be…' he paused, wanting to be honest but not unduly hurtful '…questionable.' Liza let out another choked cry. 'That does not, however, reflect on my feelings for *you*.'

'Oh?' she flung at him. 'And what feelings do you have for *me*?'

The question seemed to hover in the air between them before falling to the ground, silent and unanswered—because he *couldn't* answer. He didn't have any feelings for her, at least any that he wanted to admit to, even in the privacy of his own mind.

Yes, while they were dancing he'd admitted to himself that he cared about her—against his will—but a relationship between them was still impossible and although part of him contemplated the idea of an affair with longing he knew he wouldn't lower himself or Liza to suggest such a thing. He knew she would take offence at the idea, as would he.

'Well?' she demanded, and then she let out a harsh laugh. 'Why am I not surprised that you won't—can't—answer? Because you can't bear to admit that you might like me at all, or find me interesting or attractive or anything else!'

'I—'

'From the moment you met me you've struggled against feeling anything for me, even if it's just basic physical attraction. Well, let me relieve you of that struggle, Fausto Danti. *I* don't have any feelings for you!'

She shrugged out of his jacket, flinging it towards him, and as he caught it he found himself catching her as well, taking her by the arms and drawing her towards him.

'Don't,' she said, a jagged edge of despair in her voice, and he looked down into those hazel eyes, now possessing a sheen of tears.

'Do you really not want me to?' he asked in a low voice, and with a cry of defeat she stood on her tiptoes and pressed her lips against his. The shock of the kiss was like tumbling down a hill, or missing the last step in a staircase. Everything felt jolted and off-kilter for a heart-stopping second, and then it all felt amazingly right.

His arms came around her, his jacket falling to the ground as he drew her closer to him, her breasts pressed to his chest, her body trembling and slender against him. Her mouth opened under his as he took the clumsy kiss she'd started with and made it his—their—own.

Once again the world fell away and the stars above them seemed to sparkle with an intensity no person had surely ever seen before; the universe possessed a brilliance it hadn't a moment ago, and he saw and felt it all in one simple kiss that blew his mind apart and overwhelmed his body.

And then Liza wrenched away with a gasp, one hand to her mouth as if she'd been hurt—wounded—by him.

'Don't,' she said savagely. 'Don't…don't kiss me like that when… Don't kiss me at all!'

'Liza—'

But it was too late; she was already stumbling past him, back into the house, away from him.

Fausto stood out in the cold, still air for several moments while he tried to calm his thudding heart, his whirling mind. *What had just happened?*

Well, he'd kissed Liza Benton—and she'd stopped it. She'd rejected him! Sheer incredulity had him emitting a sound that was meant to be a laugh but most certainly wasn't. Slowly, Fausto shook his head. Of course he knew he shouldn't have kissed her. Never mind that she'd kissed him first, he'd certainly taken mastery of it. And considering that he'd apologised for the last time he'd kissed her, a second round was definitely not a good idea.

But damn it, he could not get the woman out of his mind.

He needed to, though, that much was obvious. She obviously wanted him to! Shaking his head again, he walked slowly inside. The party was still in full swing as he came into the ballroom, feeling as flat as the champagne would be tomorrow morning, should any be left undrunk.

Judging by the way Lindsay Benton was swilling it, he doubted it. His mouth twisted in a grimace as he watched Lindsay still twerking away by the string quartet. The party was over as far as he was concerned.

He scanned the crowded room for Chaz, finally finding his friend at the buffet table. He started forward, determined to make his apologies.

'Danti! Where have you been?' Chaz greeted him with his usual good cheer.

'Around,' Fausto answered brusquely. 'But I'm going to bow out now.'

'What? Oh, no, old man, you can't do that. It isn't even eleven yet.'

Fausto shrugged his words aside. 'I'm tired.'

'Tell me, though,' Chaz said, slinging his arm around Fausto's shoulders. 'What do you think of Jenna? Seriously now, because you know how much I value your opinion.'

Fausto hesitated, knowing absolutely he was not in the right frame of mind for this conversation. And yet… Jenna's planning this ball, looking at bridal magazines, seeming so restrained with Chaz… Lindsay's regrettable behaviour… Liza's abandoned kiss…not to mention his past with Amy, the way she'd taken that cheque, the smile of regret she'd given him as she'd walked away…

It all felt tangled up in his mind, a pressure in his chest. 'I have some concerns,' Fausto said shortly, and Chaz's face fell.

'Seriously?'

'Yes, seriously. Serious concerns. About her family. Surely you do as well.'

'I don't care about her family—'

'And concerns about her.' Fausto realised he meant it. He'd been duped once; he wouldn't let his friend be. 'Are you sure she feels the same way about you? Because from everything I've seen of her, she seems…unenthused.'

'Do you really think so?' Chaz looked as if he'd been kicked, and Fausto felt a flicker of remorse. But it was true, he reasoned; he'd seen nothing of Jenna Benton that made him believe she was as head-over-heels about Chaz as he obviously was about her…and too many warning signs that indicated the opposite.

And if her sister's behaviour was anything to go by, the Benton women blew hot and cold.

'I think,' he said carefully, 'that you need to think long and hard before you proceed with a woman like Jenna Benton. She might like the thrill of the chase, the heat of the moment, and of course all the advantages you might give her...' He paused, wanting to choose his words with care even as part of him resisted saying anything at all. 'But in the end, does she care about *you*, Chaz Bingham, and not everything that you might offer her?'

The words seemed to reverberate between them as Chaz regarded him unhappily. 'I suppose...' he answered slowly. 'I suppose I never thought about it quite like that before.'

'Then perhaps you should,' Fausto said, clapping his friend on the shoulder before he walked away, wondering if he'd just done his friend the biggest favour he could have—or orchestrated the worst betrayal.

CHAPTER NINE

CHRISTMAS WAS QUIET, and only kept from being completely miserable by the fact that it was in fact Christmas and Liza was at home with her family whom she loved. She did her best to take part in all the family traditions that she so enjoyed—stockings and carols around the piano, glasses of sherry while listening to the Queen's speech and hilarious charades. Throughout it all she felt a shadow of her usual self—and all because of Fausto Danti.

Drat the man. Drat him for being so arrogant, so cold… so *gorgeous*. Drat him for kissing her, and drat him for when he didn't kiss her. Liza's mind and heart were both in a ferment as she considered the damning things Jack Wickley had told her, and then the incredible way Fausto kissed. The two together were positively insupportable, and she returned to London just before New Year as miserable as she'd been before.

Jenna was miserable as well, although in a quiet way; Liza could tell her sister was flagging and she soon found out why.

'Chaz said he'd take me out for New Year's Eve,' Jenna explained with a sad smile. 'But he hasn't called or texted me once since the Christmas ball.'

A quiver of trepidation went through Liza at this revelation. 'Have you been in touch with him?'

'I couldn't. I've always waited for him to contact me first.'

'Surely you can send him a text, Jenna! It's the twenty-first century, after all. We don't have to wait by the phone any more.'

'I know, but…' Jenna nibbled her lip, her big blue eyes full of unhappiness. 'If he wanted to be in touch, he would.'

'Maybe he lost your number.'

'It's programmed into his phone.'

'Still, who knows? In any case,' Liza insisted staunchly, 'you deserve an answer. You've been seeing him several times a week for two months.'

It took several days of convincing, but Jenna finally decided to send a text. Then it took several hours of deliberating to compose all six words of it.

Haven't seen you around. Everything okay?

The reply, when it came three days later, was unhappily short.

Sorry. Been busy.

'He's gone off me,' Jenna said with a sound that was far too close to a sob. She flung her phone onto the sofa and tucked her knees up to her chest. 'I knew he would.'

'I knew no such thing! He was crazy about you. He still is.'

Jenna looked at her sceptically. 'Then why wouldn't he have called me?'

Liza didn't reply as her mind raced. She could think of no reason why Chaz would have gone off Jenna. Unless… surely, surely Fausto wouldn't have interfered? He'd been disapproving enough of her family at the ball, and he certainly hadn't denied her gold-digger remark, but even so…

Had he said something? Could he have been that judgemental, that arrogant, that low?

'Give him some time,' Liza suggested feebly, and Jenna gave her a sad smile.

They spent New Year's Eve at home, eating ice cream and watching Netflix while swearing off all men for ever.

'I always wondered if there was something between you and Fausto Danti,' Jenna said as she dug out the last of her Rocky Road. 'Things always seemed a bit intense there.'

'Intense?' Liza scoffed. 'Intensely unpleasant. I never liked him, not even one bit.'

Jenna raised her eyebrows. 'I think the lady doth protest too much.'

'No, really,' Liza insisted. She could and would not mention the two scorching kisses she'd shared with him. 'I learned some things about him... Well, I already knew he was rude and arrogant—'

'I never thought he was rude,' Jenna interjected. 'Reserved, perhaps. Distant, but maybe he's just shy.'

'Shy—?' Liza repeated in disbelief.

Jenna shrugged. 'Some people are. I am. Why not Fausto Danti?'

Because he was rich and arrogant and titled and gorgeous, and people like that tended not to be *shy*.

'What else have you learned about him?' Jenna asked.

'It's not worth repeating,' Liza said after a moment. She felt a strange reluctance, even now, to relate what Jack Wickley had said to her. She was unlikely to see him—or Fausto—again, so it hardly mattered, and yet something still made her stay silent.

'Well, I say we need more ice cream,' Jenna said with a brave attempt at a smile, and she headed to the freezer.

January felt endless to Liza—a long, dull, dark month, where all she did was go to work and go home again. The dubious highlight was a visit from Lindsay in the middle of the month; she insisted on them all going out, this time to a nightclub in Islington. Liza didn't think she could have been less in the mood for such a thing, but for Lindsay's sake she went. She was hardly likely to run into Fausto Danti at a place like that, and she didn't.

By mid-February her employer began to show concern. 'You seem to have lost your sparkle,' Henry commented wryly as he signed some letters and handed them to her for mailing. 'Although admittedly it's difficult for anyone to retain good humour at such a dull time of year.'

Liza managed a rather wan smile. 'I'm all right,' she said. She *had* been dragging, but she was reluctant to admit it. Henry gave her a small encouraging smile that suggested he didn't believe her but was too polite to say so.

A few days later, however, he did say something. 'Sometimes it takes a new perspective,' he announced.

'What does?' she asked a bit warily.

'To regain one's sparkle. I'm planning to go to my cottage in Norfolk this weekend. My grand-niece is joining me with her family. Why don't you come too?'

It was the last thing Liza had expected 'Oh...'

'The weather is meant to be good, if a bit bracing, and I promise you the walks on the beach are quite restorative. It won't be fancy—whatever kitchen suppers we can throw together, and most likely fish fingers and chips for the little ones.' He pretended to shudder but he was smiling.

Liza was on the cusp of saying no out of habit more than anything else when she remembered that Jenna was going back to Hereford for the weekend to visit some school friends. Why shouldn't she get out of the city, see something different?

For a second she wondered if Fausto might be there, but Henry would surely have mentioned it if he was. Besides, he might be back in Italy by now. He probably was—a prospect that did not make her feel sorry in the least. Or so she insisted on telling herself more than once.

'All right, then,' she told Henry, injecting as much cheer into her voice as she could. 'That's very kind of you. Thank you.'

Three days later she was taking the train to King's Lynn, and then the bus to Hunstanton, where Henry's cottage was located. He'd decamped there the day before, but Liza had chosen to come on Friday afternoon, so as not to take up all of Henry's time with his family.

'It's so good to see you,' Henry said warmly when he picked her up from the station, as if he hadn't seen her yesterday at the office.

It was a short ride through the falling dusk out of Hunstanton to his 'cottage', which Liza quickly discovered wasn't a cottage at all, but an eight-bedroom manor house with a garden rolling down to a private beach. As Henry pulled into the sweeping drive he nodded to a navy blue BMW parked next to a battered estate.

'Ah, we have a visitor,' he said cheerfully, and Liza gave him a sharp look. *A visitor...?*

'You mean besides your family?' she ventured, even though that much was already obvious.

She told herself a visitor could be anyone, from a kindly neighbour to a distant relative, but her stomach was fluttering, her heart starting to pound, as if her body *knew*. Her heart knew.

Fausto Danti stepped out of the car.

He should have known Henry was up to something. Fausto kept his expression carefully bland as Henry parked the car and Liza slowly emerged from the passenger side, her face pale as she tried not to look at him.

It had been two months since he'd seen her, and he thought she looked a bit wan. No less lovely, but there was a certain weariness to her features that made him want to comfort her, surely a ridiculous notion. She as good as hated him, it seemed, no matter that she'd been the one to kiss him last—and if two months had thawed her dislike, surely this weekend would renew it.

When Henry had called to let him know he'd be at his country house this weekend, Fausto had decided to accept the obvious invitation. The last two months had been both dreary and exhausting, and he'd found himself increasingly occupied with work—and increasingly restless. He'd told himself he'd forgotten about Liza Benton, because he certainly hadn't been thinking of her, but as he looked at her now he realised just how much effort it had taken to keep her from his mind.

'Fausto,' Henry said as he came forward to shake his hand, 'I'm so glad you could make it.' Liza stiffened and Fausto knew for sure that she'd had no idea he would be here. 'Liza, you remember Fausto Danti?'

'I do,' she said coolly, and moved past him towards the house. Henry smiled easily, and Fausto wondered if the older man could not sense the tension simmering between them, or if he knew the nature of it and that was why he'd invited Fausto along.

It was, Fausto thought grimly, going to be a long weekend—and yet he could not deny that he was glad to see her again, if just for the sheer pleasure of looking at her.

An hour after they'd arrived, they were all in the drawing room with a roaring fire and glasses of sherry; Liza had met Henry's grand-niece, Alison, and her two young children, who were involved in a game of draughts. She stood by the fire, her hair wild and curly about her face, her hazel eyes pensive as she sipped her sherry.

She'd changed from her travelling clothes into a simple knit dress of moss green that skimmed her curves and reminded Fausto of how lovely she had felt in his arms. He nodded towards the chessboard that was set up in an inviting alcove.

'We could have that rematch now.'

She let out a huff of laughter that held no humour and shook her head. 'I'm afraid I'm too out of practice.'

'You beat me easily enough last time.' She looked away without replying and Fausto stepped closer to her. Alison and Henry were having an involved discussion, catching up on their various relations, and he didn't think they would be overheard.

'I didn't know you would be here,' he said in a low voice.

'Nor I you.' She slanted him a challenging look. 'Although you probably think I've orchestrated the whole thing.'

Startled, Fausto drew back. 'I do not.'

'You reserve that judgement just for my sister, then?' she replied, and then took a gulp of sherry.

'I have never judged you in that way,' Fausto said. He had wondered, but he hadn't judged.

Liza turned back to him, eyes flashing, eyebrows raised. 'Never?'

Compelled, as always, to both honour and honesty, he answered, 'A few doubts, I admit, but that is all.' And he could admit now—mostly—that they had been unfounded doubts. Liza had never pursued him the way Amy had. Quite the opposite.

'Oh, what a *relief*,' she drawled.

'You did ask.'

'And now I know.'

He paused, sorting through the tangle of his own feelings as well as hers. 'You're angry with me for thinking you might have been after my money?'

She huffed and looked away. 'I don't like you enough to be angry with you.'

'You hardly sound indifferent.' She didn't reply. 'Is it because of that—or something else?'

'It is a whole range of things,' Liza snapped. 'But, more to the point, why do you care? You have made it clear that you're not interested in me, not really.' He was silent and she threw him a challenging look. 'You don't deny it?'

'No,' he said after a moment. 'I cannot.'

'And why is that?' Her voice trembled with the force of her feeling and she moved away from him, feigning interest in a book of photographs of the Norfolk beaches on display on a side table.

Fausto watched her, trying to school his expression into something neutral. He did not want to hurt her, but perhaps it was best if he stated his case plainly. 'I am thirty-six. I need to marry.'

She stiffened, her gaze still on the books. 'And?'

'And when I do it must be to a woman of whom my family approves, someone who is capable of managing my household, standing by my side.'

'How unbelievably quaint,' Liza said after a moment. 'How absolutely *archaic*.'

'I admit it is an old-fashioned view, but it is the one I hold. My position is demanding, and would be so for my wife.'

'And obviously I'm not even in the running.'

Again he hesitated, and then decided truth was best. 'No.'

She turned to him, a wild glint in her eyes. 'Because of my family, whom you obviously find embarrassing? Or because of me?'

Fausto stared at her in miserable discomfort, not knowing how to respond. Both—and yet neither. *Because of him*, he almost said, but he couldn't have explained that answer even to himself.

'Your silence is answer enough,' Liza said quietly, and she brushed past him as she walked out of the room.

He saw her again at dinner and, although Henry gave him a concerned look, Fausto brushed off his godfather's remarks. He was in no mood to explain the complicated dynamics between him and Liza Benton.

He determined that avoidance was the only sensible option for them both, and that proved easy enough to do—Liza had already had breakfast when Fausto came downstairs the next morning, and she was nowhere to be found when he set out on a bracing walk down the stretch of private beach belonging to Henry's property, hoping the brisk sea air would improve his mood.

It did not. As he walked along with his hands deep in his pockets, his head lowered against the wind, the confusion he'd been feeling gave way to a despondency he did not want to acknowledge.

He hated the quandary he found himself in, fighting an affection for a woman who thought he considered her not worthy of it. He didn't doubt Liza—not really—but he doubted himself. Love was a fickle emotion; he knew Amy had loved him once, and then been persuaded to change her mind. He hadn't realised she had, and he did not know if he would be able to discern Liza's feelings either. She certainly seemed one thing then another already, and who was he to know the difference? He hadn't before.

And then there was the fact that love was a dangerous emotion as well. He had been hurt before; he did not care to repeat the lamentable experience. Reminding himself that Liza really wasn't suitable felt like the sanest, safest option, even if it filled him with frustration.

And yet he could not deny, at least to himself, that he had come to care for her—her fire, her wit, the kindness and sensitivity she'd shown to everyone, even the children last night. After dinner she'd engaged them in a game of charades, and the sight of her being silly would have made him smile if he hadn't still been feeling so conflicted.

He wasn't in love with her, he decided with some relief; they didn't know each other well enough for that. But the depth of his feeling was clearly not reciprocated in the least, and that knowledge was both humiliating and hurtful.

Of course it was all for the best, since they could have no formal relationship. And yet… Fausto fumed. He did not want to end things this way. He did not want to be so unfairly disliked, and for what?

He lifted his head from his rather grim perusal of the damp sand beneath his feet to gaze out at the rippleless surface of the sea, glinting like a mirror under the wintry sun. Then he tensed as that old instinct took over; when he turned his head he saw a speck in the distance, a hunched figure on the sand that he simply knew had to be Liza.

He walked slowly towards her; her head was bent so she did not see him coming, and the wind carried away the sound of his footsteps.

Her knees were drawn up to her chest, her arms wrapped around them, her hair whipped in a wild tangle around her face. As he came closer, Fausto realised with a jolt that she was crying—and he hated that thought.

'Liza,' he said quietly and she looked up, her eyes red, her face tear-streaked.

'Of course you would find me like this,' she said with a wobbly laugh, and then sank her chin back onto her knees.

'Why are you crying?'

'It doesn't matter. You don't care, anyway.'

'I do care,' he insisted quietly, and then he decided not to qualify that statement any further.

Liza looked up at him, pushing her hair out of her lovely tear-stained face. 'Well, if you must know,' she said in a wobbly voice that still managed to sound reckless, 'I'm crying about you.'

CHAPTER TEN

LIZA DIDN'T KNOW what had made her decide in that moment to be honest. Perhaps it was because she was so tired of feeling sad. Or maybe she was just trying not to care any more, when it had become so very hard to keep disliking Fausto, no matter how many reasons he gave her.

Either way, for the last two months she'd had to drag herself through every day, and all because of this man. Even before that she'd been out of sorts, everything a tangle of longing and outrage and uncertainty. She was tired of feeling so much, and yet she felt the recklessness of her words, their implicit challenge. She stared at him now, daring him to reply.

'About me,' he repeated in that voice of cool reserve she knew so well that gave nothing away, and she let out a half wild laugh.

'Yes, *you*. Are you outraged, Fausto? Disgusted? Or is it just par for the course that a woman would shed tears over you?'

'I would never wish any person to cry over me,' he said stiffly, and she sighed wearily and wiped her face.

'No. Of course not.'

He sat down next to her, his elbow resting on one drawn-up knee. The nearness of him brought a tingle of awareness, even in her teary state, along with a rush of longing *still*.

'Last night you acted as if you hated me,' he said after a moment, sounding cautious. 'Yet it seems unlikely you would cry for someone you hate.'

'That's just the problem. I want to hate you. I want to

dismiss you from my mind, and instead I let myself be hurt. Again.' Her heart tumbled over at the blatant confession. What would he do with it? Why was she making herself so vulnerable, when she already felt so low? She didn't think she could bear his disdain now.

Fausto was silent for a moment and Liza risked a look at him, sitting so near to her. His brows were drawn together, his eyes so dark they looked nearly black. He looked so troubled and yet so handsome, and her heart ached because she knew she was halfway to falling in love with him, and the thought was terrifying.

No, she told herself rather frantically, she *couldn't* actually be anything close to in love with him. It had to be infatuation. That was all it could be, surely, considering how little they knew each other, how difficult every encounter between them had been…

'Again?' Fausto asked after a moment, and Liza shrugged.

'It was a long time ago, with someone else.' Even that was putting too much emphasis on what hadn't even been anything close to a relationship. 'Stupid of me to still be hurt, but it seems I never get these things right.'

'I have never wanted you to hate me,' Fausto said after a moment, his voice low, his head bent.

'I don't,' Liza confessed.

'And that is why you were crying? Because you *can't* hate me?' There was a lilt of humour in his voice as well as a flicker of sadness in his eyes, and both made her ache.

'It's most irritating, not to be able to do it,' she said with a desperate attempt at levity, and his lovely mobile mouth quirked in the tiniest of smiles.

'I can well imagine.'

'I have been trying so hard.'

'Indeed.' He turned his head so his face was an inch or two closer to hers, and her heart skipped a wonderful, terrifying beat. If he was toying with her now, she didn't even care. She just wanted to *feel* again—to feel that lovely, consuming desire, the wonderful certainty of *being* desired, and how together both sensations were enough to overwhelm her completely.

'And yet I keep failing,' she said, and she leaned a little towards him, both daring and pleading with him to close the small space between their mouths. Her heart was thudding now, with hard, heavy intent. 'I absolutely cannot hate you, no matter how hard I try,' she confessed in a breathless whisper.

'Perhaps you should stop trying,' Fausto murmured, leaning even closer, and then, finally, wonderfully, he kissed her.

His lips were as sweet as she remembered—as soft and hard, his kiss the most wonderful demand, the most urgent plea. Oh, she'd missed this. She'd needed it. Having it again felt as if the gates of heaven were opening. She was drowning in sunlight, overwhelmed with joy. Never mind it wouldn't last, or that he fought against his feelings even more than she did. This—this alone—was enough.

He deepened the kiss as her mouth opened under his and she scrabbled at his coat to keep her balance, and failed. They fell backward in a tangle of limbs, the sand cold and hard beneath them, their mouths still locked.

The weight of Fausto's body on top of hers was glorious, thrilling—Liza put her arms about him and drew him even closer. She felt as if she couldn't get enough of him; she wanted to infuse herself with him, solder their bodies together as if they were made of one pure metal.

He slid his hand under her coat and jumper as their kiss went wonderfully on, and she jolted at the feel of it on her bare skin.

Fausto immediately stilled. He broke the kiss, which

made her frantic, as he looked down at her with dark, troubled eyes. 'Liza...?'

'It's just your hand is *cold*.' She let out a trembling laugh; she couldn't bear it if he stopped now. She might spontaneously combust if he did—or cry. She put her hand on top of his own and, daringly for her, moved it up higher on her body.

Fausto's eyes flared hotly as his hand covered her breast. It felt intimate and terrifying and so very wonderful, and Liza knew she didn't want him to stop. She arched her body upward to kiss him again, and with a groan Fausto surrendered, deepening their kiss as his hands freely roved over her body, creating fire wherever they touched. There was nothing cold about either of them now.

The wind whipped around them but Liza felt as if they were in their intimate cocoon, their own sacred world. In one sinuous movement Fausto shrugged out of his coat and she slipped her hands under his jumper to thrill at the hard planes of his chest.

Somehow their clothes were rucked aside, their breathing laboured and ragged as their kisses became more urgent and passionate, as if already they sensed the moment was slipping away from them and they were both desperate to hold onto it, to give it its full importance.

Liza sank her hands into his crisp, dark hair as his mouth moved lower on her body, tantalising her hidden places and making everything in her ache for more.

Her hands clenched his shoulders as she urged him on, wanting and needing even more. And he gave it—her body thrilling to every intimate touch even as the very core of her cried out for yet more still.

She reached for him, pressing one trembling hand against the arousal straining his jeans, and Fausto let out a choked laugh, his face buried in her neck.

'We should stop.'

'No.'

He raised his head. 'If we don't stop now…'

She pressed her hand against him again, letting her fingers tease, amazed at her own daring and yet knowing how much she longed for this. 'I don't want to stop.'

'*Liza*…'

'I don't want to stop. Please, Fausto.'

The moment was charged with silence, importance; Fausto lay above her, braced on his forearms, his face flushed with both desire and torment. Liza hooked her arms around his neck and did her best to draw him towards her, but his body was like a band of iron.

'Give me this, at least,' she whispered, 'if nothing else.' With a muttered oath in Italian, he surrendered to her, and she to him, as his body enfolded hers and he kissed her again. She lost herself to all of it—to his kiss, his touch, his very self.

The future fell away along with the past; she wanted nothing but this moment in all of its glory—even with the wet sand, the icy wind, the roaring waves. She was overwhelmed by it all, but most of all by him, his arms wrapped around her, his mouth on hers, his hard body pressed along her whole length and yet still, *still* not close enough.

She tried to unbutton his jeans and her fingers fumbled on the snap. Fausto wrapped his hand around hers.

'You are sure about this…?'

'Yes, I am sure,' she cried, half wild, and finally, thankfully, he unbuttoned his jeans himself. Then he reached for hers, and she wriggled out of them as best she could, barely conscious of the damp sand beneath her, the awkwardness and incongruity of the moment right here on the beach—none of it mattered.

'*Liza*…' Fausto said, his voice a groan, her name a plea.

She pulled him towards her. For a second he hesitated

again, poised above her, their worlds and selves about to collide in the most intimate and sacred way possible.

Then Liza arched up and with a low, guttural moan of both surrender and satisfaction Fausto sank inside her.

He'd tried to resist. He wanted no regrets for either of them, but Liza—her body, her *self*—proved impossible to resist. Fausto buried his face in the sweet curve of her neck as he waited for her to adjust to the feel and weight of him.

He knew from that first incredible moment that she had to be a virgin, but he couldn't think further than that as the siren song of pleasure drove everything else out.

'Are you all right?' he managed after a moment, his voice strangled, and she let out a breathless laugh.

'For heaven's sake, yes—*yes*.'

Then, amazingly, he was laughing too, amazed to share such joy in this moment, until laughter was replaced by something far, far sweeter as he found a rhythm and Liza matched it, clumsily at first but then with greater assurance and fluidity, until they were both moving as one. They *were* one.

Fausto had never felt so attuned, so fulfilled and unified and utterly complete. It was beyond the physical, even beyond the emotional; to say it was sacred would have felt, out of the moment, absurd, and yet it was. It *was*.

Higher and higher they moved and strove, each stroke unified and glorious, until their oneness was made even more complete as their bodies crashed together in the final cymbal note of pleasure, before Fausto rolled over onto his back, breathing heavily, taking Liza with him.

His vision cleared and his heart began to beat more slowly as he became aware, in increments, of the cold, damp sand beneath him and something sharp poking into his back. Liza's hair was spread across his face, tickling his nose, and he felt her heart thudding against his like a bird trapped in a cage.

His jeans were rucked, rather ridiculously, about his knees, as were hers. He had a terrible suspicion that if they were to be observed from afar they would look not only absurd, but obscene. The sand really did feel very cold.

He didn't know which of them moved first, if Liza stirred or if he tensed, but as one—and yet now utterly *not* as one—they separated. Liza sat up, wriggling back into her jeans, her head bent, her hair falling forward so Fausto could not see her face.

Fausto did the same, straightening his jumper and buttoning his jeans. Neither of them spoke, and the longer the silence stretched between them the worse it felt.

Fausto tried to examine his own mind, but his feelings were so jumbled—a vague self-loathing mixed with a soul-deep satisfaction—that he did not think he could utter a single coherent syllable.

Never, not once in his life, had he lost control the way he had with Liza Benton. Not even with Amy, not with *anyone*. He'd tried, heaven knew, to keep his head—and his body—but he hadn't. In the moment he'd been more than happy to sweep aside every concern, every second for pause, every perfectly good reason not to rut like a sheep on a beach in winter where anyone could happen by!

At least it was a private beach, but *still*. What if Alison's children had run up to them? Or even Henry? Fausto could not bear to think of such horrifying possibilities, and yet he had to now, as he hadn't then.

And that, he acknowledged grimly, was just considering the *appearance* of the whole thing. What about his motive, his *honour*? Liza was—*had been*—a virgin, something he thought he could have surmised before this morning, and yet he'd felt no compunction at taking her virginity on a cold, hard beach, with little romance and even less tenderness. His stomach roiled with disgust at himself and his actions. This was not who he was. This was not who his father had taught him to be.

He glanced at Liza, who was running her fingers through her hair, trying to untangle the knots. Her expression seemed composed, and yet he still sensed a fragility about her, a vulnerability that made him long to reach out and take her in his arms—yet he knew where that would go, and he had no desire to go there again.

Although the truth, Fausto reflected, was that he *did*, far too much, and that was why he stayed where he sat.

'I'm sorry,' he said at last. She let out a huff of sound that he suspected was meant to be a laugh but wasn't.

'That's about as bad as "Forgive me".'

It took him only a few seconds to remember that was what he'd said the first time they'd kissed. 'I should have acted with more restraint,' he said. 'For that I am sorry.'

She turned to look at him, her hair still in tangles about her face, her lips swollen from his kisses. 'Do you regret it?' she asked baldly, and he heard a challenge in the question. He didn't know what answer she wanted him to give, but in any case he knew he could only give an honest reply.

'Yes—I never would have chosen this.' She looked away. 'And I can't imagine you would have either—especially for your first time.' He paused, half hoping she would deny it, but she didn't. 'It was your first time?'

'Yes.' Her voice was wooden, her face still turned away from him.

'Then I truly am sorry.'

'Is that the only reason you're sorry?' she asked after a moment, her fingers plucking at a frayed thread on her jumper. 'Because it wasn't candlelight and roses and a king-sized bed?'

A more pointed and dangerous question. Fausto sighed. 'No, it's not.'

'I didn't think so.'

'Liza—please believe me, I've never wanted to hurt you.'

'You haven't,' she shot back, her voice brittle. 'Please, Fausto, don't feel guilty on my account. I was a full participant in this.' She gestured to the expanse of sand between them. 'You don't need to have any regrets.'

And yet he did. In that moment he felt swamped by them—by his own lack of self-control, by the desire that still coursed through him. By the sure and certain knowledge that he'd hurt a woman he admired and respected, and yet still knew he could never marry.

Yet why couldn't he?

The question, so unexpected, suddenly seemed obvious. Why shouldn't he marry Liza Benton? Admittedly, she would not be his family's first choice, by any stretch. His mother would be disappointed and hurt. His father would never have countenanced such a choice.

And, he acknowledged, she would struggle to fit into his world, both here and even more so in Italy. She was not from one of Lombardy's ancient families, not by any means. Not even close.

And yet…he wanted her. He cared about her. He didn't love her, not yet, and that could only be a plus. She wouldn't be able to hurt him. And, of course, she was lovely and gracious and kind.

And, he realised hollowly, she could at this moment be carrying his child. He hadn't used protection. Amazingly, he hadn't even *thought* about protection. And he had a feeling it was far too much to hope for that she might already be on the pill.

'We should get back,' Liza said in that same toneless voice that hinted at despair. She struggled to get up from the sand, and Fausto reached out a hand to help her rise. She jerked away from him.

'Liza, please.'

'I'm… I'm sorry.' She drew a hitched breath. 'I can't. I'm trying to be sanguine and sophisticated about this, but I'm finding it hard.' Another hitched breath, this one more revealing. 'I know that's not what you want to hear.'

'This isn't about what I want to hear,' Fausto insisted. 'We need to talk about this. Properly.'

'We already have, at least as much as I want to.' She buttoned up her coat with trembling fingers. Fausto rose easily from the ground as he gazed at her frustration. Only moments ago she'd been eminently touchable; now she seemed entirely unreachable.

'We haven't,' he declared firmly. 'Not in the least. There's the matter of birth control, for a start—'

She let out a ragged laugh that was lost to the wind. 'Of course that's what you'd be concerned about. Heavens, a baby born on the wrong side of the blanket! Common enough these days, but it's the stuff of your nightmares, I'm sure.'

Irritation warred with sympathy; he could see how much she was hurting and yet he couldn't comfort her. She wouldn't let him. 'That's not what I meant—'

'Then what did you mean?' She flung up a hand. 'No, don't tell me. I don't want to know. Every time you've told me what you've been thinking it's been the worse for me, and I really don't think I can handle what you're thinking right now.'

'Liza—'

'No, Fausto, please. Let's leave it at this.' She forced herself to look at him, her face heartbreakingly lovely, her expression one of both courage and fragility. 'You don't need to feel any regrets. I won't. What happened here was—well, it was amazing.' She let out a trembling laugh. 'The most amazing experience of my life, so thank you, actually.' Another laugh, this one full of tears. 'And that's…that's all I'm going to say about it.' She started walking, hurrying past him, her head tucked low. Fausto tried to catch her arm but she shrugged away from him.

'Liza!' he called, but she shook her head and started running. Fausto knew he could have caught up with her easily enough, but that hardly seemed to be a wise course of action. And so, even though everything in him resisted, he simply stood there and watched her go.

CHAPTER ELEVEN

SHE HAD SPENT the last four hours hiding in her room and Liza knew her unsociability was bordering on rude. Thankfully, she hadn't seen anyone when she'd come back to the house; she didn't think she'd have been able to give an answer if she had.

She'd hotfooted it to her room and stripped off her rumpled clothing, trying not to burst into tears. She wasn't even sure why she felt like crying; she'd meant what she'd said when she'd told Fausto it had been the most amazing experience of her life. Perhaps that was the cause for her tears. It certainly wasn't going to happen again, and it had left her in a state of both wonder and longing.

She'd hoped half an hour standing under a near-scalding spray would have helped balance her mood but she'd felt even more despondent when she'd emerged, as pink as a boiled crab. She'd wrapped herself in the dressing gown that had been provided on the back of the bathroom door and curled up in bed while a bittersweet montage of moments played relentlessly through her head.

She knew she was tormenting herself by reliving those sweet, sweet moments with Fausto—as well as the unbearably awkward and painful moments after. She'd so wanted to be sophisticated and unruffled, as if she had sandy trysts all the time, but she hadn't been. She hadn't been at *all*. She'd been gauche and prickly and so very hurt. And now Fausto Danti had yet another reason to regret her very being.

The thought of having to see him for the rest of the

weekend was unbearable. To stumble through pleasantries as if they were merely acquaintances—she couldn't do it. She wouldn't. And yet to run away the first chance she got would be rude to Henry, and too revealing to Fausto. She wanted to show him she didn't care, even if she very much did.

Even if there had been a large, sorry part of her that had been hoping—waiting, even—for him to take her in his arms afterwards and kiss her tenderly and tell her he'd fallen in love with her. As if…! When would she learn? When would she remember that no man had ever remotely wanted to do such a thing?

Fausto had looked horrified afterwards. He'd acted as if he regretted absolutely everything about their encounter. He'd even said as much. And meanwhile she'd felt as if the universe had unveiled its secrets, as if the very atoms of her being had shifted and reformed. She was absurd, the very parody of a naïve, stupid virgin with stars in her eyes and hope in her heart.

With a groan Liza pressed her face into the pillow, wanting only to will it all away—even though she never actually would want such a thing. She wanted to hold onto all the memories even as she despised them. Oh, why did Fausto Danti provoke such a maelstrom of contradictory emotions within her? The sooner this weekend ended, the better.

And yet then she'd most likely never see him again…

Liza groaned again.

Eventually, knowing she needed to show herself, she rose from the bed, aching and weary, and dressed. She took pains with her appearance—fluffing her curls and applying understated make-up, even though she hated the thought of Fausto knowing she'd gone to such pains. Still, at a time like this make-up felt like armour.

Downstairs, the house was strangely quiet; when she

ventured into the drawing room, Henry put down his news-paper to give her a charming smile.

'How lovely to see you! Did you enjoy the beach? The wind does take it out of one, I find.'

'It was lovely,' Liza murmured, unable to look him in the eye. She glanced around the empty room. 'Where is everyone?'

'Alison has taken the young ones into Hunstanton. Fausto was taking some business calls—but I'm sure he'll be here shortly. Perhaps he'll give you that game of chess?'

Henry raised his eyebrows while Liza blushed and mumbled something mostly unintelligible. A few moments later Fausto appeared, checking his step as he caught sight of Liza before he assumed that oh, so bland expression and came into the room.

'Fausto, I was just saying you and Liza should have that rematch.' He gestured to the board while Liza fidgeted. She had never hated chess so much in her life.

'If she wants a game, I'd be happy to play,' Fausto replied after a beat. He had showered since their beach interlude; his hair was dark and damp, brushed away from his freshly shaven face, and Liza was drawn to the clean, strong lines of him, remembering exactly how he'd felt against her. She *had* to stop thinking like that.

'It's not necessary,' Liza said.

Fausto turned to her. 'You never told me how you came to be so good at chess.'

'My father is a grandmaster,' she said, unable to look him in the eye. She moved her gaze rather wildly around the room, finally letting it rest on the chessboard. 'We played all through my childhood. I competed in junior tourna-ments when I was young.'

'I had no idea,' Fausto said, and she threw him a chal-lenging look.

'Why would you?'

He acknowledged her point with an inclination of his head. 'Shall we play?'

She swallowed. The last thing she wanted to do was play a game of chess with Fausto Danti. Considering their history, it felt far too intimate—every word, every move loaded with both innuendo and memory.

'Yes, why don't you?' Henry said. Liza looked Fausto full in the face and, to her shock, his returning smile was full of sympathy. There was no mockery there, no icy hauteur, just kindness, and that nearly undid her.

'All right,' she said, her voice little more than a whisper. 'Let's play.'

Her fingers trembled as she picked up her knight to make the opening move. She could feel Fausto across the table from her—his presence, his power, the overwhelming *force* of him. It was like an undertow, pulling her down, drowning her. She could barely form a coherent thought, much less plan strategic chess moves.

They played in silence for a few minutes, the tension ratcheting up with every move, and any neat tricks Liza had been planning were just as neatly avoided by Fausto. Halfway through the game, both of them down several pieces, the game suddenly turned into something bigger, something far more important. Winning felt crucial. To lose was not to be contemplated. Defeat would be an emotional disaster, and one she didn't think she would ever recover from.

Slowly but surely, Liza felt the tide turning in Fausto's favour and she knew the game was slipping out of her control. Then, in a foolish error, she lost her queen and she bit her lip hard enough to taste blood.

'Draw?' Fausto suggested softly, and she shook her head. 'Let's play to the end.'

He won in just a few short moves, and somehow Liza managed a stiff nod. 'Well done. Good game.' She rose unsteadily from the table, feeling as if she could break. It was only a stupid game, she reminded herself fiercely, and yet it felt like just another reminder that she wasn't good enough for Fausto Danti in any way. That she never would be.

'It was a very good game,' Fausto said, rising from his chair as Liza moved blindly past him.

'I think I'll get some air,' she managed, and walked quickly from the room. She weaved through the house, finally ducking into a small morning room decorated in soothing blues and greys, although little did they help her mood. She let out a shuddering breath, willing the tears back. It was so ridiculous to cry over a chess game, and yet she knew it was more than that. So much more.

'Liza.'

Fausto's voice had her groaning aloud. 'Can you *never* let me have a moment's peace?' she demanded raggedly.

'Not when there is unfinished business between us, no.'

She took a deep breath and turned around, willing herself to have enough strength for one more conversation. 'What is it, then?'

Fausto regarded her quietly for a moment and then he closed the door behind him. 'I want to ask you something,' he said.

Liza shrugged, spreading her hands helplessly. 'What? What could you possibly want to ask me?'

'I want,' Fausto said, his voice low and firm with purpose, 'to ask you to marry me.'

As soon as he said the words, Fausto realised how much he meant them—and how shocking they sounded. He'd been thinking of proposing to Liza since their interlude on the beach, but it hadn't crystallised into both fact and desire until now. Until he'd said it out loud.

Liza's mouth dropped open and she gaped at him soundlessly for a few seconds before she shook her head. 'I was so not expecting you to say that.'

'I've said it, and I mean it.'

'Why?'

Her incredulity was understandable, and so Fausto sought to explain as clearly and concisely as he could. 'First, because I care about you. Second, because we have an undeniable physical chemistry. And third, because you could be carrying my child.'

Liza pressed her lips together, her eyes flashing. 'Why do I think it's the last one that has forced your hand?'

He inclined his head. 'Perhaps it has, but I mean it no less.'

She let out a huff of disparaging sound. 'Why not just wait a couple of weeks, Fausto? Make sure I am pregnant, because I'm probably not.'

'You have no way of knowing and, in any case, possible pregnancy aside, I still wish to marry you.'

Liza shook her head again. She still looked winded and dazed by his offer. 'You cannot possibly want to marry me.'

'It is true, I have fought against it,' Fausto said steadily. 'Considering the differences in our life situations, and the expectations my own family has for my bride, I didn't want to feel anything for you, and I did my best to avoid you.'

'Oh, you did, did you?' Liza stated with a broken laugh.

'There are obvious disadvantages to our union,' Fausto continued. He would not shirk away from mentioning the unfortunate and the obvious.

'Oh?' Liza's body tensed and her eyes flashed again. 'And what are those, exactly?'

Fausto exhaled impatiently. 'Surely they're apparent.'

'I'd still like you to say them,' she snapped, looking angrier by the second, but Fausto was no longer in any mood to appease her.

'I am the Conte di Palmerno,' he said, only to have her interject,

'I thought it was a courtesy title only.'

'Perhaps you are not aware of my position,' Fausto said after a moment, willing to give her the benefit of the doubt. 'And what it would mean to be my Contessa. The duties and responsibilities—'

'Oh, I'm sure it would be a great privilege,' Liza drawled, sounding as if it would be anything but. 'But since I didn't ask to be your Contessa, and have no desire to be your Contessa, this whole conversation is pointless!'

Fausto stared at her for a moment, shocked by her outrage as well as her defiance. He realised he had expected neither. Surprise, yes, a certain amount of caution. But to act insulted? When he was offering such a compliment and yes, indeed, a privilege? It could not be denied. 'You…you are refusing me?' he asked slowly.

She let out a hard, ugly sort of laugh. 'Is that so very hard to believe?'

'As it happens, yes.'

She let out another laugh, the sound just as unforgiving. 'Your arrogance knows no bounds.'

'I don't believe it is arrogant to be aware of all I can offer you, especially considering your own situation, and the disadvantage your family might bring—'

'*My* family!' Liza practically shouted. 'A disadvantage to you? Just because they're normal?'

'Liza, you know as well as I do—'

'And if I cared about money, perhaps—' she cut across him furiously '—perhaps I would want you to list all those obvious advantages. But, as it happens, I don't. When I marry it will be for love—because someone loves me. *Me*, and no one else, no matter where I come from or what my family is like, or whether I'll make a good *Contessa*.'

'I told you I care for you—' Fausto protested.

'Against your will! You have fought against feeling anything for me. If I were to agree to marry you, I'd be as good as dragging you to the altar with a gun to your head!'

Her theatrics annoyed him, although he strove to stay calm. 'I assure you, I would go there of my own free will.'

'Stop, Fausto, these sweet nothings are really too much,' Liza retorted sarcastically, her tone like acid. 'The answer is, and always will be, no. Absolutely, unequivocally no.'

He could hardly believe she was saying such a thing—and he was hearing it. In all his deliberations about whether to propose, he'd never once considered that Liza would refuse him. Perhaps that *had* been arrogance, but even now he considered it justified.

'May I know why?' he asked coldly.

For a second Liza looked as if she might burst into tears—her lips trembled and she blinked rapidly, drawing a shuddering breath before she stated staunchly, 'Because you are not the kind of man I wish to marry.'

'And why is that?'

'Do you find it so hard to believe? Do you think so highly of yourself that you can't imagine a woman refusing you?'

'I would not put it in such terms, of course—'

'Well, think again,' Liza cried, her voice trembling on a high, wild note. 'Everything you have ever said or done has shown me that you are a snobbish, arrogant, rude and unlikeable person, and I have absolutely no desire to spend another minute with you, never mind the rest of my life!'

Fausto stared at her, anger warring with a deep, terrible hurt. He had known Liza was fighting her feelings, just as he was, but to impugn him so thoroughly…

'In every instance I have tried to act honourably,' he said in a low voice, a thrum of fury vibrating through it.

'Then your sense of honour is very different from mine, as well as most people's.'

Anger—and that damnable hurt—pulsed through him. He'd been called old-fashioned, standoffish and, yes, proud, mostly by people who didn't know him very well. At home, with people he knew and loved, he could be comfortable and relaxed, but a need to be formal and set apart had been ingrained into him since he was child. He was a Danti. He had to be an example. And yet Liza seemed to think he was an example of everything bad, and nothing good.

'I did not realise you held me in such low esteem,' he said after a moment. For a second Liza looked again as if she were about to cry. 'Is there something in particular that has caused you to think of me with so little regard?' he asked, and she drew a hiccuppy breath.

'Jack Wickley, for one.'

'Jack *Wickley*?' He stared at her in disbelief, hardly able to credit that she'd believed that amoral chancer over him. 'You are accusing me—judging me—based on the word of Wickley?'

She tilted her chin up, her eyes flashing fire. 'Why shouldn't I?'

Fausto could not bring himself to reply. The idea that Liza would believe every word that slimy worm had said— that, after knowing him, Fausto, more than a little, she would still judge him so unfairly and harshly…

'Well?' Liza demanded, and Fausto simply shook his head. He would not stoop to defend himself against Wickley. He could not lower himself so.

'You deny what you did?' she challenged, and he stared at her coldly.

'What is there to deny?'

'That you deprived him of his inheritance and the job your own father promised him, and spread rumours about him that he wasn't trustworthy, so no one would hire him.'

He pressed his lips together as a white-hot rage threatened to consume him. 'That is what he told you?'

'Yes.'

'And you believed him?'

'Why would I have any reason to doubt him?' Liza flung at him. 'In any case, it's not just that. What about Jenna and Chaz?'

'What about them?' Fausto asked, his voice toneless, the words clipped. Fury beat through his blood but he held it in check.

'Did you warn Chaz off Jenna? I didn't want to believe it, but I know how you were looking at us all at that Christmas ball, and he dropped her like a hot potato right after.'

'I told him to proceed carefully,' Fausto conceded after a brief, heightened pause. 'And that I questioned her feelings for him, as well as her intentions.'

Liza's face flushed as she glared at him, her hands clenched into fists at her sides. 'You had no right!'

'He asked my opinion, and I gave it,' Fausto stated. 'He is a grown man, and he acted accordingly. I exerted no pressure, if that is what you're implying.'

'Your opinion is pressure enough!'

'That is hardly my fault.'

She glared at him for a full thirty seconds, her face full of hurt and anger, her eyes flashing fire and yet possessing a sheen of tears. 'I loathe you,' she choked. '*Loathe* you. And nothing would ever induce me to accept your horrible, half-hearted proposal.'

'Never fear,' Fausto returned in the iciest tones he'd ever used. 'Nothing would ever induce me to repeat it.' Not trusting himself to say any more, he inclined his head and then left the room as quickly as he could.

Unable to face Henry or his family, he went up to his bedroom and started to pack. He would not stay another moment under the same roof as Liza Benton. He could not believe she had treated his proposal—made in good faith and with honour—with such scorn and derision. And all because of a single word to his good friend—and Jack Wickley's damning recounting.

Fausto swore under his breath as he considered that wretch of a man. He had not wanted to stoop to justify himself to Liza, but he was sorely tempted. She thought him so proud? So snobbish and arrogant and rude and *unlikeable*? Perhaps he would show her otherwise.

Before he could think better of it, he stormed back downstairs, barely conscious of Henry peering out from the drawing room, and flung open the door to the little sitting room where he'd found Liza before.

She was still there, collapsed into a chair, her head cradled in her arms. She lifted her tear-stained face, her expression incredulous, as the door banged against the wall and he came into the room, fists clenched, chest heaving.

'You called me proud—well, I am not so proud as all that. I resisted telling you the truth about Jack Wickley because I had hoped that it would be enough for you to know the kind of man I was, rather than a stranger you met once in a bar.' Belatedly registering her tears, he realised she must have been crying, but he had no time to wonder at it as he continued steadily, 'Jack Wickley was the son of my father's office manager in Milan—a good man, who died when Jack was only sixteen. My father took him under his wing, brought him into our house and paid for his education through university, promising him a position with the company after he graduated.'

Liza, looking dazed, nodded slowly and, as the old hurt and bitterness coursed through him, Fausto made himself continue. 'I have known Jack since I was a child myself, and I have never liked him. Not because I am proud, but because he seemed crafty and sly. He cheated on his exams in school, and I discovered during university he was a terrible playboy and womanizer. Despite all that, I honoured my father's word and will, and I gave Jack the position of office manager here in London, over three years ago now. My father was ill, and unable to run the company, and I was consumed with family matters. However, upon my father's death, it became clear to me over time that Jack Wickley had terrorized the office staff, made unwanted advances to female employees and embezzled from the company to the tune of several hundred thousand pounds.'

Liza's eyes widened and a soft gasp escaped her, which was gratifying enough but, now that he had started, Fausto knew he had to continue. 'Moreover,' he said, 'I discovered that he had attempted to seduce my sister Francesca at a family party two years ago, when she was only fifteen. So if I dislike and distrust the man, surely you can understand why. I had no idea he was spreading the story you told me, so I can add deceit to his ever-growing list of sins.' He drew a breath and let it out, half relieved he'd told her everything, and half ashamed that he'd had to. 'If you doubt my story you can talk to Henry, who knows most of it, except about my sister, or Chaz. Or, for that matter, anyone in the London office of Danti Investments. The whole reason I have been here these last months is to repair the damage Jack Wickley wrought upon my company and my family.' He stared at her, his fury still pulsing through him. 'As for the matter of Jenna and Chaz, it is true I have had reservations about your sister. Perhaps they were unwarranted, but I have been fooled by a woman before.' He paused before making himself continue. 'I thought I loved her, and I brought her home to meet my family. Her true colours soon became all too clear.' And that was all he would say about that. 'I advised Chaz to be cautious, no more, and I still believe I was justified. If I was not, and your sister truly has feelings for Chaz, then I am sorry.' He let out a low breath before giving a terse nod of farewell. 'And now I will say goodbye.'

Without waiting for her reply, not trusting himself to

say or do something he knew he would later regret, Fausto left the room. He made his apologies to Henry, finished his packing and had left the house before Liza had even stirred from her chair.

CHAPTER TWELVE

LIZA SPENT THE next two months in a daze. Days passed, grey and alike, and she was barely aware of their coming or going. She worked, ate, slept, and thankfully neither Henry nor Jenna nor anyone else pressed her on any point, or asked her why she seemed so very miserable.

Perhaps, she reflected, she was doing a better job than she thought at seeming normal, even happy. She went out at the weekends with Jenna; she went home to Hereford twice, and had Lindsay come to stay. She even accompanied Lindsay and Jenna to a nightclub, but she didn't dance and she left when she glimpsed Jack Wickley, of all people, come through the door. That was one person she could not bear to talk to, or even to see.

And of course there was another person she couldn't bear even to think about—although for entirely different reasons. Ever since Fausto had proposed, and then explained so much to her, Liza's emotions had been in an utter tangle. Her mind went round and round in circles as she tried to make sense of what Jack Wickley had told her, to what Fausto had told her, to what she had seen—and felt—herself. The result was a very uncomfortable ferment of uncertainty, followed by a far worse sweeping sense of desolation.

What if she'd been wrong? What if, to guard her own heart and for the sake of her own pride, she'd turned Fausto Danti into someone he never had been—someone like Andrew Felton, whom she couldn't trust and had come to dislike? Yet Fausto was no Felton, and she should have been smart and sensitive enough to see that. Yes, he was proud, but he was also honourable.

Wasn't he?

In any case, Liza reminded herself more than once, it was all too late now. As Fausto had said himself, he was never going to repeat his proposal. Not that she would accept it, anyway. She might have been wrong in her assumptions about who he was as a man, but that didn't mean she wanted to *marry* him. Even if he was an honourable man, he still had old-fashioned notions of suitability and position, and he'd made it clear he was expected to marry some Italian socialite or other, from a family he'd known for about a million years. She was not remotely in the running, for so many reasons.

Besides, the possibility of her being pregnant had evaporated within a week; there was nothing, absolutely nothing, to draw them together again.

And that prospect was not something, she told herself again and again, to feel downcast about, never mind heartbroken. Her heart was not broken at *all*.

Jenna and Henry might have acted as if they didn't notice her doldrums, but someone unexpected did. At the end of April, more than two months after that weekend in Norfolk, Yvonne called her with a proposition.

'I know you must have some holiday to take, and your nan has got it in her head to go travelling. You know as well as I do that she can't go alone, so I said you'd go with her.'

'Me...?' Liza loved her nan, her father's mother, a gentle, cheerful woman with a spine of steel. 'But I don't even know if I can take time off, Mum...'

'I'm sure you can and, in any case, it's only for a week in May. I can't go, with Lindsay's exams and Marie still at home, and besides, your nan can only stand me for about ten minutes. I know I'm too silly for her.'

Her mother spoke in her usual matter-of-fact way, but

this time it made Liza's eyes fill with tears. 'You're not silly, Mum.'

'Oh, yes, I am. I'm a silly old bird, all right, and I don't mind. But your nan likes your company, and you've always wanted to see something of Europe. Now's your chance.'

'Europe? Where is she going?'

'A tour of Italy. She's got it all arranged and booked. All we need to do is book you a ticket, and make sure your passport hasn't expired. I know you haven't had any real cause to use it, but now's your chance.'

Italy… It was ridiculous to think she'd bump into Fausto in all of Italy, and yet still the prospect made her heart beat faster. 'I don't know, Mum…'

'You're going,' Yvonne said firmly. 'It'll be good for you, Liza. A change of scenery from all the grey we've been having. You need your spirits lifting.'

It was all arranged within a matter of days, and just a few weeks later Liza found herself on a flight to Milan with her nan, and then booked into a lovely little *pensione* on the shores of Lake Maggiore.

It was all so beautiful—the bougainvillea tumbling from pots on the little wrought iron balcony outside her window, the lake a deep, dazzling blue-green in the distance, the air warm and scented with lavender and thyme.

Her nan, Melanie, had informed her on the flight over that they would not be having a tour of the entire country, but rather one just of the Italian lakes.

'I've always wanted to see them, and as we only have a week we can hardly see everything in all of Italy.'

'I suppose not,' Liza agreed as a wave of trepidation— and surely not anticipation or even *hope*—went through her. Fausto's estate was, she knew, in the lakes region. Still, it was very, very unlikely that she would stumble upon him during their week-long stay. So unlikely it bordered on absurd, if not downright fantastical.

'So,' Melanie announced as she came into Liza's room, 'I thought we'd have dinner at the little restaurant down the street, and then tomorrow I want to take a tour of one of the estates nearby—some of its gardens are open to the public, along with a few of its main rooms. It's meant to be one of the most impressive properties in all of Europe.'

'Oh?' Liza asked. Then some towering sense of inevitability prompted her to go on, even while she already felt she knew, 'Who does it belong to?'

'The Conte di Palmerno,' Melanie said with a grand flourish. 'Apparently, he's someone quite important.'

The next morning dawned bright and sunny, and Liza tried to still the swarm of butterflies that had taken residence in her stomach as she took particular care with her appearance.

'You are not going to see him,' she scolded her reflection. 'He's probably not even in Italy, or if he is he'll be in Milan, working.' She took a deep breath as she smoothed her hands down the daisy-sprigged sundress she'd chosen to wear. 'Even if he's on the estate, it's completely unlikely that he'll be out wandering in the gardens when we are. So stop worrying.'

Except she didn't think she was worrying, precisely. *Hoping* was closer to the mark, which was an alarming realisation. Worry would be far more reassuring.

It was a twenty-minute cab ride to Villa di Palmerno, a beautiful drive along the shores of Lake Maggiore, with villas perched on the verdant hillsides and motorboats speeding along the calm blue waters.

'Stop fidgeting,' Melanie said with a laugh as next to her Liza shifted nervously and then checked her hair. 'We're just going to see some gardens.'

'I know,' Liza murmured, flushing, and once again she had to give herself a stern mental talking-to.

A few minutes later the taxi turned into the impressive wrought iron gates that led to the Palmerno estate. Liza drew her breath in at the sight of the endless smooth green lawns, the extensive gardens behind high stone walls and then the house—oh, the house.

She stared in wonder at the villa, with its balconies and balustrades, its turrets and terraces. Well over two dozen windows sparkled in the sunlight as the cab pulled up in front of the separate entrance to the vast gardens.

'Isn't it magnificent?' Melanie exclaimed, and Liza could not find it in herself to reply. When Fausto had been asking her to marry him, he'd been asking her to be mistress and chatelaine of all this. It was too awesome a thought to comprehend and in fact she hadn't comprehended it at all when she'd thrown his proposal back in his face.

She cringed now as she remembered just how thoroughly and thoughtlessly she'd refused him. *Absolutely, unequivocally no.* She closed her eyes and her heart against the memory as she got out of the car on weak, wobbly legs.

The gardens were beautiful, each one perfectly landscaped and surrounded by a high hedge to give privacy. They wandered through rose gardens and wildflower meadows, gardens with marble fountains and benches and gardens with trellises of wisteria and beds of lavender. They found a kitchen garden that was an acre at least, full of vegetables and seedlings. There was an orchard with every kind of fruit tree imaginable and half a dozen greenhouses where, a gardener informed them, the estate produced all sorts of tomatoes, melons and other fruits, including a unique orange that the Conte had helped to develop.

'What sort of man is the Conte?' Liza forced herself to ask in as casual a tone as she could, and the elderly gardener's lined face crinkled into a smile.

'He is *bene—molto bene!*' He kissed his fingers and then laughed. 'A very good master of the house, *signorina*. Truly the best. Some say he can be a bit reserved, but only those who do not know him truly. He is as kind and generous a man as anyone could wish.'

'I see,' Liza said, the words practically choking her, and she turned away.

Everything about the place, from the beautiful, endless gardens to the villa perched above them as gracious and lovely a building as one could ever imagine, not to mention utterly enormous, made Liza ache—not with longing for the material wealth she saw all around her, although it was unbelievably impressive.

She ached because of how quickly and completely she'd dismissed Fausto's claims about his family, his position. She'd considered them utterly unimportant, a matter not worth spending a second of thought on, and yet now she saw how understandable his concerns were.

He was lord of this place, responsible for hundreds, if not thousands, in his employ. He had a reputation to uphold, people's livelihoods to support, and naturally he would want a woman at his side who was capable of helping him shoulder such a huge responsibility, who could offer advice and welcome people from all walks of life, attend dinner parties and charity galas and press conferences and who knew what else. Of course he had to be cautious when thinking of his bride, his wife.

Yet she'd scorned it all in a moment of prideful pique. She'd scorned *him*, and now she found she deeply regretted it—regardless of his proposal or whatever future they might have had together, Fausto had deserved her to take him and his concerns seriously, rather than scornfully, and now it was too late. The bitter regret she felt was enough to choke her. She could have lain down right there in the garden and wept.

* * *

Fausto drove up and parked his navy sports convertible in front of the villa, the wind ruffling his hair as he gazed at his family home. It was good to be back; it was good to be away from London.

The last two months had crawled by, as he'd pulled sixteen-hour working days, returning to his Mayfair townhouse to simply eat and sleep. Even then he had not been able to banish thoughts of Liza—Liza, who had yielded so sweetly to him, who had rejected him so utterly. *Liza*. Why could he not forget her?

He wanted to, heaven knew. He'd even sent a reckless email to Gabriella Di Angio, a member of another of Lombardy's noble families, in order to re-establish an old connection. When she'd emailed back a blithe reply to tell him of her recent engagement to a French CEO, he'd only felt relieved. He did not want to renew his acquaintance with such a suitable woman. And yet he needed to stop thinking about a woman who was most unsuitable—a woman who didn't want him.

There had been plenty of opportunity to forget Liza in London. He'd gone out with Chaz several times, but his friend had been as dour as he was and neither of them had had any interest in the many women who'd sent all the right signals, and received none in reply.

With a sigh, Fausto stepped out of the car. Perhaps things would be better here, at Villa di Palmerno. At least he was further away from Liza, from temptation, from terrible, tempestuous memory.

He turned, and his heart seemed to still in his chest as he saw Liza herself walking through the garden gates with an older woman. For a few seconds he couldn't make any sense of it. How on earth could she be here? It was a figment of his imagination, a fantasy of his fevered mind…

But then she looked up and her eyes widened with shock

and he knew it was her. She was here in the flesh, at Villa di Palmerno, just as he'd once imagined, bringing her back as his bride.

Slowly, wonderingly, Fausto took a step towards her. Liza froze where she stood, her gaze transfixed on his face, her expression wary, even frightened. Considering how they'd last parted, he could understand her uncertainty and yet suddenly, amazingly, it all seemed so simple to him, so very easy. She was here; he wanted her here. That was all that mattered.

'Liza.' He walked towards her, both hands extended, and she stared at him in blank wonder as he took her hands in his, gave them a light squeeze and then kissed her cheek. He inhaled her light floral fragrance and it reminded him of so much—but he couldn't think about all that now.

'Fausto,' she said faintly, 'I had no idea you would be here…'

'And I had no idea you would be here,' he returned with a smile. 'How did it come to pass?'

'You know him?' the older woman said in surprise, and then recollected herself. 'But obviously you do.' She held out her hand. 'Melanie Benton. I am Liza's grandmother.'

'Fausto Danti, Conte di Palmerno. Charmed to meet you,' Fausto said, and took her hand.

'Likewise.' Melanie looked both intrigued and pleased. No doubt she was wondering just what the nature of Fausto's relationship was with her granddaughter—as was he.

'My nan wanted to…to do a tour of the lakes,' Liza explained, stammering a little. 'And I came along to accompany her. I really had no idea you'd be here. I didn't even know we were coming here to the villa until last night…'

'It's a delightful surprise.' She looked shocked as well as dubious at his pronouncement, but Fausto meant every word. He was so very glad to see her. And she looked wonderful—her wild curls pulled back with a green rib-

`bon, her sunglasses pushed up on her head. The sundress she wore was covered in daisies and her bare shoulders were tanned and sprinkled with golden freckles. He wanted to kiss every one. He wanted to kiss her—to take her in his arms, to feel her body against his, to tell her he didn't care about anything that had happened before.

The last two months had not lessened his feelings for Liza Benton in the least, he realised. They'd only grown stronger. And yet…he knew he needed to caution himself. As pleased as he was to see her, he had no intention of repeating his marriage proposal. One scorching rejection was certainly enough, if not one too many, especially considering he'd thought he'd already learned that unpleasant lesson before.

No, Fausto decided as he met Liza's enquiring gaze, he would have to proceed very cautiously—for his own sake as well as hers. He was glad she was here, but that was all. He wasn't ready to let it be more.

'We were actually about to leave,' Liza said, brandishing her phone. 'I was just going to call a cab.'

'Have you seen inside the house yet?' Fausto asked.

'No, I was hoping to see some of the rooms you have open to the public,' Melanie interjected, 'but I think Liza is a bit tired.'

Liza slid her gaze away from Fausto's and did not reply.

'Why don't you come into the house?' he suggested. 'I'll show you the public rooms myself, and then we can have some refreshments in the private apartments afterwards.'

'We couldn't—' Liza began, but Melanie was already nodding her vigorous acceptance.

'That is so very kind of you, Conte—'

'Please, call me Fausto.'

'Fausto.' She looked delighted. 'I really did want to see those rooms.'

Smiling at them both, Fausto ushered them into the villa.

His mother was in Milan on a shopping trip, and Francesca was visiting friends. They had the house to themselves, and he was glad.

'Oh, lovely,' Melanie breathed as they stepped into the enormous entrance hall, with its black and white marble floor and skylight three storeys above. Liza regarded her surroundings silently, making no comment. Fausto couldn't keep from glancing at her, wanting to know what she thought. How she felt.

'Come this way,' he murmured, and he dared to put his hand on Liza's lower back for a brief instant before he removed it and ushered them towards the villa's main drawing room, a chamber of impressive proportions, with many antiques and rare works of art.

Melanie exclaimed over everything as he took them through the drawing room, dining room, ballroom and library, but Liza said not a word. Fausto kept glancing at her to gauge her reaction, but her face was utterly expressionless. What was she thinking? And, more importantly, what was she feeling? He longed to know.

Having finished with the public rooms, he led them back to a sun-filled conservatory filled with plants and flowers that overlooked a wide terrace that led down to the villa's more private gardens.

'Oh, what a view!' Melanie exclaimed, for the shores of Lake Maggiore were glinting at the bottom of the gardens, jewel-bright. Villa di Palmerno had more lake frontage than any other lakeside property in Italy.

Fausto had rung for refreshments as soon as they'd started their tour, and they had only just sat down in comfortable rattan chairs in the conservatory when a maid brought in a tray with fresh lemonade, a selection of Italian pastries and a bowl of fresh fruit.

'Oh, you're so kind,' Melanie exclaimed. 'Really, Conte—Fausto. And I haven't yet asked...' She glanced thoughtfully at her granddaughter. 'How is it that you two know each other?'

Fausto leaned back in his chair, crossing one leg over the other as he glanced at Liza's sudden expression of alarm. After her deliberately blank looks all through their tour, it felt as if her careful veneer was finally cracking.

'Yes, Liza,' he said pleasantly. 'Why don't you explain to your grandmother how it is we know each other?'

CHAPTER THIRTEEN

LIZA FELT AS if she'd stumbled into some incredible alternate reality. Surely she couldn't be here, sipping lemonade and nibbling delicious pastries in Fausto Danti's amazing villa, while the man himself sat across from them, looking mind-bogglingly relaxed and acting so very charming? It felt impossible and yet it was happening, and she was here, and so was Fausto.

When she'd seen him step out of his car, some part of her hadn't even been surprised. Some part of her—a hopeful, desperate, wanting part—had *known* she would see him here. That secret part of her had been waiting for him all along and when she'd seen him a voice inside her had whispered thankfully, *At last*.

But what she hadn't expected was for Fausto to be so welcoming. His smile was easy, his manner assured, every word and gesture nothing but friendly. Yet the last time they'd met he'd been in a fury—and so had she.

What had changed? Why had he? Was it that he didn't care any more, and so such kindness was easy? Liza had no answers to any of it, but as she took a small sip of lemonade she knew she felt very, very cautious.

'Liza, aren't you going to explain?' Melanie asked with a laugh. 'How did you and Con—Fausto meet?'

'Well…' Liza licked dry lips as she took another nibble of her pastry, simply to stall for time. Outside, the verdant gardens tumbled down to the shining lake; she didn't think she'd ever seen anything so beautiful before. 'We met in a bar, actually.' Melanie's eyebrows rose and Liza clarified quickly, 'It was when Mum and Lindsay were visiting. Fausto was there with his friend and we all got to talking.' She glanced at him to see how he would take this explanation, and he nodded and smiled.

'Yes, and we met a few more times after that, didn't we?' His grey, glinting gaze met hers in laughing challenge, and in a panic she wondered why he was doing this. *Taunting* her.

'Yes, a few times,' she murmured. 'At a party…'

'And in Norfolk,' Fausto supplied. 'At the house of a mutual friend. My godfather, in fact. We had a lovely walk on the beach.' When Liza risked a glance at him she found he was gazing straight at her, and there was knowledge in his eyes. She felt herself flush as memories she'd been doing her best not to think about rose up in a rush. The kiss that had gone on and on…the feel of him against her…his body pressed to hers…

'I'm amazed you never said a word, Liza,' Melanie scolded. 'Considering you knew where we were going.'

'It…er…didn't seem relevant,' Liza said. She knew she sounded ridiculous. If she'd been more sophisticated and sanguine, she would have mentioned to her grandmother before about knowing Fausto in a careless manner, but she'd known she couldn't talk about him without revealing the depth of her emotion. It was hard enough now to act indifferent. In fact, it was impossible.

She didn't think she could sit here a moment more, pretending she and Fausto were nothing but casual acquaintances. She lurched upright, spilling a bit of her lemonade as she replaced it on the tray. 'It's getting late, Nan, and I'm sure the Conte is busy. We should get going.' She fumbled for her phone. 'I'll call a cab.'

'Nonsense, I'll have one of my staff drive you,' Fausto replied. 'It is no trouble. But I insist you return for dinner. Tomorrow night?'

Liza gaped at him while Melanie smoothly accepted the invitation. 'That would be lovely, thank you.'

'I don't think…' Liza began helplessly, knowing it was already too late. *Why are you doing this?* She tried to form the question in her eyes but Fausto either didn't see it or chose to ignore it.

'Let me arrange your transportation,' he said, and rose fluidly from his seat. As he left the room Melanie leaned towards Liza.

'What a lovely man,' she said in a hushed voice. 'I can't help but feel there's more to your knowing each other than you're willing to admit.'

'There isn't,' Liza replied woodenly. Nothing she wanted to relate to her grandmother, in any case.

'The car will be ready shortly,' Fausto said as he returned to the room. 'While we wait, perhaps I can show you the villa's private gardens?'

'That would be lovely,' Melanie said before Liza could frame a response.

Fausto opened the French windows that led onto a wide marble terrace. Silently, Liza followed him, while Melanie exclaimed over everything.

Steps lined with flower pots ran all the way down the landscaped hill to the lake, and Fausto led them down while Liza trailed a little behind.

As they progressed down the hill he urged Melanie forward to look at the rose bushes while he dropped back a little to walk with Liza.

'I trust you are well?' he asked quietly.

'Yes.' Liza didn't trust herself to say anything else. Having him standing so close to her, looking so unbearably handsome in his navy blue suit, was just about all she could handle. Had his hair always been so dark, his jaw so hard, his body so powerful? Yes, she was sure it all had, and yet she felt herself responding in such an overwhelmingly visceral way to him now that it took all her strength not to reach out and touch him.

'I spoke to Henry back in March,' Fausto continued, his voice pitched low so Melanie wouldn't overhear their conversation. 'I wanted to make sure you were…well.'

It took her a moment to realise he meant *not pregnant*. She swallowed. 'That must have put your mind at ease.'

'It did, for your sake.'

She glanced at him sharply; as usual she couldn't tell anything from his expression. 'And not yours?'

'Such an…occurrence would have complicated matters, undoubtedly,' he replied after a brief pause. 'But I would not have regretted it.'

Which made her feel more confused than ever. 'That wasn't the impression you gave me the last time we met.'

'The impressions we gave each other were both unfavourable,' Fausto replied and Liza fell silent. She could not make sense of him at all. As they came onto the shore of the lake she realised she would have preferred him to be his usual self—cold and autocratic.

It would have made it so much easier for her heart to heal. As it was, she felt only confused and unhappy by his seeming solicitude. It didn't make *sense*. She'd thought him one sort of man, and now she was realising more and more that he might be another, and she did not know how to deal with either. Part of her wished she had never seen him again, even as another, far greater part yearned for him still.

'This is so very beautiful,' Melanie exclaimed yet again as they came onto the wide dock where a top-of-the-line speedboat was moored. 'I don't think I've ever seen such a pretty spot.'

'It is lovely,' Liza said, because she felt she had to say something. All of it—the blue, blue lake, the fringe of grey-green mountains on the horizon, the gracious villa and its gardens—was stunning, and looking at it all made her ache in a way she didn't want to examine too closely.

'Perhaps tomorrow we could go out in the boat,' Fausto said with a nod towards the craft in question. 'Then you would be able to see the lake properly.'

'I'm afraid I'm not one for being out on the water,' Melanie answered with a laugh. 'But I know Liza would enjoy it.'

'Then it shall be done,' Fausto said, and Liza gave him a quick, sharp look.

'I'm not one for boats either,' she said quickly. 'And Nan and I were going to tour one of the other lakes tomorrow.'

'We don't—' Melanie began, but Liza shook her head. 'I want to.'

Fausto slanted her a wry, knowing look. 'Perhaps another time,' he said.

They walked back up to the villa and Liza made sure to walk ahead with her grandmother so Fausto couldn't speak to her again. His veiled references to their past stirred up far too much inside her. She didn't know how to respond to any of it. Was he being genuine? Or was he taunting her, showing her all that she could have had, but refused? She wouldn't even blame him if he was.

Perhaps he was doing both. One thing Liza knew was that Fausto's motives weren't clear, perhaps not even to himself. Perhaps he was, as he always was, fighting his attraction to her, because of her glaringly obvious unsuitability. At this point Liza didn't know if she could fault him for it. *She* didn't think she was suitable.

A few minutes later Fausto was escorting them out to the waiting luxury sedan, and he shook Melanie's hand before turning to Liza with an inscrutable smile.

'Until tomorrow evening.'

Was that a promise—or a threat? *What did he want from her?* Liza merely nodded, not trusting herself to speak. She got in the car and as it sped down the drive she forced herself not to look back, as much as she wanted to.

'So who is this woman, Fausto?'

Francesca's smile was teasing as she came into Fausto's bedroom. He was standing in front of the mirror, adjusting the cuffs of his dress shirt, frowning slightly at his reflection.

'She's an acquaintance—a friend—from London.'

'A *friend*? She sounds rather special.'

Fausto spared his sister a smiling glance. 'You have always been a romantic, Chessy,' he said, using the nickname he'd given her in her childhood. Although she was nineteen years younger than him, an unexpected blessing after years of infertility for his parents, they'd always been close. Francesca had looked up to him, and he had doted on her. He didn't think that would ever change.

'I am a romantic,' Francesca allowed, 'but, you know, your voice changes when you speak of her.'

Fausto regarded his sister with a frown. 'It does not.'

'It does, Fausto,' she answered with a laugh. 'And the fact that you don't even know it, *and* that you deny it, makes me think she must be *really* special.'

Fausto decided not to deign his sister's observation with a reply. She was always seeing hearts and flowers where there were none, and in the case of Liza Benton...

What did he feel? Nothing as uncomplicated as simple romance or affection, he acknowledged as he turned away from the mirror. In fact, he had no idea what had motivated his extraordinary invitation yesterday. Yes, it had been the simple pleasure of seeing her again—but had there been something more? A desire to deepen their so-called friendship, or a more unflattering compulsion to let her see the full extent of all she'd missed out on?

Everything felt tangled, and yet nothing had really

changed. He still meant what he'd told her back in Norfolk—he had no intention of repeating his proposal. He would not risk the kind of blistering rejection she'd given him the first time around. If that made him as proud as she'd accused him of being, then so be it.

'We should go downstairs,' he told Francesca. 'Our guests will be here soon.' His mother was in Milan until the weekend, which was just as well because he knew she would not find Liza suitable in the least. His mother was inherently proud, her dignity bordering on a reserve far chillier than anything Fausto had ever shown Liza or anyone else. He did not look forward to the two of them ever meeting, and perhaps they never would.

Downstairs, Fausto paced the drawing room, feeling more restless than he wished as he anticipated Liza's arrival. Already he was more than half regretting his invitation. How would they bridge the tension and awkwardness that existed between them? Francesca was sure to guess something of what had happened, if Liza's grandmother hadn't already. She'd seemed like a rather shrewd woman.

More importantly, he wished he had an understanding in his own mind of his feelings towards Liza Benton. As always, he felt pulled in two very different directions—a deep and even consuming desire to be with her, and a compulsion to push her away. She was not a suitable bride for him or his family, a fact that seemed even more obvious now that she was in his surroundings.

And yet…and yet…she was lovely, and kind, and gracious and smart—all very *suitable* qualities.

None of that mattered, however, Fausto reminded himself, because Liza had refused him once and he would not risk such a bitter refusal again. A man could take only so much rejection, especially when it had been given with such scathing vehemence. So, really, all of this was utterly moot, and he'd treat her as he saw her—a casual acquaintance, someone he might call a friend. That was all. That was all it ever could be.

'I think they're here,' Francesca said excitedly, and Fausto felt his heart flutter, a most unusual and irritating sensation. He straightened, eyes narrowing as Paolo, the villa's butler, went to answer the door. A minute later he was ushering Liza and her grandmother into the private drawing room reserved for family and guests.

The first thing Fausto noticed was how sophisticated she looked. She wore a flowing jumpsuit in emerald-green silk and her hair was pulled back in an elegant up-do, a few curls escaping to frame her lovely face. She'd paired the outfit with a pair of chandelier earrings and high heeled sandals and he realised, with a warm glow of masculine admiration, that she could rival any of the socialites in his circle for both sophistication and beauty.

'Thank you for having us,' Melanie said, while Fausto found he could not tear his gaze away from Liza.

'It is my pleasure, I assure you,' he promised Melanie as he continued to look upon Liza. Under his lingering gaze a blush touched her cheeks and made her only look lovelier. Then he felt someone else's eyes on him and he turned to see Francesca looking at him with avid interest. 'Let me introduce my sister,' he said, and made the necessary introductions.

Soon Melanie was asking about the history of some of the artwork and while Fausto answered he saw, out of the corner of his eye, that Francesca and Liza were chatting away. A burst of laughter emerged from their bent heads and he wondered what on earth they were talking about. They were certainly getting along, and that knowledge was both unsettling and gratifying, giving him even more of a sense of the push-pull he'd always felt with Liza.

Dinner passed more easily and with more enjoyment than Fausto had expected. Liza was a sparkling conversationalist and although she mostly addressed her comments to Melanie or Francesca she would occasionally favour him with a remark or cautious smile.

Melanie asked about various aspects of the estate, which Fausto was happy to give. 'In fact,' he said halfway through the meal, 'you are drinking Danti wines. We have a vineyard as part of the estate, a few miles away.'

'What don't you have?' Liza said with a hint of laughter in her voice, although there was a serious question in her eyes that Fausto didn't know how to answer.

You, he thought unwillingly. *I don't have you.*

After dinner they retired to the drawing room for coffee, and Liza had just sat down when Francesca asked Melanie if she'd like to see the portrait gallery upstairs.

'You've been asking about our ancestors,' she said with a smile, 'so let me show you their faces.'

'Oh—' Liza started to get up but Francesca waved her aside. 'Why don't you stay here and keep Fausto company, Liza? He doesn't want to see those fusty old portraits again.'

And before Liza could even manage a reply they were gone. Fausto smiled in bemusement; his sister's ploys were all too obvious. He glanced at Liza, who met his enquiring look with a wry smile of her own. Then she laughed.

'Are you thinking what I'm thinking?' he asked as he handed her a coffee.

'That your sister likes to play matchmaker?'

'She is a romantic. She can't help herself.'

'Does she know—about us?' Liza asked abruptly, the smile dropping from her face. 'I mean…what happened?'

Fausto took a sip of his coffee as he watched her expression turn wary and guarded. 'No, she does not. I have not told anyone about that.'

'Of course you haven't,' Liza agreed, and he raised his eyebrows.

'Your meaning…?'

She shook her head. 'Only that you wouldn't want people to know.'

'Only because I would not want anyone to know my private business, or yours, for that matter.' He searched her face, trying to discern her mood, but she rose from her seat and paced the room, her back to him as she sipped her coffee and looked out at the darkened gardens.

'Your villa—the whole estate—is very beautiful.'

'Thank you,' he said after a pause.

'I don't think I…realised what it was like when you spoke about it back in England.'

'It would be hard to imagine, I suppose.'

'It's more than that, but…' She let out a soft sigh. 'It doesn't matter now.'

He longed to ask her what she meant, yet some instinct kept him from pressing. This conversation already felt dangerous, flirting with emotions and memories he needed to suppress. As charming as Liza had been tonight, it was very clear that she was still keeping her distance, and Fausto knew he could not presume that anything between them had changed. He certainly had no intention on acting on such a presumption.

Liza's back, slender and tense, was still to him. The shadows lengthened in the room and the silence between them turned hushed, expectant. It would be so easy, so wonderful, to cross the few feet that separated them. So tempting to trail a fingertip down the bare expanse of her back, to hook a finger under the spaghetti strap of her jumpsuit and slip it off her golden, sun-kissed shoulder. Then he would bend his head and brush his lips against that spot, before moving even lower…

Fausto must have made some sound, some indication of his frustrated desire, for Liza turned suddenly, the coffee cup clattering in its saucer.

'I should go.'

'There's no need—'

'It's late, and we have an early start tomorrow. We're travelling to Lake Como and back all in one day.'

'How long are you staying in the area?'

'Till Wednesday.'

'Then you can come to our garden party this weekend.'

She shook her head as she looked at him miserably. 'Is that really a good idea, Fausto?' she asked quietly.

'Why wouldn't it be?'

'You've already made your point. I don't… I don't need to see any more. Experience any more. I get it.'

'What point is it I'm meant to have made?' Fausto asked, his tone sharpening, but before Liza could reply—not that Fausto was sure she would—Francesca came into the room, followed by Melanie.

'We've seen all the rellies,' Francesca said with a laugh. 'Some of them are so stuffy-looking it's ridiculous.'

'I was just telling Liza that she and her grandmother must come to our garden party this weekend,' Fausto told her sister. Francesca perked right up as he'd known she would, and turned to Liza.

'Oh, yes, do come. It's a tradition we have every year, to say thank you to all the staff and employees. It's so much fun—please say you'll come.'

Liza threw Fausto an accusing look before she smiled at Francesca and said stiffly, 'Of course, we'd love to. Thank you.'

Fausto could not deny the primal satisfaction that roared through him. He would see Liza again—and who knew what would happen between them then?

CHAPTER FOURTEEN

LIZA COULD HARDLY believe she was back at Villa di Palmerno again, this time for the garden party Fausto had more or less strong-armed her into. Once again reluctance warred with excitement, hope with fear. Seeing him was torture because it reminded her of how attracted she was to him and, more than that, how much she enjoyed his company. How easy it would be to let herself fall in love with him.

Yet she knew just from looking at Fausto that he had no intention of repeating his proposal, or re-establishing their relationship, not that what they'd experienced was even remotely close to that. Still, it had been the most important experience of Liza's life. She was still trying to get over it.

Even if she didn't understand Fausto's motivations for approaching her, she sensed that same reserve within him that had always been there, like a brick wall built against her, and it seemed to go deeper than his understandable concern about her suitability. She recalled his guarded remark back in Norfolk about another woman—was Fausto guarding his heart, the way she had? Too afraid to take a risk again?

In any case, Liza knew she did not have it in her to bring that wall down brick by brick, and he did not seem inclined to do so either. Guarded hearts or proud ones—what did it matter? The result was the same.

As they arrived at Villa di Palmerno the entrance was festooned with bunting and fairy lights and balloons of every colour arched over the villa's magnificent and ancient doorway. Francesca was waiting by the door to greet them, dressed in a plain white shirt and black skirt.

Liza have must looked surprised by her choice of outfit because Francesca laughed. 'Don't look so shocked—I'm dressed as a waitress. Every year when we throw a party for all the staff, all the Dantis do the waiting and serving. There's not enough of us, of course, so we have to bring in people as well—even my mother does her part.'

'And Fausto?' Liza asked sceptically. She could not picture him lowering himself in such a way.

'Oh, yes, he does as well,' Francesca said. 'It was his idea, actually—the tradition only started about five years ago.' She made a face. 'I don't think my father would have considered such a thing, but he was willing for Fausto to make his mark.'

Yet another facet to Fausto that she had not seen before—not been willing to see. 'It sounds fun,' Liza said.

'Go, have a look!' Francesca gestured to the gardens, which were crowded with people. 'There's lots of things to do.'

As Liza wandered around the gardens with her grandmother, she was amazed at every turn at all the festivities that had been arranged—there were carnival games of all kinds and stalls selling everything from plants to toys to delicate wood carvings. On the lawn there was even a small Ferris wheel and clowns on stilts offering balloons to every delighted child. It was utterly magical and she kept turning in a circle, not knowing where to look next, amazed by it all.

Even more amazing, and more humbling, was the vociferous praise she heard from every corner. All the staff attending the party were friendly, and their love for their employer was impossible to deny.

He was a good man, the best man, so kind and generous and fair. There was nothing he wouldn't do for any of them—Liza only half understood the stories several people told her because of the language difference, but the gist was clear enough. Fausto helped them all, he put them before himself, he was wonderful.

Too wonderful, she thought disconsolately, for her. Melanie had become caught up with several women she'd met, and Liza took the chance to slip away. As lovely as the party was, she didn't know how much she could take of all the good humour bubbling up, the joy and wonder and praise...not when she was feeling lower and lower herself.

She slipped through a hedge into a small octagonal rose garden that was blessedly quiet, but still felt too close to all the party mayhem. A little wrought iron gate led to another garden, enclosed by high hedges, a shell-shaped fountain in its centre.

Alone, Liza breathed a sigh of both sorrow and relief. It had been such a happy day, so why did she feel so sad? Not sad, precisely, she told herself, more just...melancholy. And she was afraid to examine its source too closely.

She sat on the edge of the fountain and ran her fingers through the water spraying from the marble shell in a graceful arc. It shouldn't hurt her so much that she'd discovered that Fausto Danti was a good man—proud, yes, but generous, kind and good-hearted. It should be a relief, because of course she'd rather he wasn't horrible. He wasn't the *snobbish, arrogant, rude and unlikeable* person she'd once declared him to be. He was anything but.

Liza let out a choked cry of dismay and bowed her head.

'You look like Venus on the half-shell.'

She stiffened at the sound of his voice, even though some feminine instinct had known he would come, or at least had hoped.

'Why do you always find me in secret places?' she asked, trying to keep her voice light, but it trembled. She forced herself to look at him; he stood in the entrance to the garden, dressed in a white shirt and black trousers, just like he had been the first time she'd met him. She'd thought the clothes like those of a waiter back then, and today he *was* acting as a waiter, and yet he was anything but. He was so much more.

Standing there, his steely gaze sweeping over her, he looked so handsome he made everything in her ache. The hooded brows...the hard line of his jaw...the lithe beauty and power of his body. She had to look away, afraid her yearning would be evident in her face.

'Why do you always go to secret places?' he asked, his voice a low thrum as he took a few steps towards her.

'I wanted to be alone.'

'Should I leave?'

'No.' Liza knew she didn't want him to. He deserved her apology, at least, as much as it would pain her to give it. 'I wanted to see you. Speak to you.'

'Oh?' Fausto sounded terribly neutral, and she wondered if he was worried she would make some melodramatic declaration. What woman wouldn't, after all she'd seen and heard today? But no. She wouldn't embarrass them both with such an unwanted sentiment.

'I wanted to thank you for today,' she said, trying not to sound stilted. 'And not just for today. For dinner the other night...and the refreshments and tour from before. You've really been so very kind.'

'It's been no trouble.'

'Yes, but...you really didn't have to.' She forced herself to continue, although her throat had grown painfully tight and every word hurt her. 'Especially...considering how we left things. The last time...in Norfolk.' She risked a glance at him but his face was blank. *Of course.* She had never been able to read him, and she wished she had some inkling as to his feelings—although perhaps she didn't. Perhaps she'd be horrified if she knew what he felt right now, about her. How little he felt.

He inclined his head. 'Whatever passed between us is in the past, Liza. It does not need to affect the present.'

'Yes.' Liza nodded, a bit too much. 'That's very gracious of you.' And even though she suspected—or at least she hoped—that he meant it kindly, those words hurt too. *The past was in the past.* She was just a friend, barely more than an acquaintance. Whatever had happened between them had been all too brief, and probably forgettable as well. *She* was the one who had given it so much importance, who had let it change her whole being, even as she'd fought against it and then thrown it back in his face.

Fausto took another step towards her. 'Why is it, then,' he asked, 'that you look so sad?'

Liza lowered her head so her hair fell forward to hide her face, the chestnut curls resting against her cheek, making Fausto itch to run his hand along her jaw, tuck those wayward curls behind her ear.

'I'm not sad,' she said after a moment, her head still bent.

'Are you sure?'

'I think I know what I'm feeling.' She spoke with humour rather than ire, and Fausto rocked back on his heels, unsure how to handle this moment, or what he wanted from it. The trouble was, he didn't know what *he* was feeling.

Part of him wanted to sweep away all the regrets and memories and simply take Liza in his arms. Forget everything else. Another part of him was wary, not wanting to risk rejection and hurt. And yet another part was trying to be wise, reminding that instinctive impulse that Liza still wasn't suitable, no matter how much she seemed so. Since he'd returned to Italy his mother had put on the pressure for him to find a bride. He had obligations, responsibilities, expectations. Yet that insistent voice was growing quieter and quieter with every moment he spent with this woman.

He strolled over to the other side of the fountain and sat on its edge. In the distance he could hear the sound of the party, laughter and music, a background of joy.

'How have you been these last few months?' he asked. 'Really?'

'Okay,' she said. She ran her fingers through the fountain's water, still not looking at him. 'Ish.'

He hated the thought that he'd been the one to hurt her. He settled more comfortably on his perch. 'How is your family?'

'The same.' She sounded bleak rather than tart. 'It's amazing, what you've done here with the party,' she continued, clearly not wanting to talk about herself. 'Everyone I spoke to sang your praises.'

'They are good people.'

'You're a good person.' She looked at him for the first time, her eyes heartbreakingly wide. 'I want—I need—to say that, especially after all the things I accused you of, back in Norfolk. You aren't any of those things. I'm sorry I said you were.'

Her apology, so plainly stated, touched him deeply, and now he found he was the one who was looking away, to hide the depth of his emotion. 'I'm still proud,' he said, trying for wryness.

'You have a right to be proud, of who you are and all you've achieved. The people I talked to today told me how you have increased the business, watched out for their welfare, navigated them through difficult times. You are a wonderful employer, by all accounts. A wonderful Conte di Palmerno.' She spoke his title with an attempt at an Italian accent that made Fausto smile even as he ached. He hadn't expected this conversation to be so sweet—or so hard.

'Thank you, Liza.'

'I... I hope there are no hard feelings between us, after everything. Most likely we won't see each other after today, but still. I'd like to part on a good note.' She smiled, her lips trembling as they curved upwards, her glinting hazel eyes searching his face, looking for answers.

He was silent, unable to agree to the assumptions she'd made—that they wouldn't see each other again after today, that they would be saying their final goodbyes.

'Fausto...?' Her voice wavered with uncertainty.

'There are no hard feelings,' he said at last. 'Although I don't like to speak in so final a tone. Today doesn't have to be goodbye.'

'Well...' she shrugged, trying for another smile '...it sort of does, doesn't it? You're back in Italy. I'm in England. And our worlds do not...intersect.' She glanced around the garden, the shadows lengthening on the paving stones as the sky slowly turned to violet. 'I realise that now—how different we are. Our worlds, our...positions. I didn't really understand what you meant. I thought you were just being snobbish, until I came here and saw all this.' She swept one graceful arm to encompass the garden, the villa, the estate, even, he thought, his title. 'I shouldn't have been so scornful about your concerns. In my own way, I was proud too. I see that now.'

Fausto pressed his lips together, fighting an irrational desire to disagree with everything she'd just said. All the things he'd insisted mattered *didn't*, not in the way he'd thought, and not in the way she was now intimating. He didn't care about their *positions*. Heaven help him, how could he have said something so stupid?

'You weren't proud,' he said in a low voice.

'Well...it doesn't matter, does it? Any more.' She made it a statement rather than a question and, unable to argue with her because he had no promises he could make, Fausto stood up.

'Come back to the party. Now that it's getting dark we have a buffet dinner, followed by fireworks. Also, I would like you to meet my mother.'

'Your mother...?' Her expression showed nothing but alarm. 'I don't think...'

'I want you to meet her.' Why, he couldn't say, even in the privacy of his own mind. Viviana Danti, the Dowager Contessa, would be coolly polite to Liza, and no more. Definitely no more.

But perhaps *that* was why. Because he was hardly going to be dictated to by his mother, especially in something like this. *And as for your father...?*

The question reverberated through him hollowly, because he knew his esteemed father would have felt the same as his mother. *Honour is everything. Remember who we are... You have a duty...*

Don't make the same mistake again.

He had promised his father he would marry a suitable woman, after the disaster with Amy. A promise he'd always intended to keep, but now he wondered if it could look different. Liza might not be from the background his parents had wanted, but she certainly had all the qualities he'd look for in a wife. She wasn't Amy, not even close, and he felt far more for her than for a woman he'd convinced himself he was in love with fifteen years ago.

And yet...he'd made promises to his father, promises he'd had instilled in him since he was but a child, and ones he had always, always intended to keep. They'd defined him. But now he felt as if he were spinning in a sudden void, wondering about the bulwarks that had been his foundation.

'Fausto?' Liza regarded him uncertainly. 'I'm not sure it's a good idea to meet your mother.'

'It is,' he said firmly. 'Come with me, back to the party.' He held out his hand and Liza looked as if it were a foreign object. Then, after an endless few seconds, she put her hand in his. It was small-boned and slender, and he twined his fingers with hers, enjoying the feeling, as intimate as a kiss.

Silently, as if neither of them wanted to break the spell that was being woven over them, they walked from the garden, back to the party.

Dusk was falling softly, a violet cloak dropping over the world. Chinese lanterns were strung through the garden, creating warm pockets of light, and torches had been brought out to the terrace so it was flickering with shadows, an enormous buffet set up by the bank of French windows.

'I'll need to do my job in a moment,' he said, nodding towards the buffet. 'But after everyone is served, I'll introduce you to my mother.'

'Okay,' Liza said, still sounding unconvinced that this was a good plan.

'Come and eat,' Fausto said, and he led her to the buffet and gave her a plate before taking his position behind, as a server. He wished he could have stayed with her, but he knew he would never shirk his position. It was important that all the people who served him so unwaveringly saw him willing to serve them in some small way.

Still, he kept his eye on Liza as she moved down the buffet, a pensive look on her face. She looked so lovely, with her hair wild about her face, her broderie anglaise top matched with a pair of bright blue culottes. Casual yet elegant, a perfect choice for the day, and as he watched her chat to some of the vineyard workers, men with broken English and rough manners, with friendly ease, something warm and sure started in his chest and spread outward. He was glad she was here.

That feeling of gladness, of certainty, only increased as the evening progressed. As Fausto served and chatted, his gaze kept moving to Liza, tracking her around the terrace as she chatted to various people, always friendly and open.

His mother had been holding court in the drawing room for most of the evening, and Fausto decided their introduction could wait. He wanted Liza to himself.

When the buffet had finished he went to join her by the balustrade overlooking the lawn where the fireworks would be set off. 'I'm sorry I couldn't be with you,' he said as he came to stand by her side and she gave him a swift, searching look.

'It's all right.'

'You've been enjoying yourself?'

'Actually, yes.' She let out a little laugh. 'Everyone is so friendly.'

'You are easy to talk to.'

She let out another laugh, this one uncertain. 'Fausto, you're so full of compliments tonight. I don't know what to do with them.'

'Stay,' he said, the word like a pulse, and she gazed out at the darkened lawn, her body so very still. 'Please.'

The first fireworks went off, showering the sky with colour and casting her face in eerie light for a few seconds so he could see how pensive she looked.

'What do you mean exactly?' she asked, her voice unsteady.

'Stay here tonight. With me.'

Another Catherine wheel exploded in the sky, followed by applause and laughter.

'My grandmother...' Liza murmured, and triumph and desire roared through him. If that was her only objection...

'She can stay as well. I will make arrangements for a guest room to be made up. She must be tired. It would be better for her to be here.'

'And me?' Liza asked, turning to look at him, a look of

such open vulnerability on her face that Fausto longed to take her in his arms.

'It is better for me,' he said quietly. 'If you stay. I want you to stay. But only if you want to.'

An age seemed to pass as firework after firework burst in the sky and Liza watched them, her expression both thoughtful and hidden. Then, finally, wonderfully, she turned to Fausto.

'Yes,' she said simply.

CHAPTER FIFTEEN

LIZA FOUGHT A sweeping sense of unreality as she and Fausto watched the rest of the fireworks, side by side and unspeaking. She couldn't believe what he'd asked of her, or that she'd agreed. This was the last outcome she'd expected, and yet some part of her acknowledged the rightness of it. She was, amazingly, not surprised.

Neither was she naïve. One night. That was what Fausto was asking of her. One night, and no more. She pushed the thought away as soon as she'd had it; she did not need to remind herself of how fleeting this one night would be. And while it was happening she wanted to savour every precious moment.

The sky darkened as the last sparks fell from it, and people began to trickle towards the front of the villa to go home. In the darkness Fausto gave her a swift searching look.

'I must go and say my goodbyes.'

'Yes. I should find my grandmother...'

'My head of staff, Roberto, will assist you with anything you need.'

Liza didn't reply because she didn't know what assistance she needed, or how she would find Roberto, and part of her just wanted to take cover in the darkness. The *thought* of being with Fausto was far more compelling than the unbearably awkward logistics of making it happen.

He strode off to make his goodbyes, and Liza went in search of Melanie amidst the crowd of happy partygoers. It only took a few minutes to find her; her grandmother had been watching the fireworks on the terrace as well. When Liza explained the arrangements for the night Melanie's eyebrows rose but she acquiesced readily enough.

'I am tired. It will be good not to have to drive all the way back to the *pensione*.' She gave Liza a considering look. 'The Conte is very kind.'

'Yes.'

A man seemed to materialise out of the darkness, smooth and urbane. 'The Conte asked me to show you to your quarters, and make sure you have everything you need.'

'Oh…er…yes.' Liza couldn't help but be flustered. She felt as if her intentions—Fausto's intentions—were emblazoned on her forehead. Roberto, however, was discretion itself and he led Melanie to a sumptuous guestroom upstairs before taking Liza to hers.

'Ring this bell if there is anything you need,' he said, pointing to a buzzer by the door, and Liza nodded. Her heart had started thumping as soon as she'd entered the room— a spacious bedroom with a huge canopied king-sized bed taking pride of place. *What was she doing?*

The door clicked softly shut as Roberto left her alone. Liza paced the room nervously for a few minutes, before she decided she might as well avail herself of the huge walk-in shower in the en suite bathroom, as well as the thick terrycloth robe hanging on the door.

Twenty minutes later she was showered and swathed in the robe—and still alone. Had Fausto had second thoughts? What if this had all been some sort of a set-up? A payback for the humiliation she'd caused him with her insults and refusal?

But no. After everything she'd learned about him today, everything she knew, she could not believe such a thing of him.

The door opened.

Liza drew her breath in sharply as Fausto stood framed by the doorway, tall and dark and powerful. He regarded her silently for a moment and Liza let out an uncertain laugh, wishing she hadn't decided to don nothing but a robe. She'd been thinking only about not wanting to be hot and sticky, but now she was thinking about being naked.

'I wasn't sure if you would come, after all,' she said.

'Truthfully? I couldn't wait to get away.' His voice was low, and her heart fluttered. She did not reply because she didn't know how to. He took a step into the room. 'You haven't changed your mind?'

'No.' Her voice wavered and she set her chin. 'No,' she said more firmly.

'Good.' Fausto closed the door behind him, and instantly Liza felt as if they'd been cocooned. They were alone, truly alone, at last. Nervously she glanced around the bedroom, conscious again that she wore only a robe.

'This is a very beautiful room, but I imagine every room in this villa is just as beautiful.'

Fausto gazed around the room, his expression indifferent. 'The most beautiful thing in the room is you.'

Liza couldn't keep from giving a sceptical laugh as she shook her head. 'You don't have to soften me with compliments, Fausto. I'm already here.'

He frowned, his dark brows drawing together. 'Is that what you think I am doing?'

'Well…yes.'

'You are beautiful, Liza. I noticed that from the first moment that I saw you.'

'Now I know you're telling lies,' Liza returned lightly, even though it hurt. After all these months, after all that had passed between them, that first little dig still possessed a needle-like pain.

Fausto's frown deepened. 'What do you mean?'

'I heard you, that first night, by the bar. "She looked as

plain and boring as the other, if not more so".' She tried for a smile. 'So don't pretend you were blown away by my beauty the first time you clapped eyes on me.'

'I said that?'

'Yes.'

'And you heard?'

'Yes.'

He sighed and shook his head. 'No wonder you took such a dislike to me right away. I did wonder.'

'You *were* rude.'

'Yes, I was. I was tired and I've never liked big social gatherings, but still there is no excuse. I'm sorry.'

Liza laughed and looked away, discomfited by the sincerity of his apology. 'I didn't tell you that to wheedle an apology out of you.'

'I *am* sorry,' Fausto said seriously. 'I never should have said such a thing. If I thought it, it was only because I wanted to dismiss you, and I couldn't, even at the beginning.'

Which brought them to the very prickly nettle neither of them wanted to grasp. Even now, when they were alone together, when Fausto had asked her here, he would still dismiss her at some point. He would still want to. But hopefully not till the morning.

'Never mind about all that,' Liza said as she moved past him to the window, its shutters open to the night air, the gardens swathed in darkness below. 'It's all water under the bridge, anyway.'

'Is it?'

'Yes.'

'Good,' Fausto said after a pause. 'That is how I would like it to be.'

She nodded unsteadily, turning back to look at him, and he glanced towards the bathroom.

'Would you mind if I had a shower first?'

First. Before what? Liza fought an urge to laugh—hysterically. This was all so very much beyond her experience. 'No, of course not.' She gestured to the bathroom, with its marble and gold taps. 'Be my guest,' she quipped. 'Even though I'm yours.'

Fausto gave her a fleeting smile and then disappeared into the bathroom. A few seconds later Liza heard the sound of the shower. Her breath came out in a rush as she sagged with something like relief. This all felt so strange, and yet she *wanted* to be here. Even if only for a night.

Still, she had no idea how things were going to go when Fausto came out of the bathroom. What if he was naked? Where would she *look*? A muffled laugh escaped her and she clapped her hand over her mouth. Assured seductress she was not.

And yet… Fausto still wanted her. Had chosen her, at least for this. And whatever sorrow or heartache tomorrow and the days after might bring, at least she would always have tonight.

Liza hoped it would be a precious, even sacred, memory. She thought it might be. And, she acknowledged as she gazed out at the darkened night, it would have to be enough.

From the bathroom she heard the sound of the shower turning off.

Fausto slowly dried himself as he gazed unseeingly at the steam-fogged mirror. He could hardly believe that he was here…that she was here. When he'd asked her to stay the night it had felt both natural and essential. All he wanted.

And while he wasn't allowing himself to think too much about any possible future, the rightness of this evening, of them being together, burrowed down deep into his soul. It felt, in a way he could not explain even to himself, like their wedding night.

Wrapping the towel around his waist, he opened the bathroom door. Liza whirled around at the sound, her lovely eyes widening at the sight of him.

'Oh…' Her gaze swept up and down the length of his nearly naked body as a rosy blush reddened her cheeks. 'Oh,' she said again, softly this time, and with admiration.

'You seem nervous,' he remarked as he took a step towards her.

'Of course I'm nervous. You do realise the only other time I've done anything like this was on that beach?'

'I wondered if there had been anyone else since.'

'In the last two months?' Liza stared at him incredulously. 'Of course not.'

'You are a lovely woman,' he pointed out with a smile at her outrage. 'You must have admirers.'

'I work all day with an octogenarian,' Liza reminded him. 'And I haven't been going out very much. So no, there haven't been any *admirers*.'

'I'm glad.'

'Are you?' She looked at him seriously. 'You must have had…other women, in the meantime. I wouldn't mind, of course—'

'No.'

'No?' She looked surprised. 'But…'

'I've been working eighteen hours a day, hardly going out at night, and the truth is, I haven't wanted anyone else.' He was amazed at how freeing that admission felt. 'Only you.'

'Fausto…'

'Why don't you believe me?'

'I don't know. Because you're so amazing and I'm so…'

'You're so what?' he asked gently.

She let out an uncertain laugh. 'Plain. Boring. The sister who isn't pretty. The one people skip over, or simply forget.' Each word vibrated with an old, remembered pain and Fausto felt a flash of anger for the idiots who had dismissed her in such a way.

'You are none of those things, Liza. None.'

'I'm not amazing,' she said, clearly trying to sound merely wry.

'You are.' He reached for her hand, because he had to touch her. 'You are utterly amazing.' He brushed his lips against her fingers, and then he gently nibbled her fingertips as he kept his gaze on her, felt his own heat.

'You make me feel amazing,' Liza admitted unsteadily. 'In a way no one else ever has.'

'I'm glad for that too.'

'You're sounding very possessive,' she said with a breathy laugh.

'I'm feeling very possessive,' Fausto answered, and then he tugged on her hand so she came towards him, willing and expectant. Her hips bumped his and heat flared in them both. He felt it in himself as well as in her. She drew a shuddery breath and then, tentatively, placed her hands on his chest, spreading her fingers wide.

'Is that okay?' she asked a little anxiously. 'Can I touch you?'

'Oh, Liza,' Fausto said with a groan. 'You can touch me all you want. Anywhere.'

She laughed as she let her hands slip down his chest, her fingertips flirting with the edge of his towel before skimming up again.

'Go ahead,' Fausto encouraged her in a low, thrumming voice. Already he was more than ready for all she could give him. 'Touch me. Take off the towel.'

'Seriously?' An incredulous smile quirked her mouth.

'Seriously.'

Her hands travelled down again, her breath coming in a gasp as she tugged the towel and it fell away. She glanced down and her eyes widened comically.

'Oh…'

'Nothing to alarm you, I hope,' he said dryly.

'No…it's just I didn't actually *see* you, before.'

'And I didn't see you.' He reached for the sash of her robe and gave it a gentle tug. 'May I?' She nodded. He undid the sash and the robe parted, to reveal the shadowy valleys and curves of a body he ached to touch and treasure.

In one sinuous movement Liza shrugged the garment off and it fell in a heap at her feet. She kicked it away, chin raised, gaze defiant and yet vulnerable.

She was lovely…so lovely, her body pale and perfect, slender and supple. Fausto put his hands on her waist, nearly spanning it as he drew her towards him so their bodies brushed—her breasts against his chest, their hips nudging one another. She let out a shuddery breath and closed her eyes.

He tilted her chin up with one finger. 'All right?' he asked quietly, and she nodded.

'Yes. Very much so.'

'Good.' And then, because he couldn't wait any longer, he kissed her, and it was as sweet as it had been every time before—no, he realised, sweeter. It meant more, because he knew this—what was unspooling between them like a golden thread now—meant more. As he deepened the kiss his mind blurred and he let the thoughts drift away on a tide of sensation.

Liza put her arms around him and as their bodies came in even closer and more exquisite contact another groan escaped him. This was torture—wonderful, wonderful torture.

Stumbling a bit, they made it to the bed. Fausto pulled back the duvet as Liza moved over, her wild curls spread across the ivory pillowcase, her body and heart both open to him. Fausto stretched beside her and hooked one of her curls around his finger.

'Your hair,' he murmured, 'is magnificent.'

She let out another one of her disbelieving laughs. 'It's too curly.'

'Too curly? No. Why do you disparage yourself?'

'I don't know. I've never thought of it that way.' She shrugged slim shoulders. 'I know I've never been as pretty as Jenna, or as spirited as Lindsay, or as clever as Marie.'

'Marie? I haven't met her.'

'No, although you might like her the best. She's quiet and bookish.'

'I like *you* the best,' he said, and then he rolled over and covered her body with his own.

She let out a little gasp of pleasure before he devoured her mouth in a kiss and her arms came around him. She arched up into him, all pliant softness, and it was almost too much.

He kissed his way from her mouth to her breasts... breasts he could feel the ripe fullness of now, could touch and savour in a way he hadn't been able to in their frenzied rush on the beach. Now he would take his time, exploring every hidden curve, every sweet dip. He kissed his way lower.

Beneath him Liza writhed as she let out lovely little mewling sounds of pleasure, her fingers raking through his hair as he kissed her soft thighs.

'Fausto...' she said shakily, half plea, half protest.

'I'm getting to know you,' he murmured, and she let out a breathless laugh as he kissed her at the core of herself and her body convulsed around him.

'Oh, I didn't *think*...'

'Now is not the time for thinking,' he advised. 'Only for feeling.' His mouth moved over her once more, and her body arched sweetly against him.

'*Fausto...*'

He could explore her hidden recesses for ever, but the

desperate ache they both felt needed to be sated. They had the whole night in front of them, and he intended to use every single hour of it. But, for now, he reached for a condom.

'Are you ready?' he asked as he rolled on top of her once more, bracing himself on his forearms. Liza nodded, her head buried in his shoulder, her body open to him.

'Yes...*yes*.'

And she was, as he glided smoothly into her, found his way home, and she met him there, thrust for glorious thrust.

It was moments, and yet it was a lifetime shattered and reborn as she enfolded him in her body, clasped him in her arms, and they both broke apart and then came together. *This was where he wanted to be.*

All his concerns about positions or pride, all the armour he'd surrounded himself with to keep himself apart, to keep from gambling on that all-or-nothing risk of loving—it all shattered in this moment.

None of it mattered. None of it mattered in the least.

All he wanted was her. For tonight—and for ever.

He kept his arms around her as he rolled onto his back, their hearts thudding hard against one another in the aftermath of their lovemaking.

'That's just the beginning,' he promised her, and she pressed her forehead against his chest.

'You'll be the death of me.'

And yet, Fausto knew as he kept his arms around her, she was the life of him.

CHAPTER SIXTEEN

LIZA WOKE SLOWLY, blinking in the sunlight, stretching as languorously as the cat that got the cream. And that was how she felt after a night of gorgeous, mind-blowing and body-altering lovemaking.

She was sore in places she'd never been sore before and her muscles ached in a way that felt delicious. As she lay there in the sunlight, in the dreamy, muted state between sleep and consciousness, a montage of lovely memories danced through her mind. Candlelight on burnished skin. Fausto poised above her. His head bent as he kissed her, her fingers in his dark hair…

And then later, when she'd felt bolder, she'd given him the same sensual treatment. She'd explored every gorgeous inch of his lean, hard body and revelled in her newfound knowledge. They'd fallen asleep in each other's arms some time towards dawn.

Liza turned her head and saw Fausto sleeping next to her, his inky lashes fanned on his cheeks, his chest rising and falling in the steady beat of sleep.

And then, as consciousness crept in, so did reality. It was over. Her one amazing night had ended. And it had been amazing—she had no regrets. Well, not many. The heartache she'd carry with her felt like a heavy yet necessary burden to bear, because she knew now that she loved him. How could she not, after all she'd learned about him? After everything he'd done for her, the kindness, sensitivity and passion he'd shown.

Of course she loved him.

And for a few precious seconds as she watched him sleep she imagined telling him so. She pictured how his face would soften in pleasure and surprise, and then he would take her in his arms and tell her he loved her too.

Of course it was only the stuff of fairy tales. In all the conversations they'd had since she'd come to Italy Fausto had never changed his position on position. On the fact that she was not suitable to be his bride—a fact Liza had felt more and more keenly, the more time she spent at Villa di Palmerno.

She was the Benton sister who had never been anything special, often overlooked or forgotten, one of many rather than a stand-out. She was the woman a man had sneeringly dismissed, had used just to get to her sister. Did she actually think she could be a *Contessa*?

No, of course not.

Slowly, Liza slipped out of bed, not wanting to disturb Fausto. Best if she showered and dressed, made her farewells as quickly as possible. Severed the connection as neatly and cleanly as she could, even if the thought of it hurt more than she could bear.

She'd just taken her clothes into the bathroom when her phone buzzed with an incoming text. Considering it was only seven in the morning, Liza frowned at the sound and swiped her screen. The text was from Jenna.

Are you awake? Need to talk.

Liza pressed 'call' and seconds later she heard Jenna's breathless voice. 'Liza? Sorry to wake you up so early…'

'It's fine, but it's only six in England. What's going on?'

'It's Lindsay,' Jenna said on a jagged note. 'We found out late last night… I didn't want to disturb you…but I couldn't wait any longer. Mum's having fits.'

Liza's stomach plunged icily. 'What's happened?'

'She's been so...oh, I can't even blame her, honestly. She's only just eighteen. Of course her head was bound to be turned.'

'What? Jenna, I have no idea what you're talking about.'

'Lindsay went to London for the weekend,' Jenna explained. 'You remember it's her eighteenth?'

'Yes...' Liza said, although she realised with a stab of guilt that, in light of everything that had been happening here with Fausto, she'd completely forgotten about her sister's birthday.

'Anyway, she told Mum she was seeing me, but she wasn't. She'd met some guy at a club the last time she was here—he invited her to some D-list party this weekend. Honestly, it sounded dire.'

'Oh, no,' Liza said softly. She could picture how thrilled Lindsay would be at such an invitation, how utterly irresponsible she might be at such an event, and also how out of her depth. Poor, foolish Lindsay.

'What happened?' she asked as dread swirled coldly in her stomach.

'I don't know the details, and I'm not sure I want to,' Jenna said with quiet grimness. 'She got involved with some minor celebrity at the party—I haven't heard of him, but Mum had.'

'And?' Liza asked, as everything in her went tenser.

'And there were photos involved. Nude photos.'

'Oh, no, Lindsay...'

'And the guy she was with, this Jack, is threatening to sell them to the tabloids—because this celebrity is apparently big enough for that—if we don't pay out.'

'Jack?' Liza knew even before she asked, 'Jack who?'

'Wick something, I think.'

'Wickley.' She closed her eyes. How could that wretched man be tormenting her family now? If she'd had any doubts about the truth of Fausto's story—and she hadn't—they would certainly have been swept away now.

'You know him?' Jenna asked in surprise.

'No, not really. It doesn't matter. What are we going to do?'

'I don't know. Mum's adamant the photos don't get published. She's worried for Lindsay's wellbeing, of course, but I also think she's afraid of her being expelled from school right in the middle of A-levels. They have a zero tolerance policy about this sort of thing.'

'And if she's expelled, no university,' Liza finished numbly. Despite her sister's seemingly scatty attitude, she had brains and she'd been offered a place studying business in Manchester.

'Her whole life could be derailed,' Jenna concluded miserably. 'Not to mention the humiliation and hurt she would feel. I know Lindsay acts shameless, but she isn't really. She's been reckless and silly, I know that, but she doesn't deserve this. She's trying to act as if she doesn't care, but I think she must.'

'Poor Lindsay.' Liza's mind was racing. 'I'll fly back today.'

'Oh, but your holiday—'

'It will be over in a few days, anyway. And this is more important.' Besides, Liza thought, her holiday already felt as if it were over. Her night with Fausto certainly was. 'I'll text you from the airport,' she promised, and then she disconnected the call.

She dressed quickly, her mind buzzing all the while, and when she emerged from the bathroom Fausto was sitting up in bed with a sleepy smile. Their night together already felt like something consigned to the past.

'Liza…' His smile vanished as he took in her agitation. 'What's happened?'

'Lindsay.' She couldn't keep it from him, as much as

she wanted to. As she related the details of the sordid tale, she couldn't help but cringe inside. If there had ever been a measure of how unsuitable she was as his potential bride, now it was taken to the full, but that hardly mattered. She had to think about Lindsay, not herself.

'That bastard,' Fausto said in a low voice. 'He never tires of ruining lives.'

'I don't know what we'll do,' Liza said numbly. 'We can't afford to pay him. We haven't any money, not like that. But I have to go home and help. I need to be there for Lindsay, for Mum…'

Fausto was already getting out of bed and pulling on his trousers. Liza watched him miserably. Could he not get away from her fast enough, now that he knew the full extent of her family's shame?

'I'll arrange for a private flight for you back to England,' he said. 'It will be quicker.'

'Oh, you don't—'

'It's nothing,' he dismissed. 'Of course I will do it.'

'Thank you—'

'I will have it arranged.'

Liza blinked; Fausto's voice sounded so cold. Perhaps he was only offering because he wanted her out of here— out of Italy—as quickly as possible. He didn't even look at her as he buttoned his shirt, and Liza realised his mind was elsewhere; he'd already forgotten her.

Perhaps he was trying to do his own damage control. If Lindsay's photos ended up in the papers and Fausto's association with Liza was discovered she supposed it could reflect badly on the Danti family. She could hardly blame him for wanting to deal with the possible fallout for his own family, and yet the realisation filled her with sadness. Their one amazing night really was well and truly over.

Everything seemed to happen in super speed after that. Fausto left the bedroom without saying goodbye or even looking at her, and when Liza had finished getting ready and gone downstairs he was nowhere to be seen. His mother, Viviana Danti, however, was. Liza recognised her instantly even though they'd never met.

'I trust you had a comfortable night?' she asked in a glacial tone that made Liza freeze where she stood in the entrance hall. She'd just asked Roberto to find her grandmother and she was hoping to make her escape as quickly as possible.

'Yes.' Bravely, a bit recklessly, she stuck out her hand. 'I don't think we've met. I'm Liza Benton.'

'I know who you are,' Viviana Danti said coldly, ignoring Liza's hand. She withdrew it, blushing at the woman's icy hauteur.

'The party yesterday was lovely,' she said after a pause, because the silence was simply too awful. Viviana inclined her head.

'I understand you feel my son has developed some sort of attachment to you,' she said. 'Please don't think it will last.'

Stung, Liza replied, 'I never thought it would, but thank you for making it abundantly clear.'

Viviana smiled, a chilly gesture that held no friendliness. 'I am trying to help you, my dear. A girl such as yourself… It is understandable that you would have hopes.'

Until Viviana Danti had said it aloud, Liza wouldn't have believed she'd had such hopes. She'd reminded herself again and again that she didn't, that she'd walked into last night knowing full well that was all it could be.

And yet.

And yet…

Looking at Viviana's icy elegance, how she looked down her nose at her in the same way Fausto once had… Liza realised painfully that she'd been hoping all along. Hoping so hard, because how could she not, after last night? After how passionate Fausto had been. How tender.

'I have no such hopes,' she stated in as cold a voice as she could manage.

'Are you quite sure?' Viviana asked coolly. 'Because we have been in this situation before, you know. Fausto brought a girl home very much like you. Amy—young, English, poor.' She paused. 'It only took a more tempting offer to make her go away.'

Liza stared at her for a few stunned seconds before she said in a thready voice, 'Are you…are you offering me a bribe?'

'I'm giving you an incentive, along with a warning,' Viviana replied. 'I thought my son had outgrown such foolish fancies, but it appears he hasn't. How much will it take? Fifty thousand? A hundred?' She smiled coolly, and Liza took a stumbling step away. No wonder Fausto worried about gold-diggers. How much had this Amy taken?

'I have absolutely no wish to take a penny from you,' she said coldly. 'And don't worry, because I don't intend to see Fausto again.' The knowledge ripped through her and she drew a shuddering breath. 'Now, if you'll excuse me, I need to find my grandmother.'

The sooner she was able to return home and forget Fausto, she thought miserably, the better.

It had been a long eighteen hours. Long, aggravating, but so very worth it. Fausto glanced at the clock on the dashboard of his car—half past six on a beautiful spring evening. His eyes were gritty and his body ached. Last night he'd barely slept.

He'd checked with his staff to see if Liza had taken advantage of his offer of a private flight, only to learn that she had left with her grandmother in a cab before Roberto had been able to secure it. That knowledge had caused Fausto a ripple of unease, but he'd determinedly dismissed it. Liza had been in a rush to get back to her family. He understood her impatience; now he was in a rush to get back to her.

Unfortunately, finding her was not as simple as he hoped. He didn't have her telephone number, didn't know her address. The only thing he knew was her place of work, but it was evening and she wouldn't be there. He knew he could call Henry and ask for her address, but he was loath to put his godfather, Liza's employer, in such a position.

But he needed to see Liza. He'd left so abruptly in his determination to address the situation, and he feared she might have been besieged by doubts—although could either of them have any doubts after the incredible night they had shared? The aftershocks of emotion and pleasure were *still* rippling through him.

Even so, he needed to see her. Speak to her. *Hold her.* Once he did that, he was sure everything would be all right. It had to be.

He ended up calling Chaz. 'I need Jenna's number,' he stated brusquely.

'*Jenna?*'

'You have it still?'

'Of course I have it.' Something about Chaz's tone made Fausto ask, a little less brusquely, 'Why did you stop seeing her, by the way?'

Chaz was silent for a moment. 'I don't know,' he admitted.

'Was it because of what I said?'

'You told me to think carefully. I did.'

'So what were your concerns?'

Chaz sighed. 'I don't know. That she didn't feel for me as much as I felt for her? It was *frightening*, how much I felt. I backed away from it, I guess.'

Fausto knew all too well how that went. 'But you've been miserable without her,' he stated matter-of-factly. 'You should call her, Chaz.'

'It's been months—'

'So? Apologise. Grovel, if you have to.'

Chaz let out a choked laugh of disbelief. 'Are you, Fausto Danti, asking me to *grovel*?'

'I am.' Because, heaven knew, he might have to grovel too. He had left rather abruptly. 'If she's worth it and, judging from the way you've been these last few months, I think she is.'

'You really want me to call her?'

'Yes, but let me call her first.'

Jenna was as surprised to hear from him as Chaz had been when he'd asked for her number.

'You want Liza's number?'

'Preferably her address. I need to speak to her.'

'She's at home with us, here in Herefordshire.'

'May I have the address, please?'

Jenna hesitated.

'Please,' Fausto said quietly. 'I want to speak to her.' He paused as the words and their truth unfurled and grew inside him. Overwhelmed him. 'I need to tell her I love her.'

Jenna gave him the address.

It was a three-hour drive to the gracious Georgian house smothered with climbing roses in a pretty village overlooking rolling golden fields.

Fausto pulled into the drive and gazed at the house in bemused surprise—yes, the roof clearly needed repairing and it looked a little shabby and worn, but in a lovely, lovable way. The garden was full of bird feeders and ragged bunting, left over from a party perhaps, was strung along the gateposts.

He'd only just got out of the car when the front door was thrown open and Lindsay stood there, hands on her hips, eyes narrowed. Considering the disaster that had been so narrowly averted, she looked none the worse for wear.

'You look familiar,' she said.

'I met you with Chaz Bingham a few months ago,' he said, and she let out a squeal of recognition and delight.

'Oh, yes, you were so grumpy then.'

Faust gave a small smile in spite of himself. 'Indeed I was.'

'What on earth are you here for?' Lindsay demanded.

'Your sister, Liza.'

'Ooh!' The squeal was high-pitched enough to hurt Fausto's ears. '*Li-za!*' she yelled.

Fausto stepped inside the house. It was as lovably shabby on the inside as it was on the outside—all mismatched chintz prints and comfortable sofas, as well as two shaggy golden retrievers who came up to him and immediately sprawled at his feet. Fausto was oddly enchanted by it all, by the homeliness of it, the comfort and care, and most of all the love that radiated from every nook and cranny like a force field. And he'd thought Liza's family would reflect badly on *him*. The realisation, one he'd held in some dark corner of his heart up to even this moment, humbled him all the more.

Then Liza came into the hall—her face was pale, her curls riotous. She wore a loose green sundress and she looked absolutely wonderful.

'Fausto…' Her voice was faint. 'What are you doing here?'

'I needed to see you.'

'Why?'

'Yes, why?' Lindsay asked, clearly having no compunction about being a part of this conversation.

Fausto looked at Liza. 'May we speak in private?'

'Yes…the garden is probably the most private place.' She led him through the house, past her gawking mother, a smiling Jenna and another sister who had to be the bookish Marie. An older man with salt and pepper hair peeped out from a study and then quickly withdrew.

Liza brought him out to a small terrace in the back that overlooked a riotous garden of blowsy roses and bountiful wisteria.

'My father's pride and joy,' Liza said, nodding towards the many roses. 'That and the orchids, but those are in the greenhouse. Nothing like yours, of course. No rare varieties.' She glanced at the kitchen window, where four Benton women were openly staring, and then she nodded towards the lawn that wandered invitingly between trailing wisteria and overgrown rosebushes to a more private space.

'I don't know why you're here,' she said in a rather wooden voice once they were free of the prying eyes and straining ears in the kitchen.

'I told you—to see you.'

'Yes, but why? Has…has something happened?'

Now that he had her here, had her attention, the words bottled up in his chest. He felt overcome with emotion, with certainty, and yet it was so hard to say it. As a boy he'd been taught all about pride and honour, dignity and respect. Not so much about vulnerability or love, yet those were what he felt—and needed—now.

'Fausto…?' The uncertainty in her voice made him ache.

'I love you.' It felt like something that could only be blurted, an admission straight from the gut—and the heart. Liza simply stared, so he decided to say it again. 'I love you. I want to spend the rest of my life with you.' It was like peeling back skin, offering his heart, still beating and raw, on a platter. It *hurt*. Then, to his amazement and horror, she slowly shook her head. This, then, was why he'd kept himself from saying the words for so long. The risk—the pain—were unbearable. 'You don't believe me?' he asked in a ragged voice.

'It's not that I don't believe you,' Liza said. 'Although, to be honest, I'm not sure if I do or not. It's that I'm not sure it matters.'

'What?' Fausto goggled at her, unable to keep himself from it—mouth open, eyes wide. 'What? How can it not? You told me you were holding out for love. That you wanted to marry a man who loved you—you, and only you. Well, I love you, Liza. I love you with my whole heart. My soul. My body. Everything. I've come to realise it—to revel in it!' He couldn't believe he was telling her so much, giving her so much, and yet she still seemed to be rejecting it. *Him*. He'd been so sure…again. How stupid could he be? How arrogant? Once again he'd thought she'd come to him with open arms.

'Yes, that's true,' Liza said after a moment, 'but Fausto, you don't *want* to love me.'

'I fought against it, that's true,' he said steadily. He would not shy away from his past sins. Perhaps now he still needed to atone for them. 'I did, because—'

'Because you didn't think I was *suitable*.' She said the words heavily rather than with scorn.

'No.'

Liza looked at him in surprise, and Fausto continued, this new level of vulnerability hurting him all the more. 'At least that was part of it, but really a small part. The truth was, I was afraid to love you. Afraid to give my heart.' He paused. 'Afraid to be hurt.'

'Like you were before.'

'Yes, although what I felt for her was nothing compared to this. Us.'

Her hazel gaze scanned his face. 'Your mother offered me money to go away.'

Fury streaked through him like a bolt of lightning. 'She's done that before.'

'Yes, she told me. And she told me that… Amy…took the money.'

Fausto's gut tightened at the memory. 'Yes.'

'I'm sorry. That must have been terrible.'

'It was a long time ago.'

'Yet these things still have the power to hurt us.' She paused, her gaze distant and troubled. 'I had a similar experience. I was hurt… Oh, it's a bit ridiculous because it never went anywhere. We only kissed.'

'What happened?' Fausto asked. He already despised whoever the man in question was.

'I met someone at uni. I thought he was interested in me. Well, he acted like he was. He flattered me…spent time with me. But then I discovered he was only interested in getting closer to Jenna.' She sighed, a wavery sound. 'He made that very clear.'

Bastard. 'I'm sorry, Liza.' Now he understood her insecurities, why she didn't believe he could love her. Her, and no other. 'Liza, I do love you,' he said in a low, insistent voice. 'Whatever happens between us, you need to know that. To believe it. I *want* to love you. Yes, I fought against it, and it was foolish of me. But I fought and I won. You won. And it is the sweetest victory, if you'll just…'

A small smile curved her lovely mouth. 'Love you back?'

'*Yes.*'

'I do love you.' Triumph rushed through him, tempered by her next words. 'But does it really change things, Fausto? I fought against loving you, just as you did with me. I can see that now. I was so angry, and that was in part because it felt as if you were making me look at my family differently, critically, and I hated that. I hated who I was becoming.'

'And I hate who I've *been.*'

'But what's changed, Fausto? Really?'

'I've changed,' he insisted. 'I've fallen in love for the very first time. I've seen a woman who is gracious and loving and kind, and I don't care if she was born a princess or a pauper. It doesn't matter.'

'It matters to your mother.'

His stomach tightened again at her despondent tone. 'My mother's concerns are not mine.'

'And yet you made it clear you wanted me gone.' She spoke matter-of-factly, yet he still heard her hurt.

'What?' Fausto stared at her in confusion. This was not part of the narrative that he understood. 'Why do you think that?'

'You left without even saying goodbye.'

'I was in a hurry—'

'Yes, I know, to do your own damage control. I do understand that.'

'My own...?' Now he could only look at her blankly. 'What is that supposed to mean?'

'Lindsay,' Liza said unhappily. 'I realised that if those photographs were published and our...association...was discovered it would reflect badly on you and your family. I'm sorry for that.'

'But the photos weren't published,' Fausto said slowly.

'No, amazingly they weren't. I don't know what happened. We weren't able to pay the money—'

'I paid the money,' Fausto said quietly, and Liza simply stared.

'You...' Then she nodded slowly. 'Because it would reflect badly on you, like I thought. I am sorry—'

'Liza, do you really think so little of me even now, after everything, that I would see off Jack Wickley simply because of how it affected me?' The pain in his voice was raw and audible, and he couldn't hide it. She'd already told him she loved him and yet she still had these doubts?

'I don't understand...'

'I did it for you, because I love you! And for Lindsay, because she is young and everyone was young and foolish once, including me. And I did it because I could not bear to see Jack Wickley get away with one thing more. I paid him off and I had the photos destroyed, and I have gone to the police with the proof of his embezzling. I didn't do it before because my father wouldn't have wanted the shame on our company and name, which is another kind of damage pride does, but I realised Wickley can't get away with things—it only encourages him to do more, and to hurt more people.' He let out an exasperated, emotional breath. 'I did all that, but I *didn't* do any of it for some sort of *damage control*. I didn't even think about that. I couldn't care less about it now.'

Liza pressed her hands to her cheeks as tears filled her eyes. 'I don't know what you want me to say.'

'Say you love me again and that you'll marry me.'

Tears spilled down her cheeks. 'I'm not…'

'What?'

'Good enough,' she whispered. 'Special enough. Sophisticated enough…'

'You are all that and more, to me. And I will happily spend a lifetime proving it to you.'

'Even though I was so horrible to you?'

'You called me out. I deserved it.'

'You didn't…'

'Liza,' he said with a groan. 'I love you. You've said you love me. We can argue about the particulars, but right now I need you to kiss me.'

She laughed and then finally, wonderfully, she came into his arms and he let out a laugh of both relief and pure joy. She tilted her face up to his and he kissed her as he'd been aching to do.

'I do love you,' she said after a long moment. 'So much. I think I fell in love with you ages ago, and I fought it as much as you did, even though I didn't realise that was what I was doing at the time.'

'Then we've both had to surrender.'

'Yes.' She smiled, her face suffused with tenderness and love. 'Sweet, sweet surrender.'

Fausto kissed her again.

EPILOGUE

Seven months later

IT WAS THE wedding of the year. A Christmas wedding and, more than that, a double wedding—two gorgeous brides and two eminently eligible bachelors. The tabloids had a field day. It was on the cover of *You Too!* with an exclusive double page spread in the magazine.

There were four beautiful bridesmaids—Lindsay and Marie, Francesca, and Chaz's sister Kerry, who had thawed when she'd realised Fausto had never even looked at her that way. The ceremony was in the village church in Little Mayton, and the reception was in a luxury hotel nearby. Fausto had rented out the entire place for the occasion.

There would be another party to celebrate his and Liza's marriage in Italy, when they returned to Villa di Palmerno. Liza was going to work remotely for Henry as well as fulfil her duties as Contessa.

It was a fairy tale of epic proportions, and Liza felt as if she had to keep pinching herself. As she took a moment alone at the reception to watch all the gaiety, she did just that. A hard pinch on her upper arm, just to see.

'What are you doing?' Fausto asked, his voice laced with amusement as he came to stand beside her.

'Pinching myself. To make sure this is real.'

'Trust me, it's real.' He nodded towards the twelve-piece band that, on Lindsay's request, was starting a rendition of the Macarena, with Lindsay front and centre leading the dancing.

Liza let out a little muffled laugh. 'You don't mind?'

'Nope.' He slid his arms around her waist. 'Look at them all dancing.'

Liza glanced at her mother, who was giving it as much of her all as Lindsay was, and Jenna and Chaz, who were laughing and dancing, their arms around each other. Her father had even joined in and Henry and, amazingly, Viviana were both nodding along. Her mother-in-law had thawed towards her, if only just, but it was enough for Liza. She understood how hard it was to let go of preconceptions, of pride and prejudice.

'Happy?' Fausto asked as he nuzzled her hair, and she leaned against him as her thankfulness and joy overflowed.

'Yes,' she said, and turned her head to brush a kiss against his jaw. 'So, so happy.'

* * * * *

MILLS & BOON

Coming next month

HIS STOLEN INNOCENT'S VOW
Marcella Bell

"I can't," she repeated, her voice low and earnest. "I can't, because when I went to him as he lay dying, I looked him in his eye and swore to him that the d'Tierrza line would end with me, that there would be no d'Tierrza children to inherit the lands or title and that I would see to it that the family name was wiped from the face of the earth so that everything he had ever worked for, or cared about, was lost to history, the legacy he cared so much about nothing but dust. I swore to him that I would never marry and never have children, that not a trace of his legacy would be left on this planet."

For a moment, there was a pause, as if the room itself had sucked in a hiss of irritation. The muscles in his neck tensed, then flexed, though he remained otherwise motionless. He blinked as if in slow motion, the movement a sigh, carrying something much deeper than frustration, though no sound came out. Hel's chest squeezed as she merely observed him. She felt like she'd let him down in some monumental way though they'd only just become reacquainted. She struggled to understand why the sensation was so familiar until she recognized the experience of being in the presence of her father.

Then he opened his eyes again, and instead of the cold green disdain her heart expected, they still burned that fascinating warm brown—a heat that was a steady home fire, as comforting as the imaginary family she'd dreamed up as a child—and all of the taut disappointment in the air was gone.

Her vow was a hiccup in his plans. That he had a low tolerance for hiccups was becoming clear. How she knew any of this when he had revealed so little in his reaction, and her mind only now offered up hazy memories of him as a young man, she didn't know.

She offered a shrug and an airy laugh in consolation, mildly embarrassed about the whole thing though she was simultaneously unsure as to exactly why. "Otherwise, you know, I'd be all in. Despite the whole abduction…" Her cheeks were hot, likely bright pink, but it couldn't be helped so she made the joke, anyway, despite the risk that it might bring his eyes to her face, that it might mean their eyes locked again and he stole her breath again.

Of course, that is what happened. And then there was that smile again, the one that said he knew all about the strange mesmerizing power he had over her, and it pleased him.

Whether he was the kind of man who used his power for good or evil had yet to be determined.

Either way, beneath that infuriating smile, deep in his endless brown eyes, was the sharp attunement of a predator locked on its target. "Give me a week." His face may not have changed, but his voice gave him away, a trace of hoarseness, as if his sails had been slashed and the wind slipped through them, threaded it, a strange hint of something Hel might have described as desperation…if it had come from anyone other than him.

"What?" she asked.

"Give me a week to change your mind."

Continue reading
HIS STOLEN INNOCENT'S VOW
Marcella Bell

Available next month
www.millsandboon.co.uk

COMING SOON!

We really hope you enjoyed reading this book.
If you're looking for more romance, be sure to
head to the shops when new books are
available on

Thursday 4th March

To see which titles are coming soon, please visit

millsandboon.co.uk/nextmonth

LET'S TALK

Romance

For exclusive extracts, competitions
and special offers, find us online:

MILLS & BOON

THE HEART OF ROMANCE

A ROMANCE FOR EVERY KIND OF READER

MODERN

Prepare to be swept off your feet by sophisticated, sexy and seductive heroes, in some of the world's most glamourous and romantic locations, where power and passion collide.
8 stories per month.

HISTORICAL

Escape with historical heroes from time gone by. Whether your passion is for wicked Regency Rakes, muscled Vikings or rugged Highlanders, awaken the romance of the past.
6 stories per month.

MEDICAL

Set your pulse racing with dedicated, delectable doctors in the high-pressure world of medicine, where emotions run high and passion, comfort and love are the best medicine.
6 stories per month.

True Love

Celebrate true love with tender stories of heartfelt romance, from the rush of falling in love to the joy a new baby can bring, and a focus on the emotional heart of a relationship.
8 stories per month.

Desire

Indulge in secrets and scandal, intense drama and plenty of sizzling hot action with powerful and passionate heroes who have it all: wealth, status, good looks...everything but the right woman.
6 stories per month.

HEROES

Experience all the excitement of a gripping thriller, with an intense romance at its heart. Resourceful, true-to-life women and strong, fearless men face danger and desire - a killer combination!
8 stories per month.

DARE

Sensual love stories featuring smart, sassy heroines you'd want as a best friend, and compelling intense heroes who are worthy of them.
4 stories per month.

To see which titles are coming soon, please visit

millsandboon.co.uk/nextmonth